COLD COMFORT

COLD COMFORT

A NOVEL BY

E. W. ABERNATHY

Save the Kittens Publishing
Morganton, North Carolina
2015

Cold Comfort

Second Edition

© 2015 E. W. Abernathy

All Rights Reserved

ISBN-13: 978-0692381151
ISBN-10: 0692381155

In Memory of J. D. W., Jr.—the *original* Reverend Jack

ACKNOWLEDGEMENTS

Many thanks to my good friends RLB Hartmann, James and Bell Lane, and Bex Aaron for their invaluable editorial assistance and handholding when the going got rough. Thank you for encouraging me, putting up with my angst, and telling me things I didn't necessarily want to hear but needed to hear to make the story better. Thank you to my mother, Laura Whisnant, for always encouraging my love of reading and for not insulting my intelligence by attempting to censor what I read—I love you.

ABOUT THE AUTHOR

E. W. Abernathy resides in western North Carolina and has worked in the legal profession for over twenty-seven years. Her favorite pastimes are writing, reading, cooking, and listening to heavy metal music. She was the recipient of The Tarheel Writers' Roundtable First Place for Best Short Story in 1978 at the age of 17 and has been writing fiction since the third grade. She is currently working on the sequel to *Cold Comfort*. Her other works in progress are a historical novel set in antebellum North Carolina, and a dystopian/futuristic novel dealing with the subject of genetic engineering in humans. She loves connecting with readers. Get in touch with her!

Facebook: https://www.facebook.com/ewabernathy1
Twitter: https://twitter.com/EllenAbernathy4
Google+: https://plus.google.com/+EWAbernathy
email: ewabernathyauthor@gmail.com

PROLOGUE

THE BACK HALF OF THE ROOM is full of people, most of whom sit or stand behind a waist-high wooden partition. At the front is a massive bench set on a platform, dominated by a woman wearing a black choir robe. I keep expecting her to burst into song, but the concert never begins, and I get the feeling that she won't be singing a tune I want to hear anyway. Sitting to her right, two women busily shuffle papers and type away at computers. Two uniformed men are positioned to her left. Interspersed throughout the room are several other men in uniforms with holstered guns at their hips.

Laurie and Mama sit in the gallery to my rear, tissues clutched in their trembling hands. Laurie has a frightened look on her face. My mother is crying. Her skin is as gray as the paint on the walls of this mausoleum where my life is about to end. She catches my gaze and offers a weak smile of encouragement, which quickly morphs into a grimace. The man in the expensive suit at the table beside me looks even grimmer. His face tightens as a group of people enter through a side door and take their seats. I am piss-my-pants terrified.

The woman in the black choir robe addresses the group, and one person rises to converse with her. I try to concentrate on what they are saying, but the Voices are rioting, and the cacophony they create blots out most everything else.

You're gonna fry, John-boy.

I hope you've got an asbestos butt.

They're gonna throw you to the wolves.

Ooowww!

"Madame Foreman has the jury reached a verdict?"

They're coming to get you.

You see how everyone's looking at you?

They all want you to get the death penalty!

"Yes, your Honor, we have."

"Will the defendant please rise?"

"I didn't do it—I didn't do it," I whisper. I feel a jab to my ribs.

"Get up," the man in the high-priced suit mutters in my ear.

I rise quickly, banging my knee on the table leg, the ankle restraints nearly tripping me. Wincing, I face the woman in the robe. Her mouth moves, but I can't hear what she's saying.

Oh man, here it comes.

You'd better bend over, put your head between your legs, and kiss your ass good-bye.

"I didn't do it. I didn't do it."

"For God's sake, John," the man in the high-priced suit says hoarsely. "Be quiet!"

You should have killed yourself when you had the chance. Now somebody else is going to do it for you.

"Shut up! Shut up!" My mind is reeling from all the commotion.

"I beg your pardon, young man!" The woman scowls down at me from her bench.

"Your Honor," the suit says, "my client is an extremely disturbed individual. I think it's fairly evident that he is not and never has been fit to stand trial."

"Be that as it may, he's been silent and disengaged throughout this trial, and he can stay that way long enough for us to finish."

My whole body is shaking—no matter how hard I try to control it. If only the Voices would cease and desist, I might be able to make it through the remainder of this ordeal with a minimal amount of humiliation. They are not about to give it a rest, however. If anything, they grow even more obnoxious.

What you do is grab the gun off that cop right there and start shooting.

Yeah, first you get that bitch behind the bench, then you plug that smug bastard next to you.

Make sure you have at least one bullet left for yourself, though.

Shoot through the roof of your mouth—that'll do it.

I glance at the nearest cop, estimating the distance between us to be only six feet. He looks toward me at precisely the same instant, his hand feeling for the butt of his gun, and I wonder if he, too, hears the Voices. Out of the corner of my eye, I notice the other uniforms come to attention, as if they are of one mind.

Well what are you waiting on?

You want them to shoot you first?

Go for it!

"Madame Foreman, what is the jury's verdict?"

Quit wasting time, you dumb shit.

This is your last chance!

"We find the defendant not guilty by reason of insanity or mental defect."

The room erupts into chaos. There are screams and shouts, and I turn to see several men rushing at me. Paralyzed by the hatred and pain on their faces, I can only watch as one of them vaults over the partition and throws himself at me, fists flailing. Then I'm being pulled backwards, and two deputies are wrestling the man to the floor.

"I'll kill you if I ever catch you out on the street, you sick scum!" he screams after me. "I'll kill you for what you did to my little boy!"

I hear similar threats as I'm pushed through a door and down a hallway, but I can't be sure if it's the Voices, the angry crowd, or a mixture of the two.

"I didn't do it. I didn't do it."

CHAPTER ONE

THE VOICES HAD BEEN QUIET for a couple of days. I knew better than to think they were gone for good—they'd been with me far too long, but at least they shut up long enough for me to shower and change clothes. It had been a while since I was clean, since I felt like being clean. Maybe, just maybe, they would remain silent and allow me to eat breakfast, too. I couldn't remember the last meal I'd eaten, but that's not saying much. I can't remember a lot of things.

When the nurse came to give me my medication, she looked surprised to see me sitting on the edge of the bed, dressed and ready to go to the dining room. "Well, John, I'm glad you decided to join the living today."

"Shh!" I whispered, finger to my lips. "The Voices might hear you and come back."

"Have I got great news for you." She smiled conspiratorially. "If you'd just take your medication like you're supposed to, they might not ever come back. And speaking of medicine, here's yours." She held up a syringe.

"I don't want a shot."

"If you'd stop being non-compliant, you wouldn't have to have one. Do we have to use restraints again this morning?"

"No." I bared a butt cheek and allowed her to inject it before the Voices had a chance to protest. "They don't want me to take drugs," I grumbled. "They think it's poison."

"Ah, but you know differently, don't you?" she asked.

Did I? I couldn't ever be sure, and it was best not to argue with the Voices. Arguing with them always got me in trouble.

"So you're going to be eating with us this morning?" the nurse asked.

"Yeah, I'm hungry for a change."

"All right. Well, you know the routine. I'll be back for you in about thirty minutes."

Right. The routine. That much I did remember. "Because of possible hypotensive effects, keep patient lying down for at least one-half hour after injection." But according to the Voices, it's to give the toxin a chance to permeate all the cells so it will kill me faster. That's okay, though, because most days I want to die.

By the time she returned for me, the venom was running its course. Hospital 1. Voices 0. I followed her down the hall to collect the rest of the guys from our ward. Dead man walking. The other staff members we met on the way seemed surprised to see me. They were no doubt wondering why the poison hadn't killed me yet. "Good morning, John. I'm surprised to see you up and about."

"Welcome back, you pervert," someone growled into my left ear, and I whirled around, surprised.

"What's the matter?" sneered the guy behind me. "Hearing voices again?"

"Daniel, quit aggravating him," the nurse admonished. "You're all here for a reason, so stop making fun of him."

"Well my bipolar disorder never caused me to—"

"That's enough, Daniel, thank you. Just stop." She ushered us down the corridor to the cafeteria.

I wished she'd let him finish. For the truth was, I didn't remember why I was here, and I hated that everyone else seemed to have that knowledge but me. I wondered if the Voices knew and decided that they must. They usually whispered and mumbled among themselves, keeping me awake for nights on end. Sometimes I tried to ignore what they were saying but vowed to pay more attention to them the next time. Perhaps they would let me in on the secret, too.

In the meantime, another voice was whispering, this one belonging to Daniel. "Freak." The hatred and disgust on his face made my stomach clench, effectively killing my appetite.

In the cafeteria I went through the line and got a tray, even though I wasn't likely to eat anything now. At our table, everyone but the nurse crowded the end opposite from me. I had long been accustomed to pretending that people's attitudes toward me didn't hurt, but I wasn't very good at convincing myself. I didn't know why it even bothered me—as far as I remembered, none of them had ever been friendly—but it did nevertheless. I pushed the food around on my plate until the nurse noticed.

"Aren't you going to eat, John?"

"No. I guess I'm not hungry after all."

"I hope you're not going to let Daniel upset you."

"I don't like other people knowing stuff about me that I don't know myself." I muttered.

"Well, I'm sure if you think about it long enough, you'll discover that you do know. You've just chosen to forget about it."

I wasn't aware of having made a choice to forget any aspect of my life. Things just refused to stay in my brain, but I decided it was best not to say any more about the matter at that point.

Back on our ward, we waited in the dayroom to be seen by our doctors. Again, the others sat as far from me as they could, occasionally casting ugly looks my way.

"Why don't you go to your room and talk to your voices like you normally do," Daniel said after several minutes, "and get the hell out of my sight."

"I'm not bothering you." I tried to keep my voice calm.

"Your being alive bothers me, you pervert. I don't know why God would bother wasting breath on something like you."

"God didn't create me, asshole—Satan did." I was immediately sorry I'd said that. Daniel's eyes grew wide and the look on his face said he'd suspected as much. To tell the truth, it was something I worried about—something the Voices discussed frequently. But it got him to shut up, and for that I was grateful.

One of the staff members came to get me for my doctor's appointment then, sparing me any further confrontation. As I was led from the room, though, I heard Daniel muttering, "I knew you were a child of the Devil. I knew it."

In Dr. Fremont's office, I waited in my usual chair while he filled his coffee cup and helped himself to a doughnut from a box by the coffeemaker in the reception area.

"Good morning, John," he said as he settled in his seat. He held up the doughnut and raised his eyebrows at me. "Would you like one? Coffee?"

"Morning. No thanks." I watched as he stirred the contents of a pink pack of sweetener into his mug.

He took a sip, then smiled at me. "I must say, I'm glad to see you moving under your own steam today. Mrs. Thompson says that you even took a shower this morning. A vast improvement. I'm pleased. Tell me how you're feeling."

I studied the backs of my hands. "I guess I'm feeling a lot better."

"You 'guess'?"

"I am feeling a lot better."

"Do you understand why that is?"

I shrugged my shoulders. "Not really."

"I've decided to put you on Thorazine, a first generation anti-psychotic medication. Sometimes old school is best. The Seroquel just wasn't controlling your symptoms satisfactorily. But the main reason is because you've been getting your medication on a regular basis since we started injecting it. I can't begin to stress to you the importance of taking your medication every day, John. Hiding your pills in your pants pockets wasn't helping you, now was it? How long has it been since you've heard the voices?"

"A couple of days, I think." I stared out the window. I didn't want to talk about them.

"Something in particular bothering you today?" He took a bite of doughnut, sending an avalanche of powdered sugar and crumbs down his tie. He flipped the tie in the air a few times with his free hand to dislodge the offending matter and waited for me to speak.

I sighed. "Well, yeah. Why exactly am I here? What is it I'm supposed to have done? Why can't I remember? Why does Daniel hate me?"

Dr. Fremont drummed his fingers against the side of his coffee cup and smiled his little smile. "To answer your first question, you're here because you've been sick, and we're working on getting you better. As to what you have done, I can't answer that, and it's immaterial to my treatment of your illness. As to why you can't remember, that may all come back to you in time."

"And until then, everyone knows but me. Am I a child of the devil?"

He frowned. "Do you think you're a child of the devil?"

"I must be. Why else would I be here?"

"You think this is hell?"

"Isn't it?"

He leaned back in his chair. "I guess after eight years it must seem that way. Which brings me to something I want to discuss with you." He watched me for several moments as if he expected me to suddenly flap my arms, fly around the room, then perch on his shoulder. Call me crazy, but he seemed disappointed when I didn't. I fidgeted with a hole in the knee of my jeans, waiting.

"I've arranged for your sister and her husband to visit you. Now that you're doing better with your medication, I decided it would be appropriate. How do you feel about that?"

I would have felt a lot happier about it if I had been able to figure out what he was talking about. A sister? I didn't remember any sister. I wondered if he was trying to trick me by asking about a relative who didn't exist. If I took the bait, would he jump up and yell, "Ha, gotcha! You're not really getting any better!"

I decided to chance it. "I would like that very much," I lied.

That must have been the right answer, because he looked relieved. "Good, good. I'll confirm the visit with her."

"Okay...thanks," I said, because he seemed to be expecting a verbalization of my gratitude. But I wasn't sure I was thankful at all. Why should I care if someone I didn't know came to see me? On the other hand, there were so few visitors on our ward that her presence would at least break the monotony. I wanted to discuss this with Dr. Fremont a little further, but he was making motions to end our session. He straightened the papers in my file, closed it, and patted it.

"Well now, I'm very hopeful that you will continue to improve on the Thorazine. Regular medication is the key to helping you get better. You do understand that, don't you?"

I nodded. I understood perfectly, however, I wasn't sure the Voices would agree.

#

Okay, this is a problem. They're injecting him with the venom again. Damn it to hell. Can't he see they're trying to poison him? They're trying to keep him crazy.

If they make him take that shit, then they'll be able to control him, and he won't listen to us anymore.

They won't stop until they control him. They'll know every time he thinks about committing suicide, every time he thinks about going to the bathroom, every time he thinks about jerking off.

We can't let that happen.

Is he going to sleep?

Don't let him go to sleep!

We've got to keep him awake.

Wake up!

How can he sleep anyway, after the stuff he's done?

He's a sick puppy.

Yeah, all messed up and no place to go.

Look, he's trying to go to sleep again.

WAKE UP!

Damn it, we can't let him have any more of that medication.

WAKE UP, JOHN!

He's trying to ignore us.

We'll just talk louder then.

#

I was crouched on a corner of the bed next to the wall, bleary-eyed from lack of sleep, when Mrs. Thompson entered my room. The Voices were back and had kept me up into the wee hours with their incessant chattering. As if that weren't enough, once I finally drifted off for a few minutes of shuteye, they awakened me with their infernal arguing.

Toward dawn, when I didn't think I could endure any more, they fell to whispering. This did not bring me any comfort, however. I was sure that their secretiveness indicated some horrible calamity about to befall me.

"Bless your heart," Mrs. Thompson said after a moment, "you look like you've had a rough night."

I nodded, afraid to speak, afraid they would launch into another diatribe, but not wanting to miss anything they said in the hope that they would let slip the reason I was here.

"Come on, now. Today's a new day. We'll make the best of it and try to forget about whatever bothered you last night. Here's your medicine."

I stood, preparing to comply, but thought I noticed something swimming in the viscous green liquid within the little vial and I climbed back onto the bed.

"Come down off that bed. This is just your medicine. See?" She held the container out for me to examine.

It appeared to be full of tiny, venomous snakes. I could almost feel their sharp, poisonous little fangs sinking into my flesh, and I couldn't help myself—I turned my face to the wall, muffling a scream.

"Don't do this to me, John. I've only been on duty for half an hour, and you're the third person I've butted heads with." She sounded exasperated, but she took the container of snakes and slime and placed it back on her cart. She stepped over to the door, and I heard her say, "I need some assistance in Colucci's room!"

A couple of male attendants rushed in and wrestled me onto my stomach.

"No! It's full of snakes!"

"Snakes?" one of the attendants muttered in my ear. "Dude, the only thing in this room that's full of snakes is your head."

My head? No wonder the Voices hadn't wanted me to take the medicine! "Kill them! Kill them!" I struggled, trying to pull the fork-tongued vermin from my head.

"Jesus Christ, he's trying to pull his hair out. Get his hands."

The three of us thrashed about on the bed, and someone said, "Get the restraints."

No restraints! If they were able to tie me down before I could kill the snakes...I didn't want to think about what would happen. I fought harder.

"All right, guys, let's see if we can get him immobilized."

They attempted to turn me over, and I managed to break free, sliding to the floor.

"Oh no you don't, John."

A wild clash of arms and legs moved around me in a bizarre dance.

"Come back here."

"You got his arms?"

"Not yet, hang on, damn it."

Someone seized my forearm.

"Got him!"

I kneed the nearest groin, and my arm was momentarily released.

"Ow! Son of a bitch!"

A pair of hands grabbed my other arm. "All right, now!"

Before I could kill any of the snakes, the attendants rolled me to one side and yanked my pants down to expose a buttock. I felt a faint sting, then the restraints were fastened securely to my arms and legs. Sure one of the snakes had sunken a fang in me, I started to cry. I could feel the venom burning its way through my flesh and into my bloodstream. I would be dead in a matter of minutes, but no one seemed very concerned. In fact, they seemed relieved.

"Whew! I'm glad that's over," Mrs. Thompson said. "He was doing so well yesterday."

They left the room, left me tied to the bed, and worst of all, the Voices were furious.

More poison!

I can't believe it. They'll have him so drugged out, he won't even know himself.

That's true, and he won't know us either.

We've got to do something about this.

What do you propose?

We get rid of Dr. Fremont! He's the one who prescribes the shit. He wants John to listen to him and not to us. He's been trying to lose us for months.

Fine. The next opportunity we get, we'll remedy that little problem.

The Voices continued to whisper, plotting and planning among themselves for a time, then gradually quieted down. I was about to doze off when one of the male attendants returned to my room.

"Is everything cool now?" he asked. "Ready to get up and stay in reality for a while?"

I waited to see if the Voices had any snide remarks to make, but they didn't. "Yes."

"Great." He unfastened the straps and helped me to my feet. "You feel like something to eat? You missed breakfast, but I can round up something if you're hungry."

"No thanks. I kind of lost my appetite."

He shrugged his shoulders. "Your doctor's going to see you in about an hour, so don't run off."

Ha, ha. Like I could if I wanted to. I worried, though. What did the Voices have planned for Dr. Fremont? I didn't think they were likely to be a problem at least for a couple of hours, but what then? I didn't like the idea of hurting Dr. Fremont and indeed had no intention of hurting him. Yet the Voices could be so persuasive—when they spoke it was inconceivable that I would not listen.

A dreadful thought occurred to me—perhaps I was here because I had hurt someone. If the Voices were planning Dr. Fremont's demise, then it was within the realm of possibility that they had done the same to someone else. And it was possible that I had carried out those plans. The very idea that I may have been responsible for harming someone made me sick to my stomach. It would, however, go a long way toward explaining why I was an unwilling, long-term guest in one of the State's finest institutions.

I hoped that my sister could shed some light on the subject for me during our visit. I tried to imagine what she would look like, how she would act. Had we been close before...before whatever it was that brought me here? Oh God, this was never going to work—I couldn't even remember her name. I did good to remember my own. Colucci, John Edward. But would I know that if I hadn't seen it on the label of the file folder on Dr. Fremont's desk? I wasn't sure and that scared me.

#

The morning of my sister's visit I was already jittery, nervous. In my room, I paced in front of the window, stopping occasionally to look out on the grounds, wishing my brain functioned normally so I could at least recall her name. I could sense it lurking in the cobwebs, but when I tried to drag it into the light, it broke free and skittered away deeper into the shadows, leaving me even more frustrated.

To compound my frustration, Mrs. Thompson came by with her little medication cart. "Good morning, John," she said. "Want to bare a cheek for me?"

"Do I have to have a shot *now*?"

Mrs. Thompson sighed. "Yes. You know this. We have to make sure you're getting your Thorazine on a regular basis."

"Couldn't I wait until later to take it? It always makes me so jumpy, and my sister's supposed to come later. I want to be able to concentrate when she gets here."

She rolled her eyes as if I were trying her last bit of patience. "John, in order for you to stay well, you have to take your medication on time. Dr. Fremont increased your dosage, and you can't afford to miss it."

"But please. If you checked with him, I'm sure he wouldn't care."

"Dr. Fremont is out of town, and he won't be back until Wednesday. Now are you going to bare your hip or do I get someone to help you?"

Angry, I toyed with the idea of baring something else, but I knew if I did, I would have to endure a session with Dr. Fremont saying how disappointed he was in my behavior. So my frustration stayed where it belonged, and Dr. Fremont would have been proud of me.

I unzipped my jeans and held them at half-mast while she injected me with the venom. Maybe it was my imagination, but it seemed she jabbed the needle a little harder than necessary.

It was nearly nine-thirty when an attendant came for me and I did the Thorazine shuffle down to the cafeteria. I wasn't very hungry—the medicine had cured that—but it was something to do. I selected a cinnamon roll since it didn't require a lot of coordination to eat. I only dribbled a little milk on my shirt, but it didn't make a very noticeable stain. I was brushing crumbs from my lap with shaking hands (also compliments of the Thorazine) when a voice close to me said, "There he is, Randy. My God, it's been so long."

I looked up to see a couple approaching my table. The woman looked very much like the person I saw in my mirror on those days the demons weren't visiting. The nose and mouth were the same, the blue eyes and brown hair the same, but while my face was longer and more angular, hers was rounder, fuller. She was a beautiful woman.

For a moment I could hear a teen-aged girl, saying, "John, can't you eat a cookie without making so many crumbs?" Then I heard that same girl, older, a young woman, crying, "Oh my God, John, what have you done?" I trembled.

But that girl, that woman, was smiling now, reaching to put her arms around me. I allowed her to embrace me, trying not to tense up, all the while praying that my foggy brain would remember more.

"Take it easy, Laurie," the man said. "Can't you see he doesn't know who you are?"

Laurie dropped her arms and stood back, surveying me. "Is it true, John? Don't you recognize me? Don't you remember me?"

And I did recognize her at last. "Yes," I said. "You're the lady in the chicken soup commercial. 'Even Mom's never tasted this good.'"

Randy burst out laughing. He was a big man and his voice carried all over the cafeteria. No one turned to look at us, though. They were used to loud laughter here. "Well, you did ask if he recognized you," he said to Laurie and there was a hint of derision in his voice.

I could tell my answer upset her. "You're my sister," I said to her.

"Yes, I'm your sister. But if you'd met me on the street, you wouldn't have known that, would you?"

"Maybe. I'm not sure." Another image flashed in my mind. "Toasted Twinkies!"

"You do remember me!" She threw her arms around me again.

"Excuse me?" Randy said.

Laurie laughed. "I was babysitting John one afternoon while Mom and Dad went out shopping. John wanted a snack. Twinkies were his favorite. He couldn't have been more than six years old, and he got this bright idea that he'd like his Twinkies toasted. He climbed up on the counter and stuffed his Twinkies in the toaster. Obviously they were too thick for the slots, and he had to cram them in. Well, his Twinkies got toasted all right. The cream filling ran out and started smoking, then the sponge cake caught on fire. I came in the kitchen and discovered him getting ready to pour a glass of water down into the thing. I stopped him just in time to keep him from being shocked."

Funny how the memory of my sister and the Twinkies evoked memories of electric shock therapy. I hadn't remembered anything about her past the flames leaping out of the toaster and her yelling at me to stop, but I didn't think it necessary to tell her that. Those memories might be forever lost to me, having leaked out of my brain during the shock treatments which were forced upon me by Dr. Fremont's predecessors, although they claimed the shock treatments had nothing to do with my memory loss.

According to the doctors, the shock treatments had been very humane—before each I was given medication to prevent muscle contractions and the procedure had been done under anesthesia. Or so I had been told. If the toaster had shocked me, I wouldn't have been afforded the amenities the state had to offer. Perhaps if I had been shocked as a child, I would not be in here today. But that kind of thinking was crazy, right?

"Poor John," Laurie murmured, squeezing my shoulder. "It hasn't been easy for you, has it?"

"There's a lot I don't remember," I told her truthfully.

She tried to look cheerful. "Dr. Fremont says you're doing very well on your new medication. I don't know why your other doctors didn't try it."

"They were having too much fun frying my brain one piece at a time."

Randy snorted. "Yeah, and there are some people who would've liked to fry your ass."

"Randy!" Laurie looked mortified. "I thought we weren't going to talk about that."

"He might as well know the truth, especially if Dr. Fremont is thinking about releasing him."

"Dr. Fremont is going to release me?" I could hardly believe my ears.

Laurie cast a sidelong glance at Randy before replying. "If you continue to do well, he plans to."

"That's great." I surprised myself by smiling, then the rest of Randy's words sunk in and I felt the smile turning into a frown. "Who would want to see me fry?"

"Don't worry about that." She put on her happy face again. "You just keep taking your medication and concentrate on getting better. That's the most important thing you can do right now."

"And if you thought it was bad in here, just wait 'til you get out there," Randy muttered under his breath.

I pretended that I hadn't heard him, yet something kept grating on my conscience, something my frazzled brain was trying to remember. I decided I didn't like him very much, and it appeared that the feeling was mutual.

Perhaps sensing the tension, Laurie stepped between us and sat down next to me, forcing Randy to take a step backward. "Dr. Fremont thinks he may be able to release you by mid-March. We'll celebrate your birthday then. I know it will be a couple of weeks late..."

She didn't finish the sentence, but I knew what she was thinking. The atmosphere on the ward did not lend itself to celebration. "That's fine," I told her. I hadn't celebrated a birthday in at least eight years. What would it matter if I missed one more? When was my birthday anyway? I wasn't even sure how old I would be.

Laurie placed a hand on my shoulder and peered into my eyes for so long that I finally had to look away. "I'm glad you're back," she whispered and kissed my cheek.

CHAPTER TWO

"HOW ARE YOU TODAY, JOHN?" Dr. Fremont sat behind his desk smiling at me, hands clasped around his ever-present coffee mug.

I didn't smile back.

"Having a bad day?" he asked after a few moments.

"More like a bad life," I replied.

"Why do you say that?"

"Well, for starters, I'm living in a nightmare, and have been, according to you, for eight years now. I wasn't fucked up enough, so you fry my brain. Then, when that stopped getting you bastards off, you fill me full of drugs."

"You sound rather angry."

"You're damned right I'm angry. I'm royally pissed."

Dr. Fremont put his cup down on the desk. "Let's talk about it."

I jumped up to stand by the window next to my chair, where I could look out at the traffic going by on the street below. I didn't realize that I was systematically plucking the leaves off a potted plant until Dr. Fremont came over and gently removed my hands from the now bare stems.

"Shall we talk?" he asked.

I wanted to choke him—the Voices would have approved. "Why couldn't I remember her?" I yelled instead. "Why couldn't I remember my own goddamned sister? My birthday? My age? And just what am I doing here anyway? Those damned shock treatments fried my brain cells, and now I don't even know who or what I am!" I punched the padded back of the chair I had been sitting in, and it scudded across the floor, striking a bookcase and causing several figurines to topple over.

"Calm down, John. Now, as I have explained to you several times, the general consensus in the medical community is that electroconvulsive therapy is not a very efficacious treatment for schizophrenia, although some of your former doctors thought that it might prove helpful in treating your underlying depression. And as I have also explained to you, the shock treatments did not cause your long-term memory loss. At the most, they would have affected your memory of what took place immediately before and after the treatments."

"How many treatments have I had? Fifty? And why couldn't I have waited to take my medication until after Laurie's visit? You know it makes me jumpy! How can I remember anything if I'm climbing the walls? I swear, I think you want me to stay crazy!"

"Sit down, John." Dr. Fremont pulled my chair back over in front of the desk and pointed. Furious, I stomped over and dropped onto it, and he perched on the edge of his desk, fingers drumming the crease of his slacks as he studied me. "First of all, I think you will agree that your behavior just now is hardly an incentive to delay your medication for any reason. Secondly, I do not want you to 'stay crazy'." Here he made quotation marks with his fingers. "More than anything else, I want you to get well so you can leave this place. As for your memory, I think that as time goes by, you will begin remembering more about why you came to be here. That's all part of the process of getting well. Perhaps the visits with your sister between now and then will help speed up that process. Didn't you remember anything while she was here?"

"A little—not enough to count," I muttered.

"Well now, that's a start. It's not going to come back to you all at once, John. It took years to bury each memory; it will take you a while to uncover it. Don't be discouraged. You've made outstanding progress in the last month."

"Will there be any more shock treatments?"

"Not as long as I'm treating you."

"How long will I have to take the drugs?"

Dr. Fremont clasped his hands, steepling his forefingers. "To stay well, you're going to have to take them indefinitely, barring tardive dyskinesia. In fact, that's going to be one of the conditions of your release."

"What is tardive dys—dys—what the hell did you call it?"

"Dyskinesia. To explain it simply, it's abnormal, uncontrolled movements, mainly of the face, tongue, mouth and neck that can be caused by prolonged treatment with antipsychotic drugs."

"Well that's just great. If you can't fry my brain, then you'll turn me into a spastic!"

"If you're going to stay well and stay out of the hospital, John, you have to take your medication. Perhaps you're the one who doesn't want you to get well."

"That's not true." An urge to cry was threatening to overwhelm me, and my voice shook with the effort of trying to control it. "I do want to be well. I want to be normal again, and I want to leave this place."

Dr. Fremont rested his hand on my shoulder. "That can happen. Keep working with me, and it may happen sooner than you think."

When our session was over, I waited on a bench in the hallway outside Dr. Fremont's office for the attendant to use the restroom before taking me back to the ward. Weak winter sunshine filtered into the hallway from tall, arched windows, and in the distance, snow clouds stacked up on the mountain peaks. I leaned back and closed my eyes, going over my conversation with Dr. Fremont.

Was I really that close to blowing this hellhole? He'd said I'd made outstanding progress, my thinking was clearer, and the Voices weren't quite as vocal as they had been. Still, it was difficult to imagine an existence on the outside. I had only the vaguest memories of life elsewhere. Where would I live once I got out? What would I do for money? And what had Randy meant about people wanting to fry me?

As if on cue, one of the Voices said in a low, hateful tone, "Well, well. What kind of perversion are you dreaming up today, you monster?"

"Shut up," I hissed. "Just stop it." The Voices could always be counted on to ruin any peaceful moment.

"Who are you telling to shut up? I hope you're not telling me to shut up, 'cause I don't need any other reason to beat your ass."

"What?" Never had the Voices threatened me before. I opened my eyes to find Daniel standing at the opposite end of the bench, one hand balled into a fist and the other in his pants pocket. Where had he come from?

"You heard me."

I looked around, but saw no attendants in sight, and stood warily. "Why don't you go away? I've never done anything to you."

"You're breathing, that's enough."

"I can't see how that's hurting you."

"Just like you couldn't see how you were hurting those—" his voice broke off in a choked kind of fury, "—those little kids."

"What—"

"Don't act like you don't know what I'm talking about! I know all about you, about what you did. They should have given you the death penalty, you pervert. Instead they send you here, and decent people like my family have to pay taxes to keep you alive. The least they could have done was to lock you away so you'd never see the light of day again. But no, now they're talking about turning you loose so you can prey on other children!"

"What—" I barely got my mouth open when he lunged at me. There was no time to brace myself and down I went, the back of my head colliding with tile-covered concrete.

For a moment the light dimmed and things grew a little hazy, then a solid, well-placed blow to my stomach brought it all back into sharp and painful focus. My breath left me in an agonized wheeze, and I figured my stomach contents wouldn't be far behind.

Daniel's face hovered above me, and he waved a shiny pointed object within my field of vision. "Ever think about suicide, John? Let me help you. All it would take is just a few strategic cuts and you could bleed to death in a matter of minutes. How about it?"

He swung the object at my throat, and I reacted by blocking the motion with raised arms. There was a burning sensation in my right forearm. A split second later, a rush of something warm and wet soaked my shirtsleeve. He made another slicing motion, this time at my face, and I wrenched my head to one side, though not quickly enough to avoid the same sensation to my cheek.

Daniel shifted his weight to make another jab at me, and I was able to free my left leg. I kicked hard, my foot connecting with the side of his head just above his ear. He fell over with a grunt and lay there several beats as if dazed.

I placed a hand to my face, surprised to find that it was also wet. The surprise turned to anger when I realized that I was bleeding. "You son of a bitch!"

Scrambling to my feet, I rushed at Daniel, who was also picking himself up from the floor. I grabbed his wrist and twisted. In turn, he seized a handful of my hair and yanked me closer.

"I'm gonna cut out your black heart and feed it to you," he snarled.

I managed to slide my foot behind his and rammed my shoulder into his rib cage. He sat down abruptly, and I fell on top of him, swinging.

Footsteps and shouts resounded in the hallway, and I felt myself being lifted off of Daniel by my shirt collar. An assortment of staff members surrounded us, mouths gaping and eyes wide. Dr. Fremont pushed his way through to me.

"What's going on here? What are you—John, you're bleeding!"

"I know." I put a hand to my cheek again, and it was then that I noticed the rip in my shirtsleeve and blood oozing from the nasty cut on my arm. "Oh, Jesus." My head filled with helium, and I felt that morning's breakfast clawing its way up out of my stomach. I don't remember aiming for Daniel, but splattered him nevertheless.

"Let's get John to the infirmary," Dr. Fremont said to one of the attendants, "then I want to know what the hell was going on and why these two were alone. Someone had better be coming up with some good answers. Don't think there won't be write-ups over this."

"It was self-defense," Daniel yelled, brushing at his clothes, a disgusted look on his face. "The schizo attacked me! He was talking to his voices or something—maybe they told him to do it. He just walked up to me and started waving that blade. I got it away from him...God only knows what he would have done to me if I hadn't."

"I'll talk to you later," Dr. Fremont said to him. He sounded angry. When he turned back to me, however, his voice was gentler. "Do you think you can make it to the infirmary?"

"Yeah, I'm fine," I lied.

He and an attendant walked on either side of me anyway, which was a good thing, because my equilibrium had mysteriously disappeared. And when I puked again, this time on my knees in the bushes near the door leading to the infirmary, they waited politely by the sidewalk and hauled me to my feet when I was finished.

"You're not going to pass out on us, are you John?" Dr. Fremont looked into my eyes, concern evident on his face. I had to admit that I was lightheaded.

They got me into the examining room and pulled off my shirt. I felt queasy again when I got a good look at my arm, and even queasier when I glimpsed my face reflected in the mirror over the sink.

"Doing okay?" the attendant asked as one of the infirmary doctors began cleaning my wounds. "You're a little green."

I thought I was doing okay until they began sewing. The sight of it was more than I could endure, and I closed my eyes so I wouldn't have to watch. When I opened them again, I was stretched out on one of the infirmary beds, bandages on my arm and cheek. Dr. Fremont stood nearby talking with a nurse.

When he saw me stirring, he came over and sat down beside me, smiling. "You conked out on us there for a bit. We've got you all patched up now, though, and we're pretty sure you're going to live."

I didn't smile back. "It wasn't my knife, you know."

"I never thought it was," he replied.

"He tried to kill me. He was going to cut my throat."

Dr. Fremont nodded soberly. "He'll be dealt with on that score."

"He called me a monster. He said that I hurt little kids." I watched for his reaction.

He pretended to be studying something outside the window.

"Is it true?" I asked.

This time he looked directly at me. "You're the only one who can answer that, John."

"God damn it, why can't you shoot straight with me for once?"

"I've always shot straight with you, but that's not a question I can answer. I'm not a judge or a jury. As far as I'm concerned, you're here because you suffer from schizophrenia and anything you may have done is directly as a result of that. I'm sorry this happened to you. I've called your sister to let her know. She's going to be up on Friday morning, and we're all going to have a little chat about your release."

"Oh, and I suppose you're not going to release me now, because this just proves I'm not ready!" Angry, I rolled over, my back to Dr. Fremont.

"On the contrary," I was surprised to hear him reply.

#

On Friday I was released from the infirmary and taken directly to Dr. Fremont's office. There I found Laurie and Randy already seated in front of the desk, Randy in the place where I usually sat. He surveyed me with a critical glance and a sneer by way of greeting. Laurie, however, jumped up to throw her arms around me.

"Are you okay?" She hugged me, then stepped back to inspect the bandages and bruises. "I was so upset when Dr. Fremont called and told me you'd been attacked." She brushed hair from my forehead with trembling fingers.

"He really ought to get that mess cut," Randy muttered. "Anyone who sees him will know he's a lunatic."

"Randy, please," she whispered.

I said nothing, but seated myself on the metal folding chair Dr. Fremont offered me.

"You're looking much better," he said, taking his place behind the desk. He opened my file and flipped through it for a few moments, then looked up. "I've been talking with your sister and brother-in-law this morning, John, and I told them that I'm releasing you next week."

I could not hide my astonishment.

"Overall, you've done very well on the Thorazine. It's done more for you in the past few months than everything else that has been tried in the past eight years. I see no reason why you can't continue to improve at home. But for you to continue to improve, you must keep taking your medication, and I can't release you unless I'm certain that you will. Do I have your word?"

"Yes!" Afraid that my response had been too hasty, I paused. Lowering my voice, I said more deliberately, "You have my word."

"Excellent, but I want to make it clear that if you stop taking your medication for any reason, you run a high risk of being involuntarily committed again. Do you understand?"

Before I could reply, Randy spoke up. "If he quits taking his medicine, I'll bring him back myself."

Irritation flashed across Dr. Fremont's face, but he ignored Randy and repeated, "Do you understand, John? You must keep taking the Thorazine even though you are feeling better. You have to take it consistently for it to have any benefit."

"I understand."

Dr. Fremont smiled. "Good deal." He glanced at his watch. "Why don't you go on to lunch with Laurie and Randy? I'm sure you have some things you want to discuss with them. I'll see you again tomorrow for our regular session."

I followed Randy and Laurie out of Dr. Fremont's office and an attendant led us downstairs to the cafeteria. We went through the line where they both selected a sandwich and coffee. I got a Pepsi.

"Don't you want something to eat, John?" Laurie asked.

"Not really," I told her.

"But you're so thin already."

"Oh Christ, if he doesn't want anything to eat, leave him the hell alone," Randy snapped.

We found a table and sat down. I took a sip of my drink, then a deep breath, and said to Randy, "You don't like me very much, do you?"

"Oh, it's not that at all!" Laurie protested before he had a chance to answer truthfully. "He's just on edge because—well, because it's going to take us a while to get used to the idea of having someone else in the house. It's not that we don't want you, but it's just been the two of us for years now. I'm sure you can understand."

I wasn't entirely convinced that was the reason for his attitude toward me, but I nodded anyway. "So I'm going to be staying with you?"

"Where did you think you were going to stay?" Randy asked in the same hateful tone of voice. "By yourself? You haven't got any way of making a living. You can't take care of yourself. Hell, you can't even bathe yourself half the time."

My stomach wrenched into a tight, nervous ball. I found myself thinking it would be a happy coincidence if I were able to projectile vomit on the one other person I liked least in my sordid little world. "I don't have to stay with you," I said, struggling to keep my voice steady.

"Yeah, John, you do. Besides, who else is going to take *you* in? Why do you think they're turning you loose? They don't want you in here anymore. Your presence antagonizes the other patients—they want to kill your ass. You can't be sent to a halfway house for fear of the same thing happening there. People haven't forgotten a high profile crime like yours. Just where else would you stay?"

"Randy..." Laurie was crying silently, large tears sliding down her cheeks, streaking her make-up.

A sense of dread stole over me. "What did I do? Why do people want to kill me?"

"Oh, knock off the bullshit. You know good and well why."

I jumped up from the table and headed for the door.

Behind me Laurie was saying, "Damn it, Randy! John, please wait! Don't go yet!"

"Let him," was Randy's gruff command.

#

"I am *not* going to live with them," I said to Dr. Fremont.

He put a hand to his head as if seized by a sudden, severe headache and looked up at me, clearly exasperated. "You don't have a choice. I can't release you if you're not going to live with them. They are your legal guardians because you've been adjudged incompetent. There's no one else I can release you to, and I can't release you on your own."

I experienced a heaviness in the bottom of my stomach. "I'm incompetent?"

"You've been suffering from schizophrenia in varying degrees since you were fifteen, John. Until very recently you've been unable to care for yourself or make decisions that affect your well-being. This can hardly be news to you."

"But 'incompetent'—that makes me sound like I drool and wear diapers."

"If you wore diapers, then you'd be incontinent." He grinned at his little joke, no doubt trying to lighten my mood. It didn't work.

I stood on the pretext of looking out the window, ashamed that I was crying. "I don't understand why Randy hates me," I said when I was able to speak again.

"I doubt that he hates you, or you wouldn't be going to live with him."

"If it was all up to him, I wouldn't be."

"Well then, thank God for that, John. After eight years, I would think that you'd be glad to get out of here any way you could. I'm glad you're leaving, it makes me feel like I've made a difference in your life."

I turned to face him. "Randy says you're releasing me because my being here antagonizes the other patients."

Dr. Fremont picked up a pen from the desktop and rolled it between his fingers. At last he said, "There's no escaping the fact that your presence has antagonized at least one other patient, but the truth of the matter is budget constraints are forcing the state to cut back services and release patients. That being said, if I didn't see a remarkable improvement in your condition, I couldn't ethically or legally release you."

I wanted to ask him exactly what I had done to make Randy and Daniel despise me so, but I knew I wouldn't receive an answer I wanted to hear. I sat down, rested my head in my hands, and closed my eyes. Was I ready for this?

CHAPTER THREE

"HI, JOHN." Laurie entered my room, a shopping bag on each arm and a smile on her face, and stopped to give me a hug. "Well, today's the big day, isn't it?"

I felt my muscles tense at her touch but forced myself to hug her back, wishing I could share her enthusiasm about my release. Now that the day had finally arrived, rather than being happy, I felt only a cold, numbing fear.

"Being afraid is only natural, John," Dr. Fremont had told me the previous morning. "After all, this has been your home for eight years. I would be more concerned about you if you weren't afraid."

"These are for you." Laurie placed the bags on my bed and began pulling out new clothing—jeans, long-sleeved pull-over collarless shirt in a soft blue-gray fabric, a pair of Doc Martens boots, leather belt, coat, even underwear and socks. She indicated the shirt. "That really brings out the color of your eyes."

At first I was angry because I felt that she was ashamed to be seen with me in my 'institution' attire. Then I felt guilty because I realized she was trying very hard to show me she cared, and the rest of my clothes had definitely seen better days. So I traded the worn, faded things I had been wearing for the new, tossed the old clothing into the trash can, and prepared to go out and face the world a better dressed, if not better, man.

"Are these all of your things?" Laurie asked, glancing about the room to see if we might have missed something.

"That's all I have," I told her as I finished pulling on the boots. It seemed a sad statement that eight years of my life would fit into one small carry-on bag.

"You look great," she said when I finally stood. "Do the boots fit?"

"They're fine. Thanks."

She squeezed my hand and said, "Are we ready?"

I picked up my bag and nodded, not trusting my voice to answer her, but I wasn't ready. I didn't like not knowing where I would be tomorrow morning. For nearly as long as I could remember, I woke up in the same room (when I was able to sleep), to the same view outside my window. I followed the same routine, with few exceptions, almost every day. And while the people may have come and gone over the course of eight years, there were at least several faces that were familiar to me at any given time. Even knowing the things that had happened to me here, I was now reluctant to leave.

In the institution, I had a good idea who my enemies were, and I also knew that they had limited access to me. But out there—if Randy was correct—I was unprotected, vulnerable to attack at anytime, anywhere, from anyone. My stomach was experiencing a bad case of turbulence, and I could taste acid at the back of my throat.

But ready or not, I followed Laurie from my room. Some of the staff members we passed waved good-bye, and Mrs. Thompson stopped me at the dayroom door to hug me and whisper, "Good luck, hon."

Over her shoulder, I saw Daniel sitting in a chair near the window. He sneered and pointed his index finger at me, pulling an imaginary trigger. "Lots of luck, you pedophile," he called. "You know I won't be in here forever either. Be seeing you around."

Laurie's face was white as the attendant took us to the administrative wing of the building where Dr. Fremont greeted us in his office, coffee mug in hand. "Care for any?" He gestured at the coffeemaker.

My stomach was so unhappy, I didn't dare chance it. Laurie declined his offer as well, and we took seats across from his desk.

Dr. Fremont smiled at me. "John, you look great! I guess you're ready to get out there and start living."

"Not really," I muttered, but if he heard me, he didn't acknowledge my comment.

He explained the dispensing of my medication to Laurie, adding, "Should he become noncompliant, his new doctor can certainly resume injections. But that won't be necessary, will it, John?"

I shrugged. "You give me shots here."

"Yes, but we're not going to be with you out there, so we're relying on you to take it on your own. That's item number one on the list of conditions for your release. You do understand how important your medication is, don't you?"

I studied my new boots and entertained the idea of saying no, to see what would happen. Maybe I wouldn't have to leave after all. But they seemed so sure that I was ready, I didn't think I could disappoint them. Besides, if I stayed, I'd have to give back the new clothes.

"You do understand," Laurie repeated. It was a statement, not a question.

I took a deep breath and said, "Yes. I do."

She and Dr. Fremont appeared relieved—I had passed their test—and they discussed the doctor I would see on the outside and what Laurie should do if I experienced any problems.

At last, Dr. Fremont rose and held out his hard to me. "Good-bye, John, and good luck. No offense, but I hope we don't ever see you here again."

"Thanks." I shook his hand and attempted a smile, but my face was frozen with the effort of trying to keep from breaking down.

"I appreciate all the help you've given John," Laurie said to him.

We left his office and an attendant walked us down the corridor to the main entrance of the building. There a uniformed man unlocked the door for us, and we stepped out into the frosty winter air. I thought being free would be a more joyous occasion, but experienced only a deep sense of foreboding instead.

Laurie led me to a low-slung black sports car and unlocked the doors. I put my gear in the back, and she waited for me to get settled in, then started the engine. We were out on the highway before she spoke. "Are you feeling all right, John? You haven't had a lot to say this morning."

"I'll be okay."

"Would you like to listen to some music?" She seemed to understand that I wasn't able to talk at that point and sang along softly.

I scrunched down in the seat and closed my eyes, content to listen to her voice, pretty and delicate like a butterfly. If Dr. Fremont was correct, I had been hospitalized for at least eight years, and I had been suffering from schizophrenia since I was fifteen. A good portion of my life had been spent in hell and hearing her sing was like remembering another existence altogether.

Someone soft and fragrant murmurs soothing words. "It's all right, John-John, you just had a bad dream, that's all." Gentle lips touch my cheek and hands brush the hair from my brow. "Go back to sleep now, baby. Mommy's right here. Would you like me to sing you a lullaby?"

It had been a long time since I'd thought of my mother, and I wasn't prepared for the emotions that were unleashed. I knew she was gone, but I couldn't remember what had happened to her. Big, bloody chunks of memory had been ripped from my consciousness and were scattered across the littered floor of my mind. Even if I were able to sweep them up, would I ever be able to piece them back together?

Laurie placed a hand on my shoulder. "John, are you sure you're all right?"

"Please keep singing," I whispered without opening my eyes.

"Why don't you try to nap? I'll wake you when we stop for lunch." She began singing again, this time to a song about a bridge over troubled waters.

I must have slept, though it didn't seem like any time at all had passed before she was jostling my elbow and saying, "Wake up, John."

Sitting up abruptly, I banged my head on the roof of the car, causing little pinpoints of light to dance in front of my eyes.

Laurie laughed and said, "Ouch! That's not a good way to wake up."

"Oh, I don't know. It beats waking up in restraints and having an itch you can't scratch."

"I guess it would at that," she grinned. "Are you ready to get something to eat?"

I climbed out of the car and stretched. We had been traveling toward the mountains and here the air was colder, with a wind that bit through my clothes. Patches of white clung stubbornly to the hills surrounding us, and the sunshine had disappeared behind low gray clouds.

I shivered, grateful for my new coat. "Looks like snow."

"I think you're right. Come on, let's get out of this wind." Hand on my arm, Laurie steered me into the restaurant.

In the dining room we were seated next to a blazing fireplace. A waitress brought two cups of coffee straight away, saying, "It's so cold outside, I'm not even bothering to ask anyone if they want coffee today. I'm just assuming the answer is yes."

"Thanks," Laurie laughed. "It's freezing out there."

We sipped our coffee for a few minutes then the waitress came back to take our order. When she left our table, I leaned closer to Laurie and said, "If I ask you a question, will you please tell me the truth?"

Her smile vanished and a strange, frightened look crossed her face. "I'll try, John."

I swallowed hard and held my trembling hands under the table where she couldn't see them. My throat felt tight, constricted. "What happened to our mother?"

Her relief, mixed with pity, was evident. "You've been thinking about her, haven't you?"

"Yes, but I can't remember what happened."

"She was diagnosed with breast cancer not long after you first got sick, but she kept it to herself for a long time—she was so worried about you. She had some chemotherapy and they did a double mastectomy, but it was too late. She died three months after you were hospitalized. I wanted to tell you, but you were so sick yourself when she died that your doctor said we shouldn't even attempt it. Then, when you finally started getting better, so much time had passed, I just couldn't tell you and risk setting you back."

"You should have told me when it happened. I can remember wondering why she didn't come to see me, and thinking that she hated me." The tears I'd been fighting off all morning were getting ready to make an appearance.

"Oh, John, I'm so sorry." Laurie squeezed my knee and blinked back tears of her own.

I could feel a cloak of sorrow enveloping me as I sat digesting this bit of news. "Tell me one more thing." I was barely able to force the words out. "How old am I?"

She watched me for a moment before answering, probably wondering if she should take me straight back to the hospital. "You'll be twenty-eight on February twenty-fifth."

"Thank you." I stood from the table and headed for the restroom. There was no one else around when I entered, and I gazed at myself in the mirror for a long time, watching the anger and hurt roll down my face. Eventually, the storm passed, though my emotional sea was far from calm. I washed my hands and scrubbed at my face with a scratchy brown paper towel before returning to the dining room.

"Is everything okay?" Laurie asked as I sat down again. Worry lines bracketed her eyes.

"I'm all right now," I told her.

"I'm sorry things happened the way they did, John. I wish—"

"I said I'm all right, so just drop it!" I could tell that my curt tone wounded her. Softening my voice, I said, "I'm sorry. It's just that...I feel so overwhelmed. I don't know how to act, what to think. I need some time to sort out my head."

"Fair enough." She pointed to the steak I had ordered. "You'd better eat before it gets cold."

It was the first steak I'd had a chance to eat in at least eight years, but I couldn't do it justice. I kept thinking of my mother dying from cancer while I was locked away in la-la land, oblivious to her suffering and unaware of even my own existence. I also thought of the thirteen years I'd lost to this damned disease, and who knew how many more I might lose before it was all over.

"Are you finished?" Laurie asked, and I knew that I had been staring at my plate. "We really need to be going. I don't want to be caught driving in snow."

Back on the road the sky was even more threatening. "How much farther do we have to go?" I asked.

"An hour if the weather holds off; God only knows how long if it doesn't."

A little over ninety minutes had passed when we pulled in Laurie's driveway. Snow was coming down in big sticky flakes, and as Laurie cut the engine, the front door of her house flew open and Randy stalked out onto the porch.

"Where the hell have you been?" he shouted at her as we exited the car.

Laurie winced at the sound of his voice. "It took longer than I expected due to the snow."

I reached into the back of the car for my bag and followed her up the sidewalk.

"Why in God's name did you drive the Corvette if you thought it was going to snow?" Randy stomped into the house behind us, slamming the door and causing me to flinch.

"If I thought it was going to snow, Randy, I wouldn't have."

"Why don't you listen to a damned weather report once in a while?"

I was ready to run for cover, but Randy, frustrations vented, flopped down in his recliner. He picked up a beer bottle and tilted it to his lips, eyes already locked on the television.

Welcome to your new home, loser.

#

A portion of the first night in my new home was spent doing a complicated dance with the bedcovers, while the clock on the nightstand glowered at me, jeering my inability to sleep.

I had turned in early, too uncomfortable with Randy to sit in the living room. At nine-thirty, I heard him lumbering through the hall, followed moments later by the sound of water splashing tile on the other side of the wall. At ten-thirty, the television went off, the door slammed once more, and a car engine started.

I could hear Laurie moving through the house, her steps light, as if she were trying to keep from disturbing me. She came to my door and stood looking into the room for a few minutes. After that the house grew quiet, and it was just me and the clock from hell, its numbers burning an angry red.

I tried not to stare, but my eyes were drawn to it like moths to a porch light, minute after everlasting minute. I got out of bed and turned the thing so it faced the wall, yet still the red glow taunted me. Down on my hands and knees in the dark, I fumbled for the electric cord and yanked it from the outlet, half expecting it to electrocute me in revenge.

The demon clock died a quick death, but I didn't trust it. Sitting in the middle of the carpet-covered floor, I kept vigil to make sure it didn't resurrect itself. Through a space between the curtain panels, I could see the falling snow backlit by amber colored streetlights. I was still sitting on the floor when the streetlights winked off, the sky lightened to a dull gray, and traffic began to move slowly through the subdivision as its residents traveled to work and school. And I was still there sometime later when Laurie knocked on the door and peeked in.

"Good morning." She sounded surprised to see me awake. "How long have you been up?"

"Since early yesterday morning," I replied.

She frowned. "You didn't sleep at all?"

"Sometimes I can't." I didn't tell her about the clock. Some tales are just better left untold, especially when crazy people are the ones doing the telling.

"Well, since you're up, come on, and we'll get some breakfast."

Legs stiff, I rose and followed her into the kitchen, where she pointed me to a bar stool. Taking a bottle of water from the refrigerator and setting it and a glass on the counter in front of me, she said, "First things first." Opening a pill container, she shook out one tablet and handed it to me.

I unscrewed the cap on the water bottle, poured some water into the glass, and made sure she was watching as I placed the pill in my mouth and washed it down. I don't know what she was expecting and perhaps it was my imagination, but she seemed relieved there was nothing more to it.

She got herself some orange juice. "What would you like for breakfast? I could fix some scrambled eggs or pancakes, and I have both sausage and bacon. Or there's cereal if you'd rather have that."

"Could I just have some toast?" The institution had done a good job of turning me against breakfast forever, and the thought of overcooked, rubbery eggs and underdone, limp bacon made me want to gag.

"Are you sure that's all you want?"

"Yes...please."

She fixed two slices of toast with butter and placed them on a plate before me. "If you want anything else, I'll be glad to—"

"No. I mean thanks, but this is fine."

"Okay." She smiled. "I guess I sound like Mom, huh?"

I nodded my head, but had to take her word. It was quickly becoming obvious to me that the Voices relinquished only those memories they deemed fit, and they didn't bother to let me in on their reasoning for the ones they chose. I wished I could explain this to Laurie in a way that wouldn't make her think I'd missed a couple of doses of medicine. But there was a lot I didn't understand myself—such as why the Voices had been appointed guardians of my memories in the first place.

Laurie finished the rest of her juice. "Well, if you don't need anything else at the moment, I think I'll go take a shower. There are towels and stuff for you in the hall bath whenever you want to bathe."

She left the room, and I messed with my toast for a while, cutting it into tiny pieces with the butter knife, eating maybe half of it. Outside the snow was coming down thick and fast, with at least half a foot already on the ground.

I picked up my dishes to carry to the sink, pausing at the window to look out into the back yard. At the house across the way, I saw two kids making a snowman and throwing snowballs at each other, and faintly heard their excited yelps. I watched them, envious of the fun they seemed to be having.

Hearing movement behind me, I turned, thinking Laurie had finished her shower and had come to check on me. But it wasn't Laurie. Some part of me was aware of the plate and glass slipping from my hands and shattering on the tile floor at my feet, but it was not a part of me that could react.

A collection of blue lights congregates outside the windows, and their reflections swirl around the interior walls of the room. I know, somehow, that they have come for me, and I have a bad feeling in my gut, but I hold my position and continue to rock the broken, abandoned doll in my arms.

It occurs to me, after some moments, that I am crying, and it is only then I become aware of the words I am chanting. "Poor baby. Loving you was like loving the dead, and the dead tell no tales. I'm so sorry."

There is commotion in the hallway—yelling, shouting, stomping, pounding. I kiss the doll's cool china forehead and whisper, "Don't worry, they won't hurt you. No one can hurt you anymore."

The door flies inward and slams into the wall behind it, and a legion of Satan's finest pours into the room, a single gleaming eye peering from the left breast of each demon. "Oh God, John, what have you done?" one of them asks me.

Frightened that a demon could be on a first name basis with me, I cuddle the doll tighter and continue my chant. "Poor baby. Loving you was like loving the dead—"

"John, release the child."

"—and the dead tell no tales. I'm so sorry." Then faster, louder.

"John, please listen, before you get hurt. Release the child—"

"Can't you see?" I scream. "God damn it! Can't you see? The doll's already broken."

A subconscious sense of self-preservation belatedly kicked in, and I bolted out the door. Vaulting over the deck railing, I found myself crouched in the back yard, feet bare, snow above my ankles. One of the kids making the snowman called to me, "Hey, that was cool! Do it again!"

I glanced up to find that Laurie and Randy had followed me as far as the edge of the deck, Laurie pleading, "Back off, Randy. Please, just back off."

Randy rolled his eyes and returned to the house, shaking his head as he went. Laurie picked her way down the deck steps carefully, and held her hand out to me. "Please come back in, before you freeze to death. Everything will be okay, I promise. Randy's not going to hurt you."

I wasn't sure she would be very effective in stopping him if he did try to hurt me, but I returned to the warmth of the kitchen anyway.

Laurie trailed behind me, asking, "John, are you all right? What did you say to him, Randy?"

Randy was in the process of cleaning up the mess in the floor. "I just walked into the room, for Christ's sake, and he started losing his shit! Watch where you step, there's glass everywhere."

"I'm sorry." I was trembling, my t-shirt wet with sweat, my pants soaked from the snow.

"What's with you, man?" he snapped.

Strange emotions were still surging through me, and it was hard to look at him, much less talk to him. "I didn't know you were a—a cop."

"The hell you didn't. You know I was there when you were arrested." He finished wiping the floor and stood, the kitchen light reflecting off the handcuffs on his utility belt.

My mouth went dry and my heartbeat picked up. "I think I'll go to my room for a while." I edged my way toward the hall.

"Are you okay?" Laurie sounded worried. She peered into my eyes, and I could see part of the terror I had been feeling mirrored in her expression.

"That's a stupid question," Randy muttered.

"Randy, please. You've done enough for one day."

"I haven't done a damned thing!"

"Why can't you just—"

I ran to my bedroom and closed the door on their bickering, hoping neither of them followed me. I drew the drapes tight across the window, making the room as dark as I could, and pulled off my damp clothing. Climbing into bed, I wrapped the blankets and comforter around me in a pseudo-cocoon. And whether it was from fear or cold, or a combination of the two, I shivered for quite some time.

#

It snowed off and on for two more days, and by the fourth morning I decided that I was getting out of the house for a while, snow or no snow. In the hospital everything was planned out for me, but at home, my days became chasms—I barely struggled through one before another lurked on the horizon, fangs bared.

It was frustrating to watch television for any length of time—images flashed past too quickly, and I couldn't keep up with plot lines. My only source of entertainment, indeed the only thing I seemed to be doing well, was staying out of Randy's way. This wasn't too hard to do, though, since he had third shift duty and slept most of the day. When he got up in the evening, I found an excuse to go to my room and stay there until he left for the station.

As amusing as this was, I was becoming very bored. I knew Laurie would not want me to go out walking on my own, and I was sure that Randy would have some snide comment to make, but I figured what they didn't know wouldn't hurt them.

It was still dark out, but there was no point in trying to sleep—I had slept maybe a total of eight hours in the time I had been home. Being careful not to wake Laurie, I got up and got dressed. I was grateful I wouldn't have to worry about Randy since he would still be on duty.

Outside the air was cold and still. I stood in the yard, breathing deeply, enjoying the snow-induced hush. The roads had been scraped and salted, but the snowplows had pushed the mess onto the sidewalks, and I was forced to walk in the street. There wasn't much traffic out at this hour, however, so I wasn't too worried about getting splattered by a car.

By the time I reached the downtown area, my hands, face, and ears were almost frozen. I found an open diner a couple of blocks up the street and patted my pants pockets to make sure I hadn't forgotten the twenty-dollar bill I'd pilfered from Laurie's purse.

It was crowded but warm, and I took a seat at the end of the counter near the back. Most of the patrons were clean-cut, middle-class types, probably on their way to work. Several of them glanced at me. One woman in particular seemed to be paying me an inordinate amount of attention—a beautiful, strawberry blonde, sitting at a table toward the front of the restaurant. I could tell from the faces of the other patrons they were probably wondering what disgusting thing the cat had dragged in.

Self-conscious, I ordered coffee and toast and sat with my hands around the ceramic mug, trying to get some feeling back into my fingers. I was aware of the Voices grumbling softly among themselves and prayed that the situation wouldn't escalate into something embarrassing.

Remember what Randy said? If any of these people knew what you'd done, they'd kill you in an instant.

They think you're scum anyway.

That old coot sitting next to you? He's checking out that tattoo on the back of your hand and thinking you must be some kind of freak.

I glanced at my hand then at the old man sitting to my right. His gaze met mine for a split second, and he turned away. I couldn't even remember when I'd gotten some of the tattoos. They seemed to appear overnight. The scenes depicted were colorful...and hellish. The Grim Reaper, vampires, Satan, snakes, all interwoven. They told the sordid tale of the progression of my disease—a manifestation of the chaos and turmoil inside me. The demons were marking me as one of their own, and it scared me that they were so successful.

"Excuse me," a voice said to my left, and I jumped, spilling some of my coffee. The strawberry blonde stood next to me, her hand held out. "Hi—Caitlin Murphy. Sorry, I didn't mean to startle you."

I wiped the coffee from my hands with a paper napkin before shaking hers. "That's all right. I had my mind on something else." What little mind was left, anyway.

She brushed her hair behind one shoulder and flashed me a dazzling smile. "I know this is going to sound like the worst pick-up line in the world, but don't I know you from somewhere?"

"I don't think we've ever met." As bad as my memory was, I didn't see how I could forget anyone like her. I knew I was staring, but it was hard to take my eyes from her face.

"Are you sure? I could swear I know you," she persisted.

Her scrutiny was so intense that I had to turn away at last. Why was she even talking to me?

"I don't think so," I murmured.

She placed a hand on my arm, compelling me to look at her once more. "Do you at least have a name?"

"John Colucci." I could feel the corners of my mouth trying to turn up in response to her grin.

"It's good to meet you, John. Hopefully I'll be seeing you again." She stopped at the register to pay her bill, and I watched as she waved good-bye to some of her friends and disappeared through the door.

Our entire conversation had lasted maybe two minutes and yet I couldn't quit thinking about her. I was amazed that a woman would look at me, let alone talk to me. In fact, the only other women I could remember talking to me in the recent past were the ones serving as caregivers. It was good, for once, to be recognized as human and not just a receptacle for pills.

Encouraged by my brief exchange with Caitlin, I got up to pay my check. Not ready to go back home yet, I set about wandering the sidewalks and thinking of her. I had already made up my mind that I would return to the diner tomorrow morning and see what transpired. Who knew? I might get lucky and make a friend. I didn't dare dream beyond that—that was asking a lot—but I really needed a friend. Laurie was too much like a mother and Randy was just—well, an asshole. It had been me against the world for so long, I couldn't even remember the last person I had called friend or lover. I guess Dr. Fremont would come the closest to being a friend or an ally, but he was getting paid for it.

I must have rambled around for a couple of hours, fantasizing about Caitlin, when I passed the police station. A handful of officers were gathered in the parking lot. I froze and it became hard to breathe or swallow....

Cold metal bites into my wrists—somewhere in the chaos of my mind, I've been made to understand that I am being detained and that it has something to do with the broken doll. I remember telling them that the doll was destroyed when I found it, but my words are met by hostile, hate-filled stares. They fingerprint, photograph, and strip-search me, and by the time they lead me to an interrogation room, I am on the verge of hysteria.

Standing on one side of a large conference table, their faces grim, are several uniformed officers and two men in suits. I'm shown to a lone chair on the opposite side and told to sit down and be quiet. The men gather in a knot and began speaking to each other in low tones, occasionally glancing my way.

Frightened, alone, I rock back and forth in time with the ever-present music in my head and try to calm myself. There is a knock on the door and one of the suits breaks away from the little clique to see who it is. Words are exchanged and then he steps back to allow someone to enter. A feeling of doom settles over me when I see that this someone is Randy.

"I never would have believed he was sick enough to do something like this, Peter," he says to a tall, muscular fellow officer, his head in his hands. "Jesus, I feel responsible somehow. What am I going to tell Laurie? Hi honey, I'm home—oh, by the way, we arrested your little brother for murder tonight."

Peter claps him on the shoulder. "Take it easy, man. You're not to blame." His voice is full of concern and sympathy. "Listen...are you sure you want to be in here while they're questioning him? It might not be such a good idea."

Randy looks up, a malevolent expression on his face, and my blood congeals. "No, I want to hear this," he insists. "I want to hear what he thought the voices were telling him this time. And maybe this time it'll get him locked up in a nuthouse where he belongs." And that's when the fun really begins.

The Voices are in rare form, and even paying close attention, I don't understand a lot of the questions the cops are asking me. I'm unable to make the connection between their inquiries and the broken doll. All I know is that something serious is going down. Something that involves me.

After firing off a barrage of questions I can't comprehend, let alone answer, one of the three-piece Gestapos bangs his fist on the table, causing me to jump, and shouts, "God damn it, I'm tired of dicking around, John. Let me put this in a way that even someone like you should be able to understand—did you kill that child?"

I stare into each of the faces peering down at me. What are they talking about? I'm going to puke any second. I heave a few times and everyone takes a step backward. When I can finally speak, I ask, confused, "What child?"

In an explosion of movement, Randy lunges across the table. "You sick piece of shit!" His fist comes from nowhere, crashing into my mouth, and I find myself in the floor, blood trickling down my chin from a busted lip.

"Oh my God." I moved away from the cops as fast as I could, until I was well out of their sight. Ducking into a narrow alley between two buildings, I hunkered down, my back to a wall. The temperature had not risen much since my walk into town, but sweat ran down my face and soaked the underarms of my shirt. Hugging my sides, I rocked back and forth.

"Oh my God," I whispered. "I killed a little kid." Even as I said it, though, something inside me was rebelling. I had only just begun to grasp the seriousness of my illness. Although I had apparently been arrested and tried for murder, I didn't want to believe that things had ever been bad enough for me to kill a child.

My hands were shaking. It was no wonder Randy hated me—no wonder people wanted to see me dead, and having this knowledge, did I really want to live anyway? I continued to crouch there, crying for the loss of the child's life and the virtual loss of mine, until the sun was no longer directly overhead and clouds began to darken the sky. Then, staggering to my feet, my legs aching, I wiped at my face with my coat sleeve and set off toward home. A great weight seemed to have fastened around my ankles, however, slowing my pace.

Another winter storm was moving in, and it was snowing again heavily as I made my way to Sheridan Boulevard—big sticky flakes that came close to creating a white out. I couldn't ever remember seeing it snow as hard. Without a cap or hood, my hair quickly became plastered to my skull. I walked as fast as I dared, but had to wait for a long line of traffic to pass before I could attempt to cross Sheridan to get to the entrance to Laurie's subdivision. Meanwhile, I might die from exposure.

The last car passed and I stepped off the sidewalk and into the general area of the marked pedestrian crossing, guessing at the true location since it was all but obliterated by snow. In the next second a black sport pickup truck appeared out of the swirling blizzard, travelling much too fast for conditions, bearing down on me like a bullet train. The driver obviously didn't see or care that I was in the road. Panicked, I anticipated the impact, but paralyzed, I was unable to move. God, he had to see me—he was right on top of me! At the last second, the driver swerved to the left, thundering past me so close that the rear bumper brushed my thigh and sent me sprawling in the slush. The driver of the vehicle never even tapped his brakes, much less stop to see if I was okay.

Shaking and cursing, I scrambled to my feet before another car could come along and finish the job. I limped to the opposite side of the road and brushed the loose snow from my clothes, which were now also thoroughly soaked. I would have a huge bruise come tomorrow. Why hadn't that driver slowed down or stopped once he realized he was about to hit me? Had it been intentional? I felt a chill crawling up my spine, but this one wasn't due to the frigid weather. Should I report the incident to the police? But no, that would involve voluntarily talking to cops, and there was no way I was doing that.

I looked down the road in the direction the truck had sped off. It was hard to tell, but I thought I saw the black outline of the truck farther up, pulled to the side of the road. Waiting to make another pass at me or preparing to come back and make sure I was okay? I wasn't waiting around to find out. I broke into a run for the entrance to the subdivision, cutting across lawns and keeping away from the street, not looking back.

I knew I was a mess as I trudged through Laurie's front yard. She would be sure to comment on my appearance and fret over me, I thought as I stamped my feet on the concrete stoop to dislodge the snow from my boots and tried to stop trembling. I barely got the door open when a hand grabbed the front of my coat and yanked me into the foyer. Thrown off balance, I slammed face first into the opposite wall and felt a jolt of pain, followed by something warm gushing over my lips and down my chin. I righted myself and turned to find Randy, still in uniform, a murderous look on his face. We glared at each other while blood dripped from my nose, staining my coat.

Finally he said with a disgusted snort, "Don't just stand there bleeding all over the place, go get some paper towels."

Grabbing a wad of tissues from the box on the counter in the hall bath, I started to my bedroom. Randy met me at the doorway, blocking my entrance.

"Do you have any idea how upset your sister is? She's out looking for you right now." His words were clipped. "I was getting ready to send patrol cars out after you, for Christ's sake."

I held the tissues to my nose and said nothing.

"What the hell did you think you were doing, John? Do you honestly think you can make it out there on your own?" He stepped closer, and I could feel his breath on my forehead. "Tell me!" he shouted. I flinched but still said nothing, watching him carefully over the sodden mass of paper I held clutched to my upper lip.

"You're hopeless." He shook his head. "You didn't take your medicine, you missed your doctor's appointment—and don't tell me you didn't know, because Laurie's reminded you at least twice and wrote it on the kitchen calendar. You just walk out of the house and don't let anyone know where you're going. What if something had happened to you?"

He didn't know how close he was to guessing the truth. "I guess your prayers would have been answered then, wouldn't they?" I replied, the hate in my voice shocking even me.

A sneer worked its way into his expression. "One of them, anyway."

"Fuck you." I spit on him, though the look on his face told me that this wasn't a particularly smart thing to do.

He wiped the mixture of saliva and blood from his eye, and grabbed the front of my coat, yanking me toward him. "I'm going to tell you something," he said, breathing hard, "and you and all those so-called little voices in your head had better listen up. I don't know what you were up to today, but while you're on the outside—and I'm not convinced that you're going to stay on the outside—I'm responsible for you. Anything you do is going to reflect directly on me and Laurie. The very first sign of any weird shit going on, your ass is going right back to that hospital, and it's not coming out again. You understand me?" He stomped off and I slipped into my room, slamming the door shut behind me.

My nose was still bleeding as I shrugged off my coat and lay down on the bed. Laurie came in a short time later and sat on the edge of the mattress next to me.

"Is everything okay?" she asked, gently removing the tissues from my hand. "Randy said you tripped and fell."

Tripped and fell. Anger prevented me from speaking. I sat up and looked out the window, hoping she would get the idea I didn't want to talk and leave.

She sighed but made no move to withdraw. "I understand you need some independence, John, but that wasn't a very smart way to go about it. Do you realize that you missed your first doctor's appointment? If something had happened to you, if you'd needed medical attention...you don't even have any identification! How would anyone know to contact us?"

"I've already had this little talk with Randy," I muttered, "or didn't he tell you?"

"Don't act hateful with me, John. This is your doing. I only want what's best for you—I only want you to be safe."

"And I'm safer with you—with Randy—than I am out there on my own?"

Laurie's eyes narrowed. "What is that supposed to mean?"

"Nothing." It was obvious that she didn't suspect Randy as being the cause of my 'mishap', and I was damned if I was going to tell her. Nor was I going to tell her about the incident with the truck, which would give them yet another reason to hold me captive. I had already figured that Randy was out to make my life a living hell, and I refused to give him any more ammunition.

"You need to take your medicine now," she said, standing to leave.

Swallowing hard, my heart thundering in my chest, I put a hand on her arm to stop her. "Why didn't you tell me?" My voice sounded the way I felt, small and betrayed.

A panic-stricken look came over her face. It was the same look I had seen before at the slightest mention of my past. "Tell you what?" she asked, and her voice quavered.

It was now or never. "Why didn't you tell me that I murdered a child?"

She stared at me as if I'd slapped her, and I could see tears forming in the corners of her eyes. "How could you *ever* forget something like that?" she whispered.

How could I forget that my name was John Edward Colucci and that I was almost twenty-eight years old? How could I forget I had a sister, or that my mother was dead? How indeed.

CHAPTER FOUR

IT WAS TOWARD DAWN that I woke to find myself sitting on the floor, propped up against the bed. I couldn't have slept for very long, because the clock in the kitchen had read 4:37 when I went to get a drink of water. At any rate, there was no going back to sleep now.

My doctor's appointment had been rescheduled for ten o'clock, and I decided that I might as well go ahead and get a shower. Maybe the warm water would soothe me and I could go back to sleep for a short while before I had to leave. I needed sleep in the worst kind of way but could never manage more than a couple of hours a night.

I went into the hall bath and stripped off the t-shirt and sweatpants that served as pajamas. Making the water as hot as I could without scalding myself, I stepped under the spray. I realized, though, that it was not having the desired calming effect, and I understood just as suddenly why this was so.

Caitlin. I could recall the perfumed scent of her reddish-blonde hair and the warmth of her palm against mine when we shook hands. I was relieved that the thought of her aroused both emotion and a physical response I had long ago given up for dead. I didn't know how I would manage it, but I was going back to the diner whether Randy and Laurie liked it or not.

Stepping out of the shower, completely wide awake, I dried off and dressed. No one else was up yet, and the sun was just beginning to lighten the sky as I wandered into the living room and switched on a lamp. I sat there on the couch, trying to imagine what it would be like to have a place of my own. From Mommy and Daddy, to the hospital, to big sister, I had always been looked after by someone else. Was it possible that this would always be the case? I didn't like to think so.

Restless, always restless, I stood and paced the length of the room. Stopping at the wall of bookcases, I saw a thick photo album covered in brown leather. Curious, I carried it back over to the couch by the lamp.

On the first page were a few wedding photographs of a young man and woman. Judging from the clothing and hairstyles, they had been taken some thirty-five years earlier. There were more pictures of the couple holding a newborn baby. These followed the growth of the baby—a pretty little girl with light brown hair and blue eyes.

Then came photos of the little girl, perhaps seven or eight now, beaming at the camera, a baby propped in her lap. This baby was a boy with the same coloring.

There were more snapshots of birthdays, Easter, Christmas—the baby boy growing from a fat-cheeked, chubby toddler to a tall, thin teen-ager in the space of the pages, the girl from merely cute to exquisitely beautiful in turn. Some minutes passed before I understood that I was viewing my own family. Myself.

I studied the rest of the pictures with horrid fascination before flipping back to the beginning and going through them again. I was trying to force my brain to remember the events depicted, and in a panic, I realized I couldn't.

That the pictures were of me, I was sure, but it was as if they had been taken in another life. A life where I'd inhabited the same body, but not the same mind. I was older and there were a few lines on my face now, but it was the change in my eyes that bothered me. In the photographs, they were clear, even mischievous, and while I didn't look exactly cheerful, neither did I have the haunted appearance I saw in the mirror each morning.

Studying the prints, I chose one of me as a teen-ager, a rare, genuine smile on my face, and slid it from its plastic sleeve. On the back someone had written, "John—14th birthday." Life, intelligence, and promise lay behind those eyes. I had not yet become acquainted with my good friend, schizophrenia. How sad to think that shortly after this picture was taken, all promise vanished, like smoke in the wind.

Hearing noise from the direction of Laurie's bedroom, I slipped the photograph into my shirt pocket, closed the album, and laid it on the coffee table. I didn't feel like talking to her at that moment, so I grabbed my coat from the closet, and stepped out onto the deck.

The sun was up, though this side of the house was still in shadow. I leaned against the railing and watched birds pecking in the snow at the edge of the yard. At the house across the way, one of the kids came out carrying a bag of birdseed and proceeded to fill an empty feeder.

He noticed me, waved, and started through the yard toward me. When he reached the deck, he held up the bag of seed and said, "That's the third time this week I've had to fill up the feeder. Mama says we've got every bird in the neighborhood eating here."

He looked to be about seven or eight years of age. Blonde hair peeked out from under the hood of his Green Bay Packers coat and he wore round, metal-framed glasses. He grinned, and I could see his breath in the cold air. "I'm Adam Wade. I guess you're visiting Laurie—uh, Mrs. Kimbell?"

"Yeah, I'm her brother, John Colucci. I'm going to be living here now. But just call me John."

He laughed. "Mama says it's impolite for kids to call grown-ups by their first names. Laurie gets mad if I call her 'Mrs. Kimbell'. She says it makes her sound old, so I call her Laurie when I come to visit, but don't tell Mama."

"Your secret's safe with me," I told him. "I like your snowman, by the way. You looked like you were having fun building it."

"Oh that." He waved a gloved hand in the direction of his creation. "That was my little brother's idea. I wanted to build a Tyrannosaurus Rex, but ever since we saw *Jurassic Park*, he's had this thing against dinosaurs."

I thought I vaguely remember a movie by that name, but I didn't want to seem ignorant, so I said, "A dinosaur would have been cool. Maybe you and I could make one."

"Hey, yeah—a T. Rex or maybe a velociraptor!"

Just then we heard a woman's voice calling, "Adam! Hurry up or you're going to miss your bus!"

The kid grimaced. "That's Mama. I've got Cub Scouts after school today, but I'll try to come back tomorrow afternoon and we can get started."

"Okay, I'll see you then."

"Bye, John." He ran back across the yard to his house clutching the bag of seed. Already the birds were beginning to gather on and under the feeder.

Behind me, I heard the kitchen door opening and Laurie saying, "Oh, there you are!"

"Don't worry," I mumbled, brushing past her into the kitchen. "I didn't run off again."

She ignored my comment and went about fixing some coffee. "Would you like anything for breakfast?"

I thought about the diner...and Caitlin. "Just coffee."

Laurie was silent as she put the filter in the coffeemaker and began measuring the coffee into it. She added the water, flipped the switch and turned to me. "John, I'm sorry about yesterday. I guess we should talk about what we expect of you and what you expect of us."

"I'm not a child," I said, thinking that was exactly what I sounded like.

"I know that, but you'll always be my little brother." She removed two mugs from the cabinet. Placing them on the counter, she offered me a little smile. "I just want to protect you."

"I can look after myself." The words came out sounding harsh, though I tried hard to keep my voice neutral.

"You don't know how much I wish that were true."

"Well, it is," I snapped.

"No." She shook her head. "It's not." She sat down at the bar stool next to me and placed a hand on my arm.

I wanted to slap her, hurt her as she'd hurt me with that statement, but I refrained.

"I know you don't like feeling like you have to answer to us, and I don't particularly enjoy this role either. But you've been in a mental institution for eight years, John. It wouldn't be fair to just turn you out with no supervision or guidance."

"But I'm getting better," I said. "Dr. Fremont said so."

"That's true," she agreed, "but better compared to what? You were catatonic for days at a time—you didn't speak or move. Anything would be an improvement over that. Look, I know you feel as if you have to make up for lost time, but give yourself a chance to adapt. I don't want to see you hurt."

I watched as she got up to pour our coffee, knowing she was right and resenting her just the same. Anger built into a hot, hard knot beneath my rib cage. "So what you're saying is, if the institution won't keep me locked up, you will!"

"That's not what I'm saying at all, and don't shout at me." She looked irritated as she placed a steaming mug in front of me. "All I'm saying is that you don't need to be out roaming around on your own. It's too dangerous."

"And I'm so obviously incompetent."

"I didn't say that either."

"But it's what you're thinking!" I swept the coffee mug from the counter with my arm. The liquid flew in a high arc before splattering on the floor, the cup in hot pursuit.

"What the hell's going on?" a voice said behind me, and Laurie and I both jumped. "Have you got something against us having unbroken dishes?"

Randy was lounging in the doorway between the living room and kitchen. He looked less than happy to be home.

"Tell me something, John, are you just naturally a fuck-up or is it something you have to work at?" He walked toward me.

I tried to slip past him and into the hall, but he stepped into my path, and we were face to face.

"It's all right, Randy," Laurie said. "John's just feeling a little frustrated."

"Well, you know," he glanced at her and then me, "I'm beginning to feel that way, too."

I tried moving around him again, but he put his hand on my chest. "You can go off and talk to your voices in a minute. Right now you clean up that mess."

"You make me." This time I stood my ground, waiting for him to strike me, wanting him to do it with Laurie as a witness. True to his nature, he did raise a fist, but after glaring at me a few seconds, he turned and stalked from the room.

"Take your medicine, John. Maybe it'll calm you down." Laurie's voice was short, almost angry, as she stooped to pick up the pieces of the broken mug.

Ashamed, I, too, bent down and reached for a shard.

"Just go in another room, okay?" she whispered, pushing my hand away. "That's the best thing you can do right now."

Chastised and feeling guilty, I went into the living room and sat on the couch, thankful that Randy was nowhere to be seen. On one hand I regretted the way I had acted, and on the other, I was furious with both of them for treating me like an imbecile. The Voices, of course, had to interject their two cents' worth.

Well after all, John, you are an imbecile. How could you expect them to treat you any other way?

You might as well go ahead and kill yourself. Save somebody else the trouble of having to do it.

Randy's got a gun. All you would have to do is slip it out of the holster sometime while he's asleep and blow your brains out.

End it all. No more schizophrenia, no more Randy, no more hatred—no more anything.

Wouldn't that be nice? And it would certainly make a lot of people happy.

What do you say, John? Is it a date?

No? Well, let's look at this realistically. What good would be served by you living?

Do you think things are going to get better between you and Randy?

Do you think Laurie's going to want to look after you for the rest of your unnatural life?

And you don't honestly think that Caitlin Murphy would have anything to do with you!

Besides, you know what's going to happen if you stay here, don't you? They're going to spy on you.

Hell, they're already doing that. Randy's a cop. He knows all about surveillance techniques.

He'll know where you're going—what you're doing—before you will.

You're not going to have any secrets from him. You're not going to have any peace either.

A hand on my shoulder startled me. I stopped rocking.

"Are you ready for your doctor's appointment?" Laurie asked. "Let's go or we're going to be late."

We didn't have much to say to each other in the car, and I guessed she was still as upset as I was about our argument.

"You don't have to wait for me," I told her as she pulled into a parking space. "I know you have better things to do. I can walk home from here." I was trying to make concessions for my earlier behavior, and I desperately wanted some time to myself.

"We've been through this once already this morning, John. I'm not discussing it again. Besides, since I'm your guardian, the doctor will need to speak with me." Lips pressed into a narrow line, she got out of the car and slammed the door.

I had no choice but to follow her into the building. In the lobby, I slumped down on a chair next to her, feeling once more like a scolded child. I just couldn't fucking win.

The doctor called for her, and I could imagine what she was telling him. I fidgeted, picking up one magazine after another, incapable of concentrating on any of them long enough to make out the titles of the articles. The Voices hissed and mumbled. I did my best to ignore them, though I was unable to resist muttering "Shut up" a few times, which earned me some strange looks from the people sitting nearby. Even though we were all sitting in a psychiatrist's waiting room, it was apparently bad form to actually act crazy.

When Laurie returned, she was in a better mood and even smiled at me. The doctor beckoned, and I followed him. He shut his office door behind us and pointed to a chair. Not even offering to shake my hand.

"Mr. Colucci." He nodded his head toward me. "I'm Dr. Steele." Then without preface, he continued, "Your sister tells me that you're having some trouble adjusting."

Somewhat taken aback by his brusque manner, I stared at him. "I'm doing my best."

"She's worried that you may be reluctant to confide in her if you're experiencing problems."

"She's right," I said.

"It must be hard for you to go from a structured environment to one with very little structure at all."

I didn't know what he was getting at, but I was fairly certain I wouldn't like it. Nervous, I cleared my throat and glanced around the room. I hadn't known him for two minutes and already I didn't trust him. Dr. Fremont was the only doctor I'd ever liked or trusted. I kept my eyes moving, refusing to look at him as we played every psychiatrist's favorite game—twenty questions.

"How are you feeling?"

"Fine, I guess."

"Have you experienced any problems with depression?"

"No." I was as depressed as I'd always been.

"Are you sleeping well?"

"No."

"Why do you think that is?"

"I don't know."

"Are you getting any exercise?"

"Not really."

He scribbled on his note pad. "Why is that?"

"My sister and brother-in-law don't want me out walking by myself."

"Walking is good exercise."

"Yeah, tell them that."

"Are you taking your medication on a regular basis?"

"Yes." Lie.

"Hmm. Your sister tells me you've missed a couple of doses of Thorazine and that the difference in your behavior is apparent to her when you have."

Damn, busted. I shrugged, feigning indifference. "Why are you asking if you already know the answer?"

Dr. Steele frowned. "You have to take your medicine."

"Yeah?"

"I can instruct her on how to give it to you by injection."

"Is that a threat?"

Crossing his legs, he gazed at me, perhaps trying to gauge my mood, then wrote something on his notepad. "Do you feel threatened by the fact that you have to take medication?"

I snorted. "No, but I do feel threatened by people who tell me that if I don't take it orally, then someone will force it into my body with a needle."

"Your medication is important, John. This has surely been explained to you in detail."

"For the one millionth time, *I understand*."

He jotted something else on his notepad. "Have you been hearing voices?"

"Occasionally." Okay, frequently.

"Have you been eating well?"

"I haven't had much of an appetite."

"It's just as important for you to eat well, exercise, and rest as it is for you to take your medicine. Do I need to give you something to help you rest?"

"No, I figure the medication I'm on now is the reason for the problems to start with. I don't want any more."

"Fine, but you need to make a conscious effort to do these things. Next week I can teach you some relaxation techniques that may help."

"Okay."

"What have you been doing to occupy your time?"

"Nothing much, and I'm bored out of my skull."

"Nothing?"

"There's not much I can do. It's hard for me to watch television, and I can't even read anymore."

"Yes, that's to be expected."

Now it was my turn for some questions. "Why is it to be expected? I used to read all the time—I loved reading. Does schizophrenia turn you into an idiot?"

He wanted to laugh, I could tell he did—Dr. Fremont would have. It might have gone a long way toward helping me trust this prick if he had been able to laugh. Instead, he briefly covered his mouth with his hand before launching into some textbook explanation of schizophrenia and a pharmaceutical pamphlet description of the side effects of my medication, either of which, according to him, could have contributed to my reading predicament.

Discouraged, I yawned without meaning to and felt my attention slipping away by degrees. Had he kept on in that vein, I might have actually fallen asleep.

Maybe he was demonstrating one of his relaxation techniques. I had already closed my eyes when I heard him say, "There's a program sponsored by the library here in town that helps people with reading problems. Maybe you should enroll in it. You could meet some new people, work on trying to overcome your reading problem, and get some time away from your sister in the bargain."

Hope fluttered in my chest for a moment before plummeting to its death. I shook my head. "No way. She'd never go for it. She's afraid if she lets me out of her sight, something terrible will happen." I could hear the venom in my voice and felt frustration boiling just under the surface of my skin.

"Maybe you should sit down with her and explain why you'd like to do this."

"I can't talk to her. She's too much like a parent."

"Would you like me to speak with her again before you leave?"

I finally allowed my eyes to meet his, trying to determine whether or not I should let down my guard and trust him. I wasn't particularly interested in being stuck in some remedial reading program, but it did present a way out of the house. "Sure," I said.

Dr. Steele nodded. "All right, then, and next week we'll practice some of those relaxation techniques I mentioned." He still did not offer to shake my hand.

"John," he said, as I reached for the doorknob, "you need to understand that if you don't take your medication, you run the risk of being involuntarily committed again."

I resisted the urge to tell him to commit an unnatural act upon himself. The heady scent of freedom was in the air.

CHAPTER FIVE

RANDY CAME IN FROM WORK as Laurie was preparing breakfast the next morning. She and I had been discussing the library program in which I was going to enroll, and she interrupted herself to accept a kiss from him.

"Dr. Steele said it would be all right for you to walk into town or catch the bus on the days you go to the library," she continued. "Randy or I will pick you up, though, since it will be dark by the time you're through. You'll need to have an ID card made."

Randy's loving mood apparently vanished when he saw me. He gave me an evil look as he took the chair next to mine. Reaching to spear a piece of sausage with his fork, he said to Laurie, "You're not seriously going to let him wander around town by himself, are you?"

Muscles tightened in my shoulders and neck, and I realized I'd made a foolish mistake in sitting where I had. With the table in front of me, window to my right, wall at my back, and Randy to my left, there was no escape route. I felt panic trying to claw its way out of my stomach.

Laurie stopped what she was doing and frowned. "Randy, we discussed this yesterday. His doctor thinks it will be good for him to get out and do a few things for himself."

"And does this doctor know about John's past?" Randy asked.

"I'm sure he's got a copy of the hospital file. Besides, I've got some jobs lined up beginning the first of February. John's going to be by himself part of the day anyway; he might as well be at the library."

"Yeah, and you should have thought of that before you brought him here. Is that quack going to take the blame if something happens? Are you?"

I wanted to bang my fist on the table until the dishes clattered and scream, "Quit talking about me like I'm not even in the room!" I did neither of these things. Instead, I tried hard to force the anxiety and anger back down out of my throat and remain calm. The longer Randy sat beside me, though, the more threatened I felt.

I wasn't aware that my agitation was so obvious until he whirled to face me and snarled, "Sit still!"

Laurie's eyes flashed. "Don't speak to him as if he were a dog!"

Randy stood, smiling slyly. "I have too much respect for dogs to speak to them that way."

He withdrew from the kitchen, and I waited for my hands to stop trembling. Laurie looked miserable and I didn't know whether to feel sorrier for her or me. "Why does he hate me so much?" I asked when I could trust my voice not to quaver.

She refused to meet my eyes. "I wouldn't say that he hates you."

"I would." Sickened by the sight of the food on my plate, I left the table. So much for Dr. Steele's admonition that I make a conscious effort to eat right, I thought as I retrieved my coat from the hall closet. I put it on and stepped back into the kitchen, where Laurie was now washing dishes.

She opened her mouth as if to ask where I was going, and I said, "You know, I didn't ask to be released from the hospital, and I sure as hell never asked to come here." I went out the door, slamming it behind me.

Hands jammed down into my coat pockets, I crossed the back yard and passed Adam's house, coming out on the next street over. The more I thought about the way Randy had spoken to me, the angrier I became. The Voices were in a near riot also, screaming and shouting and demanding retribution. I prayed he wouldn't come after me, because I was really afraid I would hurt him.

The few people I passed on the streets gave me wide berth, casting sidelong looks my way. They could tell, just from looking at me, that something was not quite right. I wanted to scream at them and watch them turn and run back down the street as if Satan were after them. For all I knew, I was Satan.

It was like I had told Laurie—I hadn't asked to be released from the hospital. I hadn't known it was possible, and after eight years, I was reconciled to being there forever. Neither had I asked to live with her, hadn't remembered I had a sister. That idea had to have been hers, and I felt sure that had she known what would be involved, she might not have been so eager. So where did this leave me?

I had nowhere else to go, no one else I could turn to. Suicide was beginning to look pretty good. The Voices were right. One bullet from Randy's gun, straight through the roof of my mouth, would do it. I would be free—free from Randy and Laurie, free from fear, free from schizophrenia, and free of the Voices. Or maybe I wouldn't. Maybe the Voices were really demons and while I was still alive, their power over me was minimal. But after I passed out of this existence, their power over me might be immeasurable, and I would be doomed to suffer all eternity. I was screwed either way.

Screwed. The word swirled in my brain like a demented bird. No, not just screwed, but fucked. Royally fucked. Being screwed was life's way of politely messing with you, but there was nothing polite about being fucked. Getting fucked was life knocking you down in the dirt and taking you from behind. You weren't sure what happened, you just knew it hurt like hell.

"I'm tired of being fucked," I mumbled, shaking my head and almost colliding with a man in a three-piece suit. He sidestepped me and gave me a nasty look over his shoulder.

"Damned freak," I thought I heard him say, but I couldn't be sure if I'd actually heard him speaking or one of the Voices.

I looked up to find myself in front of the diner. I had not been conscious of traveling in this direction; nevertheless, I took a deep breath, squared my shoulders, and went in.

The early morning crowd had thinned out by this time, and I sat down at one of the booths near the front window. A quick glance told me that Caitlin Murphy was not there, and resigned, I ordered a cup of coffee. In my coat pocket I discovered the pack of Marlboros leftover from my last trip to town. I laid the pack on the table, thinking it was too bad health laws prohibited smoking in restaurants.

The waitress brought my order and tried to engage me in small talk. It was difficult, though, for me to respond to her, and she gave up after a few moments. I sat there sipping from my mug, studying the pattern on the table top. Depression threatened to engulf me and sweep me downriver in a flood of self-pity. I was about to let myself be carried away when the door to the diner opened.

"Hi, Edie," a female voice said. "Did I leave my gloves here by any chance?" I looked up and saw Caitlin Murphy standing by the counter addressing the waitress.

Grinning, Edie reached into her apron pocket and held out a pair of black gloves to her. "I wondered how far you would get before you remembered them."

"Thank you so much!" Caitlin sounded relieved as she accepted them from Edie. "Those were a Christmas present from Mackenzie. She figured I'd lose them before the end of January."

"The month's not over yet," Edie laughed.

"Oh ye of little faith—you sound just like her! I'll see you tomorrow morning."
She gave a wave and turned to leave. Our eyes met before she got to the door,
and she smiled, came over, and slid into the seat opposite me.

"Well, hello. It's John, isn't it?"

"Yes, hello," I said, and I wasn't sure, since the action was so foreign to my
face, but I may have been smiling also. A cloud of fragrance—perfume,
shampoo, soap—settled around her, and I breathed deeply, drinking in her
scent.

"Are you certain we don't know each other from somewhere?" she asked,
leaning forward.

I shook my head. "I really don't think so."

She shrugged. "Well, we know each other now." Noticing the pack of
cigarettes lying on the table, she pointed and said, "May I have one for later?
Shame on you, by the way. I'm trying to quit, but sometimes it's just so hard."

"I know what you mean." An unexpected tightness in my groin caused me to
shift in my seat. I pushed the pack toward her and watched while she fished
one out and stuck it behind her ear. I found the gesture incredibly sexy.

The Voices were immediately on red alert.

Hot damn! What a piece!

What's that delicious scent?

God, that's her! She smells good enough to eat!

Whoa, John. How did you manage this?

*Check out that hair—wouldn't you just love to grab a handful and bury your
face in it?*

Well why stop at that?

Wouldn't you just love to kiss those lips?

The ones between her hips....

Oh, Jesus. I prayed that she hadn't noticed my discomfiture. I needn't have
worried, because she was talking about the cold weather.

"I wouldn't mind it nearly as much," she was saying, "if I could get in a little skiing. I haven't been once this season, and last year by this time, I'd already been four or five times."

"Why haven't you been able to go this year?" I sounded halfway normal and waited for the Voices to pop out with something obscene. To my everlasting relief, they had clammed up again.

She rolled her eyes. "Work. I mean, don't get me wrong, I like what I do, it's just that it's all I seem to do."

"And what do you do?" I was amazed that I was able to carry on a dialogue with her.

She grinned. "I'm not sure if I should admit it, considering the reputation it's got, but I write for *The Kingsville Herald*. I also do volunteer work for the local literacy council."

"So you're a reporter?"

"Well, yes, and I occasionally do columns on arts and entertainment—book reviews, movie reviews, music reviews, that kind of thing."

I tried to imagine being in her position, being able to read a book or watch a movie from beginning to end in order to review it. It didn't seem like asking too much to be normal. "That sounds like fun."

"It can be. Tell me, what do you do?"

I could feel the heat rising in my face and frustration rising with it. Now what? Tell her I didn't have a job since I was fresh from the nuthouse—that there weren't too many career opportunities in the field of basket weaving?

Caitlin evidently sensed my discomfort this time. "I'm sorry," she said. "You don't have to answer that; I didn't mean to be nosy."

"No, it's okay. It's just that I'm...unemployed." *Oh great*, I heard one of the Voices mutter, *now instead of thinking you're a mental patient, she'll think you're a derelict.*

"I'm sorry." She touched the back of my hand with her fingertips.

I was like a thirsty desert plant, draining every drop of compassion from her through that brief physical contact, soaking up her kindness. God, but I was lonely. I wondered what her lips would taste like, what her body would feel like pressed against mine. I wanted to follow the suggestion of the Voices and bury my nose in her red-gold hair.

She glanced at her watch. "I've got to go, now," she said, as if reluctant to leave, "but could we meet here tomorrow for lunch—say one o'clock, when I have more time to talk?"

"That would be great."

She flashed me one of her brilliant smiles as she stood to go, and I felt my insides dissolving into mush. "I'll see you tomorrow then, John."

After she had gone, it took several minutes for my breathing to slow down and things to return to normal. By the time I finished my coffee, I was capable of standing without embarrassing myself.

Outside, snow was beginning to fall in the same big, sticky flakes that had marked my return home. As much as I hated the idea, I decided that I should probably head that way. By now, at least, Randy would be in bed, and I wouldn't have to listen to his mouth.

When I was two blocks from Laurie's house, the wind picked up and began dumping the snow with a vengeance. I was thinking how glad I was I didn't have much farther to go when I heard someone calling, "Hey, John! Wait up!"

I looked but didn't see anyone and figured the Voices were having some more fun at my expense. I shrugged and kept walking.

"Wait up, John!"

This time I saw a small figure hurrying toward me across the slick pavement. It drew closer, and I recognized the Green Bay Packers coat as belonging to Adam.

Wiping snowflakes from his glasses with a mittened hand, he grinned up at me. "Hi, John."

Surprised to see him, I asked, "What are you doing out in this mess?"

"They let school out early 'cause of the snow. What are you doing out? Don't you have a car?"

"Wouldn't do me any good if I did," I told him.

He shifted his bookbag to the opposite shoulder. "Why not?"

"Because I couldn't drive it."

"Why not?"

I looked down at him. "You ask a lot of questions."

He grinned again. "That's what my Dad says. Why couldn't you drive it?"

"Because I don't have a license—and don't ask me why, I just don't."

"Okay."

He was trotting, trying to keep up, so I stopped and said, "Want a piggyback ride?"

"Cool!"

I stooped down so he could climb on my back, and we marched off through the blizzard. When I deposited him in Laurie's front yard, he dropped his book bag and quickly scooped up a handful of snow, patting it into a ball. I didn't realize he was going to throw it at me until it was flying toward my face. It caught me between the eyes, some of it falling into my shirt collar.

"Hey," I yelled, grabbing my own handful of snow, "is that the way you say thanks?"

My snowball caught him above the ear, and he ran around the house to the back yard, shrieking with laughter. The fight was on, and I had no choice but to follow. Of course, he was waiting in ambush and managed to bombard me with more snow missiles before I could dive for cover. I was preparing to pelt him with a few Arctic specials when the kitchen door opened.

"Well hello, Adam," I heard Laurie say.

Adam dropped the snowball he had been fashioning. "Hi, Laurie," he said, all innocence and politeness. "John and I were just talking."

"Oh, is John back?" she asked, and I detected a note of confusion in her voice.

"Yes, ma'am. He's under the deck."

Glancing up, I found Laurie peering at me over the railing.

"What are you doing under there, John?" She sounded even more bewildered and a little suspicious.

Feeling sheepish, I crawled out and dusted the snow off my clothes. "I—uh—we—"

"Aren't you two cold out here?" she asked, shaking her head, not waiting for my answer.

"No, ma'am," Adam spoke up. "John's going to help me build a snow dinosaur. Is that okay?"

Laurie hesitated, then directed her gaze at me. Her brows furrowed. "Well, I suppose, but try not to be too loud; Randy's sleeping. When you get through, why don't you come on in the house and I'll make you both some hot chocolate."

"That would be great." Adam beamed at her, and she finally turned and went back inside.

We started on the "Tyrannosnowrus Rex," as Adam christened it, and in between a few minor snowball skirmishes, managed to build a halfway decent-looking dinosaur.

"You ready to go in and get warm?" I asked when our teeth were chattering and our fingers and toes numb.

In the house, we peeled off our coats and pulled off our shoes. I caught Adam staring at me as I removed my damp outer shirt.

"That's cool," he whispered in awe, coming closer to examine the tattoos on my arms. "Where did you get those? They're like sleeves."

I shrugged. "I don't remember." Trying to change the subject, I said, "Do you want some cocoa?"

But Adam wasn't about to let the subject be changed. "They remind me of a nightmare I had once. How did you get them? Did they hurt?"

How did I tell him about the demons? It seemed a shame to worry a little kid with it, and I was thankful when Laurie called us to the table and distracted him.

"Do you want marshmallows?" she asked him.

"Sure," he answered, "if John's having some."

She dropped the marshmallows into our mugs and said, "I think you forgot to take your medicine this morning, didn't you, John?"

With a sinking feeling, I realized that I had neglected to do so. I accepted a pill from her and swallowed it with a big gulp of guilt and the glass of water she provided.

Adam, the tattoos now forgotten, asked, "Why do you have to take medicine?"

"He takes medicine because he's sick and it helps him stay well." Laurie was speaking more for my benefit than his. "But it won't do him any good if he forgets it."

Adam nodded knowingly. "My little brother has to take medicine 'cause he sometimes has seizures. Medicine's important, John."

I glimpsed a smile on Laurie's face as she busied herself with the few dishes in the sink.

"You too, huh?" I muttered in Adam's direction.

"What?" He cocked his head toward me, wriggling his eyebrows, a frothy brown mustache outlining his upper lip.

I couldn't help laughing.

CHAPTER SIX

THE ALARM WENT OFF, but I was already awake, or to be more precise, I had never gone to sleep. On any other morning I would have been a little on the cranky side, annoyed that I hadn't been able to rest. However, this morning I was excited about my lunch date with Caitlin.

I showered with care, washing my hair and soaping every square inch of my body. I took my time shaving and nicked my chin only once. I even remembered to brush my teeth and put on deodorant and clean underwear. The only problem was that by the time I finished dressing, it was just 6:30 AM, and I had six-and-a-half hours to go before meeting Caitlin.

For lack of anything better to do, I went back into my bedroom. Catching sight of my image in the dresser mirror, I tried to see myself as Caitlin would see me. The reflection did not reveal a refugee from a mental institution as I feared it might. It showed, instead, a melancholy but otherwise decent-looking young man, tattoos and hair aside. I stared even harder, convinced that I was seeing someone else—an imposter wearing my clothes. But that was ridiculous. Who would want to wear *my* clothes? Who would want to risk being mistaken for John Colucci?

This person didn't particularly look like the type who sat in a corner for hours on end without moving or speaking, barely blinking his eyes. Nor did he look like the type of person who roamed hospital halls, carrying on lengthy conversations with himself. And he certainly didn't appear to be the type of person who could harm little kids. Wouldn't it show? Wouldn't he somehow look different from other people—with glowing red eyes, horns, cloven hooves?

Caitlin must not have thought I resembled a lunatic. If she had, then she never would have spoken to me, and I couldn't decide if this was good or bad. On the one hand, if I had, in fact, done the things I was accused of, she was better off not knowing me. On the other hand, if I had not done those things, I deserved some companionship...I deserved a friend. Granted, no one else would see it that way. Being accused of something was the same as having done it. Someone like Randy would say that not only did I not deserve a friend, I didn't deserve to live.

So what business did I have agreeing to meet Caitlin? What would I talk to her about over lunch? My last eight years in a state hospital? She could tell me about her more memorable ski trips, and I could tell her about my favorite electric shock therapy sessions. She could tell me about her work at the paper, and I could tell her what I did to end up in the hospital. If only I could remember.

I was an idiot to have agreed to this. Why would she want to have lunch with me? Did she feel sorry for me? I had to be missing something. Maybe she thought I was homeless, and feeding me was her good deed of the week. Afterward she could go back to her office and tell everyone how she'd fed some poor loser. The thought disgusted me. If that's the way it went down, I would be out of there so fast her head would spin. I didn't want to be a charity case. I wanted a friend.

I had almost talked myself out of the whole thing when an image of her popped into my head, and I remembered her warm, sweet scent. The truth was, whether she thought I was a charity case or not, I knew I would be there. I was desperate to connect with someone, to have an ally.

But she's got to have an ulterior motive for even looking at you, John. Let's face it; you're not the type of guy women would fall all over themselves to meet.

She thinks she knows you, that's all it is.

Either that or she feels sorry for you.

She just sees this sad-looking dude who's all alone—sits alone, walks alone. She pities you, thinks of you as an abandoned puppy.

And you know women can't resist stray puppies. It's the mothering instinct.

She's a do-gooder, and she'll pat herself on the back for this all week.

She probably belongs to some club where they tally up all their good deeds at the end of the year. Then they hold a banquet, present a trophy to the winner, and write her up in the newspaper—call her "Woman of the Year."

Smug, self-serving bitch.

"That's not true," I said, not because I knew this to be a fact, but because I felt obligated to defend her.

Is too, and you know it. You just won't admit it.

What do you think, John? Maybe she's heard of your sexual prowess?

How do you suppose she could have found out about that? From your right hand?

Talk to the hand.

Har-har-har.

"Shut up!" I banged my fist on the dresser top, causing the mirror to teeter on its frame.

The truth hurts, doesn't it? She's just like everyone else. As soon as she finds out you've spent time in the Macadamia Mansion, she'll get this glazed look in her eyes, murmur something stupid like "Oh my, look at the time—good talking to you," and she'll be on her way.

You don't have anything to offer her. Never did, never will, and as soon as she finds out about your past, she'll leave your ass in the dust.

"That's not true! She's not like everyone else. If she was, she never would have spoken to me to start with."

Maybe she's just incredibly naive.

Yeah, or she's incredibly determined to do her good deed. She wants that "Woman of the Year" award so bad she can taste it.

And you're going to help her get it, John.

"Why don't you shut up? I'm tired of listening to you! There's no way you could know her motivation." I was trembling, working my way into a rage.

And you do? But of course you have such a wealth of experience to draw on. I keep forgetting that.

Tell us about your last relationship with a woman.

Can't do it, can you? Know why? Because you've NEVER had a relationship with a woman.

So tell us, Mr. Experience, just what is her motivation?

Oh, I know! She took one look at you, and she could tell what a stud you are. Decided she had to have you and nothing else would do.

"Shut up!" I clapped my hands over my ears, pacing between the dresser and the bed. "Shut up! Shut the hell up!"

Not to be outdone, the Voices decided to try a different tack. All at once they were solemn.

You know, John, there's a simple way to solve all your problems. Why do you keep ignoring it?

It's going to come down to that sooner or later, and sooner would save everybody a lot of grief.

Think of the burden Laurie's under—you would be releasing her. Think of your own unhappiness—you would be releasing yourself, your soul.

Do it, John.

No one cares. You'll be another statistic on the evening news, and in a day it will all be forgotten.

Do it, John, do it.

Do it, John.

DO IT.

I was no match for The Voices as they continued their maddening refrain. There were many more of them, and they were louder and more raucous, by far, than my own miserable wailing. So it was no great surprise when Randy stormed into my room, followed by a frightened Laurie.

"Please be gentle with him," I thought I heard her say, but if she had spoken, it was hard to distinguish her soft voice from all the obnoxious ones.

Randy placed a hand on my arm. His voice was strident, more resonant than Laurie's. "Let's go for a ride, John."

He's going to take you and put you out of his misery.

He knows you're a worthless piece of shit, and he's going to get rid of you.

Fight him. You've got to do it yourself, otherwise there will be no absolution.

You have to kill yourself. Don't let somebody else do your dirty work for you.

Grab his gun, stick the barrel in your mouth, and pull the trigger.

Randy tugged on my arm again, and I jerked away from him. He turned to Laurie. "Call the station and ask them to send someone over to help."

Laurie began crying. "Oh, no, Randy."

"Call them *now*," he said, not taking his eyes from me.

Laurie left the room, and he positioned himself between me and the door and said, "Let's go for a little ride, John."

I stared at his handgun. Could I get it away from him? And more importantly, would I be able to use it on myself before he could stop me?

My gaze wasn't lost on him. "Believe me," he whispered, "I would like nothing better than to blow your ass away."

"Then do it and make us both happy."

"Hell no. I'm not using *my* piece. Too damned much paperwork involved. Besides, how would it look, my own beloved brother-in-law? No, if you get shot, it's not going to be by my gun."

"Please," I was reduced to tears and ashamed of my desperation. "You can tell them I committed suicide."

"You don't know how tempting that is."

You chicken shit! I told you—you have to do it yourself.

There's no absolution if you let him do it.

"I don't care!" I sank to my knees in supplication. "I don't have the courage to do it myself...please, Randy."

"I can't believe they let you out of Broughton." He wiped perspiration from his upper lip with the back of his hand. "Get up off the floor. I'm taking you to the emergency room. Maybe they can give you something to calm you down."

"I'm not going to any more hospitals, and I'm not taking any more medicine!" Leaping to my feet, I attempted to push my way past him and into the hall. He caught me around the waist, and I flailed at the doorframe for purchase.

He forced me back down to the floor, pushing my face into the carpet and digging his knee between my shoulder blades. "You want me to spray you, man?" he asked, punctuating each word with a thump to the back of my head. "You ever had pepper spray in your eyes?"

Infuriated, I clawed at the carpet and bucked in an effort to relieve Randy's crushing weight on my back.

"Hold still," he said, sliding his knee forward so that it pressed into the base of my skull.

I felt the metal fangs of a demon viper brush my right wrist, and I fought harder.

"Randy—handcuffs?" Laurie was sobbing hysterically. "Can't you see he's terrified?"

"Get out of here," he bellowed at her, "before you get hurt."

"Randy—"

"Now, damn it! Go wait for the patrol car."

I tried to yank my left arm out of the viper's reach but was not quick enough to prevent it from coiling around my wrist. Twisting to one side so that Randy slipped from my back, I screamed, "Get it off! Get it off!" and thrust my arm at him, my fist connecting with his eye.

He clutched at the snake's dangling body, provoking it to bore deeper into my flesh, and twisted my arm behind my back. We continued to wrestle, he to keep me pinned to the floor, and me to rise to my feet.

"What the hell's going on?" I heard a male voice ask. I struggled to see if there was a new arrival or if I was merely hearing a new Voice, but from my position it was hard to tell.

"Still serving your specialty, I see," continued the newcomer. "Carpet sandwiches."

"Normally, I would laugh at that remark," Randy replied, which was a good indication that someone else had arrived, "but it's kind of hard to find the humor in a psychotic episode."

"Oh, is that what this is? And here I thought you two were just having an intimate moment."

"Very funny, Peter. I hate to interrupt your stand-up routine, but do you think you could help me get him cuffed?"

With the viper's cooperation, they bound my hands behind me and dragged me, kicking and thrashing, out to the patrol car. Twice they tried to force me into the back seat, but I pushed against the rear quarter panel with my feet, thwarting their progress.

"No more snakes," I told them.

"Shut up, John, and get in the car." Randy panted from exertion, and even in the frigid air, sweat rolled down his face.

Their third attempt to ensconce me in the back seat met with the same defeat. Finally, they threw me down in the snow at the edge of the driveway.

"Grab an arm and a leg," Randy said to Peter, pressing my face into the snow so hard I could barely breathe. My clothing soaked up moisture, chilling me to the bone.

"Want to make a wish?" Peter asked.

"Don't tempt me," Randy huffed.

They each grasped an arm and a leg and shoved me headfirst into the car, banging my head on the opposite door. This stunned me long enough for them to snap the seatbelt tight around me, but as soon as I recovered, I began writhing.

"No more snakes," I chanted, kicking the seat in time with the words. It was important to ward them off for as long as possible. The longer I kept them at bay, the less potent their venom.

Peter started the engine, and Randy turned to face me. "Cut the shit if you know what's good for you."

Hmmm...interesting statement. "Snakes are not good for me," I told him.

"Shut up, John," he said again. "You're talking crazy."

I burst into laughter. "I am crazy! Or did the stupid sons of bitches forget to tell you that? I'm two sandwiches shy of a picnic; two cantaloupes short of a fruit salad!"

"You're also going to be a few teeth short of a full set if you don't cool it," he grumbled.

Peter whistled under his breath. "Laurie wasn't kidding when she called to say he was out of control, was she? He's scary."

"Among other things."

Peter glanced at me in the rearview mirror. "Will the local hospital know what to do for him?" he asked Randy.

"They'll pump him full of Thorazine, wait 'til he calms down, and then send him back home."

"Lucky you."

"Yeah. If he'd take his medicine like he's supposed to, though," Randy said, looking pointedly at me over his shoulder, "we wouldn't be doing this right now."

"No more snakes, please," I begged. "The venom is poisoning me."

Peter's brow furrowed. "Why does he keep talking about snakes?"

"Who the hell knows? He's living in a perpetual nightmare."

"Poor guy."

Randy snorted. "Let me tell you about this 'poor' guy."

Peter shook his head. "I know all about that I was with the department back then, too, remember? All that happened a couple of months before I moved to Raleigh. Still, it's got to be tough when you can't distinguish between what's real and what's not."

"The snakes are real," I whispered. I heard them hissing under the car seats, and in all the excitement, I'd forgotten to put on any shoes. Terrified that they would slither out at any moment and bite through my socks, I squirmed and tried to tuck my feet underneath me.

Of course, if the snakes in the car didn't attack me, I knew for certain there would be more waiting at the hospital. If Randy and Peter were able to get me into the emergency room and restrain me, I would be helpless against them. Therefore, I had to make certain this did not happen.

When we arrived at the hospital entrance, I was ready. I came out of the car willingly enough, but as soon as Peter turned to shut the door behind me, I began complaining that the handcuffs were cutting off my circulation.

"Oh, for God's sake," Randy muttered, taking out his keys, "quit acting like we're killing you." He unfastened the cuff on my right wrist and I wasted no time in wrenching my arm from his grasp and taking off across the parking lot.

"John, you son of a bitch, come back here!" he yelled after me.

Crouching down beside a car, I realized my stupidity. My socks were sopping wet from the snow and my feet were freezing. There was no way I was going to get very far like this. I wasn't even wearing a coat. This called for a new plan of action.

Still squatting, I pulled at door handles. Locked. My only sanctuary from the snakes was to hide until they got tired of looking for me and left. Crawling through the parking lot slush, my hands icy and my jeans now drenched from the knee down, I went from car to car. Surely, in all these hundreds of automobiles, there would be one with an unlocked door.

I scuttled along to the next vehicle and was reaching for the door handle when I saw a pair of black patent leather boots next to the front tire. Glancing upward, I saw that the boots belonged to Randy. I shifted into reverse. My avenue of escape was blocked by another pair of boots, though—these belonging to Peter.

"Are you through jerking off?" Randy asked, sounding somewhat testy.

I couldn't contain the sobs that leapt from my throat. The knowledge that the vipers had won again was almost more than I could bear.

"Come on, dude, let's get you some help." Peter sounded sympathetic, but I didn't dare trust him.

"Please don't make me go in there." I begged and pleaded with them, trying to push their hands away. Yet for each one I dislodged, another took its place. I made my body as limp as I could, but they simply dragged me between them.

"He's scared," Peter observed.

"I'd be scared, too, if I were him," Randy said.

"What does he think they're going to do to him?"

"Maybe he's afraid someone will do something that should have been done a long time ago."

#

After an ugly battle, with me the consummate loser, I sat huddled in a chair in one of the examining rooms, shivering, a blanket pulled tight around me. My wet clothing, which had been replaced by a hospital gown, lay draped over the examining table. I was covered with bruises and scratches inflicted upon me during my skirmishes with Randy, Peter, and various hospital personnel.

My face felt feverish, chapped, scalded by the angry tears I had shed earlier. I was beyond humiliation, beyond rage, beyond hope, merely smoldering now, the fire all but extinguished, leaving a charred husk in its wake.

A nurse popped her head into the room to ask, "Everything okay in here?"

Our eyes met and I looked away, unable to rouse myself to answer her.

She lingered a few moments as if waiting for a response, then said, "Your brother-in-law left to file a report, but your sister is on her way to get you."

I nodded once to indicate I understood, but this was the extent of my communication. I felt drained emotionally and doubted I could have spoken even if I were inclined to do so. I closed my eyes and leaned my head against the tile wall.

The Voices, perhaps realizing the gravity of the situation in which they had placed me, reduced themselves to whispers so faint that even I couldn't hear what they were saying. I wanted to sleep in the worst kind of way, but each time I began to doze off, something in my subconscious caused me to jerk upright and a sad, lonely feeling to crest in my stomach. I wasn't really sure whether three minutes or thirty had passed before the nurse came back with Laurie in tow.

"You're all set to go," the nurse said to me, her voice a little too bright, a little too loud. To Laurie she added *sotto voce*, "He's pretty drowsy from the sedative; he'll probably want to sleep for a while."

"I hope so," Laurie replied, her voice also low. "He needs to rest."

The nurse left the room and Laurie came over to me. She gave me a pained smile and asked, "Feeling okay now?"

It was too much trouble to answer her—my vocal chords felt as if they were encased in granite, my jaws and tongue made of lead.

She placed a small duffle bag on the counter, and pulled out a few pieces of clothing. She helped me dress, steadying me when I got my shirttail caught in my fly and nearly toppled over struggling to free it. It was stuck fast. "The hell with it," I muttered and flopped back onto the chair.

"Let me help you with your shoes." She knelt beside me and began working my feet into my boots. "There." She stood and patted my knee. "Are you able to walk or should I ask for a wheelchair?"

A wheelchair would have made more sense, but I stood anyway, my balance precarious and my gait unsteady. I was determined to shuffle out of there with at least a modicum of dignity, and surprised myself by remaining upright until we reached the car. We rode home in complete silence, the world moving past me in a blur.

Once back at the house, I got as far as the living room, where I sank down onto the sofa, too lethargic to go any farther. Laurie brought a blanket and tucked it around me.

"Try to rest for a while," she whispered.

Without being aware of it, I must have finally fallen asleep. The next thing I remembered was opening my eyes to find a small figure sitting in the recliner next to the couch. From the slant of light entering the room through the windows, I figured the time to be three or four o'clock.

Disoriented, I sat up and rubbed my eyes, trying, but failing, to dispel the blurry vision.

"Hi, John," Adam's voice said from the shadows.

"Hi." I yawned, still trying to gather my senses. "What's up?"

Adam stood from the recliner and came over to sit beside me on the sofa, where he peered up into my face. "I came to see if you wanted to make another snow dinosaur, but Laurie said you were sick. She said you had to go to the emergency room." He continued to stare into my face. "Are you okay now?"

Ah yes, the emergency room—I shuddered involuntarily, not wanting to remember. But there was something else, something important that I did want to remember, something that wouldn't reveal itself while Adam's worried gaze continued to scrutinize me for signs of illness.

I attempted a half-hearted smile. "Yeah, I'm okay." But this wasn't entirely the truth, as I found out when I tried to stand. The room spun in circles, tilting first in one direction and then another. This was complicated by the fact that I had to piss like a racehorse.

Adam jumped up to help balance me, placing an arm around my waist and positioning my hand on his shoulder.

"Thanks," I said. "Think you can help me to the bathroom?"

With his assistance, I made my way to the toilet, where I tried to unzip my jeans, only to realize that my shirt was still stuck fast in my damned zipper. "Can you help me out here?" I asked.

Adam had both hands on my zipper when Laurie burst into the room. "John, what are you doing?"

I jumped, nearly falling backward into the tub. "I'm trying to get my zipper undone—what the hell does it look like?" I shot back, annoyed, and then I realized why she was concerned and felt sick with shame.

"Adam, why don't you go back in the living room? I'll help John." Laurie shooed him into the hall and shut the door.

"I don't want your help," I mumbled, embarrassed. "Haven't I been humiliated enough for one day?"

Laurie shut her eyes and whispered, "Oh God, please don't let this be happening again."

"Nothing happened." I hated the defensive tone in my voice. Damn her anyway.

She looked up at me, her eyes tearing. "You can't be doing this, John. I never should have invited Adam in. I'm so stupid, but I never wanted to believe this of you. You cannot do this." She put a hand to her mouth, looking distressed. "Oh God, Randy would kill you if he knew." Her hands trembled as she reached for the doorknob, and she ran from the room.

"Nothing *happened!*" I yelled after her, sour panic rising in my throat, suffocating me. Was I still so sick that I had no concept of my actions? I guessed it was possible, and this thought filled me with such dread that it became hard to draw a breath. What sort of atrocities was I capable of committing unconsciously? If only my damned brain would work in such a way as to allow me to determine the truth.

I knew there were intervals I couldn't account for, when hours—indeed days—had disappeared without a trace, as if I had been elsewhere, too busy to take note of their passing. But that hadn't happened in the recent past...or had it? Oh God, I didn't know. I just didn't know.

I found Laurie sitting at the kitchen table, her face in her hands. "Where's Adam?"

Laurie raised her head to stare at me. "I sent him home. I told him you still weren't feeling well. Stay away from him, John."

"I told you nothing happened!"

Her mouth opened, but I careened out of the room, not giving her the opportunity to reply. Snatching my coat from the back of the couch, I headed out the door.

Now that the sun was lower in the sky, the chilliness of the day was dissolving into frigid night. I crept along the street, dizziness prompting me to measure my steps with care. This was precisely why I didn't like taking anti-psychotic medication. Not to mention the fact that once the sedative wore off, I would be awake for days on end.

After a couple of blocks, I was chilled to the bone. A car slowed as it neared me and someone shouted, "Hey, skell, why don't you go curl up somewhere and sleep it off!" This was followed by laughter and the sound of an engine revving as the car drove away.

I tucked my chin closer to my chest and pretended that the remark hadn't hurt. Still and all, I had rather be mistaken for a drunk or a crackhead than a schizophrenic or a—I couldn't even say the words to myself, wouldn't allow myself to think them.

Eventually I arrived at the diner a few degrees short of hypothermia. There were only three other customers present, and the waitress, a petite older woman with salt and pepper hair, was one I had never seen before. She hesitated; perhaps she, too, thought I was drunk or high.

Nevertheless, she took my order for coffee and a BLT. Having missed both breakfast and lunch, hunger was beginning to gnaw at my stomach like an angry demon. But it was not until the coffee cup was placed before me that I realized I had missed more than lunch. *I had missed my date with Caitlin.*

The expression on my face must have given the waitress a scare, for she set the coffee carafe down on the countertop and frowned, "Are you all right?"

I nodded, but I was having a hard time reining in my emotions. Uncertain, she continued to stare at me until a cook stuck his head through the window separating the kitchen from the dining room and said, "Pat—order up!"

Keeping one eye on me, she collected the food and brought it over. Sliding a plate in front of me, she asked, "You sure you're okay?"

"Yes." I forced the word out of my mouth and, at the same time, pulled the plate toward me on the pretext of eating. Pat did not appear convinced by the charade but focused her attention on the remaining patrons.

When she turned her back, I put my head in my hands. I wasn't sure why the failed date depressed me so, but it did, and to my everlasting disgust, I felt tears forming at the corners of my eyes. I tried hard to force them back, tried thinking of a happier time—of something that gave me pleasure. Then I realized that I was trying to conjure up something that had never been, something that would never be. There would only be this unending grief, always and forever.

"Oh, Jesus." I rubbed at my eyes with my palms, dispersing the dampness as best I could. When I glanced up to find Pat staring at me once again, however, I felt a few remaining tears slip down my cheeks.

"Listen," she said, her voice low, "I don't know what's wrong, but if there's anything I can do, I wish you would tell me."

I tried to smile at her but feared it was more of a grimace. "Can you give me a new life?" I whispered. "Or at least take this one away?"

"You want to die?" Her face told me that such an idea was foreign to her. Then again, she wasn't schizophrenic.

"You don't understand. I'm already dead—I want to live."

She frowned, seeming to think this over. "It sounds like you need help."

I snorted without meaning to. "No thanks. I've had eight years of help. I've had every kind of help you can imagine. I've got help coming out my ass. What I need is a friend; someone I can talk to besides my damned sister."

Pat grinned. "You're doing a pretty good job of talking to me."

"I didn't mean to bother you. Sorry." I pushed the sandwich away and collapsed back into my misery.

She slid the plate back to me. "Sorry? For what? For needing someone to listen to you? Don't apologize for that. Just means you're human. Now eat that. Didn't your mama ever tell you not to waste food? Besides, it'll make you feel a little better to have something in your tummy. Be back in a sec." She walked off to wait on a couple who'd entered the diner.

I picked up the sandwich and took a few bites. Magically, it transformed itself into the best thing I'd eaten in months.

I tried to remember my mother and if she'd ever told me not to waste food, but the exercise was futile. As far as my memories went, she may as well have never lived. How much better off I would have been if she hadn't. But she had, and here I was. Now what?

By the time Pat returned, I had finished the sandwich. "Good for you," she said, picking up the empty plate. "Now, don't you feel better?"

I admitted that I did. It occurred to me only after they ceased, that the dull pains in my stomach had been hunger. And now that I had eaten, I felt a few degrees less depressed.

"Thanks for talking to me," I murmured.

Pat laughed. "Honey, you don't have to thank me for that—I love to talk. I'm sure my husband sometimes wishes I would do a little less of it."

She poured more coffee in my cup and leaned against the counter while I sipped it. "Are you going to be okay now?" she asked after a few moments.

I shrugged. "Maybe. Maybe not. I haven't been okay for a long time. I'm not even sure I know what that means."

"Lord, you're going to have me worrying about you. By the way, what's your name? If I'm going to be reading about you in the obituaries, I would at least like to know who you are."

I smiled in spite of myself. "John—John Colucci."

"Well, John, honey, if you need somebody to talk to, you remember I'm here Monday through Friday from two 'til eight. Promise me you won't do anything stupid without at least stopping in to tell me 'bye. Okay?"

"Okay," I agreed, standing to leave. I pulled a few crumpled bills from my pocket, but she waved me away.

"It's on me this once, but I'll expect you to hang in there so you can make it up to me sometime."

#

The sun had long since gone down when I left the diner. Most of the snow had been pushed from the sidewalks and streets and mounded against the curbs. A savage wind gusted between the drifts, driving pieces of trash ahead of it and swirling the slag into winter dust devils. I entered a bus shelter on the corner of the block to keep my skin from being sandblasted off my body and lit a cigarette. Only when I'd smoked it down to the filter was I ready to brave the weather. Though I'd missed my lunch date with Caitlin, I remembered that the reading program met that night, and I was determined that I would at least attend that.

Coat collar turned up and hands crammed into my pockets, I set off once more. The wind continued to buffet me from all sides, making each step even more difficult. Walking as fast as I dared, I had only gone a couple more blocks when I heard a car. Glancing over my shoulder, I saw a police cruiser creeping steadily along after me.

I sucked in my breath and the aching cold with it, and my heart throbbed to life in my chest. If not for the medication-induced vertigo, I would have broken into a run and gotten the hell out of there. If I could make it to the next block without being accosted by the cop, I could slip into an alley where he couldn't follow me except on foot. By the time he got out of his car, I'd be on the next road, where I could duck into an open business.

I crossed a side avenue against the traffic light, slid on a patch of ice and tripped on the curb. It happened so fast, I wasn't even sure what had occurred until I felt pavement under the now-skinned palms of my hands. I heard a car door open and then footsteps beside me.

"Are you all right?" a man's voice asked. "What the hell are you doing out here anyway?" Peter stood scowling down at me.

"Why are you following me?" I sat up, brushing my hands gingerly across my knees to dislodge the grit.

"You ought to be glad I did. This isn't the best place for someone like you to be at night by yourself."

"Yeah? Why don't you define 'someone like me'?" I didn't feel very grateful.

He had the grace to look embarrassed as he stammered, "Well, I—uh—just meant that you're...well, vulnerable. You'd be easy prey for some of the goons that hang out in this area."

"Why do you care?" I tried to stand, without success.

"I guess I feel sorry for you." He took my arm and helped me to my feet. "Look, John, I apologize. I didn't mean that to sound the way it did."

"Forget it." I shrugged my coat sleeve out of his grip, wanting to be on my way.

"Why don't you let me take you home?" Peter asked, gesturing at the car.

"No, thanks. I'm not ready to go home."

He rolled his eyes heavenward and shook his head. "Dude, I'm telling you. This is not a good place for you to be. At least let me take you wherever it is you're going."

Great, I thought, now Randy and Laurie have recruited Peter to rag my ass. "*No thanks.*"

"Man, I'm trying to say I'm sorry. Humor me."

"All right. Fine." I listed in the direction of the car and reached for the handle on the back door.

"No, get in the front seat. You're not in custody now."

"That's good," I said as I climbed in. "Once a day is usually my limit."

He fastened his seatbelt, motioning for me to do the same, and started the car. "I hope we didn't rough you up too much this morning."

"Oh, just a few cracked ribs and a mild concussion. Nothing to worry about."

He cut his eyes toward me for a split second and his forehead furrowed.

"I'm kidding," I told him.

A smile slowly spread across his face. "No offense, but I don't see how you can keep a sense of humor in your situation."

I shrugged. "Sometimes I don't."

"I'm amazed at the difference in you since this morning. I guess the medication works, doesn't it?"

"Oh, it works all right. And later on tonight, while everyone else is snoozing in their beds, I'll be climbing the walls—literally—and wearing holes in the carpet from pacing."

"Side effect?"

"One of many."

"Hmm." Peter braked for a red light. "Where do you want me to drop you off?"

"At the library."

He signaled for a left-hand turn. "Randy's kind of rough on you."

I didn't say anything, but it was my turn to look at him.

"I mean, I think he is," he said when we were moving again. "The way he talks, I get this mental picture of some two-headed monster, some sideshow freak. And then this morning I was almost believing it."

I snorted. "Hang around long enough and I have a feeling you'll see that two-headed monster again."

"You seem pretty normal right now."

Normal. He couldn't know how much that word hurt, simply because it was something I would never be. And the fact that I appeared to be that way at the moment was just another cruel joke life had at my expense. The price for being quasi-normal was too high—the side effects of and dependence on medication, having to rely on people who resented being relied upon. Looking like a regular human on the outside and being a fucked up mess on the inside.

"Stop the car."

He turned his head toward me. "What?"

"Stop the car."

"I thought you wanted me to drop you off at the library."

"I changed my mind. Stop the car."

"Did I say something wrong?"

"Stop the car, or I'm jumping." I hit the release button on the seatbelt, and it thwacked against the doorframe as it sailed back into its slot. I reached for the door handle.

"Jesus Christ, John. Hold on a damned second." He braked quickly, and I had to brace myself to keep from tasting the dashboard.

"The library's two blocks up on the corner," he said as I stepped from the car. He pulled away from the curb shaking his head and no doubt mumbling under his breath. I felt reasonably certain that he was reconsidering his observation on the state of my mental health.

CHAPTER SEVEN

I WATCHED THE CAR move down the street until the taillights resembled the glowing red eyes of a disembodied demon, then shuddering, I lurched along to the library and through the front doors, my teeth chattering.

Warmth and silence rushed to greet me, enclosing me in their embrace, and I was glad the Voices had shut up for a while. The tranquility seemed too pristine, too pure, to be defiled by their irreverence, and I allowed the blessed quiet to wash over me before proceeding further.

A woman sat behind a desk opposite the entrance, frowning as she glanced in my direction, her gaze like a white-hot laser, appraising me. Her eyes lingered on the now rust-colored bloodstain on my coat. Then she stood and squared her shoulders in determination, preparing to meet a battle, a battle she had fought—and won—many times. The heels of her shoes clicked across the hardwood floor, and a condescending smile played on her lips. Her expression said that she clearly thought I was white trash.

"I'm sorry," she said, and I imagined a blast of icy air erupting from her mouth, freezing me on the spot, "but the shelter is on the corner of Devinney and 8th."

It took me several long moments to realize what she was saying, and when it began to sink in, I felt my face heating up in embarrassment.

"I'm here to enroll in the reading program," I said with as much dignity as I could summon under the circumstances.

"Oops, sorry," she replied, not looking very apologetic, "we have a lot of homeless people trying to come in and camp out. We do have to be careful." Great. In addition to being crazy, now I looked homeless.

She led me past her desk, up some stairs, through a hallway and to a meeting room. "Here you are," she said at the doorway. She offered me a phony smile, and then she was gone.

I stepped into the room where two other people—a man and a woman—were both seated at a round wooden table. The man said, "Hello," but the woman stared at her hands, which she held clasped before her.

Noticing a coffeemaker and a stack of foam cups on the counter at the rear of the room, I went over and poured some. I wasn't going to sleep tonight anyway, so a little more caffeine wouldn't hurt. Self-conscious, I removed my coat and draped it across a chair. As soon as my ass hit the seat, though, the woman came to life.

"You can't sit there," she snapped. "That's where the teacher sits."

"It's cool, Grace," the man told her. "He's new. He didn't know."

She glared at me until I moved to another seat, then went back to studying her hands. From what I could glimpse of her face in the few seconds she had turned it up to me, there were permanent creases outlining her scowl. I wondered if she, too, were mentally ill. For that matter, both she and the man looked as downtrodden as I felt. What a fine cross section of humanity we made. Life had held us down in the dirt with its foot on our heads for so long, it was impossible for us to get back up.

I took a sip of coffee, nearly spilling it in my lap when a loud, bright voice said behind me, "Hi guys! Sorry I'm running late tonight."

Grace's expression softened slightly and the man smiled at the late arrival.

"Well," said the same voice, and a woman stepped into my line of vision, "look who's here!"

"Caitlin?" I thought perhaps I was hallucinating to find her grinning down at me.

"Are you here to enroll in the class?" She placed an armload of books on the table.

Flustered, I could only stammer, "Yes."

"Great," she said, still grinning. "Let me get Jimmy and Grace started, and I'll be right back."

She moved between the two of them, laughing with Jimmy, murmuring to Grace. I watched her hand linger on Jimmy's shoulder as she stood over him, pointing out several passages in one of the books, and her slender fingers as they rested lightly on Grace's forearm. After an eternity, they selected a book from the stack and opened it, and Caitlin, gathering a handful of papers, came to sit beside me.

The scent of her perfume made me want to move my chair closer to hers and lay my head on her shoulder. I was so caught up in the fantasy that I didn't realize she was speaking to me at first.

"So what happened to you at lunch today?"

"Pardon me?"

"What happened to you at lunch today? I thought we had a date."

"We did...I'm sorry." Wonderful, now what do I tell her? Oh yes, I was getting pumped full of anti-psychotics and sedatives right about then; maybe some other time. Unable to come up with anything more creative, I blurted out the truth, "I was at the hospital."

Her expression went from quiet expectation to concern. "The hospital? I hope everything's all right."

"Yeah, nothing major. I'm fine now." As fine as I could ever hope to be.

Relief crossed her features. "Well, in that case, I guess I'll have to offer you a raincheck. How about tomorrow? Same time, same place?"

"I'd like that. Thank you."

"Great! Now, in the meantime, how can I help you with your reading?"

Feeling embarrassed again, I shrugged my shoulders and muttered, "I'm not sure."

"Are you able to read at all?"

She put a hand on my forearm, and I thought my brain would explode with an orgy of sensation. Read, hell, I couldn't even think. One touch of her palm and I was reeling out of control. I wanted to stroke her hair, to rest my hand on hers, to place my mouth over hers, but an alarm clamored in my head, warning me against this course of action.

"There's nothing to be ashamed of, John," she was saying, unaware of the effect her touch was having on me, "but I can't help you if you don't answer my questions."

Nothing to be ashamed of—God, if she only knew. Never mind the thoughts I was having about her, there were things I had done—unspeakable things— things so bad that I couldn't even remember them. And if that weren't cause enough for shame, how did I tell her about my reading problem without telling her what I was?

It was hard to find my voice. I worked my mouth a few times, but nothing came out. I was aware that Jimmy and Grace had both looked up from their books and were watching me with curious expressions.

"John, it's *okay*. It's no big deal." Caitlin squeezed my arm gently.

A strangled noise worked its way past my frozen vocal cords, and I leapt from my seat and bolted from the room.

In the hallway, I stood trembling. I didn't mind telling her that I couldn't read, but I just couldn't tell her that I was schizophrenic. I was tired of the label and the stigma attached to it. If I ever stood a chance of making it on the outside, it had to be without the brands of "Schizophrenic", and "Incompetent".

Caitlin stepped into the hall and pulled the door closed behind her. I took a deep breath and prepared to face her. I wasn't sure how to explain my behavior and fully expected her to tell me to hit the road.

Instead, her face kind, she said, "Please, can we start over?"

Relieved, I said, "Yes."

"Good. I really wasn't trying to be nosy. You don't have to tell me anything you don't want to. It's just that I was trying to determine a starting point. I don't want you to get bored or frustrated, that's all."

"I didn't think you were being nosy. I can read...a few words at a time, but when they're strung together in long sentences—in paragraphs—I get overwhelmed. I feel like such an idiot. I don't even know if it's anything you can help me with." My pulse thundered in my veins with the admission. There...it was out. It probably wouldn't take her long to put two and two together and come up with the truth.

But instead of recoiling, she patted my shoulder. "We'll work it out, John. Come on back in, and we'll see what we can do to get you started."

I followed her into the room and took my seat as she rummaged through her stack of books. She pulled out a thin primer with a brown and white puppy on its cover and handed it to me.

I stared at the round-headed puppy with the curlicue tail, frustration mounting. "It's a *child's* book," I said, and I'm sure annoyance was evident in my voice.

"I know," she replied, "but let's try it anyway. We'll start with it and work our way up."

Reluctantly, I opened the cover and turned to the first page. And though there were far fewer words on this page than there were in my novels at home, they still danced and swam. I could pick a couple out of the murk—"fence" and "meadow"—but none of the rest of it made any sense. Angry, I snapped the little book shut.

"John," Caitlin was at my side, bending toward me, her hair hanging down between us, "please don't get upset. We'll work it out, but it's not going to happen immediately."

I closed my eyes and breathed in, allowing her fragrance to fill my nostrils and thinking it was a sin for any woman to smell as good as she did. How could I concentrate on anything with her standing so close? To make matters worse, she sat next to me, her thigh pressing against mine, and reached to open the book, her breast brushing my arm.

"Let's look at the first page," she said, but I could focus only on the delicate bone of her wrist and the thin gold chain fastened around it.

Would it be so wrong to take her hand and gently taste each of her fingers, to savor that pale gold skin from the palm of her hand to the soft hollow at the base of her throat?

"John—the book?"

Reluctantly, I shifted my gaze once again to the round-headed puppy.

"Let's start with the first sentence. Just take one word at a time. Don't worry about the other sentences now. One at a time." She placed her palm on the page, covering all but the very first sentence.

I tried to concentrate on the first word only, but the others were pushing, crowding, trying to climb over it, fighting for attention. Frustration continued to mount.

"One at a time," I told myself. "Concentrate." But the first word didn't want to be by itself and joined the others in the swirling haze. "Stop it," I whispered, enraged. "Don't make me out to be a fool."

You don't need any help with that, John.

No, you play the fool quite competently without our help.

The only thing you're competent at, we might add.

Give it up; you can't read.

And worse than that—you can't have Caitlin.

Close the book and leave.

You can't read!

"I can, too," I muttered, staring hard at the page, willing the words to stop moving.

Jimmy and Grace are laughing at you.

They figure if they can read, you must be a real dumbass if you can't.

I jerked my head up to glare at Jimmy and Grace, but if they had been watching me, they quickly averted their eyes. I felt my face coloring, and accompanied by the laughter of the Voices, I gritted my teeth and turned yet again to the round-headed puppy.

You couldn't read that book if there was only one word in it.

Hell, you couldn't read it if there were no words in it.

I've seen babies who could read better than you.

The sound came out of my mouth so fast, it was almost a shout. "Five!" I laughed. "The first word is five!"

"Good." Caitlin urged me onward with a squeeze on my arm.

"Little...puppies. Five little puppies dug a—hole—under the—fence. Five little puppies dug a hole under the fence." I was grinning ear to ear, and I knew it. It didn't matter that the words were once again going into the spin cycle, I was able to read some of them and that was all that mattered at the moment.

"I knew you could do it." She looked as triumphant as I felt. "One word at a time, just keep that in mind. We'll start small and improve on that. You're just going to need to retrain you brain. Why don't you keep working at that for a while and then we can go on to something more challenging?"

I continued to examine the little book. Struggle as I might, however, I was unable to decipher any more about the five little puppies, although occasionally a word surfaced in the melee long enough for me to identify it. I didn't realize how long I had been grappling with the second half of the first sentence until Grace and Jimmy stood and said their goodbyes to Caitlin.

I stood, too, and reached for my coat as Caitlin gathered the books and stacked them in a large pile.

"I could carry those for you, if you'd like," I told her as she attempted to lift the assortment, which threatened to topple over.

"Well, thank you." She took a small armful anyway. "Are you sure you don't mind?"

Anything to be with you, I wanted to say. "I don't mind," was what I did say.

I followed her downstairs to the front desk where we deposited the books in the return bin, and she said goodnight to the library staff. Together we walked through the double doors and into the cold night air.

"I can't believe I've lost my gloves again." She shivered and shoved her hands in her coat pockets as we stood on the steps.

"I can't believe I don't have any," I replied, and she laughed.

"So, I'll see you tomorrow at the diner at one o'clock?"

"Yeah." I held my hand out to her. One last touch and I would be on my way. "Thanks."

Freeing her right hand from its coat pocket cocoon, she placed it in my outstretched palm. "I'll see you tomorrow then."

Tomorrow seemed a long way off as I picked a path down the steps over several icy spots. I still had the rest of the night to get through—a night with no sleep. A night with the Voices. A very *long* night. And, of course, the Voices had already begun their litany, though they hadn't reached their peak.

I drifted off down the street, wishing I'd had the sense to call Laurie to pick me up. After only a block, my hands and feet were so cold that they ached, and my eyes, stung by wind and grit, poured a constant stream of tears. I wondered idly if I would make it home alive or if someone would find my frozen body lying in an alley, and decided that I didn't much care one way or the other. I seemed to remember from something I had read—back when I could read like a normal person—that people who froze to death first got drowsy and then felt warm all over, wanting nothing more than to lie down and sleep. But I was so damned cold and wide awake, I figured I was a long way from that.

Another block and the cold-induced pain was almost unbearable. I thought about finding a phone to call Laurie and realized that I didn't even know her number. I supposed I could go to the police station and tell them who I was—

ask them to call Randy or Peter, but I knew I wouldn't do that. I would rather die no matter how long it took.

Traffic was moderate, vehicles swooshing past, tires crunching on random patches of ice. I tried not to think of all the people in their nice warm cars, hurrying to their nice warm homes. And when I heard a car slowing behind me for the second time that night, I tried not to think about that either.

Sure that it was Peter again, I kept walking, determined to ignore him. But when the horn blared, causing me to jump, I whirled, ready to chew his ass out. It was not a police cruiser stopped at the curb, however, and the driver was definitely not Peter.

It was Caitlin who leaned over the seat to open the passenger door. "Get in the car before you freeze," she ordered in a mock-stern voice.

I slid into the seat next to her. The warm air blowing from the heater vents was a welcome relief.

"Are you crazy, out there walking?" she asked. "The wind chill factor's got to be below zero."

I winced at her choice of words. "I didn't have a ride."

"Well, I'm glad I happened to be going in this direction and spotted you."

"So am I."

She signaled and maneuvered the car into traffic. "Where to?"

"Windflower Lane—in Stratford Hills. It's off Sheridan Boulevard."

She turned an astonished face toward me briefly. "You would have frozen solid trying to walk there."

"I've walked there before."

"Not on a night like this, I'm willing to bet."

"True," I admitted. "Thanks for picking me up." I settled back in my seat and studied her profile as it swam in and out of the illumination of streetlights. I also entertained the fantasy that instead of returning me to the relative safety of Laurie's home, she would keep driving out into the county where we would find a secluded back road to park. We'd climb into the back seat, and I'd....

And you'd what, John? Take her against her will?

You'd have to, 'cause that's the only way you're going to get a piece of her pie.

But, boy, wouldn't she taste good?

Stolen pie's always the best.

It took everything in my power not to reprimand the Voices in Caitlin's presence, and I felt my face grow hot with embarrassment at the things they were saying. I gritted my teeth and "silently chanted, "Shut up, shut up."

"Is my driving that bad?" Caitlin asked, grinning. "It must be. You've got a death grip on that armrest, and it looked as if you might have been saying a prayer."

"No, no," I told her, making a conscious effort to relax my hold on the armrest. "It's not that at all. I was just thinking about something else."

"I don't think I'll ask what that something was."

"You don't really want to know," I agreed.

She slowed the car as we approached the turnoff for the Stratford Hills subdivision. "You'll have to direct me from here."

We pulled into the driveway a few moments later, and I noted, with dread, that Randy's car sat in its customary parking place and every light in the house was on. He hadn't yet left for work and there would be no way of sneaking past him.

"Thanks for the ride," I told her, my mouth suddenly dry, the words sticking in my throat.

"You're welcome." Her gaze lingered on my face until, reluctant, I turned my attention back to the house.

Later, when I was alone, I could ponder the significance of that look, but for now, I had a gauntlet to run. The front door opened, and I could see the outline of Randy's bulk silhouetted against the foyer light.

"Thanks again," I said, reaching for the door handle.

"See you tomorrow at one." She was smiling as I climbed out of the car and shut the door.

"If I live that long," I muttered and began the trek toward my doom.

I reached the porch, and Randy bowed from the waist and swept his arm in a great arc in the direction of the interior. "Why look, honey," he called in a loud, sarcastic voice as I entered the house, "it's your dear brother, John, come to pay us a visit!"

He slammed the door shut behind me, and I flinched when a framed painting fell off the wall and clunked to the floor. Laurie stood in the middle of the living room, one arm folded across her chest and a hand covering her mouth. Her eyes twitched from Randy's face to mine.

Stalking over to a chair, he patted the back and said in the same sarcastic tone, "Please, John, won't you have a seat and stay for just a little while? Please?"

From the dangerous glint in his eyes, I knew that I had been given a command rather than a request. I swallowed hard around the grapefruit-sized lump in my throat and sat down.

With another gallant flourish, Randy motioned Laurie to the sofa. She sat obediently, and he sat next to her.

Clasping his hands together, he looked around the room. "Well, now, isn't this cozy? Tell us, John, what have you been doing with yourself lately?"

I raised my eyes to meet his and felt my hands tremble. "I haven't done anything wrong." My voice was barely above a whisper, but in the dead quiet of the room, it might as well have been a shout.

He was quick. Damned quick. I saw only the flash of his palm before it collided with my face, snapping my head back. The echo of skin on skin reverberated through the room. I fought the urge to rub my cheek and sat frozen, rage burning white-hot within me.

"I thought we'd had this conversation before," he growled into my ear.

Laurie was sobbing, "Please, don't hit him. He can't help the way he is."

"He's lucky if a slap is all that happens to him, especially out there on the street. That was a wake-up call, by the way—a reality check. You'd better start listening to what we tell you, and the first rule you need to get straight is don't go running off without telling someone where you're going and when you'll be back. The second rule is don't be hitchhiking. If you need a ride, call and we'll pick you up."

If he hit me again, I knew the fight would be on, so I struggled to keep my voice low and neutral. "Laurie knew where I'd be—at the library for the reading program. We talked about this the other day. And I didn't hitchhike. The lady who runs the reading program gave me a ride."

Laurie looked dismayed. "Oh no, tonight was the reading program, wasn't it?"

"God damn it!" Randy slammed his fist down on the coffee table. "You two had better get your schedules straight, because I am not going through this shit every night. It's a good thing I hadn't called the department yet—then we'd have two or three more people out there wasting their time."

"Meaning, of course, that I'm a waste of your time," I retorted. All bets were off now.

Randy gave me another of his evil sneers and said, "John, as far as I'm concerned, you're a waste of life."

Laurie gasped and the color drained from her face. "I can't believe you would say that."

"And I can't believe a child-molesting murderer is living in my house!" he bellowed at her.

Laurie cried harder.

"Just a minute!" They both turned to stare at me. "I didn't ask to come live with you. I didn't even remember I had a sister." Laurie's tearful face registered pain, but I continued, too angry to worry about her feelings now. "And since my being here is such a burden on your otherwise happy home life, then I'll leave!"

"You leave here and you'll go right back to the hospital," Randy warned.

"Fine!" I screamed at him. "I was a hell of a lot happier there!"

"You ungrateful bastard."

"What do I have to be grateful for?" I was on the verge of crying myself. "Should I be grateful that you decided to take me into your warm, cheerful home? Should I be grateful that you hate me?"

"I don't hate you, but I sure as hell hate what you did," he said quietly.

"Which is the same thing with you!" I couldn't keep my voice from cracking. "There is no 'love the sinner, hate the sin'. And just what is my sin anyway? That I'm schizophrenic? That I'm not perfect, like you?"

Laurie stepped toward me, her arms outstretched as if to embrace me, but I put up a hand to stop her. "Don't touch me!" And before either of them could make another move, I ran to my bedroom and locked the door behind me. Then as an added measure of security, I barricaded it with the chest of drawers.

#

I crept out of the house late the next morning while Laurie was busy in the laundry room, Randy's rules be damned. This time I was prepared for the cold, wrapped tightly in my coat and wearing a toboggan and pair of gloves scrounged from the bottom of the dresser drawer in my room. I was also prepared for lunch with another twenty-dollar bill borrowed from Laurie's purse in my pocket.

Halfway to town, I realized that I'd forgotten to take my medicine. Again. Damn. And amongst all the Voices that grumbled constantly, I could hear Dr. Fremont, Dr. Steele, Laurie, and Randy saying in unison, "If you don't take your medicine, you'll go back to the institution."

"Fuck all of you," I muttered and walked even faster.

The hospital wasn't such a bad place. I hadn't been abused, or, in any event, couldn't remember it if I had. Someone had seen to it that I was clothed and fed. I probably could have done without the ECT, but had no recollection of the specific shock treatments themselves.

Being sent back to the hospital would be no threat to me with the exception of matters regarding Caitlin. It was pretty obvious that I didn't belong out here and never would. I did, however, want to see where things went with her. I would at least like to know if I were capable of having a relationship with someone besides a caregiver. And with that thought in mind, I arrived at the diner.

Pushing into the lunchtime crowd, I found one vacant seat at the counter where I waited until I could procure a table for Caitlin and myself. According to the clock on the wall, it was ten 'til one, and the closer it got to the hour, the faster my heart beat.

At five after one, I caught a glimpse of her red-gold hair as she entered the diner and thought I might be going into cardiac arrest. She spied me at the counter, and her smile was one of genuine delight. I resisted the urge to look behind me to see if it was directed at someone else.

I stood as she neared me to offer her my seat until the place cleared out a little. She clasped my hands in hers, and it was all I could do to keep from panting.

"I'm glad you came! I wasn't really sure whether to expect you or not." She perched on the stool, shoulder against my arm, and her fragrance wafted up to me—far more appetizing than the food smells around me.

"I would have been here yesterday, only I ended up at the emergency room," I said by way of apology.

"Oh, I'm not complaining about that! I'm just glad you were able to come today." She glanced down the length of the diner where a couple was preparing to leave. "Look, there's a table. Let's grab it!"

We slid into the booth, pushing dirty dishes to the table's edge where the waitress could get to them.

"Was everything all right last night?" she asked. "You seemed really nervous about something when we got to your house. I worried about you all night."

I was touched that she would have wasted any time contemplating my problems, and I could feel my soul opening up to her. "I live with my sister and her husband," I blurted out, "and he can be a real asshole sometimes."

She nodded knowingly. "Isn't that the job of in-laws everywhere?"

"With him, it's not just a job, it's a career."

She laughed, then turned to greet Edie, the waitress, as she arrived.

"Hi, Cait. Let me get these dishes out of the way, and I'll take your order."

She stacked everything on her tray, then pulled out her order pad and flipped it open to a fresh page. "Who's your friend?" she asked.

Caitlin grinned at her and said, "Nosy butt. This is John Colucci. John, this is Edie Morgan."

Edie shook my hand. "Glad to meet you, John." When she turned back to Caitlin, I thought I saw them exchanging a glance that seemed to indicate approval. Approval of what, I wasn't sure.

When we had given our orders and Edie had gone off to tend to other diners, Caitlin focused on me once again. "I just can't shake this feeling that I ought to know you. Maybe we met in a former life?"

"If we did, I sure hope it was a better life than this one," I replied.

She sat forward again, propping her elbows on the table. "I sense a story here."

I waved a hand at her. "Too depressing. I don't want to bring you down, too."

"Sometimes it helps just to talk to someone."

I studied her for a moment, trying to gauge her sincerity. I couldn't remember anyone ever being genuinely interested in what I might have to say. The exception to this, of course, being doctors who were trying to determine whether or not to fry my brain or load me down with more anti-psychotics.

I wanted to trust her. I needed to trust her. But then there was the problem of how much to tell her without revealing that I was schizophrenic. For I felt certain that if she knew, then she, like a lot of other people before her, would hightail it out of my life at light speed.

"I guess my biggest problem right now is my sister and brother-in-law," I said. "Things just aren't working out with me living at their house. Seems like every way I turn, I'm butting heads with Randy. Nothing I do is right, according to him. Last night we had this big argument, and he told me I was a waste of life."

Caitlin frowned. "What a jerk!" She paused while Edie delivered our lunch, then continued. "You don't have to stay there, do you? Couldn't you find a place of your own?"

"Kind of hard without a job to pay for it."

"Oh, no. That's right!"

To her credit, she didn't ask why I didn't just get a job. Still, I felt that I had to explain myself somehow.

"I'm disabled," I ventured, "so it's not like I can just go out and go to work."

For some reason she seemed to brighten at this news. "But then you'd qualify for some kind of assistance. And if you don't qualify for disability, then it must mean that you have money or property in your name that makes you ineligible."

Good point. Neither Laurie nor Randy had ever mentioned a word about a disability check or money of any kind whatsoever.

Caitlin frowned once more. "Don't tell me they're getting your money and not telling you about it."

Again, I said nothing, but anger was beginning its slow boil beneath my skin.

"You need to check into that, John. Don't let them rip you off."

They wanted me to think I had to stay with them. They wanted me to believe I had no choice in the matter. Sure, take his money and treat him like a red-headed stepchild. He's a schizo—he'll never figure it out.

Caitlin must have sensed the change in my mood. "I hope I haven't upset you." She touched my hand and smiled at me.

"You haven't." I wanted to concentrate on the sensation of her fingertips against mine, but the Voices were beginning to stir and make themselves known.

Imagine that. Randy trying to take advantage of you.

Who'd've thunk it? Certainly not a genius like you.

And don't forget, Laurie's his accomplice.

Hell, they could just kill you, hide your body somewhere, and collect that money without having to hassle with you.

Randy would rather see you dead anyway. It's his life's ambition.

You know, other people have aspired to a lot less.

"You're sure I haven't upset you?" Caitlin was pulling at my shirtsleeve, concerned.

I shook my head as much to stun the Voices into silence as to answer her question. "It just pisses me off to think they might be taking advantage of me."

She put a hand to her mouth, looking distressed. "I shouldn't have insinuated that they would. I'm sorry. I don't even know them. It's just that...well, I've heard so many horror stories in my line of work, and I wouldn't want to see it happen to you."

"Neither would I, but don't worry about it. I guess it wouldn't upset me if I didn't think it might actually be true."

"Want to change the subject?" she asked.

"Yeah. Let's talk about you; someone whose life isn't completely fucked."

She gave a short laugh. "Everyone's got their share of problems, and I'm no exception. But let's talk about this. Do you snow ski?"

"I don't know. I've never tried it."

"Well, I'm dying to get some skiing in before winter's over. Although at this rate," she said glancing toward the window, "I'd say that's going to be a long time in coming. I was thinking about going up to Beech Mountain next Friday evening, and I'd love the company. Would you like to come?"

Would I ever! Trying not to act too eager, I said, "Sure, that is if I can get the guard dogs off my back."

"We'd go up Friday night and come back late Sunday afternoon. They couldn't object to that."

"Ah, but you don't know them, remember? They've set themselves up to be my parents." I didn't bother to explain the whole incompetency thing.

"And how old are you?" she asked.

What age did Laurie say I was? Twenty-eight? I would have to take her word for it. "I'm twenty-eight," I told Caitlin.

"And they still treat you this way?" she asked, incredulous. "I'm not sure if I want to know them."

"You don't," I agreed.

We continued to talk until she glanced at her watch and said, "Well, as much as I hate the thought, I have to get back to work now." She gathered her things and stood to pull on her coat.

I jumped up to help her and said, "Can I walk you back?"

"That would be great." She reached for the check, but I plucked it from her hand.

"I'll get it."

On our way out, I stopped at the register to pay, then hurried to the door to catch up with Caitlin. She slid her arm through mine, causing me another mild coronary, and we stepped out into the cold sunshine.

We walked five blocks to the newspaper building, Caitlin assuring me that she would have me skiing like a pro in no time. I had my doubts, but it didn't matter since my interest was in her, not skiing.

Stopping at the corner, she said, "Check with the guard dogs about the ski trip and let me know." Then she tilted her chin and lifted her lips to mine.

I responded almost greedily, tasting her mouth, drinking her in. For once the Voices were speechless, as if an electric current had run through me, stopping all vital body functions for a brief interval.

CHAPTER EIGHT

AS EXPECTED, getting Laurie and Randy to agree to the ski trip wasn't as easy as it sounded. "Our reading group is supposed to leave Friday night," I reminded her as she was putting supper on the table Wednesday evening of the following week.

"I still fail to see how that relates to reading," Randy said. He was already seated at the table and nibbling out of each serving dish she set down.

She shot him a warning look then turned back to me. "It does sound like fun."

"Yeah, I'd really like to go."

She considered this for a minute as if it were the first time we'd discussed the subject. "Do you know how to ski?"

I sighed impatiently. "I can learn."

"Ski, hell. You can't even learn to take your medicine like you're supposed to," Randy interjected.

"Bite my ass," I said. "You're not my father."

"Thank God for that!" he whooped. "No, John, I'm something worse. I'm your guardian! And you can't even breathe unless I say so."

Laurie banged a pot on the stove. "Does everything have to be a power play with you, Randy? Let him make some friends. Let him have some fun. Heaven knows he hasn't seen much of that in his life. Please—leave him alone."

Randy waggled a fork at me and asked, "How are you going to pay for this little trip? Skiing costs money, you know. Or maybe, as usual, you just didn't think about that."

I was in his face in a second, anger making me forget my fear of him. "I intend to pay for it with *my* money. I either have money of my own or I draw disability. One way or the other I have money. And don't pretend you don't know what the hell I'm talking about!"

He gave me one of his infuriatingly smug smiles. "The going rate for crazies isn't very high, and it costs something to house, clothe, and feed you. What makes you think there's anything left over after that?"

I was overcome by an almost overwhelming urge to punch him right in the middle of his hateful face. I didn't realize I had drawn back a fist to do just that until Laurie placed a hand on my arm, forcing it down by my side.

"Both of you stop! You can go skiing, John," she said. "It's okay. You have enough money." She glared at Randy, and then added, "Dinner is ready if anyone has an appetite left."

When Caitlin came to pick me up Friday evening, Laurie pressed a wad of cash into my hand and gave me a quick hug. "I hope you have a great time."

I was beginning to think I was home free when she turned to Caitlin and asked, "Is the rest of the group meeting you at Beech Mountain?"

I froze, knowing that the jig was up the minute Caitlin voiced confusion. But she was quick on her feet. Much quicker than I could ever hope to be.

She never cut her eyes at me, nor hesitated, before replying, "Yes, they went up earlier in the day. I wasn't able to get off work until five o'clock, though, and didn't want to drive up by myself. So I asked John if he would ride with me."

I couldn't tell if Laurie bought the lie, or if, in fact, Caitlin was even telling a lie. Perhaps a group of people were to meet us there; maybe I'd misunderstood her invitation. It was still hard for me to understand what, if anything, she saw in me—why she would want to be alone with me. And suddenly I was angry with Laurie for asking the question.

Before she could think of anything else to interrogate us about, I said an impatient good-bye and ushered Caitlin off the porch to her car. Flinging my carry-on bag into the back, I climbed into the passenger seat beside her and said, "Let's go."

Caitlin waited until she had backed out of the driveway and turned onto the main road before saying, "So...I take it you didn't want sis to know we were going up alone?"

"It's none of her business," I muttered, fiddling with the cuffs of my coat sleeves so I wouldn't have to look her in the eye.

"You're an adult, John."

"Tell *her* that."

"Maybe *you* should."

I stole a glance at her, and her eyes met mine momentarily. Where I thought I might see disgust, however, I saw only challenge.

"What's the worst that could happen if she finds out you and I went alone?"

"She'd tell Randy and then I'd have to listen to the two of them bitching about how I'm—" I stopped. About how I'm incapable of entering into a relationship. About how I can't even take my medication like I'm supposed to. About how, if I'm not careful, I'll go back to the institution. *About how I'm schizophrenic.*

Caitlin's voice was firm, authoritative when she spoke. "You're old enough to make your own choices."

And I was, at that. I had made the choice to be with Caitlin. "You're right."

Grinning, she said, "Your sister's not that bad, John."

I snorted. "You don't have to live with her."

"Touché."

By the time we stopped for supper, I was thoroughly overwhelmed by Caitlin's charms. In a booth at the back of the restaurant, we laughed and cut up, neither of us eating more than a few bites. I wasn't sure how much time had passed when she said, "I guess we'd better be going, though I doubt we'll get in any skiing tonight."

I was about to answer when she placed a hand on my thigh. The words in my mouth evaporated and the air in my lungs solidified. An unseen force took my hand and placed it on hers, sliding it up higher between my legs. She uttered a little noise that was a cross between a gasp and a soft moan, and I grew harder in response.

We stared at each other, only our eyes asking and answering the questions there. I didn't remember standing but we were moving toward the register, then out the door into the winter moonlight to her car.

The ride up the mountain was slow torture, patches of ice and hard-packed snow making the drive perilous at best. She whispered, "Damn" a couple of times as the car slid in a turn, otherwise, neither of us spoke.

I watched her hand on the gearshift and the movement of her legs as she worked the clutch, gas, and brake pedals. I imagined those legs wrapped around my hips, those hands pressing against the small of my back, driving me deeper inside.

When the hotel finally loomed in the distance, I wanted to shout with relief. I silently cursed the length of time it took to get checked in, the time it took the elevator to get to our floor, and the minutes spent searching for our room. But once the door closed behind us, I was unsure of what to do with myself.

As cold as it had been outside, the room seemed stifling, and we both shed our coats immediately. I wanted to push her down on the bed and rip the rest of the clothes from her body, but suddenly I was afraid I'd misread her cues. So I stood in the middle of the room, trembling with want, until she approached, encircled me in her arms, and our lips met.

Removing my outer shirt and undershirt, she placed her palms against my bare chest. I groaned and closed my eyes as her hands wandered lower, behind the waistband of my jeans, across my abdomen, and down to my crotch. I may have murmured, "Sweet Jesus," as her fingers stroked me, but with all the words swirling through my malfunctioning brain, I wasn't sure which of them I had spoken.

"Open your eyes." Her voice was soft and low, the seductive command of a she-devil to her helpless slave.

I didn't want to obey, afraid that I would discover I was merely having an hallucination. Afraid that it was all a wet dream. But when I opened them, she was still there, smiling now as she released me and began unbuttoning her blouse.

The garment floated to the floor, her bra not far behind. Hands shaking, I touched her cheek and chin, shocked by the heat of her smooth flesh. With great restraint, I traced the outline of her collarbone, beginning at the base of her throat, running my fingertips across her shoulder and down her arm. The tightness in my groin begged to be alleviated, and yet I wanted to inspect every inch of her, to prolong this sensation since it could be another eight or nine years before I had the opportunity again.

The fragrance she wore drifted up to me, an enticement to bend my head and place my mouth first on one breast and then the other. Her back arched, muscles tensing, and she hooked her fingers through my belt loops, pulling me toward the bed.

She sank onto the down comforter, and I knelt beside her, covering her mouth with mine. She reached for the front of my jeans, struggling with the button before sliding the zipper open. In turn, I pushed her skirt up, and when she lifted her hips to assist me, I took the opportunity to slip her panties down.

I touched her tentatively between the legs, thrilled when she moaned, "God, yes," licked her lips, and spread her legs wider. Needing no further invitation, I lowered my head. For the next while, my thoughts were simply of pleasing her. I ceased to exist—I became part of her. And it was only when I felt her shudder, felt her pelvis thrusting against my face, that I regained my own identity.

"Oh, my God," she gasped as I kissed my way up the length of her body. "Oh, my God, John…."

Our lips ground together, Caitlin no doubt tasting herself on my mouth, and I struggled to rid myself of the remainder of my clothing. She reached between us, guiding me inside, and I did some shuddering and gasping of my own, trying not to hyperventilate. For a change, I was enjoying the tight, anxious sensation between my legs, knowing that blessed release was soon to follow. If I had died at that precise moment, I would have died a happy man. Or at least as happy as I knew how to be—happiness being such a relative thing and all.

Of course, if your name is John Edward Colucci, happiness is a short-lived or nonexistent phenomenon. And this was certainly no exception.

I was moving toward the *coup de grace*, when I stalled abruptly on the downstroke. There was no warning, no gradual loss of interest. One moment I was poised on the precipice and the next moment I was at the bottom of the cliff, without ever going over the edge. "*Shit!*"

"What's wrong?" Caitlin asked as I withdrew from her, climbed out of bed, and began searching the jumble of clothes and bedding for my pants.

"I'm sorry," I muttered, as I pulled on my jeans. "I don't know what happened." I located my shirt and boots, donning them as well, before stepping out on the small balcony. I was angry with myself and angrier still with the Voices who could now be heard snickering.

I was sure they were at least partially responsible for my inability to consummate my first night of passion with Caitlin. Of course the balance of blame rested with me, owing to my overall incompetence. Or was that impotence? I could imagine the fun Dr. Fremont would have with that play on words. At any rate, I should've known that it would be impossible for me to accomplish anything as normal as making love to a woman.

In frustration, I struck the wrought iron railing with my fist and felt it vibrate with the impact, dimly aware of the pain in my hand and elbow.

Behind me the sliding glass door opened, and Caitlin joined me. She took my hand, kissing my knuckles, and I was surprised by her satisfied expression.

"Don't be so hard on yourself," she whispered. "No pun intended."

"I let you down."

Her grin widened. "You didn't let me down. I got mine. Remember? Besides, we've got all weekend to practice."

#

"John!" I pretended not to hear this new Voice, but it echoed across the slope again, much louder this time. "JOHN!"

"John." Caitlin nudged me with her elbow and pointed to a huge figure dressed in black ski apparel.

Our attention now focused in that direction, the figure raised its hand in a wave, gave a push on its ski poles, and shooshed down the incline toward us, stopping mere inches from me in a smooth, practiced move.

"Hi there." Peter Barrington grinned at me and gave Caitlin an appreciative once-over. He worked his hand out of his glove before offering it to her and introduced himself, adding, "I'm a friend of John's."

Caitlin shook his hand. "Caitlin Murphy."

He reluctantly turned his attention back to me. "So, what brings you up here, wild man? Did Randy and Laurie turn you loose?"

I had a sudden, uneasy sense that he had been sent to spy on me and that having met Caitlin in the bargain, he was plotting to lure her away from me. "What are *you* doing here?" I asked, not bothering to answer his questions.

If Peter detected my hostility, he didn't let on. "I'm here with a group of kids from Wheeler Elementary—Police Athletic League."

He'd no sooner gotten the words out of his mouth than I heard a second Voice shouting, "John!" A smaller figure in a Green Bay Packers coat, dark green with yellow trim, made its way unsteadily down the slope, wobbling to a shaky stop beside me.

"Hi, John." Adam grinned up at me from under his hood, his glasses fogging with the heat of his breath.

"Hey, kiddo," I replied, and couldn't help smiling at him in spite of my irritation with Peter's unwelcome appearance.

"Know what?" he asked. "We could make a whole lot of snow dinosaurs up here!"

"A whole mountain full," I agreed.

Peter frowned at me and asked, "How do you know Adam?"

The question caught me off guard, and the defensive response it triggered in me was even more of a surprise. Visions of half a dozen angry police officers facing me across a table flashed through my mind. "We're—we're neighbors."

"We're friends," Adam interjected. "He helped me build a T. Rex. It was cool!"

Caitlin slipped her arm through mine and looked up at me, obviously amused. "You didn't tell me you built snow dinosaurs, John!"

Adam tilted his head to watch her for a moment, then asked, "Are you John's girlfriend?"

Caitlin and I glanced at each other, and she laughed. "I guess you could say that," she replied, giving my forearm a light squeeze. My heart beat a little faster.

Peter prodded Adam's backside with the handle of his ski pole. "We need to catch up to the others. It looks like the instructor's getting ready to start."

"I wish I already knew how to ski," Adam grumbled, "instead of having to stay on the beginner's slope with all the little kids."

"Don't feel bad," I told him. "I don't know how to ski either."

"You don't?" This news cheered him up for some reason. "Then come with me and we can learn together."

"I don't know..." I wasn't all that eager to break my neck.

"Aw, come on, John. Please?" Adam executed an about-face in a series of jerky motions and waggled a hand at me. "Come on!"

I felt Caitlin's hand on my arm once more. "Why don't you go with him? You can pick up a few basics, and I'll make a couple of runs without feeling guilty about abandoning you."

So I took my place on the beginner's slope with fourteen children, the only other adult being the instructor. Though I'm sure he thought I was an imbecile, he was polite enough not to say so. Very patiently, he taught (or tried to teach) us how to turn, how to slow down, how to stop, and most importantly, how to fall without killing ourselves. I tried to pay particular attention to the last part, since I was sure I would be doing more of that than anything else.

After about an hour, the instructor allowed us to put our newly found knowledge into practice, which was a big mistake. I did okay with the turning part, but I gathered too much speed going down the incline and when I tried to slow down, my skis managed to get crossed and jettisoned me directly into the path of another skier. The impact sent us both sprawling, and I winced at the immediate sharp, hot jolt of pain in my left wrist. I fell back in the snow, clutching my arm to my chest, an involuntary whimper escaping from the back of my throat.

Adam was the first to reach me. He tossed his ski poles aside, struggled to release his skis, and dropped to his knees next to me. The other children had grown quiet and anxious looking and seemed relieved when the ski instructor appeared.

He, too, knelt down beside me, asking, "What's the damage, dude?"

"I think it's broken. I am so done with skiing."

A few minutes later, a member of the ski patrol joined us. Together he and the instructor splinted my wrist as a precaution and hauled me to my feet. By the time we got back to the lodge, someone had located Caitlin.

"I am so sorry," she said for the tenth time on our way back from the local emergency room. "I feel responsible."

"But why?" I asked her. "Besides, it's only sprained, not broken."

"Well, I invited you up here, knowing you didn't ski, and I encouraged you to take a lesson."

"I'm the one who was stupid enough to actually put on a pair of skis."

"Oh, John, I am so sorry!" She was beginning to sound distressed.

"It's not your fault," I told her. "But if it makes you feel better, you can make it up to me later on."

"I can do that," she answered with a sly smile. And she did.

Between her ministrations and the painkillers the ER doctor prescribed, I was feeling very fine. So it was late that night, with the pressure off and Caitlin on top, that I was able to consummate our relationship. And if the sounds Caitlin was making were any indication, I wasn't the only one who was satisfied.

Then, for the first time in months, perhaps years, I slept the whole night through.

#

Out on the slopes again early the next morning, I was still feeling good. My wrist continued to ache, but I was on an emotional high. While Caitlin took a last couple of runs, I sat in the sun at the little outdoor cafe near the lodge, a big mug of coffee in front of me. I kept remembering the previous night, and I knew I was grinning like an idiot.

I probably would have sat there all morning, continuing to grin like an idiot, except that Adam and his friends happened to spot me and came flocking over. They clustered around me, asking how I felt, then, spying the skull tattoo on the back of my hand, Adam turned the talk to the subject of my other tattoos. The army of yard apes began chanting, "Show us! Show us! Show us!"

So nothing would do except for me to take off my coat, push up my shirtsleeve, and show them. Gathered in a tight huddle around me, oohing and aahing, they stared at my arm.

"That one's the best."

"No, it's not. That one is."

"That one's ugly."

"Where did you get those?"

"How do they do that?"

"My uncle says they stick needles with ink under your skin!"

"Ugh, that's gross."

"Didn't it hurt?"

"I hate needles!"

"They go all the way up his arm, like a sleeve," Adam told them, sounding self-important.

"How do you know?" one kid asked.

"Because I've seen them. He's got them on both arms!"

"I wanna see them, too," the kid said, and all the other little kids chimed in.

Had Peter not walked up at that moment, they would have had me down on the ground, my shirt ripped off, studying my tattoos. They all crowded around him, talking at once as usual.

"Officer Pete, have you got any tattoos?"

"John's got lots!"

"Wanna see?"

"Why do you want to look at tattoos?" Peter asked them. "You guys need to run on and play. We'll have to leave soon."

He waited until they had scattered, then turned back to me. "What are you doing?" he asked, his voice low.

"I was showing them my tattoos...why?"

"Do you really think it's wise for you to be showing your tattoos to little kids?"

I felt my throat constrict from that all too familiar sick shame, and my heart began beating faster. "What do you mean?" Each word wanted to stick in my throat, and I had to force them out.

"Well, shouldn't you be off somewhere showing them to Caitlin?"

His expression was so stern, that at first I didn't grasp his meaning. It was only when I felt my face heating up that he broke into a smirk.

"Or has she already seen them?"

Highly embarrassed, I looked away from him, studying the slopes and wishing an avalanche would come along and sweep him down the mountain. I hadn't realized that my satisfaction would be so evident to him.

He laughed and seated himself in the empty chair at my table. "There's nothing to be ashamed of, John. If I were you, I'd be crowing like a rooster. Cock-a-doodle-doo—no pun intended."

"Yeah," was as much of a response as I could muster.

"I guess it had been a while for you, huh?" he asked. He flagged down a waitress and ordered an Irish coffee. I hoped he choked on it.

"Unless you count the times I was raped by the male attendants in the hospital utility room," I said, rewarded at last by the blanching of his face.

He gave me a strange look that I couldn't interpret. "That's not really funny."

I let him stew a few more moments before finally admitting that it had been a bad joke, and he turned the topic of conversation to a safer subject. He looked relieved when Caitlin showed up and we excused ourselves.

Back in our hotel room, I began packing my things with no real enthusiasm for the chore. When I had finished, I sat on the edge of the bed, watching as she gathered a small pile of her clothing.

A pair of panties fell to the floor by my foot. I bent to retrieve the small, lacy triangle of fabric, pained that I would not be spending that night at her side.

"You know, I really hate for this weekend to end," I said as I held the lingerie out to her.

"So do I," she answered. Her voice was low, but there was a crafty little smile on her lips. She pressed gently on my shoulders, pushing me back on the mattress, and as I watched, she reached for my belt buckle. I was hard in an instant.

She laughed as she undid my zipper. "Just like a Boy Scout. Always prepared." She put her hands on my hips, and whispered, "Now tonight, when you're in bed by yourself, I want you to remember this," and I felt her wicked lips close around me.

#

It snowed for the next three days after we returned to our respective homes, dumping another foot on the city. Monday brought blizzard conditions, with the wind chill below zero all day. Drifts accumulated against houses and covered cars; trees and power lines were down in the neighborhood. Tuesday was spent huddled in front of the fireplace trying to keep warm. Wednesday, even though the power was back on, I still couldn't get out to see Caitlin because the temperatures were in the single digits. I was really beginning to hate snow.

The only good thing about the whole mess was that Randy had to work double shifts those three days in order to ride herd on all the accidents. I was glad for the chance to avoid him, but I knew it was too good to last. And it didn't.

When he arrived home late Wednesday afternoon, he gave me a sly smile and said, "Peter told me about your weekend."

When I was unable to come up with an intelligent reply, he added, "Why did you lie to us?"

"I didn't lie," I blurted out, cringing at the petulant tone in my voice.

"'I'm going skiing with the reading group.' That's a lie in my book."

"I didn't lie. Caitlin's in the reading group."

Randy wiped a hand across his face. "All right, stop. Back up here. Let me put this another way. You lied to us. That's not good. Don't do it again."

I'm not sure where it came from, but when I opened my mouth the words popped out before I could stop them. "Did it occur to you that if you didn't act like such an almighty prick then I wouldn't feel the need to be so secretive about what I'm doing?"

He stared at me as if one or both of us had lost our minds, and he wasn't sure which. He gave me a tight little smile and said, "What?"

I smiled back. "Fuck you."

Thunderclouds filled the horizon. Randy frowned and shook his head as if trying to dislodge water from his ears after a swim. "I'm sorry. It sounded as if you said, 'Randy, I need a major ass whipping.'"

"No, you heard wrong. *Fuck you*. I'm not a teenager. Don't be telling me what to do."

"You may not be a teenager chronologically, John, but you sure don't exhibit any more sense of responsibility than a teenager would. Christ, do you not think anything through?"

"What's to think about?" I bellowed. "I went skiing. Period."

Randy nodded. "There you are lying again. That's exactly what I mean. You didn't stop to think that if you go skiing with little or no instruction, you might get hurt—which you did. Now you've got a hospital bill to pay. And I'd be willing to bet that when you jumped into bed with Caitlin, you didn't think about using any protection. What if she gets pregnant? What if she gave you something you can't get rid of? If she screwed you, she'd screw anybody."

"What are you talking about?" Although I knew *exactly* what he was talking about it, and I didn't like it.

Randy gave a short, harsh, barking sort of laugh and slapped a hand to his forehead. "My God, you're screwing around and you don't even have a clue how to protect yourself or someone else. Reality check here, John. Have you ever heard of sexually transmitted diseases? Condoms? Do you know where babies come from? I can't believe I'm having this conversation with someone who's nearly thirty years old. Does Caitlin know that you're mentally ill?"

My brain was on fire but my body was cold and numb. "What has being mentally ill got to do with anything?"

"I'll bet you didn't mention that to her, did you? Do you think she would even look at you, let alone touch you, if she knew the truth?"

So there it was, out in the open now. The question I had asked but didn't want to allow myself to answer. I could no longer pretend that I didn't hate Randy. I knew that he would beat my ass for what I was about to do, could, in fact, already feel my flesh bruising, but that didn't stop me.

"You are such a piece of shit." But this time I didn't wait for him to strike first. My hand clenched into a fist and leapt through the air between us to land dead center in his face.

I felt the cartilage in his nose give way and blood gushed with a sudden, explosive force. The split second look of surprise on his face was priceless. Of course he reacted much as I suspected he would, with a roundhouse to my jaw that sent me sprawling and caused my vision to blur and then dim. But even as the pain in my head swelled like a mushroom cloud, threatening to push my eyeballs out of their sockets, I lurched to my feet and headbutted him in the stomach.

He fell backward over an ottoman, striking the floor hard, the breath whooshing from his lungs. There was now a fierce roaring in my ears, but I wasted no time in bolting out the front door. There was no way I would *ever* spend another night in his house.

CHAPTER NINE

ALREADY I WAS FREEZING as I slipped and slid through the snow. My left eye was quickly swelling shut, making walking even more difficult because it screwed with my depth perception. I didn't intend to walk for long, though. As soon as I got out to Sheridan Boulevard, I stuck out my thumb.

Two cars passed me, exhaust from their tailpipes swirling frosty circles in the frigid air. The third vehicle, a pickup truck, stopped and an older man leaned across the passenger seat to open the door. "Young man, get in before you freeze to death. Where is your coat?"

I climbed in and fastened the seat belt. Unfortunately, the interior lights were on long enough to allow him a good look at my face.

He whistled and said, "I hope the other fella looks worse 'n you!" He laughed and put the truck in gear. "Where to? You reckon maybe you need to have that eye looked at?"

I shook my head, but even that slight movement threatened to make it explode. "No, I'm good. If you're going into town, could you drop me off at the diner near the newspaper office?" I figured if nothing else, Pat would be there and I could get some ice to put on my face and get some ibuprofen for the pain. What I would do for the rest of the evening, I had no idea, but I would not go back to Laurie's house.

When we got into town, the man parked near the diner and said, "Guess I'll go on in with you and have a cup of coffee."

We walked in together and sat down at the counter. Pat was on duty and came over to us immediately. She looked at me and did a double take. "John? For goodness sake! What happened?"

I grimaced and said, "It's a long story."

The older man leaned over to peer closer at me and said, "Your eye's done swelled up twice the size it was when you got in the car. Might want to put some ice on that."

Pat's own eyes were huge. "John, that looks really bad. Let me get you some ice, hon." She went into the kitchen and returned a few moments later with a large clump of ice cubes wrapped in a kitchen towel. "You all come back here and sit in one of these booths. Can't have you scaring off other customers, can

I?" she said, motioning us to the back, but she patted me on the shoulder to let me know she was sympathetic.

"That bad, huh?" I muttered.

"And it's turning purple, too," the older man said helpfully.

We got settled in the booth and Pat brought over some coffee before going off to tend to her other customers. The man stuck out his hand to me and said, "I'm Tom, by the way, and I take it you're John?"

I shook his hand and we sat quietly for a few minutes while I held the ice against my skin, listening to the chatter around us. My face throbbed with each beat of my heart, and after a few more minutes I began to feel queasy. I tried my best to ignore the sensation, but it quickly became apparent that it was not going away. I muttered, "Excuse me" to Tom and stood to make my way to the restroom, but the diner shifted on its axis, and I stumbled into the wall and went down on my knees.

Suddenly, Tom was there, pulling me to my feet and steering me in the direction of the men's room. "You really need to go to the emergency room, young man," he said as we pushed through the door. I did not make it into the stall before upchucking. On the bright side, there was not much in my stomach to come back up.

Leaning over the sink, I splashed some water on my face and noticed that my hands were trembling. Tom grabbed some paper towels and began wiping the mess from the floor.

"Dude, you don't have to do that," I managed to croak between dry heaves.

"Like you're in any position to do it," he replied matter-of-factly. He finished and came over to me, took a handful of clean paper towels, wet them, and held them out to me saying, "You got some on your chin."

I wiped at my chin and looked at myself in the mirror. "Holy shit!" My left eye was, of course, swollen completely shut and my cheek was an angry purple.

"You ain't kidding," he snorted. "I'm hoping you at least gave the other guy as good as you got."

"I'm pretty sure I broke his nose." Another wave of nausea washed over me, and I crouched down against the tiled wall.

"Good for you," Tom chuckled, then said, "Well, hell" as the floor shifted, and I tipped over. "John, my friend, we're gonna have to get you out of here. How about letting me take you to the ER?"

"No!" I said, a little too loudly, the memory of my last trip still very fresh in my mind.

"All right, then, where?" Tom sat me up and watched me, hands on his hips. "Is there somebody I can call for you? Mom? Dad? Girlfriend? Boyfriend?"

The dry heaves took over again for a few minutes, making speech impossible. "Caitlin," I whispered when they finally subsided.

"That your girl?" he asked. "What's her number?"

I realized I didn't know it, and felt like a total loser. How do you have a girlfriend and not know her phone number? "She just got a new phone, and I don't remember the number," I lied. "Ask Pat to call Edie—Edie'll know it." I tried to stand but ended up facedown on the bathroom floor instead.

#

"John, wake up." The voice was soft and sweet, as was the hand on my forehead. "John, open your eyes or I'm calling an ambulance."

I opened my eyes—or to be more precise, I opened my right eye. My left one wasn't opening even with a crowbar. Caitlin was peering down at me anxiously.

"Damn, it hurts," I said struggling to sit up. "I feel like I kissed a moving freight train."

"I hate to tell you this," she said, "but you look like you did, too." Some of the tightness left her face though. "John, what the hell happened to you? You weren't mugged, were you?"

I sat up and looked around, surprised that I was no longer in the diner. "Where am I?"

"My apartment. God, you scared me to death. I got a call from Edie saying you were passed out in the men's room at the diner and that you looked like someone had taken a sledgehammer to your head. What *happened*?"

I had no memory of leaving the diner or traveling to Caitlin's apartment. "How did you get me in here by yourself?"

"Tom followed us over and helped, otherwise you'd still be on the men's room floor. He's a nice guy, by the way. He said you refused to be taken to the ER. We should have taken you anyway. Are you going to tell me what happened, or do I have to beat it out of you?"

I grimaced. "Randy's already done that for you."

"You're kidding! Your brother-in-law did this?" She looked and sounded outraged. "John, that's assault! You can't let him get away with this. Oh my God."

"I'll be honest," I told her, "I popped him first. He started running his mouth about you, and I'd had enough. I think I broke his nose."

Caitlin slapped a hand over her mouth. "*John!* Oh my God!" And then she started laughing.

And after all the pent up tension of the evening, I started laughing, too, but the more I laughed, the more my head hurt, so that I was alternately laughing and moaning in pain.

Wiping tears from her eyes, she said, "I don't even know him, but I would have loved to have seen the look on his face."

"It was pretty priceless," I agreed.

"And you were defending my 'honor'. How sweet." She knelt down on the couch beside me. "Thank you," she whispered and placed her lips over mine. My pain miraculously vanished.

#

I woke up the next morning to Caitlin's alarm clock. She hit the snooze button and reached for me, wrapping her arms around me. She kissed me and hooked a leg over my hip, laughing when she felt my response. She allowed her mouth to wander down the length of my torso, stopping between my legs.

A breathless and extremely satisfying fifteen minutes later, she kissed me on the mouth again. "Just my way of saying thank you," she whispered, then, her voice rising, "Oh my God, I'm going to be late for work!"

She leapt out of bed and ran into the bathroom, where I heard the water come on in the shower. I followed and stepped in behind her, exploring her body with my hands. Now it was my turn to pleasure her. Lowering my head, I placed my mouth over her right nipple, pulling gently with my teeth, teasing, then performing the same ritual with the left, until she was moaning. Following a ribbon of water down her stomach with my tongue, I slowly worked my way to that soft, moist place between her legs, and kneeling in front of her, I pulled her toward me, burying my face.

"I'm going to be so late for work—" she began and then gasped when my tongue found its target, and I worked my magic.

She clutched the back of my head to pull me closer and whispered, "Oh God, John, *now.*"

Standing, I slid her into position and, bracing her back against the shower wall, I entered her. Our hips moved together in that age-old rhythm, and when we had finished the dance, we stood under the water trying to catch our breath.

"And that's my way of saying thank you for coming to my rescue," I murmured, nuzzling her neck.

"If that's your way of saying thank you for coming to your rescue, then I hope you get your ass beaten every day," she laughed.

"And if I get to do this each time, then I will gladly suffer it being beaten."

"I don't suppose you could make some coffee while I get dressed," she asked.

"Sorry," I said, "I'm kind of out of practice."

"Well," she replied, "if you're going to be living here, I suggest you make yourself useful and learn."

She left for work a half hour later but not before giving me a proper good-bye. When the door closed behind her and the scent of her perfume began to dissipate, I looked around the apartment happily.

"If you're going to be living here...." I heard those words over and over again in my mind, and I knew I was grinning like an idiot. I looked at her clothes hanging in the closet, inhaled her fragrance lingering on them. "If you're going to be living here...."

#

I felt her lips on mine and opened my good eye to find her kneeling beside the sofa where I'd fallen asleep.

"I'm sorry I woke you," she said, grinning. "Even though your face looks like a train wreck, your lips were irresistible."

I pulled her to me and gave her a deep kiss in return. "You can wake me up that way any time you want."

She settled herself beside me, snuggling under the arm I held out to her. "I thought about you all day at work. In fact, you're *all* I thought about at work. I almost missed a deadline daydreaming about you." But she was smiling and looked so happy that I felt a surge of emotion I had not experienced before.

Taking her hands in mine, I asked, "Did you really mean it about me living here?"

"Absolutely! John, you can't go back to Laurie's house—Randy will end up killing you or you'll end up killing him. I'm not sure which, but you're not safe there. But more than that," she smiled, "I could not wait to leave work today. The thought of coming home and you here waiting for me—I can't describe how exciting that was. But I guess I'm being selfish or presumptuous and I should ask you—would you want to live with me?"

"God, yes. I can't believe you'd even have to ask that after this morning. But it's been so long since I got to decide anything for myself, and you know I'm...." And that was just it. She *didn't* know, and I was so caught up in these new emotions that I couldn't risk telling her the truth. Because what if the truth scared her? What if the truth caused her to feel differently about me? What if Randy was right?

Never had anyone told me that they had spent all day thinking about me, and never had I spent all day thinking about someone else. Never had anyone else made me feel the way I felt about Caitlin.

"I know you have a disability," she said. "I know you're in danger if you go back to your sister's house. And I know that I think...I'm in love with you."

She looked up at me, perhaps to see how I would receive this statement, her smile tentative. Maybe if I had been a nobler person, I would have disabused her of this notion. I was not, however, a noble person, and the words were out of my mouth before I could think better of it. "I love you, too." I only hoped that I was not dooming her with this declaration. Unaware that she may have been headed for the gallows, she smiled up at me and lifted her mouth to mine.

The next thirty minutes duplicated the way our day began, and we were both panting and sweaty when we were finished.

"I'm going to keep you chained to the bed as my sex slave." Caitlin leaned over to kiss me.

I groaned and pretended to shoo her away. "Are you trying to kill me?"

She straightened up and gave me a mock-stern scowl. "Can I help it if you're so damned hot? Train wreck of a face and all!"

"You're not exactly a mercy fuck yourself," I laughed.

"Well, that's a good thing." She frowned. "I think."

"Yeah, it's a good thing," I agreed, kissing her again before reaching down beside the couch to find my jeans among the tangle of clothing. "So," I said when I was partially dressed again, "how about showing me how to work the coffeemaker so I can earn my keep. If that pleases my master."

She fished in the pile of discarded clothing and grabbed my t-shirt. "It pleases your master immensely." She pulled it over her head. "Come with me, slave." She stuck a finger behind the waistband of my jeans and pulled me along with her to the kitchen.

"Talk about leading a guy around by his cock."

"Generally not a hard thing to do," she snorted in a most unladylike manner.

"Is that supposed to be a pun?"

She laughed when she realized what she'd said. Rummaging through a kitchen drawer, she pulled out a booklet and tossed it to me. "Coffeemaker instructions," she said. "When all else fails, read the instructions, slave."

Ah, the first chink in our post-coital bliss. I held the booklet in my hands and though I knew she wasn't aware of what she'd said, I could feel the heat rising in my face.

She opened a cabinet door and took down two wine glasses, then removed a bottle of wine from the fridge. She held up the bottle and said, "Muscadine? I like my wine like I like my slaves—sweet and sticky—" She stopped short when she saw my expression and looked from the booklet in my hands to my face.

"Oh my God. John, I'm so sorry. I didn't mean that—I didn't even think!" She came to me and took it from my hands, peering up into my face. "Please forgive me."

"There's nothing to forgive," I said, but I had a hard time looking her in the eyes. She'd brought it all home. I wasn't normal.

"I sure know how to kill a mood, don't I?" she asked.

I sighed. "No more than my lame ass does."

She laughed. "Well, bring your sexy lame ass over here and I'll show it how to work the coffeemaker."

When she was satisfied that I had mastered the operation of the thing, she held up the wine bottle again. "Wine?"

I shook my head. "I'm not supposed to drink with my medication—", and I had to slap a hand over my mouth. Awkward moment number two. Not only had I walked away from Laurie's without my medication, now I had to explain what I took and why.

Caitlin looked at me, lifting an eyebrow. "No medication?"

"No medication," I said. "*Shit!*"

"No worries," she said. "Who's your doctor? Just tell them you lost it. Although if it's a controlled substance, you're going to have trouble getting a duplicate prescription. It's not pain medication, is it?"

"No, it's not pain medication." I scratched in my feeble brain for an answer and finally came up with it. "The doctor's name is Steele."

"S-t-e-e-l or with an 'e' on the end?" she asked.

I merely looked at her.

"Oh, yeah. Right," she said after a couple of beats, and this time we both laughed. "Well, don't worry, I'll find his phone number, and we can call about it."

"And what can your humble servant do in your absence tomorrow, milady?"

"Cook supper?"

"Your wish is my command. I will enthrall you with my culinary skill in preparing canned gourmet tomato soup with delectable grilled artisan cheese sandwiches on premium sliced white bread. Served, of course, with the house wine and your humble servant for dessert."

She narrowed her eyes and licked her lips. "I like to eat my dessert first."

"You can eat your dessert any time you like. In fact, it's ready right now."

And so began my indentured servitude as manservant and sex slave to the fair lady, Caitlin.

#

The Voices were raging, and I tried my best not to reveal how much this upset me, but Caitlin was very much attuned to my wavelength now, and we weren't even out of bed before she asked, "John, what's wrong? Is it your eye?"

My eye had gone from red and purple to a nice glossy black—guaranteed to get looks from people everywhere I went. It still throbbed to a lesser degree, but I shook my head. "No, it's not my eye. I just—I just really need my medication." And it occurred to me how delighted Dr. Fremont and Dr. Steele would be to hear me say that, but I didn't know how I could tell Caitlin what I was experiencing without scaring the ever-loving piss out of her.

"Let me locate your doctor, and then I'll go get your prescription." She climbed out of bed and stretched.

A particularly strident, hateful Voice reverberated in my head like a sharp pop of thunder, and I grabbed for her hand.

She sat back down beside me and put a hand on my shoulder. "Tell me what's wrong. Are you in pain?"

Tell her what you are.

Tell her.

Do you think she'll keep you around for even a minute when she finds out what you are?

She thinks you're a hot piece of ass, but she wasn't counting on crazy as a bedbug to boot.

There's no orgasm worth that.

Tell her what you are.

Tell her.

Tell her!

And goddamn it, I couldn't help it. I was crying.

She pulled me to her, holding me in her arms. I could smell her hair, her skin, the fragrance that was her.

Tell her, tell her.

Tell her, you selfish bastard.

Tell her what you are.

Tell her what you've done.

Tell her where you've been for the past eight years.

Tell her!

I jerked away from her and fell to my knees. I could feel the knife edge of hysteria pressing against my flesh, cutting, piercing.

"John, you're scaring the hell out of me." I could tell by the look in her eyes that she was as terrified as I was.

"I'm schizophrenic, okay?" I screamed at her and saw her jerk as if I had punched her. I hated myself, but I couldn't stop. "I'm crazy! I've been in a mental institution for eight years. And, oh yeah, *I'm fucking incompetent!*" And then just as suddenly as they'd come upon me, there was complete and total silence of the Voices.

Caitlin trembled, tears rolling down her face.

"I'm sorry," I whispered. "I'm sorry. I didn't mean to scare you."

She didn't move, just continued to sit there, jerking with sobs.

I pushed myself to my feet and started grabbing up my clothes. "I'm sorry," I said one last time. "I'll leave." I pulled on my t-shirt and stepped into my jeans. I could only find one sock. I grabbed my boots and headed toward the bedroom door.

"John?" Her voice was shaky.

I turned to her, prepared for her to tell me that she hated me and to get the hell out and never come back.

"You aren't going to scare me off that easily. Not when I've just managed to acquire a slave of my very own."

I didn't know whether to laugh or cry some more.

She touched me tentatively on the arm. "I'm sorry. I can't imagine what it would be like to live with an illness like that. I want to help you. Let me. Please. We'll get through it together." She smiled at me and brushed my cheek with her fingertips.

I felt on the verge of hysteria again, but the happy kind this time.

CHAPTER TEN

LIKE A GOOD SLAVE and manservant and to make up for my nuclear
meltdown, I tried to please my master. While Caitlin was at work each day, I
either cleaned like a demon or watched Food Network or the Cooking
Channel, trying to figure out how to make something for us to eat besides
canned soup and sandwiches. I was really to the point where if I never saw
another sandwich again in my life, it would have been entirely too soon.

That's not to say that Caitlin couldn't cook, because she did that like she did
everything else—exceptionally, but I knew it wasn't fair for her to come home
each day after working and have to fix something, especially when she had
probably been used to going out a lot to eat with her friends. So to make myself
seem not so dependent, and to keep the Voices at bay, I cleaned and cooked.
And burnt the hell out of a lot of food at first.

I also listened to a lot of music. Caitlin had hundreds of CD's, and I was
surprised at her widely disparate tastes. Heavy metal, Celtic, classical, pop,
rap, jazz, Broadway musicals. I listened to it all. Wasn't so much a fan of rap
and jazz—heavy metal was my hands down favorite—but the rest of it I could
get into.

Truthfully, I was getting cabin fever. I hadn't ventured out of the apartment,
mainly because I knew that everyone would stare at my face, which was now
in a putrid green stage. And which, of course, Caitlin couldn't resist teasing
me about, calling me "Hulk" and taking every opportunity to say "Hulk
smash!" at the top of her lungs when I walked into a room. Then she had to
play *The Incredible Hulk* DVD, nudging me and giggling every time the Hulk
made an appearance in the film.

We watched umpteen movies those first couple of weeks—some
action/adventure (my favorite) and some romantic comedies (her favorite).
Watching *Slingblade* bothered me, because I could see the parallel between
myself and Karl, between Randy and Doyle, and because Karl was returned to
the institution at the end. Something I worried about on a daily basis.

"Tell me what it was like being in the hospital," Caitlin said, switching off the
DVD player after the credits began rolling.

"You might think I hated it, but it was all I knew for eight years, so in a way
it was home." I told her about Daniel, about the patients who sat or stood in
corners and rocked all day, strings of drool hanging from their mouths. The
monotony of the days I could remember. Being frightened because there were
days, weeks, and months I couldn't remember. The certainty that I would die

in the place alone and unloved and my surprise when Dr. Fremont said he was releasing me.

"Did Laurie and Randy come to visit you often?" she asked.

"Until a few months ago, I had forgotten I had a sister. I sure don't recall her coming to see me, but I was there eight years, Caitlin. And there's just so much I *don't* remember. I remember the Voices ranting and raving and sometimes I'd just started screaming to drown them out. There were days and weeks when I didn't talk to anybody, when I didn't move off my bed, because if the Voices were quiet, I was afraid I would rile them, and if they weren't quiet, I was afraid I would kill myself with the first thing that came to hand to shut them up."

She looked distressed. "What do they say to you?"

"What don't they say? They tell me everything I do wrong; they tell me what other people are thinking; they tell me what to think, what to say, when to breathe. And none of it is nice. They tell me to kill myself. They tell me to kill other people."

"How do you stand it?" One lone tear escaped her eye and ran down her cheek.

"I honestly don't know. It's something I've lived with half my life. There have been times I wanted to end it all, and I'm sure I would have if I'd had a weapon handy."

"Have you—have you ever wanted to kill someone else?"

I looked at her. "I have to tell you, there are some people who think I have."

"Did you?"

I exhaled. "I don't remember. I've tried to. 'How can you forget something like that?' That's what Laurie asked me one time." I couldn't read the look on her face. "Caitlin, if you want me to leave, I'll understand. What do you see in me, anyway?"

"Is that you talking or the Voices?"

I sidestepped the question, for wasn't it one and the same? "What would your family say to you if they knew about me?" I asked her. "What would your friends say?"

"I don't have any family close by that counts, and the friends who know are jealous. They put rulers on my desk with sticky notes that say 'It was *this* big'. They make jokes about me walking funny."

"I can tell you what Randy would say. Better than that, I can tell you what Randy did say."

"Screw Randy."

"No, thanks. I'll leave that job to Laurie."

#

Our life settled into a comfortable, pleasant routine for the next several weeks, and I dared to think I had finally found happiness until the Tuesday night Caitlin came home from her library reading group and went straight to our bedroom. I had been trying to get supper ready (not burnt for a change) and when she didn't greet me in her usual manner, I knew something was up. I found her staring out the window, frowning.

"What's wrong?" I asked.

"I'm not sure." She turned back to look at me. "The head librarian said there was a cop at the library looking for me earlier today."

This news brought me up short. "No name? No description?"

She shook her head. "No, she said he didn't tell her and he didn't leave a card. She didn't pay any attention to his name tag. She just said he was big and had a military haircut. She told him when I would be there. He told her he would come back Thursday night."

"That could describe either Randy or Peter."

"Peter?"

"Peter Barrington? You met him on our ski trip. He's one of Randy's cop buddies."

"They're looking for you." It was a statement, not a question.

"Yeah."

"What do you want me to do?"

I sat down on the bed. "Randy's going to try to get me to come back to their house or harass the hell out of us, one or the other."

"What's in it for him if you're there?"

"Control?"

Caitlin nodded her head. "There is that."

"I may as well go talk to him. He won't leave us alone until I do."

"Oh, hell no," she said. "Not on your own."

I grinned at her. "I'll be okay. I can take care of myself."

"How long did it take you to stop looking like a lizard? No, huh-uh. I'm coming with you. He wouldn't dare try anything with me there. Besides, I've got to protect my investment. Maybe we can talk to Laurie—get her to have him back off."

"She doesn't have a lot of power in that relationship."

"But she managed to talk him into having you come live with them."

"Pussy whipped."

Caitlin gave me a sly grin. "Speaking of pussy whipped...."

Dinner that night got burnt anyway. And yes, okay, I admit it. I am.

#

So we decided to go see Laurie the next night when I was fairly certain Randy would be at work. His car was gone when we drove up and I'd be lying if I said I wasn't relieved.

She must have seen us arrive because she was standing at the open front door when we came up onto the porch. She hugged me without saying anything and gestured for us to come inside. In the weeks I had been gone, the skin between her eyebrows had taken on a drawn, pinched quality and her mouth now turned down at the corners. I felt like an asshole because I knew she had been worried about my disappearance, and she didn't deserve the aggravation. She'd only tried to help me.

We followed her into the living room, Caitlin and I sitting together on the couch.

"Do you want some coffee?" Laurie asked.

Caitlin said, "Sure, thanks."

Laurie looked at me. "John?"

"Yeah, thanks."

We waited while she went in the kitchen and after a few minutes I could smell the coffee brewing. She came back in carrying two large mugs and set them on the table in front of us, then went back for the creamer and sugar. I loaded both in my cup until I felt the two of them watching me.

"What?"

Caitlin grinned. "Like a little coffee with your sugar and creamer?"

"Well, you know—I like my coffee like I like my master—"

"Sweet and sticky," we said in unison and laughed together.

Laurie looked from me to Caitlin and said, "I don't want to know."

"Probably not," I agreed.

"I assume you've been with Caitlin then," Laurie asked.

"You assume correctly," I said, "but I understand that Randy may be out beating the bushes for me."

"Why do you think he would be looking for you, John? Could it be that you disappeared off the face of the planet?" The sarcasm was out of character for her. I knew she was upset, and I felt for her, but not enough to come back and partake in more of Randy's crap.

"Will you ask him to back off? Please."

She put her hands over her face and shook her head. "I can't do that, John. We're legally responsible for you."

"That can be changed. Can't it?"

"Not without a lot of effort on the part of a lot of people. Not to mention legal fees and court hearings. Does Caitlin even know about—"

"I know," Caitlin said.

"And you know he's incompetent?"

"I know that's what you say."

Laurie gave a short, sharp laugh. "It's not what *I* say! It's what the *court* has said."

"And I know what I see. John's got problems. I've seen that firsthand myself, but as far as making decisions for his own well-being and functioning on a daily basis, he's doing that. In fact, he functions exceptionally well in a lot of areas."

"And how long have you known him?" Laurie asked. "Maybe a total of eight weeks? How can you possibly know how he'll function in the long-term?"

"There's only one way to tell." Caitlin stared her down.

Laurie turned her attention back to me. "Randy is never going to agree to this, John. We'd be legally liable if anything happened."

Caitlin and I spoke at the same time.

"I'm not coming back—"

"He's not coming back—"

Oh, and then wouldn't you know it—dear God in Heaven—the front door opened and in walked the Devil himself.

I shot to my feet and moved in the direction of the foyer, all to no avail, of course, because he was blocking my exit.

He jerked his chin at me and said much more cordially than I would have believed he could manage under the circumstances, "John." I got a good look at his mangled nose and smiled in spite of my nervousness.

Caitlin was on her feet, too, and moving toward the two of us. She walked right up to him and held out her hand, invading his personal space so that he was forced to step away from the door. "Hi, I'm John's girlfriend, Caitlin Murphy. I believe you were looking for me at the library yesterday? And by the way, I know the story, so you can save your crap for somebody else."

"Ok, I'll save it then." He clapped his hands and rubbed them together. "So, am I missing out on the party? Why didn't you invite me?"

"Party's over. We were just leaving," I said.

"*No.*" That one word carried a hint of menace.

Caitlin's hand went immediately to the front pocket of her jeans where she yanked out her keys and tossed them to me. "Go to the car now, John."

I didn't wait. I went. And as I did, I heard her saying, "He doesn't want any problem with you. He just wants to be able to live his life."

And I wasn't fast enough to miss Randy's reply. "He forfeited that right a long time ago."

Then I was down the sidewalk and into the passenger seat, leaning over to stick the key in the ignition and crank the engine. Caitlin came out the door and started to the car, Randy close behind her, and I gripped my knees reflexively. He reached out as if to stop her, and I grabbed the door handle, prepared to launch myself into full-on assault mode if he so much as laid a finger on her, but he lowered his arm, stopped next to the left front quarter panel, and allowed her to open her door.

"This isn't over," he said.

"Bring it," she told him. "Tell me, what are you going to do if he and I decide to get married?"

I choked.

"You're kidding, right?" he asked. "No? Well, as his guardians, Laurie and I would file an action to have the marriage annulled. That's about the only grounds for annulment in this state—incurable insanity."

"You just can't stand it that someone else sees John as a human being—with needs and wants. With feelings."

"Humans don't do the things he's done—monsters do. I really hope to God you two aren't planning to have kids because the world just really doesn't need any more of his kind."

"Is that why you haven't reproduced?"

Randy looked at her for a minute, then patted the car hood. "I've got your license plate number, so I'll have your address shortly."

Caitlin's face darkened, and I threw open the car door and went to stand beside her.

Randy looked to me. "What do you think you're doing? You want your ass beat again?"

"I'll take your nose *off* this time," I said, my voice low and steady, notwithstanding the fact that my body was shaking.

"Do *not* use your badge to harass us, you dick. John hasn't done anything."

Randy grinned at her, that shit-eating grin of his I knew so well. "Nothing that you know of, anyway."

"Asshole." Caitlin got in the car and I followed suit. She fastened her seatbelt and popped the car into gear.

I waited until we were out of Randy's neighborhood before asking, "Did you say *marriage*?"

"I've got to make an honest slave out of you somehow."

"You're serious about marriage?"

"My love, one thing you will have discovered about me by the time we celebrate our 50th wedding anniversary is that I don't kid about the serious stuff. Unless you don't want to be made an honest slave?"

"It's a dream come true," I said. "I've been waiting all my life for someone to come along and make an honest slave out of me."

"Well, there you go."

"So when's the big day?" I asked, half in jest.

"As soon as we can get to Las Vegas."

I laughed. "Now I know you're kidding."

"Do you have a photo ID and your Social Security card?"

"Yeah, Laurie took me to have an ID made a few weeks back. I've got my wallet with me. Why?" I wasn't sure where she was going with this.

"We're going to Las Vegas for a wedding."

"How can we afford to travel to Las Vegas?"

"John, I have money. Are you up for this?"

"I'm always up."

"That's the God's honest truth." She gave me a crooked smile.

"Are you doing this just to annoy Randy?"

She pulled the car quickly off the side of the road and we rocked to a stop. "I don't know how else to show you that I love you, and I will stand by you. Maybe it's part lust, because you make me feel the way no one else ever has. I think I've had more sex in the past few weeks than I've had in the past several years, and I can't ever imagine a time that I wouldn't want you. I know we've known each other less than three months. I also know there have been plenty of successful marriages between people who've known each other for less time. But if you're not ready to do this, I can't force you, obviously."

We looked at each other. "Mrs. John Colucci," I said. "I like the sound of that."

She shook her head, a wicked grin tipping the corners of her mouth. "Oh, no. Mr. Caitlin Murphy. Get it right, slave."

#

Word to the wise, folks—if you're schizophrenic, airplanes and Las Vegas are not the places for you. With respect to the airplane, maybe it was the change in air pressure or maybe it was the fact that I had never flown before, or perhaps a combination of the two, but by the time we landed at McCarran International Airport, the Voices were in full riot mode, and if someone had come up behind me and said, "Boo!" I would have shot two hundred feet straight up into the air. There were so many people in the airport that I kept being jostled from all sides, and the noise outside my head was as cacophonous as the noise inside.

Caitlin could tell I was disturbed, and she grabbed my arm and held on tight. "Whatever the Voices say to you, just remember, I'm marrying you so you must not be such a bad guy. No matter what, just remember that."

I nodded and tried to remain calm, but other people were giving me strange looks, and I know I probably resembled someone on the verge of totally losing his shit. When we finally got checked into the hotel, after the scariest damned taxi ride ever, I went straight over to the bed and sat down.

Caitlin said, "Let me have your coat and your shirt," and helped me remove them. She pushed me back on the bed and then lay down beside me, rubbing my chest with her hand. "Breathe in—deep. Hold it. Breathe out. Keep on."

Breathe in—deep. Hold it. Breathe out. Over and over until the Voices ceased, one by one, my fists unclenched, and my jaw muscles relaxed. And then the next thing I knew, I was startled awake by knocking on the door.

Caitlin leaned over and kissed me, saying, "Stay there, it's just room service. I'll get it."

She opened the door and a waiter pushed a cart into the room and over to the table next to the window and began offloading the dishes and a bottle of wine in a silver wine bucket. When he was finished, she slipped him some money and he left.

She came over and ran her fingers through my hair, pulling my face between her breasts. "Better?" she asked.

"Yeah." I nuzzled her, breathing in her scent. And that's when I knew—really knew—that I loved her.

I tried to pull her down on the bed with me, but she pushed on my shoulders and said, "No. It's bad luck to screw the bride the night before the wedding."

"Where did you hear that?" I asked. "I thought it was bad luck for the groom to see the bride in her wedding gown before the wedding."

"That, too."

I laughed. "You're making this up as you go along."

"Pretty much, yeah," she agreed.

"So we're really going to do this?" I asked.

"Unless you've changed your mind."

"Never." I reached for her again and she slapped my hands.

"You're disobeying your master. You need to come eat now."

I tried to look chagrined. "Yes, ma'am." She led me to the table, pushing me onto a chair, then opened the bottle of wine and poured a small amount into my glass and a healthier measure into hers.

"A little bit won't hurt you," she admonished when she saw that I was about to protest. She tilted the glass to my lips. Some of the wine trickled into my mouth but the majority of it ran down my chest and stomach.

"Did I do that?" she asked. "Here, let me clean that up."

She knelt on the floor between my legs and began licking the wine from my stomach, slowly working her way up to my nipples, tracing my collarbone with her tongue before nibbling on my earlobes. When she had me ready to scream, she straddled me in the chair and ground her pelvis against mine, and I popped my wad before she could even finish her lap dance. She laughed a wicked little laugh and said, "That's all you're getting until you say 'I do'."

"I am so pussy whipped," I breathed.

"You are. Now eat."

"But master, you haven't had your wine yet either." I stood and took her glass in my hand, holding it to her lips, making sure a little dribbled down her chin and across the base of her throat. "Clumsy me, I spilled it on your blouse. Let me help you." I pulled her top over her head. "Oh, damn. It soaked through to your bra. I'll get that." I unfastened the undergarment, pulled it away from her breasts, and let it fall to the floor. I let my knuckles brush against her nipples, already hard as small pebbles. She whimpered.

"None of that, now." I placed a mouth over her right breast, sucking on the nipple until her back arched and she let out a gasp, then moving to the left breast and repeating the motions. I slipped my hand down the front of her jeans and past her panties. She was wet and ready as my fingers touched that magic spot, and then she was grabbing for the front of my jeans, trying to get the zipper undone. I pushed her hands away, saying, "No."

"Please, John." She reached for me again.

It was my turn to slap her hands. "I said no." I unfastened my jeans and pulled them down, touching myself, teasing her. Her own jeans quickly came off and she put her hand between her legs. "Oh my God, John, please, I am *begging* you."

I took a handful of her hair and pulled her head back gently so that she was looking me in the face. "Now who's the slave and who's the master?" I asked her.

"You're the master, definitely," she panted, reaching for me.

I moved my hips so I was just out of her reach. "I didn't hear you."

"You are the master...you are." I actually thought she was going to cry and I relented a little and allowed her to grasp me before pulling away again.

"I think we ought to save it for after the wedding," I said as she clutched my chest.

"No, please. Master." She trembled against me.

I scooped her up, carried her to the bed, and proceeded to rock her world.

#

The next morning we left the hotel for the Clark County Register of Deeds to pick up the marriage license application and pay the necessary fees. We had to wait about an hour and a half for the application to be processed and when we had the license in hand we went back to the hotel to get ready.

Caitlin dressed in the bathroom while I attempted to tie my tie in front of the dresser mirror, and when she came back into the room and I caught a glimpse of her in the mirror, I was stunned. She wore a cream colored dress with a delicate lace overlay and long sleeves that fell to points at her fingertips. The dress hit her about mid-thigh and she wore sexy matching shoes with an impossibly high heel, which made her long legs look even longer.

We gaped at each other for a few minutes before she straightened my tie and said, "You look so hot, I'm not sure if we're going make it to the wedding chapel."

"We'd better hurry, then, because I'm thinking that dress may end up in shreds on the floor."

At the wedding chapel there were three other couples ahead of us, so we waited our turn, and ended up witnessing for the couple directly ahead of us. They agreed to remain after their ceremony to act as witnesses for ours.

The official asked if we wanted traditional Christian wedding vows. Caitlin looked at me and I shrugged. "Sure."

We lined up across the front of the little chapel, the male witness to my right and the female to Caitlin's left and the official began:

"Now repeat after me. 'I John—'"

"Slave," whispered Caitlin in my ear.

"I, John—"

"Take thee Caitlin—"

"Master," whispered Caitlin.

"Take thee Master—" I actually said 'Master'. The minister looked at me quizzically. "Take thee *Caitlin*—"

Her shoulders were shaking, no doubt in an effort to keep from laughing, and she put a hand over her mouth to hide her grin.

The official continued.

I repeated after him. "To be my lawful wedded Wife, to have and to hold from this day forward, for better for worse, for richer, for poorer, in sickness and in health, to love and to cherish, till death us do part, according to God's holy ordinance; and thereto I pledge thee my troth."

"You said *troth*," Caitlin snickered in my ear, but when the official began her vows she was suddenly very solemn, and I watched as tears formed in her eyes.

"I, Caitlin, take thee, John to be my lawful wedded Husband, to have and to hold from this day forward, for better for worse, for richer, for poorer, in sickness and in health, to love, cherish, and to obey, till death us do part, according to God's holy ordinance; and thereto I give thee my troth."

"You said troth *and* obey," I murmured, and she elbowed me in the ribs.

"Are you exchanging rings?" the official asked and Caitlin held out a jeweler's box to him.

"Where did that come from?" I whispered. She gave me only a "wouldn't you like to know" smile in return.

He removed a slim, white gold band and held it out to me, instructing me to place it on Caitlin's ring finger.

"With this Ring I thee wed, with my body I thee worship, and with all my worldly goods I thee endow. In the name of the Father, and of the Son, and of the Holy Ghost. Amen."

He repeated the ritual with Caitlin and she placed a wider matching white gold band on my ring finger. The official then said, "I now pronounce you husband and wife. You may kiss the bride."

I kissed her long and hard as the other couple clapped. We walked out of the chapel together and shook hands with them on the sidewalk. Later, back at the hotel, Caitlin grinned and said, "Now comes the fun stuff. Were you paying attention to the part of the vows about 'with my body I thee worship'? I'm getting ready to worship the hell out of you with my body, but first I wanted to show you something. Take off your wedding band for a minute."

I removed the ring and held it between my thumb and forefinger. She pulled hers off and held it likewise. "Look at the inscriptions." Engraved inside her band was the word "Master" and inside mine was the word "Slave."

"When did you get these?" I asked, but then she reached for me, and I didn't care anymore.

#

We boarded the plane, Caitlin in the aisle seat to my left and me in the center seat. I could feel the anxiety building in anticipation of the take-off, but she reached over, grasping my hand in hers and said, "Remember, breathe deeply. Breathe in—hold it. Breathe out." I concentrated on our clasped hands and my wedding band. Breathe in—hold it. Breathe out. And I was able to get through the take off without coming completely unglued.

There was a lot of turbulence on that flight, though. When the plane wasn't dropping abruptly down through the clouds without warning, it bumped along like a hyperactive frog.

"I'm gonna be sick," I whispered to Caitlin. She quickly grabbed for the emesis bag in front of her and thrust it at me. "Hold this over your mouth," she said, prying my hand from the armrest and pushing the bag into it. Even though I've never professed to be a religious man, I found myself swearing on all that was holy that I would never fly again. I guess it's true there are no atheists in foxholes.

The businessman in the window seat next to me didn't look very happy. When I stopped heaving into the bag, he said, "First flight, huh, buddy?"

"Second," I wheezed, "and *last*."

"Been to Vegas to play the slots?" he asked.

I shook my head. "Got married."

"Hey, congratulations!" he said, slapping me on the shoulder just about the time another wave of nausea hit me and I bent over the bag again. I had purposely not eaten anything that morning, fully expecting just such a problem, but that didn't matter to my stomach. I spent the rest of the flight with my face jammed in the bag, retching until my chest and abdominal muscles burned, Caitlin rubbing my back at intervals.

I think everyone in my immediate vicinity was as relieved as I was when the flight was finally, mercifully over and we could disembark. I was in total misery as Caitlin parked me and our carry-on bags in the waiting area while she went to get the car.

I was sitting there, face in my hands, silently pleading with my gut to settle down, when I heard a male voice say, "John, is that you?"

I hoped against hope that someone else named John was being addressed. But luck has never been my friend. Peter Barrington stood there. *Fuck.*

"Been a while since I've seen you," he said offering me his hand.

I shook it reluctantly.

"You're not looking so hot," he remarked and then, glancing pointedly at my suitcase, he added, "Going somewhere?"

"Coming back," I said rubbing a hand over my face. "Rough flight." I noticed him studying my left hand and realized too late that he was staring at the wedding band. *Double fuck!*

"Motion sickness? Man, that sucks." He didn't make mention of the ring, but I figured he'd be calling Randy and Laurie to tell them before I even made it home.

"Something sickness." And my stomach gave a few more weak flips to make sure I hadn't forgotten it.

"Where did you go?" he asked, but I was saved from answering by Caitlin's reappearance.

"Short weekend ski trip to Vail," she lied smoothly.

"Slopes still in good shape this late in the season? Though I guess they still get a lot of snow out there even in April."

"The slopes were perfect," Caitlin replied. "Well, it's been nice seeing you again—Peter, is it? But we had a really rough flight and John's kind of worse for the wear, so we need to run."

She grabbed me by the elbow with one hand and our bags with the other and steered me to the car. She stowed the luggage in the trunk and waited for me to get situated.

"As far as Randy, Laurie, and Peter are concerned, what happened in Vegas, stays in Vegas," she said as she merged the car into traffic.

#

Back at the apartment, at long last, it was immediately apparent that someone had been in it in our absence.

"What the hell?" Caitlin said as she looked around. Nothing appeared to be missing but things had obviously been moved, as if whoever had done it wanted us to know for a fact that they had been there.

"Check the kitchen," she said to me as she went toward the bedroom.

I noticed the refrigerator and freezer doors standing open, the lower door propped open with a kitchen chair, in fact. All of the food would, of course, have to be discarded. I was pissed, but not as pissed as when I went into the bedroom after hearing Caitlin say, "John?" in a frightened voice.

Her personal papers—bank statements, tax returns and the like—were scattered across the floor. Her clothes had been dumped out of the dresser drawers and pulled from the closet still on hangers. A pile of her panties lay at the foot of the bed. Someone had taken a knife or pair of scissors to every item she owned. None of my clothes had been touched.

"What the hell?" I grabbed up handfuls of the clothing, not quite believing my eyes.

I heard a sob and found her sitting in the floor crying, clutching ruined garments in each hand. I squatted down next to her, embracing her tightly. "It's okay," I whispered. "It's okay."

She leaned into my chest, releasing the rags to grasp my sleeves. "Who would do this?" she wept. Then, "Why?"

"I don't know. I don't know. Shh...." I stroked her hair and let her cry it out, her tears dampening the front of my shirt.

"We need to call the police," she said, and suddenly everything clicked into clear and painful focus.

We looked at each other a split second, and I jumped to my feet. "Oh, no! Oh, no, he did *not*." I paced the room, clenching and unclenching my fists, feeling truly impotent with rage.

My first inclination was to find Randy and kill him, or, at the very least, beat him within an inch of his miserable life. I was operating on pure adrenalin and unadulterated hatred, and stomped out to the living room, snatching my coat from where I'd tossed it on the couch.

"I'm going to his house, and I *will* kill his ass," I said to Caitlin.

"No." She grabbed my arm. "John, that's exactly what he wants you to do. He's setting you up to come to him, and then he's going to have what he needs to get you where he wants you—back in an institution."

"God damn it, this is *bullshit*!"

"I know. And there's not a damned thing we can do about it. Not one damned thing." She wiped her face with her hand and said, "I'm calling a locksmith and then a security company."

"I don't suppose it would do any good to move?"

She shook her head. "He'd just find us through the DMV or the tax collector. And let's face it, as a cop he's got access to information most people don't have."

I closed my eyes and leaned my head against the wall. "This is bullshit." But there was nothing for it except to get out the trash bags and start picking up the mess.

"I'm sorry I brought this on us," I said to her, handing her the ruined clothing to put in the bag.

"I'm not," she smiled. "I've been wanting a new wardrobe."

CHAPTER ELEVEN

AT LAST THE SEASON moved more certainly into spring, the days growing warmer, and the snow finally melting. Plants and trees started budding out, and I felt like a newcomer to the planet, seeing it all for the first time and with a reason to finally enjoy it. The three weeks since our wedding had gone by in blur—yeah, mostly in the bedroom, but sometimes in the living room, and once in the kitchen.

I was getting fairly adept in the kitchen as cooking went—not proficient, mind you—but enough that I didn't slice my fingers off or poison us, and usually the food was edible. And of course the best part of every day was when Caitlin walked through the door in the evening and we held each other, laughed, watched movies, or made love.

Caitlin came home for lunch that day, carrying a newspaper. I could see from the masthead that it was not her paper, but *The Asheville Journal,* a rival paper. I was in the kitchen at the time, making a sandwich, and offered to make her one but she shook her head and said, "John. I need you to stop what you're doing and sit down a minute. There's something I need to show you."

"What?" I sat down next to her. My mouth was suddenly dry, but my palms were wet.

She unfolded the paper and laid it on the table. I had no trouble deciphering the three words printed in large type above the fold: "Suspected Killer Released!" Directly below that was an old photograph of me. I swear my heart did not beat for a full minute, and I felt my forehead break out in a sweat. I ran a hand over my face. "Oh, hell." I glanced over at her. Her stricken expression made my gut churn harder. "Read it to me. Please." I don't know how I managed to sound so calm when my world was imploding.

Caitlin picked up the paper and began. "On December 3, 2004, suspected killer, John Edward Colucci, then nineteen years old, was found not guilty by reason of insanity or mental defect of the murder and molestation of eight-year-old Hunter Jernigan, despite having confessed to the crimes. He was also a suspect in the murder of nine-year-old Gavin Beasley, which occurred around the same time, although he was never formally charged in that murder. In a separate hearing following the trial for the Jernigan murder, Colucci was determined to be incompetent and was subsequently committed to Broughton Hospital in Morganton, North Carolina. He remained institutionalized until January 15, 2013, at which time he was released to the custody of his sister, Laurie Kimbell, and her husband, Randall Kimbell, a public safety officer with the Kingsville Police Department, his legal guardians. The families of the victims were not provided any notice of Colucci's release. Because he was tried and found not guilty, he cannot be retried, nor can he be required to register as a sex offender. It is unknown where Colucci is currently residing. Attempts to reach the Kimbells for their comments were unsuccessful."

I felt as if the life had slowly drained from my body while she read, and I was now a hollow shell sitting in her kitchen. "It's raining shit," I whispered, "and me without an umbrella."

Caitlin placed a hand on my arm. "This is bad, really bad, and I'm scared. Scared for you, scared for me. I'm even scared for Laurie and Randy. This is going to bring the crazies out."

"Ha, ha," I said without mirth, "the *other* crazies you mean."

"Bad choice of words." She wrapped me in her arms. "I've started going through all the articles in the newspaper archives from your trial, and I'm going to be writing a few articles of my own."

"Not like that one, I hope."

"You know that I would never do anything to hurt you intentionally. You know that, right?" She pushed my hair out of my face and her palm remained on my cheek.

I nodded and placed my hand over hers.

#

If I'd thought that article was the beginning of a shit storm, I was unprepared for the Category 5 shit hurricane that was brewing.

Two days later Caitlin brought home an article that appeared in *The Asheville Journal* about two boys who were missing after leaving their homes in Kingsville to play in a neighborhood park. They drew inference to the cases I had been involved in ten years earlier, and while they didn't come out and accuse me, anyone with half a brain could tell what they were getting at, and they made sure to mention again that I had been released from Broughton Hospital earlier in the year.

Then, a few days after that, Caitlin brought home yet another front page article, once more above the fold, in large font: "Missing Boys Found Dead" with the subtitle "Kings County Sheriff Confirms Boys Also Sexually Assaulted." Again they rehashed the old cases and my involvement. Caitlin finished reading the article to me, which ended: "With all of the similarities to the previous murders and his recent release from Broughton Hospital earlier in the year, sources at the Sheriff's Department have expressed an interest in speaking with Colucci."

"My God. My God." I couldn't think, couldn't move for several long minutes. If she had pulled out a baseball bat and smacked me upside the head with it, I would not have been any more stunned. My nightmare was slowly but surely beginning again. "How much worse can this get?" I whispered.

She knelt in the floor next to me. "I've learned to never ask that question, because the answer is always 'infinitely worse.'"

"Say the word," I told her, "and I will leave. I hate that I've brought you into this mess." I knew that deep down she had to be wondering what she'd gotten herself into. And then, because I couldn't help myself, I said, "Caitlin, you don't think I had anything to do with this, do you?"

"Don't you dare talk about leaving me! And no, I don't think you had anything to do with the deaths of those boys or any boys. Ever. But this is bad and I'm scared. You know the Sheriff's Department is looking for you, and they're going to use any excuse to pull you in and question you. When that happens, and rest assured it will, do not talk. Don't say anything. If they arrest you, do not talk, and know this—they'll tell you anything to get you to talk. Promise me you won't talk."

I promised her I wouldn't and the waiting game began. We didn't have to wait long, though. The next morning at 7:15 there was a loud rapping on the door. We were both in the kitchen making breakfast, and I froze, instantly on edge. We looked at each other.

"I'll see who it is," Caitlin said, sounding as nervous as I felt. She went to look through the peephole, but immediately came running back. "It's the Sheriff's Department, John," she said in a low voice. "You might want to go get your shirt and shoes on. I've got to go let them in before they break down the damned door." She kissed and hugged me as the door shuddered in its frame.

I had just finished pulling on my shoes when they clattered down the hall and into the bedroom. One deputy stayed in the doorway, but the other strode into the room. "John Edward Colucci?" He was at least as tall as I was—6'1", but he probably outweighed me by a hundred pounds, all of it muscle. He already had one hand on his utility belt, removing a set of handcuffs. "We have a warrant for your arrest. You'll have to come with us."

Caitlin tried to push past the deputy standing in the doorway, but he blocked her access. "Wait!" she said. "Why is he being arrested?"

"He's been charged with assault on a government official."

Caitlin peered over his shoulder, we frowned at each other, and I said, "*What*? Who?"

"The warrant says you assaulted Officer Randall Kimbell of the Kingsville Public Safety Department," the officer replied, snapping the cuffs on my wrists and pushing me toward the door.

Caitlin said, "*What*? That was weeks ago—" and immediately slapped a hand over her mouth. "I'll be working on bonding you out. Remember what I told you yesterday," she murmured as they led me out of the apartment.

It was the beginning of a very long day and night. They left me in a holding cell for at least an hour before they processed me. I was having flashbacks to the last time I had been arrested and I knew I was not in for a treat.

After taking me to the interview room and telling me someone would be right with me, they left me sitting another hour. By the time an officer did show up, the Voices were mumbling and grumbling, and I was doing my level best to ignore them.

The officer introduced himself to me as Detective Whisnant and offered me a drink and a snack, like we were at some freaking party.

"Just water," I told him and then, when he left the room and didn't return for another half hour, I wanted to kick myself.

Eventually, he did return carrying a plastic water carafe and cup, which he set down on the table, and indicated that I should help myself. He settled himself in his chair, took out a pen and notepad, and made a production of fiddling with this for another ten minutes before clearing his throat.

"We've got some things we want to ask you about, Mr. Colucci. We know you were involved in an incident several years ago where two boys were sexually assaulted and murdered. We know you were recently released from Broughton Hospital down in Morganton. And we've got a problem, John—can I call you John? And I'm Garrett, by the way. Garrett Whisnant. Anyway, we've got a problem and we're hoping you can help us."

I didn't say anything. He played with his pen, tapping it on the table and drawing invisible circles.

"Here's the problem," he continued. "We've got two more boys who've been sexually assaulted and murdered, and we're wondering if you have any information on that you want to share with us. We're not accusing you of anything, understand."

"Why would you think I know anything?" My leg jiggled nervously of its own accord and the Voices hissed and muttered. I made a conscious effort to stop the jiggling.

A protracted silence passed, and he tried a different tack. "We know you've had some mental health issues in the past and we know you'll want to clear this up. So we just wanted to give you that opportunity."

I studied my hands.

"If you know anything, it might help us to get rid of this assault charge. Just talk to us, John."

I looked up at him and moved my lips as if to speak but said nothing. He tapped the pen on the tabletop in a quick staccato. He continued to try this routine in several variations for the next hour. And my mouth stayed firmly shut.

"All right," he finally said. "I'll be back in a few minutes, then."

Another hour passed and I really regretted drinking the water.

A different officer came in the room and introduced himself as Detective Samuels.

"Before you start with the bad cop routine," I said, "I have to go to the restroom."

"Sure, sure," he said, exuding cordiality. "Let me show you where it is."

Once we were seated again he gave me a big shit-eating grin—I swear to God they must teach that in cop school. Randy and this guy would have been at the top of their respective classes. "Well, I guess Detective Whisnant explained our problem to you."

I said nothing. Again.

"I gotta tell you, this isn't looking so good for you right now." On we went. Another hour. Then two hours. Three hours. By the fourth hour Detective Samuels wanted to throw something at me, and by the fifth hour I wanted to throw something at him. When the sixth hour rolled around Detective Samuels yawned and stood up.

"Excuse me for a few minutes," he said. Aw, shit. Here we went again.

I put my arms on the table and laid my head down. And went to sleep. But not for long. Oh, no. They let me sleep just long enough so that I would be confused and cranky when I woke up, more likely to talk.

Detective Whisnant shook me awake. When he had me sitting up again, I made the mistake of saying, "I'm really tired. Are you going to take me to a cell, let me post bond—something?"

He clasped his hands together. "Well, now, we can get you to a cell or let you make a phone call, but we need you to talk to us first. We really need your help, John."

Oh. My. God. And we were off and running once more. I glanced at his watch. It was now 8:36 PM. Christ. On a crutch. Then Whisnant switched off with Samuels. Then they tag-teamed me. By the time Whisnant's watch read 11:17, I was, literally, crying from exhaustion.

Samuels took this to mean that I was near the breaking point of confession. He put a hand on my shoulder and said, "Just tell us what you know, John, and everything'll be okay and we'll get you home."

"Okay," I said, wiping my face, and they both sat forward expectantly. "Here's what happened—*nothing*. I did nothing. I know nothing. Nothing. No. Thing." And I put my head down on my arms.

Whisnant threw down his pen. "Have his ass hauled to lock up," he said to Samuels. Off I went to booking to trade my street clothes for a lovely orange jumpsuit. It was not until after noon the next day that I appeared before the judge, had my bail set, and Caitlin was able to bond me out. I crawled into bed immediately upon returning home and slept until the following morning, when I awoke to an apocalypse.

#

Caitlin left for work shortly before 8:00 AM but returned to the apartment a few minutes later clutching a neon green poster board. She couldn't have looked any more shocked if she had been hit by a bus.

I experienced an overwhelming sense of dread when I saw the expression on her face. "*What?*"

She turned the poster board around. Scrawled upon it in large black letters were the words "CHILD MOLESTER LIVES IN APT. 4-E!" She was crying.

"This was taped to the front entrance of the apartment building. Oh my God, they know where we live."

Without comment, I turned, went to the bedroom closet, took out my suitcase, and started tossing my stuff into it.

She followed me into the bedroom, asking, "What are you doing?"

"I'm leaving," I said. "I'll go back to Laurie and Randy's. I'm not putting you in the middle of this any longer. It's not safe."

"*NO!*" She stamped her feet. "*NO!* We're a couple! You don't get to make that choice unilaterally."

She struck me in the chest with her fist and began pulling things out of my hands, then tipped the suitcase off the bed.

"Caitlin, if something happens to you because of me, I *will* kill somebody. So I'm leaving. Period."

"No, you're *not*," she screamed, and then drawing in a big breath, "We're *both* leaving. *Together*. And I know where we can go." She grabbed her own suitcase out of the closet and began filling it.

Later that morning we were worlds away at Fontana Lake, near Bryson City. As we drove down a narrow, rutted dirt road, I watched the water sparkle through the trees.

"God, I'd forgotten how beautiful it is," Caitlin said. "I haven't been up here in at least a year. We've got a property management company that's supposed to look after the place, so I hope we don't go in to find that raccoons have taken up residence."

"It is beautiful." We turned into a clearing and a pretty little cottage came into view. Clad in silvery-gray cedar shingles with bright blue trim, it featured a long screened-in porch across the front, with views out onto the lake and a boat dock. From what I could tell, it stood in a secluded cove.

"This is yours?" I asked as we got out of the car and stood under trees looking down toward the water. I took a deep breath, drawing the woody scent of pine into my lungs. Inexplicably, I felt the tension of the past five months leaving my body, and I felt *alive*.

"I own a one-fourth interest in it with my three cousins. It belonged to my grandmother—she passed away almost two years ago and left it to us." She grabbed my hand and pulled me down a path to the lake.

"You've never told me about your family." We walked out onto the boat dock and sat down.

"There's not much left to tell you about," she replied. "My dad died of a heart attack when I was a freshman in college and my mother died of breast cancer when I was a junior. It's a wonder I managed to graduate. So now it's just me, an aunt and her husband, and the three cousins. They're all out in California. But you've never told me about your family either except Laurie and Randy."

"They're it as far as family goes. My mother also died of breast cancer—while I was in Broughton. My dad committed suicide when I was fifteen, just about the time I started hearing the Voices. He had schizophrenia, too." I wasn't sure where that memory had suddenly reemerged from, and I found myself wishing it had remained buried.

Caitlin gripped my hand. "God, your life has been so tragic."

She wasn't being sarcastic, but I felt uncomfortable anyway. "Doesn't sound like yours has been a picnic, but no, my life's just been a freaking slow motion train wreck."

She smiled. "Like your face after you and Randy got in that fight?"

"Hey, now."

"Your face is fine. Better than fine." She leaned over and touched her lips to mine, and we stretched out in the sun, holding hands. There wasn't any sound except for the water lapping on the little beach and the leaves moving in the breeze.

Caitlin broke the silence in which I had almost fallen asleep. "What's on your bucket list, John?"

I turned my head to look at her, squinting into the sun. "My *what*?"

"Your bucket list. Things you really want to do before you kick the bucket."

"God, Caitlin," I said. "I think I've spent so much of my life trying to find a reason to keep from kicking the bucket or having it kicked out from under me, that I've never put any thought into what I wanted to do before I actually did."

"You have to have a bucket list, John. What about traveling to Europe?"

I lifted my arm across my eyes to block the sun and laughed. "Do you really want to spend a nine hour flight listening to me being sick? I'd be on the permanent 'no-fly' list—never mind a bucket list. They'd open the door on the plane over the Atlantic and push me out."

"What about kids? You'd make beautiful babies."

I sat up and looked at her, but she was staring into the sky and didn't meet my eyes. "So would you, but seriously? You'd want to have kids with me, knowing what you know about me? About my dad? Our kids might be beautiful, but they would be sick in the head. Besides, I would suck as a father."

My stomach growled just then and she laughed. "Are you ready for some lunch?"

I stood up and helped her to her feet, steadying her while she slipped her shoes back on. "Yeah, I'm hungry, and I think I've got a splinter in my ass."

Caitlin was delighted that the house was clean and raccoon free, although she did discover there wasn't enough firewood for that night and the next morning, so while she fixed lunch, she sent me to the woodshed on the upper part of the property to split some of the firewood stored there. "You'll need to take the key off the hook by the back door there to unlock it," she said as I went out.

I've always heard that wood warms you three times—when you cut down the tree, when you split it, and when you burn it, and I'm here to tell you that at least part of that's true. I stripped off my outer shirt, then my t-shirt, and probably would have been in my undershorts had Caitlin not called me to lunch right about then.

"Sexy beast," she said as I stepped onto the screened porch, wiping myself off with my t-shirt.

"Don't start with me, woman. I'm hungry."

She'd laid everything out on the porch picnic table and we sat and ate, listening to the water and the wind. When we'd finished, I took the dishes back into the house and put them in the sink, then beckoned her to the swinging bed suspended from the ceiling at the far end of the porch and we curled up for a nap. I thought I could get to love a place like this.

#

Caitlin got permission from her paper to work from home for the foreseeable future, and set up her computer at a table in a corner of the little living room. She spread out a stack of papers, booted up, and started opening files. She'd been hard at it for about ninety minutes when she suddenly said, "These articles make it sound as if there wasn't much of anything in the way of evidence to be able to charge you.

"What?" I looked up from the couch where I was sprawled watching *Forrest Gump*.

"They took your confession and then tried to make it fit the facts. We've got to look into that."

I reached for the remote and switched off the DVD. "Why? That's all over and done with. We can't go back and change it now."

She turned from the screen. "It's true we can't go back and change anything, but it makes me wonder. If the police had someone who confessed to a murder and the scant evidence they had tended to support that confession and the only 'witness' is a police officer, how hard did they look at anyone else? And how hard will they be looking now? New murders occur shortly after their prime suspect in other murders is released from a mental institution. What would *you* think?"

We stared at each other, and then she went to her purse and pulled out her cell phone. She handed it to me. "I have the name of the attorney who represented you in 2004. I'm going to look up his phone number, provided he's still practicing, and I want you to call him and make an appointment. I'll go with you, but I need you to do this because he's not going to talk to me without you there."

Back on the computer she clicked on a website and a few minutes later she said, "Okay, here he is on the NC State Bar website. David Webster. He's still practicing and his office is still in downtown Kingsville." She read off the phone number, and I punched it into the phone without any great enthusiasm.

"I really don't want to do this," I said. "That was an extremely bad time in my life."

"I know." She came back over to sit next to me on the couch. "But we have to."

"What are you hoping he'll tell you?"

"He can tell us the moon is made of green cheese for all I care, but we're walking out of there with a copy of the discovery from your case. I want to know just what evidence they had. Let's say a prayer that he hasn't destroyed your file since then."

So I spoke with Webster's receptionist, and she made an appointment for me the following Thursday. I was just as glad it wasn't any sooner so I could work up my nerve to face the past.

#

If Kingsville had been my own personal hell, Fontana Lake was my Utopia. I took long walks while Caitlin worked at the computer hour after hour. During one of those walks, I heard a new voice say, "Afternoon," as I came around a large poplar tree. Startled, I jumped. I had never encountered anyone else and certainly didn't expect to see an old, bald man sitting there propped against a tree trunk, a pair of binoculars in one hand, a notebook in his lap, and a canvas sack by his feet.

"You scared it away," he said, although he didn't sound particularly annoyed that "it" was gone.

"I'm sorry. Scared what away?"

"Pileated woodpecker." He laid down his binoculars. "Been years since I've seen one of them. With all the clear cutting for timber, forests are disappearing, and the pileated woodpecker won't be far behind."

"Sorry," I said again.

"It'll be back later," he said confidently. "See that dead pine tree over there? Full of beetles. Good eating for a woodpecker. Besides, I heard its mate calling to it." He reached into his canvas sack and pulled out a can of Sprite and a package of sugar wafer cookies. "Here." He handed me the can and took another from his bag. "Always bring two along. Never know when I'll get the opportunity to share. Have a seat."

I sat in the pine needles and leaf litter beside him. He pulled the tab on his soda can and motioned me to do the same. We sipped our drinks and then he opened the package of cookies and held it out to me. I chose a pink one—strawberry.

"That's my granddaughter's favorite flavor, too," he said, and we sat munching cookies. I felt like I had known him all my life instead of merely ten minutes.

"Have you noticed that group of ferns down at the bottom of that hill there?" He indicated the direction to which he was referring. "Very rare. Northern Beech Fern—*phegopteris connectilis* and they're growing right here."

"I wouldn't know a fern from a water buffalo," I told him.

"Well, now. We can't have you tromping around the woods uneducated, stepping all over rare flora and fauna." He introduced himself then. "Jack Woodrow. And who might you be?"

I shook his hand. "John Colucci."

"Where are you staying?" he asked.

I tried to explain to him where the cottage was in relation to where we sat. He nodded his head. "The old McFalls place. Gray, dark blue trim. I knew Patsy McFalls. She's been gone a couple of years now. Guess that place has been passed down to her daughter in California."

"It went to her grandkids," I replied. "I'm married to her granddaughter, Caitlin Murphy."

"Are you, now? It doesn't hardly seem like Cait should be old enough to be married, but I expect now that I think about it, she'd be about twenty-seven or -eight." He sucked on his teeth a minute. "Kids sure have a habit of growing up quick. How long have the two of you been married?"

"A little over a month."

"Newlyweds. Well, congratulations. Cait's a fine young woman. I've done a lot of marrying in my time." He noticed the funny look I gave him and laughed. "I'm a retired Presbyterian minister. Thirty-five years in the pulpit. Performed a lot of marriage ceremonies."

"Caitlin and I got married at a wedding chapel in Las Vegas," I said, "but we used traditional Christian vows." I don't know why I felt compelled to offer this bit of information, but I did.

"Christian's always good." He laughed again. "Better than a satanic ritual."

"Yes, sir," I agreed.

"Well, it's good to meet you, young man." He started gathering up his things. "Walk on down the hill here with me, and I'll show you those ferns."

We walked down the hill together, and he showed me the cluster of ferns growing near a pile of rocks that marked the place where an underground spring bubbled up out of the earth. "If you're still here in a couple of weeks when they're blooming," he said, "I'll show you where a patch of lady slippers grows. They're not so common anymore either."

#

Caitlin and I returned to the apartment in Kingsville the day before our appointment with David Webster, so that we wouldn't have to drive three hours the morning of the appointment. As we came down the hall, we could see three pieces of paper taped to the door. Caitlin handed me the keys and pulled the papers off. I opened the door, but the alarm didn't sound. We immediately looked at each other and then glanced around the apartment.

The place was a wreck. Dishes were smashed, potted plants overturned. Books, CDs, photographs, and decorative items had been swept off the shelves. It was that way throughout the whole house—kitchen, bathroom, bedrooms, and closets. Caitlin didn't cry this time. She merely walked from room to room, her lips white. I sat on the sofa watching her.

She finally said, "I'm calling those morons at the security company. I know that alarm was set when we left. Someone is getting a major ass chewing." I was glad I was not that someone.

I listened as she got them on the phone, and I'll give her this much, she was polite, but there was a barely controlled fury underneath her words. She gave her name and our address, then said, "There's been a break-in at our apartment, and I would really love it if someone at your company could explain to my satisfaction why no one responded to that break-in and why I wasn't informed immediately that there was a breach in security."

She listened a moment to the person on the other end and I saw her indignation falter a bit. She cut her eyes to me, then looked away quickly, and I knew it wasn't good news. "What do you mean, it was the Sheriff's Department? My home has been vandalized. I want to know why I wasn't informed. A search warrant? But that still doesn't explain why I wasn't informed—yes, we've been out of town. I told your office that—no, I've had my cell phone with me at all times...."

I leaned my head back and closed my eyes.

But the hits were still coming. "The apartment management office? You're damned right I'll call them, and you can cancel my service as of this very moment." Cell phones are so inadequate for ending upsetting phone calls— you can't slam down the receiver. She stabbed the end button savagely with her index finger, then punched in another number and gave her name and apartment number again and basically went through the same spiel. She was silent a moment and then said, "Evicted? *Evicted?* What the hell for?" There was another grim silence and her voice took on a slightly hysterical timbre. "'*That person*' is my *husband.* He is not a registered sex offender. He was found *NOT* guilty. And in this country you are supposed to be presumed innocent until proven guilty in a court of law—not in the pea brains of a bunch of redneck vigilantes. I will *GLADLY* vacate the premises."

She threw the cell phone against the wall so hard it shattered, then stalked over to the console table near the entrance, where she'd laid the papers that had been taped to the front door.

"A search warrant," she said shuffling through them. "An eviction notice." She picked up the third piece of paper, and I saw her face harden. "And a death threat. I don't believe this."

"Welcome to my perpetual nightmare." I rubbed my hands over my face. "Cait, you can walk away from this any time you want. I'll understand."

She whirled to glare at me, and I knew I had stepped in it. "John, would you, *for God's sake*, stop saying that? Walk away from what? From you? From our marriage? From injustice? Do you think I married you for a joke? Were you even paying attention to our wedding vows? In sickness and in health, for better or worse, until death do us part? Why can't you just accept that I love you and I'm *not* going anywhere?"

"Maybe because I've been told all my life that I'm not worthy, that I'm defective."

She shook her head vehemently. "That's just not true. Stop believing it right now. You're funny, you're sweet, and you're damned sexy and good-looking. None of us are perfect, John. Some of our imperfections just aren't obvious. You *are* worthy, and you're deserving of all the good things life has to offer, although I think we'd both agree there hasn't been much of that lately."

She held up the third paper. "This is serious, John."

I took it from her, not sure that I'd be able to make anything out of it, but I needn't have worried. There were only nine words: "Evildoers—and the vermin who harbor them—will perish." My skin crawled.

Neither of us slept that night. She lay curled up close beside me, her hand clutching the front of my shirt. We didn't even bother picking up the mess.

"No, leave it," she'd said when I went to the kitchen to get some trash bags. "I'm hiring a cleaning crew and a moving company before we leave town tomorrow. Let them earn their fee."

Neither of us felt like eating the next morning either, and we left earlier than we'd originally planned so that Caitlin could buy a new cell phone before our appointment. I waited in the car while she was in the store. When she came back out, she handed a phone to me and grinned. "I got the family plan."

I have to admit that the word "family" had never meant much to me before that day. Now it took on a whole new meaning.

#

We arrived at Webster's office about thirty minutes early, and I spent those thirty minutes doing my breathing routine in an effort to quell the anxiety that was building. Once in his office, he led us to his conference room and told us to have a seat. On the table were three cardboard file boxes, each marked "State vs. Colucci, 04 CRS 51118". I looked at Caitlin, who grinned and gave me a thumbs up.

"How are you doing?" Webster asked, shaking my hand as he sat down. "I've got to say, you look one hundred percent better than the last time we saw each other."

"Thanks," I replied. "I appreciate you talking to us. This is my wife, Caitlin Murphy."

He reached over to shake her hand. "Good to meet you. So, how can I help you?"

Caitlin was off and running. With regard to the first order of business, she talked for nearly an hour non-stop, with Webster interrupting occasionally to ask questions. "And we were really hoping to be able to get copies of John's file, including the discovery."

"Well, as you can see, there's quite a lot of it." He indicated the boxes. "According to the State Bar, I'm only required to keep a client's file for seven years, but for this type of case, I keep them indefinitely. I'll be glad to give you copies, but I'll have to have a service make it for you, and there will be a minimum fee of $250. They'll put everything in electronic format on a flash drive, though, so it'll be easy for you to search for specific things."

Caitlin was already pulling her wallet out of her purse. "And while we're on the subject of money," she said, "we'll need your representation on several other matters. John's been charged with assault on a government official—his brother-in-law Randy Kimbell. He's a city cop."

Webster nodded. "So, Kimbell finally got what was coming to him." And he smiled. "It'll be my pleasure to help you with that."

"I've also been served with an eviction notice." Caitlin handed him the paperwork. "And we want to petition for John's competency to be restored."

Webster thought for a moment. "With the Sheriff's Department looking at you for these newest murders, I'm not sure restoring your competency would be the best thing. With your competency restored, you know you could be looking at the death penalty. Why make the state's job easier for them?"

Caitlin sat back in her chair, the wind taken out of her sails. I looked out the window, digesting this bit of news, and wished myself back at Fontana Lake.

Webster continued. "We'll get started on these other issues. For now, John, the best advice I can give you is don't talk to the Sheriff's Department about these newest murders. If the worst happens and they arrest you, call me, but don't talk to them under any circumstances."

After we left his office, Caitlin made the arrangements for the movers and the cleaners, and we were on our way back to Fontana Lake. Not a moment too soon if you asked me.

#

We pulled into the yard at the cottage, and while Caitlin went straight into the house, I made a detour down to the boat dock to sit and think. It had turned into a really warm day for early May in this part of the state, and I ended up stripping to just my boxer briefs, so I could dangle my legs in the water. And though this was my "happy place", I couldn't help but think about what Webster had said, and I was *not* happy. "If the worst happens and they arrest you...." I wouldn't survive a second trial and I wouldn't return to the hospital—I *would* be eating a bullet. I was really tired of being a pariah.

Caitlin came out onto the dock, and I heard her say, "There you are. I wondered where you'd gotten to."

I didn't respond. I couldn't—not then. She sat down next to me and put an arm on my shoulder. Eventually she kissed me on the cheek and left. When the sun was lower, just to the point of dropping below the horizon, she returned with a picnic basket and two blankets, one of which she spread on the dock. She began taking out food, plates, utensils, a bottle of wine and two wine glasses.

"Come eat," she said. "You haven't had anything since lunch yesterday." She held her hand out to me. "Please."

I moved over to the blanket while she lit the tiki torches lining the edge of the boat dock. The reflection of the light from the torches flickered on the water's surface. She sat down next to me, nuzzling my ear and kissing my neck. She'd made my favorite meal—garlic chicken, potatoes with onions and green peppers, and a salad—and filled both our plates, then poured some wine in both glasses and held one out to me. I drank it down, not really caring at the moment what interaction it might have with my medication, and felt an immediate warmth spreading from my stomach outward. It was sweet and delicious—both the wine and the sensation—and I asked for more.

She noticed I was just pushing my food around. "You have to eat, John. If we both eat garlic and onions, we cancel each other out. And I've got plans for you tonight. You know it's our six week wedding anniversary." I had to smile then, and I did try to eat a little so I could cancel out her garlic and onions.

"I'll be glad when it's warm enough to swim," she said as she poured more wine. "Then we can go skinny dipping."

"Something to look forward to." I raised my glass to her. She raised hers and clinked it against mine.

"We have a lot of good things to look forward to, like this for instance. Come here." She crooked her forefinger under my chin and pulled me toward her, covering my mouth with hers.

CHAPTER TWELVE

CAITLIN TRIED TO GET ME to go with her to Kingsville to look for a new place, but I refused. "I'd really like your input since you're going to be living there, too," she said.

"Caitlin," I told her, "for the past eight years I've lived in one room in a hospital with very few furnishings and my clothing as my only possessions. I could not care less what you pick out, but I'd just as soon not have to go back to that hell hole ever again."

"I know." She put a hand on my arm. "But we can't stay here forever. The cottage is rented out from mid-June through Labor Day. We can't be here after June 12th."

Just a little over one month left in Utopia. "I don't see why we have to live in Kingsville at all," I said and left the house to put an end to the conversation.

She tried to broach the subject with me again the next morning before she was due to leave. The Voices were gearing up for fun at my expense, and with all the yammering in my head, I couldn't deal with her in a rational manner. "Caitlin, I cannot have this conversation with you right now. Please."

"But, John—"

"Shut up!" I shouted. "*Now*! Just shut up. All of you. For Christ's sake! Shut *up*!" I was out the door and down the path to the woods. God damn it, I hated myself for causing the surprised, hurt look on her face. I hated my damned diseased brain and all the loud, hateful Voices contained therein, and I stayed in the woods until long after I was sure she would have left before I returned to the cottage.

She'd left a brief note stuck to the refrigerator with a watermelon magnet:

John,

I'll call later. Please turn your cell phone on.

Love,

C

But it was a really bad day with the Voices and I did not turn my cell phone on. Grabbing a towel from the linen closet, I went to the boat dock, peeled off all my clothes and plunged straight into the cold water of Fontana Lake. The shock of it took my breath away and I came up gasping for air. But lo and behold, it also shocked the Voices into complete and utter silence, and I swam as far out as I dared go and swam back even faster, fairly leaping up onto the dock. Dried off and dressed again, I sat there in the sun to get warm once more. And each time the Voices started up, off came the clothes and in the water I went until, by late afternoon, I was sure that they had decided to shut up for the day. Anybody watching me would have concluded, quite correctly, that I was fucking insane.

By the time the sun was going down, I trudged to the cottage for something to eat. I heated some of the leftover garlic chicken and potatoes in the microwave, but made the mistake of sitting on the couch to wait for the timer to beep and fell asleep without eating. I woke up around two o'clock to a noise that was out of place. I sat up thinking perhaps Caitlin had returned early. All of the lights in the living room and kitchen were on as I had left them, but the front door was now standing wide open. A shadow moved across the porch, the wooden steps creaking under the weight of somebody or something, and I felt my heart kick into overdrive. I forced myself to stand and move to the door and out onto the porch. The shadow—definitely a man with broad shoulders and a military-type haircut judging from the silhouette—moved quickly down the drive toward the road but had too much of a head start for me to have any hope of catching up. Not that I particularly wanted to.

I slammed and locked the front door, then checked all the windows—pulling the curtains shut—and double-checked the back door. I wondered for a moment why the kitchen reeked of garlic, then remembered the food I'd left in the microwave. I threw it in the trash. In the living room, I started a fire, but I couldn't get warm and I couldn't go back to sleep. I wasn't safe in my Utopia anymore.

After the sun came up, I made a sandwich, grabbed an apple and a bottle of water, stuffed it all in a backpack and took off in the direction I had seen the shadow traveling. I don't know what I expected to find—but I felt a compulsion to do this. I freely admit that my mental illness may have been responsible for the compulsion, but I did it nevertheless. I found some shoe prints and tire tracks that looked as if they belonged to a large vehicle—either an SUV or a full-sized pick-up truck, but as far as telling me *who* they belonged to, well I was out of luck there. I continued roaming the woods until eventually I was so exhausted that I sat down underneath a pine tree surrounded by rhododendron and slept.

When I woke, it was mid-afternoon and I was momentarily confused until I remembered what I had been doing. I ate the sandwich, munched the apple, and drank some of the water. I hadn't realized how far I had traveled, and by the time I entered the clearing surrounding the cottage, another couple of hours had passed. The sun was lower in the west, and Caitlin's car was back in the driveway. I ran up onto the porch, fully intending to grab her and hug her to me—make sure she was safe. She met me at the door but before I could reach for her, she drew back and slapped me across the cheek. Hard.

Instinctively, my hand went to my face, as if the pressure of my fingers could stop the stinging. She raised her palm again and I caught her wrist and held it. "Stop," I said.

"You bastard." She burst into tears and fell against me, wrapping her arms around my waist. "I thought something had happened to you. I've been trying to call your cell phone ever since I left—you've probably got four thousand missed calls—and I left so many voice mail messages that your mailbox is full. Why the hell didn't you answer your phone?"

"I didn't turn it on," I admitted and held up my arms in case she felt the need to slap me again. In light of recent events, I realized how foolish it was not to have it on and with me at all times. What if she had needed me? "I'm sorry," I added. "I was having a bad day with the Voices and then I was a little freaked out after what happened last night, and I didn't even think about the phone anymore."

"Oh my God." Her voice was full of dread. "What happened?"

I told her what had taken place, but because she looked so terrified, I added, "Maybe it was just someone looking to burglarize the place and when they came in and saw me, it scared them off."

"Maybe." But she didn't sound any more convinced of that than I felt, and we spent the week being hyper-vigilant—me jumping at every little creak of the old house and her checking and double-checking the door and window locks. When the week had passed and nothing further happened, we both began to relax, and I began enjoying my time there again.

Caitlin returned to her writing, and after receiving the flash drive containing the discovery from my case, she continued her research. While she was otherwise occupied, I continued my walks through the woods. I ran into Rev. Jack almost every day, usually walking with him. Often we talked, but on the days the Voices were bothering me and I didn't feel like talking, it wasn't an awkward or uncomfortable silence, and he maintained a one-sided dialogue, telling stories, naming plants, trees, and birds. He taught me how to fish, taking me out on the lake in his canoe, fishing with bamboo rods he crafted himself. He taught me how to identify the different species of fish, how to clean and fillet them, and best of all, how to grill them. He was the grandfather I'd never had and I knew it would be hard to leave him behind when we had to return to Kingsville.

He invited us over to his cabin several times to eat and we invited him to eat with us, usually out on the boat dock, where we sat and talked until late in the evening, after which he would snap his fingers at his little dachshund, Winnie, and off they'd go through the woods back to his house.

Even though we were in one of the most amazing places on earth and would only be there a couple more weeks, I had trouble getting Caitlin away from her research during the day. I tried not to complain—the research was for my benefit after all, but I was lonely. Even when we were in the same room, she was worlds away, wrapped up in a past I'd just as soon never visit again.

#

"Come swim with me," I said to Caitlin, nuzzling her neck. "You've been at this for hours. Take a break."

She kissed the air near my face distractedly. "I will in a minute, I promise."

"You've been saying that all day," I told her. I was getting a little pissed off.

"No, really. Just a few more minutes and I'll be down."

So I waited a bit on the dock, then stripped and dove into the water, which had finally warmed up in the June sun. I swam to where the cove opened up into the lake proper and swam back. Twice. Still no Caitlin. I climbed out of the water and lay down on one of the folding lounge chairs on the dock, waking up an hour later. Still no Caitlin.

Retrieving my fishing pole from the boathouse, I fished off the dock for a while. I caught two nice-sized lake trout, which I thought would be good grilled for supper. Back up the hill I went to the shed where there was an old wooden bench I used for cleaning fish. And I had an evil idea.

With the fish cleaned and filleted and my mess picked up, I took the fillets to put in the fridge before continuing to the living room, where Caitlin was still hunched over the computer.

I went up behind her and nuzzled her again. Eyes still on the computer screen, she turned her head slightly toward me.

"Give me a kiss," I said, and she obligingly puckered her lips and kissed the fish head I held out.

Her nose registered the smell, her eyes locked on the fish, and she let out a scream and shot straight up out of her chair. I chased her all the way to the boat dock, where she jumped into the water to get away.

Laughing, I flung the fish head far out into the lake and jumped in after her. "And if you continue to ignore me," I told her, "you'll find one in bed with you."

"You're an asshole, John," she said, splashing water on her face and rubbing at her lips, but then she started laughing, too, and swam over to me and we spent some time making a few waves.

Later that evening I grilled the fish á la Rev. Jack, and we took everything down to the boat dock to eat. The night remained warm and pleasant, and we lit the tiki torches, then sat and watched the lightning bugs.

"I've learned some interesting things about your case," Caitlin said, taking a sip of her wine and stretching out her legs.

I really hated to spoil the mood by discussing that unpleasantness, but I was curious. "What's that?"

"There was evidence attributable to you. A hair, some tears, and saliva. And of course there's Peter Barrington's account of how he was investigating some suspicious activity in the area and came into the warehouse and found you with the victim. How you kept repeating, 'I'm so sorry.'"

Sick shame washed over me. Had she finally begun to doubt my innocence? I felt my chest tighten. Was this where she told me we were through, that she couldn't live with someone who'd been accused of such a horrendous act?

"It's obvious that the child wasn't murdered or sexually assaulted there. There was no semen found on the body. No condoms. Nothing. There were ligature marks on the child's wrists and ankles, but no restraints were found. The child's body was as if it had been bathed, redressed, and transported after death. But that's not what really bothers me. There was some evidence left at the scene that didn't belong to you or the victim."

I sat up on the lounge chair. "What kind of evidence?"

"Two small blood smears on the victim's underwear. Like a skinned knuckle might make if it was brushed against something. And John, in the video of your arrest, it appears that Peter Barrington has Band-Aids on the knuckles of his right hands."

The skin on the back of my neck prickled. I wasn't sure how to receive this information. "I'm sure the prosecutors had a convenient explanation. Didn't they?"

"I don't know that it was ever brought out in your trial. I've got to read through the trial transcripts to be certain, but none of this makes sense. This was all evidence of an organized and calculating mind, and—how can I say this politely—yours was anything but. Yet they were convinced that you were responsible. Like they're convinced that you're responsible for these newest murders. They're just waiting to lower the boom."

"So what do we do?"

"That's a really good question, my love, and I hope to find out the answer. I can tell you this much—I don't trust Peter Barrington for one second. There's something just not right there. I can't help but think that he's involved in some way." She came to sit in my lap, draping an arm over my shoulder. "I'm sorry I've been ignoring you."

I kissed her. "I guess I'm glad you have been."

"I won't ignore you tonight. Come on, let's go back to the house." And she was as good as her word.

#

"My first article on your case is going to be published tomorrow," Caitlin said the next morning over breakfast. She'd fixed omelets and a fruit salad, and I was actually ravenous for a change—of course we'd burned a lot of calories in the bedroom the previous night after returning to the cottage, so that might have had something to do with it.

"About the lack of any significant evidence?" I asked as I got up to pour more coffee.

"Yes, sir. There's going to be a lot of shit hitting a lot of fans, and I hope at least part of it splatters the Kingsville Public Safety Department."

"Aren't you afraid it'll do more than that? We've already got somebody pissed off." Wrong thing to say.

"I'm not afraid to let the truth be known, John. There's no place for vigilantism and terrorism in a civilized society."

"There may be no place for it, but it's there," I replied, sounding much calmer to my own ears than I felt. "It's there whether we want to acknowledge it or not. You see proof of it every single day."

"I'm not going to live my life afraid."

"Babe, I've lived my whole life afraid."

"Then it's time to stop. You can only die once, John."

"I'd like to have lived a little first before I do."

"If it makes you feel any better, I'm not naming names in this article."

"No names have been named yet," I said, "and someone is still gunning for us."

She frowned. "You don't think Randy's messing with us?"

I shook my head. "I don't think so—the notes? That's not Randy. He wouldn't suddenly begin leaving chicken-shit notes; he'd say what he was going to say to my face. He always has."

"Who do you think it is?"

"I have no idea. The family of one of the victims, maybe?"

"So we're back to vigilantes."

"Sure seems that way."

"Well, I'm tired of it." She shook her head and flipped her hair back over one shoulder. "If we hunker down and keep quiet, then they win and we lose because we're afraid to have a life."

"Caitlin, what if one of these screwballs decides that a life for a life is the way to go here? It's kind of hard to have a life when you're dead."

"Then that's the price of loving you."

"No!" I pounded my fist on the table and the dishes jumped and clattered. Caitlin jumped, too. "You really need to drop this now. The more attention you draw to it, the more you're going to antagonize whoever's behind this."

"John, as you just pointed out, whoever this is doesn't need any encouragement. They're already on the warpath. My articles might help—they might get people to actually think before they act."

"You're not helping me if you get yourself killed! I couldn't live with that. Just let it go."

"I'm not going to do that, John."

"You are so hard-headed." I stood up from the table.

She gave me an impudent smile. "You know that's what you love about me."

I slammed out of the house and down the porch steps, and did what had become my panacea of late. I stripped off my clothes, dove into the lake, and began swimming. Caitlin came down to the dock and beckoned to me, but I turned and swam even further away and eventually she walked back toward the cottage. When I stopped being angry and started being exhausted, I pulled myself up out of the water and dressed again. I knew I would continue to butt heads with her over the subject, but didn't have any fight left in me at the moment.

She greeted me as if we'd never argued and pulled me down on the couch with her to watch a movie—*Benny & Joon*. Another movie to draw some parallels from—a lot of parallels.

"We're giving a party," Caitlin said as the end credits were rolling. "Call it a wedding reception."

"Seriously?" I asked. "We've been married two months now."

"Not unheard of." She stretched out her leg and ran a foot under my shirt and across my stomach. "Besides, everyone at work is dying to meet you."

"Why would they want to meet *me*?"

"Because they've heard me sing your praises—because I'm married to you."

"Because I'm notorious?"

"Stop it. Why do you assume that you're not worth knowing?"

"Because not many people do know me. People aren't exactly lining up to meet me."

"And you don't exactly put yourself out there either, do you?"

She had me there. I'd learned long ago that the fewer people who knew me, the less chance for disappointment and hurt—but also fewer opportunities to create new relationships. "So tell me about the party."

"It's going to be all day Saturday, and I'm having it catered. We're going to set up tables near the boat dock, and I've hired a local band to play. It's going to be fun—we need some fun for a change."

"Sounds like you've been planning this for a while."

She grinned. "I have. For two months."

"And how many people are coming?"

"About thirty-five have RSVP'd. There's still about ten I haven't heard from."

I was beginning to feel that another swim was in order. "That many? God, what am I going to talk to them about? I have nothing in common with any of them."

She sat up and frowned at me. "How do you know?"

I put my head in my hands. "Caitlin, I've been in a mental institution."

"And how long are you going to use that as a crutch?"

Okay, ouch, that hurt.

CHAPTER THIRTEEN

THE DAY OF THE PARTY was perfect, owing to Caitlin's luck and not my own, I'm sure. The sky was a deep, clear blue—no clouds anywhere—and it was warm without being oppressively hot or humid. I went for a swim before things began rocking and rolling, and the water was a perfect temperature also. I spent more time swimming than I had intended to, and the caterers and equipment rental company had already arrived by the time I got back up to the cottage. Caitlin was in her element, directing them as to where to place the food and tables and chairs, showing them how she wanted things set up. She pressed me into service immediately, so that I, too, was dragging around tables and chairs.

After moving the same table four times at her direction, I said, "Right here's fine. This is where it's staying. Now, what next?"

She handed me an armful of tablecloths and pointed to a box with candleholders, candles and vases. "You can start putting these on each table."

I rolled my eyes. "Really? You want *me* to decorate tables?"

She studied me a moment, then took the tablecloths from me. "No, maybe not. Why don't you go shower and get dressed. Edie and a couple of girls from work will be here to help me any time now."

I gladly retreated, shuddering at the thought of having to decorate tables and grateful for the reprieve. I stripped in the bathroom and stepped into the shower, but began having doubts about the party again. For the better part of the day, there would be potentially forty to fifty people I didn't know hanging out. I had no idea if they all knew about me or not and wasn't sure if I was more or less comfortable if they *did* know about me. If they did know, would they be watching me for some kind of sign that I was a nut job, and if they didn't know, would I act in some way so as to disturb them? To say I was really nervous was an understatement.

Back in the bedroom I put on the clothes Caitlin had chosen for me—khaki cargo shorts, a short-sleeve button up plaid shirt, and Topsiders (sans socks). I might be crazy, but damn it, I would be a well-dressed crazy. Outside, I could hear another delivery truck arriving and additional female voices laughing and chattering—Edie, *et al*—and there was nothing else for it except to dive in.

Caitlin was standing in a group of women talking and laughing and she waved me over to them. "John, you remember Edie from the diner." Edie reached out and gave me a hug. "Hey, sweetie," she said. I hugged her back awkwardly—

I've never been much of a hugger with the exception of Caitlin. Sandy, Jennifer, and Mackenzie, thankfully, were not huggers but handshakers, and after greeting me, they went about their business. Caitlin sent me to take a stack of beach towels down to the boat dock, check the fuel in the tiki torches, and set up a few more lounge chairs. By the time I finished, it was nearly noon and she went in to shower and change before the guests started to arrive.

She came back dressed in an emerald green top with spaghetti straps, which showed off her lovely shoulders, and a short white skirt, which showed off her long legs now tanned by the time we'd spent in the sun. She dragged me around by the hand introducing me to everyone, but in all honesty, the only other person whose name I remembered was her editor, Will Lackey. My brain was on sensory overload—talking, laughing, shouting, music, smells of food, aftershave, and perfume, and all the people moving in and out of my field of vision. I really wanted to go for another swim but knew this would be rude and Caitlin would strangle me if I did. Of course she would strangle me when I lost my cool and starting yelling, too.

My anxiety was apparently obvious to her and she pulled me off to one side. "You're doing fine," she whispered. "Remember to breathe—deep in, hold it, and release slowly."

I nuzzled her ear and said, "There's something else I'd like to have deep in and release slowly."

She laughed and squeezed my crotch. "We'll get to that later, my love."

She steered me toward a group of guys, Will Lackey at the center, who were laughing loudly at some joke. "John," Will beckoned me to join them, closing one arm over my shoulder. Great, another hugger. "So tell us," he said, "how's married life treating you?"

"It's been great," I said.

"Caitlin's an excellent young woman," Will said, "and she can be like a pit bull when she gets her teeth into something—a story like yours for instance."

"Yeah, I've found out the hard way how persistent she can be," I muttered and everyone laughed.

"It's a shame we didn't meet before you got married," Will said, "I could have told you some real horror stories—given you an idea what you were getting into." I was relieved when he launched into some of her exploits so that I didn't have to make an attempt at small talk. I had to admit that the stories were pretty entertaining and I learned a lot about Caitlin through them. I found I was laughing despite myself, and when I next looked up, the caterers were announcing that the food was ready to be served and everyone was forming a line to fill their plates.

I was too anxious to eat much but the barbecue smelled so good, that I had to try some, although I could only manage two bites before I started feeling sick. Caitlin had also thought to provide a fully stocked bar and with one of the caterers acting as bartender, the alcohol flowed freely. I got a large glass of muscadine wine and then joined Caitlin at the table.

"You're not eating?" she asked as I sat down.

I made a face. "Tried that. It's not happening."

"Don't tell me it doesn't taste good, or I'm going to be so pissed," she said picking up a forkful of barbecue and sniffing it suspiciously.

"It's fine," I told her. "I just can't eat right now."

She pointed to the large glass of wine I held. "You'd better take it easy with that then."

"I'll be okay." I finished that glass and was working on another when Caitlin called me over to one of the serving tables where the caterer had set out a small wedding cake. We went through the ritual of cutting it and mashing it in each other's faces while Edie took pictures with a digital camera and Mackenzie used another digital device to record it. Normally I would have been uncomfortable at being the center of attention, but with a good start on the second glass of wine, I was feeling kind of mellow and when I finished it, I went in search of a third.

The sun went down and everyone moved to the small beach. Me and a couple of the other guys, whose names I couldn't tell you if you offered me a million dollars, went up to the woodshed and brought down a bunch of firewood to make a bonfire on the sand. The caterers set out roasting forks, hot dogs, marshmallows, chocolate bars, and graham crackers and some of the guests busied themselves with this activity while others stripped down to bathing suits and jumped in the water.

Since other people were swimming, I figured Caitlin couldn't get mad at me, so I stripped to my swim trunks, too—worn especially for the occasion and with a nod toward propriety, as I usually wore nothing at all when I swam—and jumped in. The tiki torches on the boat dock and the lights strung through the trees on the shore all reflected in the water, which remained warm and pleasant even though the sun had set. I swam out beyond the others and floated on my back for a while until I heard Caitlin calling for me. I reluctantly swam back to the dock to do my master's bidding. More firewood.

As I went up the hill to the woodshed, I hit up the bar for another glass of wine, and drank it on the way. I finished adding the wood to the fire and had the glass refilled. By the time the guests began leaving after 1:00 AM, I was feeling no pain.

The last of the guests had started up the hill to the driveway and Caitlin and I were gathering towels, soda cans, and beer bottles. She'd also had too much to drink and was obviously having trouble with her balance.

"You know what?" I said to her. "Before you fall in the lake and drown, let's just go to the house. We can get all this stuff in the morning when it's light and we're both a little more clear-headed."

"Okay." She bent over for a bottle and fell on her face.

I picked her up and happened to glance toward the woods to the right of the dock. A figure was standing there. A huge broad-shouldered man. I frowned, thinking one of the guests had gotten turned around. "Hey," I yelled, "the driveway's in the other direction!" The figure raised an arm and I saw the brief flash of a red beam and a red dot simultaneously appeared centered over the left pocket of my shirt. I was confused for a few seconds as to the significance of this red dot, then the implication filtered through the alcohol and I was half pulling, half dragging Caitlin so fast she had trouble getting her feet under her.

"John, for God's sake, what's the hurry?" she asked, slightly slurring her words.

"You didn't see him?" I asked, knowing she hadn't. "That man—there!" We stumbled to a stop. The figure had disappeared by that point, of course.

"See who? What are you talking about?"

I shushed her and listened. Nothing. I was sweating now and feeling more than a little out of it. Maybe I had imagined it. Somebody was just fucking around with a laser pointer. I had been pretty stressed out all day, and I'd probably imbibed a couple of bottles of wine by myself. When we reached the cottage, however, I sent her into the bedroom to get ready for bed, and I made sure the windows and doors were locked tight, which made the house hotter than hell, but there was no way I was making it easy for someone to get in.

The next morning, after cleaning up the remnants of the party and helping the equipment rental guys load their table and chairs, I packed a sandwich and a bottle of water in my backpack, checked on Caitlin, who was still in bed nursing a hangover, and set off down the path in the opposite direction of the driveway. I saw no evidence that anyone had been through the area but I continued walking until I heard Rev. Jack's little dachshund barking. A few minutes later I heard crashing through the underbrush and saw a doe and fawn leaping up the hill, Winnie close behind.

Rev. Jack came along presently. "Well, morning there, John. Didn't figure I'd see you up this early after last night. Sounded like some party."

"Yeah, sorry if it kept you up, although I thought we'd see you there."

"Feeling a little under the weather or I would have been, although I doubt you needed an old man hanging around."

"I wish you had been there—it would have given me someone to talk to. I didn't know any of those people."

"Pshaw," he said, but I could tell he was pleased that his company was missed.

There was some more crashing through the brush and Winnie came bounding back down the hill, her tongue hanging out. We both laughed at her.

"What do you suppose she intended to do with the deer if she caught it?" I asked.

"Probably gum it to death," he chuckled. "She's getting old like me and she doesn't have too many teeth left, but speaking of deer reminds me of something I wanted to ask you. You or Cait know of anyone who's been out here hunting?"

"Hunting? No. It's not even hunting season, is it?"

"No and that's just it. I saw a man going through the woods on the ridge above my cabin early this morning. He was carrying a rifle with a scope on it. Most of the land 'round here is private. My cabin sits on ten acres, and I've not given anyone permission to be hunting. Didn't know if you all had told someone they could hunt yours and maybe he was just crossing over."

"Not us," I replied, and it made me uneasy to think about someone running around with a rifle and scope, given the incident from the night before.

We walked on a while and sat down a bit to rest, and I said, "If I don't see you again before next week, I just wanted you to know we'll be going back to Kingsville. The cottage is rented out until Labor Day, so I imagine it'll be September before we see you again."

"Well, now, I'm sure going to miss our walks and our talks and our dinners out on the boat dock."

"You won't miss it nearly as much as I will," I told him. I really hated the thought of having to give up the cottage—of being stuck in Kingsville with no access to the lake or the woods—without a friend.

#

I heard the noise in my sleep and I was up and moving into the living room before I was fully awake, barking my shins on the coffee table. I can't explain how I could be so sure, but I knew the sound had come from the front porch. I yanked open the door and flung the screen wide but it collided with something lying on the porch and came slamming back toward me. I sidestepped the screen door, nearly tripping over the thing, but managed to leap over it at the last second, half falling, half sliding down the porch steps.

I scanned the yard in all directions, trying to detect movement among the trees. Nothing. With a feeling of dread, I turned back to the thing on the porch. In the dim early morning light, I couldn't make out what I was seeing at first. Grayish fur, pointed ears, long bushy tail, and trailing from it a dark, thick-looking substance and several feet of what looked like knotted rope. Its head was canted at an odd angle, neck broken. A wolf? Were there wolves in the wild in western North Carolina? I didn't think so. A coyote then, or someone's dog. That the thing—whatever it was—was dead, I was sure.

Closer, I could see that its stomach had been slit open and its organs were spilling out onto the porch. A hunting knife jutted from the animal's rib cage, and I was trying really hard not to throw up when I noticed the note pinned between the hilt and the creature's hide.

Bending down so I could see the note, but trying not to get too close, I read: "Sometimes the predator becomes the prey." I jerked upright and grabbed for the screen door handle. It took me a couple of tries to get hold of it.

In the bedroom, Caitlin was still asleep. I seized her by the arm. "Caitlin. *Caitlin*! Wake up! *NOW*!

She tried to shrug me off, murmuring, "John, it's too early for that. You had your chance last night. Go back to sleep."

"Caitlin! Get up now!" I was shouting by this point and the tone of my voice finally penetrated her consciousness.

She sat up, looking wild-eyed. "What? What? What's wrong?"

I got both our suitcases from the closet and started grabbing clothes left and right. "Get up," I said again. "Get up, get dressed, and get your shit. We're gone."

She stood there wobbling a moment, trying to get her bearings. "Have you lost your mind?"

I just looked at her, my hands full of clothes.

She rubbed at her face and said, "I'm sorry—I'm sorry," then she too began grabbing up clothes and toiletries and slinging everything into the suitcase haphazardly. She pulled on the clothes she'd worn the day before, still a little wild-eyed, while I threw on my own clothes and shoes.

Finished, I gripped her elbow. "Come on. We're out of here." We went down the hall trailing the suitcases after us, and she started for the front door. "No!" I tightened my grasp and steered her to the kitchen and the back door.

"What the hell is going on?" She tried to pull away from me.

I had to have been hurting her as I pulled her along with me, my hand wrapped around her upper arm in a death grip. It was a little lighter outside now, and I went out first, checking to make sure no one else was close by and no other nasty surprises awaited us. "Give me the keys."

She fumbled in her purse, drawing out her key ring and handing it to me. I released her arm to put our suitcases in the trunk.

"John, are you going to tell me what's going on?" She turned toward the front porch as she spoke, and I saw her stop and frown.

"Caitlin, stay where you're at," I commanded.

There had been plenty of times in the last several months that I had thanked God, or whatever deity was in charge of the universe, for sending me a headstrong, persistent woman, but this was not one of those times. I unlocked the passenger door and tried to shove her in, but she caught sight of the furry lump and started for the porch.

"What is *that*? Is it a dog? Is it hurt?"

"Goddamnit, Caitlin. Do *not* go up there!"

She moved much more quickly than I would have thought given her sleepy, confused state, and she was up the steps before I could get to her. I saw her stop. There was silence and then she started screaming. I ran to her side and forced her away from the animal's corpse, down the steps, and into the passenger seat.

I hadn't been behind the wheel of a car in over eight years, but I prayed that it was like riding a bicycle and I would still remember how to drive. Not quite. I started the engine, put the car in gear, and let the clutch out too fast. The car gave a mighty hop and the engine died. Three times. I cranked it once more and managed to get everything synchronized and the car moving forward, and then I drove like a demon.

We made it back to Kings County in record time, and Caitlin looked up as if aroused from a coma. "You'd better slow down, John, or you're going to get a ticket."

No sooner had these words left her lips, than a highway patrol car pulled out behind me from a side street, lights flashing and siren blaring.

I slowed down and pulled the car over onto the shoulder of the road. "Fuck my life," I said, banging my head on the steering wheel.

#

The state trooper was convinced that I was under the influence of an impairing substance and administered a field sobriety test, then had me blow in a portable breathalyzer. When that didn't satisfy him, he took me to the hospital to have my blood drawn for testing before delivering me into the clutches of the Kings County Sheriff's Department, this time charged with DWI, speeding 95 miles per hour in a 35 mile per hour zone, driving while license revoked, careless and reckless driving, and probably ten or twelve other offenses. And this had to have tickled the shit out of Detectives Whisnant and Samuels because they wasted no time in finding me down in booking and dragging my sorry ass off to an interview room once more.

"Where were you going in such a hurry this morning?" Whisnant asked, settling back in his chair. "It wouldn't have anything to do with the dead boy we found last night, would it?"

"*No!* You wouldn't fucking believe me if I told you," I made the mistake of saying. Whisnant took this tidbit and made a meal out of it.

"Well, now, John, just try us. You might be surprised how understanding we can be. Why don't you tell us and let us decide? Your girlfriend—or is she your wife—looked pretty shaken up. Of course that may have been due to the fact that you were going nearly a hundred miles an hour. Did the two of you have a fight? Maybe she was trying to get out of the car and you didn't want her to? We know how it goes in situations like that. You get a little angry, do stuff you shouldn't. Get a little rough."

"Wait—what? Are you saying I *hurt* her?"

"Well, she does have some nice bruises on her upper arm, about the size of your hand, I'd say."

"Well, yeah, from where I dragged her out to the car this morning—"

"So you admit you made those bruises on her arm."

"Well, yes, but—" Too late I remembered to keep my mouth shut.

"You may be looking at a charge of assault on a female, too."

"*What?*" Fuck my life. "I did *not* assault her."

"You talk to us John and we might be able to see our way to help you out here."

"Shit!" They charged me with assault on a female, too, and put me on a forty-eight hour hold, nearly every minute of which was spent in the interview room with them or their counterparts. Belatedly, I clammed up, but this just encouraged them to go at me harder.

Which is how I came to be back in Kingsville for two whole days before laying eyes on our new "home". I have to say that Caitlin did all right by us in that regard—not that I had ever doubted that she would. It was a much nicer and larger apartment than the previous one and she'd bought a lot of nice furniture to go in it. I felt a little guilty because it appeared that she had rented it in an effort to appease me or as a peace offering for having to leave Fontana Lake.

"What do you think?" she asked as I walked around getting familiar with the place.

"It's pretty awesome," I said, stopping in front of a 65-inch flat screen television. "Especially *this*."

She grinned. "I thought you'd like that. The complex also has an indoor pool and a fitness center."

I sat down on the new sofa and kicked off my shoes. "That's good, but I'm really tired right now, and I'd just like to sit here for a while." I handed her the wad of paperwork from my latest visit to the Sheriff's Department. She flipped through it until she came to the warrant for assault on a female.

"What the hell is this?" She waved the paper at me. "How can they charge you with this without me making some sort of complaint against you?"

"I don't know," I yawned and lay back against the cushion, "but apparently they can."

"They're getting desperate now."

"Maybe so. I hate living my life looking over my shoulder, waiting to be arrested for shit I didn't do when I'm being arrested left and right for shit I did do."

"John, if they had any hard evidence on the murders, they would have arrested you already. Why do you think they have to play these games? They've got nothing. And they'll continue to have nothing. Because you've done nothing. That's why they keep harassing you—they're hoping you'll give them something to hang you with so they don't have to do their jobs. Just like they didn't do their jobs the first time. But they're not going to be so lucky the second time, because now they've got to contend with *me*." She sighed and got her cell phone out of her purse. "I guess I'll put in another call to Webster. I hate to think how much this is going to cost."

I put a hand over my face. "I'm sorry." I was at the place where tears were next on the list.

"We'll get through this." She sat down beside me, placing a hand on my shoulder. "If it wasn't so damned serious, it would be funny." And then she started laughing, and I started laughing until we were both bordering on hysteria.

When we'd calmed down again, I wiped at my eyes and said, "I don't know how much more I can take, Caitlin. I really don't."

"We'll get through it," she said again. "You're a much stronger person than you realize. Look how much you've been through already and you're still alive and kicking."

"Don't forget—any time you decide you've had enough—you can walk away."

"If you say that again, John, I swear to God I will give you a reason to assault me."

I found myself thinking that if I lived to be a hundred, I wasn't sure I'd ever understand what I'd done to earn her love and devotion.

CHAPTER FOURTEEN

"THE MAD MAULER", which is how I came to think of our stalker, had gone to ground once more. Three weeks had passed since our hasty return to Kingsville, and Caitlin and I settled into a new routine. I swam in the complex pool every morning after Caitlin left for work, but it was not like swimming in the lake. For one thing, I couldn't swim nude, and for another I was forced to share the pool with a couple of older women and young mothers with squealing, pre-school aged kids.

In the evenings before we ate supper, Caitlin and I made use of the weight resistance machines and treadmills in the fitness room. I was pleased to see more definition in my abdominal muscles, and Caitlin commented more than once on my "six pack." I, of course, took every opportunity to let her know how much I appreciated her nice, firm ass.

We were usually back in our apartment by 7:00 PM, but that night we got there late and it was close to 9:00 before we finished. Caitlin struck up a conversation with another couple who were also exercising and when we all walked into the parking lot, the sky in the west was still glowing a very faint pink. We stopped on the sidewalk outside the front door while Caitlin said good night. I lifted the hem of my t-shirt to mop the sweat from my face when the flash of a laser beam from the edge of the lot caught my eye. Just like that night at the lake, a red dot appeared on my shirt.

I opened my mouth and turned to shout a warning to Caitlin when two sharp cracks split the night open, and I felt as if I had been punched in the chest. I staggered and went down on my knees at the same instant I heard the glass shatter in the window behind me.

The three of them fell to the ground beside me, Caitlin's friend with cell phone already in hand, dialing a number. I could hear a voice on the other end of the line saying, "Kings County Emergency Services. Do you need police, fire or ambulance?" and the woman was yelling out the address of the apartment complex and saying, "We need the police and an ambulance. Someone's been shot!"

"John?" Caitlin's voice had a strange hysterical pitch to it. "John—oh, Jesus!"

"Who's hurt?" I asked, looking at each of them to see who had been injured. Please God, not Caitlin.

They stared back at me with horrified expressions, and then Caitlin was pulling at me, saying "Get down!"

I knocked her hand away and attempted to get to my feet, but for some reason I could not persuade my legs to cooperate, and there was now a fierce burning sensation moving throughout my chest. I felt my heartbeat ratchet several notches higher when I saw that the left side of my shirt was covered in blood. "Am I bleeding?" I recognized it for the stupid question it was as soon as it left my mouth.

"John, you need to sit down. *Now*." Caitlin's eyes were on my chest and her chin quivered.

I could feel the blood, warm and viscid, wicking my shirt to my body, and then I was having trouble getting my breath and collapsed onto the sidewalk. People were gathering, staring at me, and I could hear voices shouting "Someone's been shot", and running feet. Another woman came up to Caitlin. "I'm a nurse. What's his name? I'll stay with him until the ambulance gets here."

Caitlin's response was strained. "His name is John."

The woman knelt beside me. "Hi, John—I'm Amy. Are you having trouble breathing?

I could only nod. I didn't understand how the inside of me could be on fire and my skin could be so cold.

"Yes? Okay, let's check you out." She placed her fingers over the pulse point on my wrist. "Pulse is a little fast, but that's to be expected. Does anyone have a flashlight?" Someone handed her one and she pulled up my shirt and shone the light on me. Blood bubbled from the wound each time I attempted to breathe in or out. She looked up at Caitlin. "The bullet's penetrated the chest wall."

I tried to speak, but what came out didn't resemble a human voice.

Amy patted my arm. "It's going to be hard for you to talk right now. Don't try, okay?" She pulled out her own cell phone and punched in three numbers, identified herself, and asked to be patched through to the ambulance in route. Snippets of her conversation filtered through the panic. "…gunshot—we may be looking at a tension pneumothorax…fast pulse, labored breathing…shock setting in…no, he's conscious for now." She listened for a moment then hung up and turned back to me. "They'll be here soon, and we'll get you to the ER, get you taken care of."

I tried unsuccessfully to pull in more oxygen and felt the terror rising. There was now a weird sucking noise in the area of my chest each time I attempted to inhale or exhale, and the pain was a wild rabid animal inside me searching for a way out. I pushed away the blanket someone had placed over me.

"Where is the ambulance?" Caitlin asked. "The hospital's only ten blocks away. Where the hell are they?" She scooted closer to me. "You hang on, John."

I wanted to tell her that I loved her, but I could make no sound other than the horrible gurgling noise as I struggled to draw air into a lung that no longer worked. The pressure in my chest was so great that I didn't see how my heart could continue to beat properly. I clawed at my shirt, ripping it in a futile effort to relieve the pressure.

Amy placed her hands over mine. "I know you're scared, John, but listen, the ambulance will be here any second. We need you to hang on for us." She tried to calm me, but the pain was unbearable. Writhing on the ground, I was only vaguely aware when the ambulance and half the city's police force finally screeched into the lot. Then the medics were kneeling beside me, slapping on monitors and blood pressure cuffs, and pulled off what was left of my shirt. They cut away my shorts, and poked and prodded, tormenting me until I would have screamed had I been able to get my breath.

Randy's face peered down at me. Oh God, help me. I didn't want to die with him standing there watching me draw my last breath. Then I saw Caitlin's tear-streaked face and tried to reach for her, but the medics and other police officers pushed them both out of the way.

The medics fitted an oxygen tube in my nose and a stiff collar around my neck, slid a board under me, and lifted me onto the stretcher. I descended to a new level of agony as they talked over me. "Blood pressure's dropping…needle aspiration…intubate…have Life Flight on standby…trauma unit at Mission…need to make it snappy." The pain was accompanied by a roaring in my head as if all the Voices were screaming in unison on my behalf. It occurred to me as the siren started up that I was praying for death and I was already sliding down that slippery slope toward it. It seemed so much easier to die than to live.

"John, stay with us, dude," a medic said.

"Pain." It took a phenomenal effort to force out that one word.

"Hang in there. We're gonna get you to the ER. Then we're sending you on to Mission Memorial by Life Flight. They'll take good care of you. You ever been in a helicopter?"

I thought of the flight to Las Vegas. My wedding. This must be the part where my life flashed before my eyes.

"It'll be over so quick you won't know you were even in the air. Promise. Stay with us now."

The ER was another nightmare—more poking and prodding, more agony, people rushing around the stretcher in a dizzying dance. I thought I glimpsed Caitlin, heard her crying, heard someone saying, "You can't be in here now, ma'am. Let us work on him."

"Cait," I wheezed.

"His wife," someone else murmured.

"All right, folks, let's get the crash cart in position."

"Okay, John." A man in scrubs leaned over into my field of vision. "You're going to be a busy fellow for the next little bit. We're going to put in a tube to help you breathe, then we're going to have to do a needle decompression, get some of that air out of your chest. You've got a collapsed lung. After that you're off to Mission. Bet you didn't think you were going to have to work this hard today, did you? The good news is, you get the really good drugs for this. Ready? Here we go."

I registered the prick of the needle as it pierced my skin, and my eyelids began closing almost immediately. Then something akin to a white-hot ice pick was probing my chest, but miraculously the pain began loosening its tight-fisted grip on me. A grim voice said, "Get his wife in here, stat. We've got to get him in that copter."

There was more rustling and bustling, more footsteps, then I sensed her standing nearby and I forced my eyes open. Her face was pale and scared, and I could tell she had been crying. As she clutched my hand, I saw more tears rolling down her cheeks. I squeezed her fingers and she squeezed back.

"Love." It took a mighty effort to force that word up from my diaphragm, through my throat, and past my lips.

"I love you, too—" The words broke off in a sob, and she held my palm to her face and kissed it, leaned over and kissed my forehead. Then she was being pushed from the room.

"Okay." The doctor bent over me again. "Here comes the best stuff—saving the best for last. Another little stick—it's gonna put you out for a while." And then I was falling, falling, falling down into the darkness.

#

I didn't know how much time had passed before I was fully aware of my surroundings. Unfortunately, my first conscious vision was not of Caitlin but of Randy, the bastard, and I said, "What the fuck?" My voice sounded raspy, rusty, and my throat was sore.

"Hello to you, too." He moved closer to the bed.

I looked around the unfamiliar room, taking in the flowers and get-well balloons. A TV mounted on the wall was broadcasting an old episode of Law and Order—how appropriate. "Where am I?"

"You're at Mission Memorial, Asheville. They just moved you out of ICU. I guess you're going to live after all."

"Too bad for you."

"Yeah," was his reply, but I didn't detect the rancor that was usually present in his conversations with me, or maybe I was just too tired to really give a shit.

"Where's Cait?"

"She and Laurie went downstairs to get something to eat. They'll be back shortly."

I shifted around in the bed until the stabbing in my chest made me decide that wasn't wise.

"You need something?" Randy asked.

"I'm really thirsty." It wasn't until he poured some water into a cup and brought it over to me that it occurred to me how unusual this was—normally he wouldn't have pissed on me if I was on fire. I drank the water in two big swallows and held the empty cup out to him again. He refilled it and handed it back. "Thanks."

"Yeah." He cleared his throat. "So what do you remember about getting shot?"

"I remember not being able to breathe and thinking I was dying."

"You were in surgery nearly nine hours. You coded on them once, but they resuscitated you."

"I'll bet *that* pissed you off," I said.

"Shut the hell up, John. You know, it's been a really bad week for me if for no other reason than because I love your sister and she's been a total basket case."

"Well, we both know you wouldn't waste a minute's worry about me otherwise."

"And if the situation were reversed, you wouldn't waste a minute on me either."

"Damned straight."

But before we could continue sniping at each other, we heard Caitlin and Laurie in the hallway. Caitlin entered the room first, her eyes immediately on me. "Oh my God!" She ran over and jumped onto the bed, grabbing me in a bear hug, then saying, "I'm so sorry" when I groaned from the pressure. Then she was crying and holding me again and I was crying, too. Laurie sat down in a chair next to the bed wiping her own tears, and I held out my hand to her. She grasped it tightly. Randy was *not* crying, but then I've never known an asshole to cry.

#

Caitlin had gone down to the hospital gift shop to get a magazine when Laurie and Randy entered my room a few days later. "You talk to him," Randy said, "because I'm not going to be nice about it." He went to stand by the window, and Laurie sat down in the chair next to the bed where Caitlin had been sitting earlier.

I could tell she was nervous. "Talk to me about what?"

He said, "Well, go on. Waiting won't make it any easier."

She didn't look at me as she said, "We think you need to come back home with us."

I struggled to sit up. "Why the hell would I do that?"

Randy couldn't resist jumping in anyway. "Because we're your guardians and Caitlin is obviously taking advantage of you—putting you in jeopardy."

I laughed. "You're kidding, right?"

"When have you ever known me to kid?" We were back to asshole Randy.

"I'm *not* going with you."

"Listen, you moron—"

"Shut up!" I swept the food tray from the rolling bedside table with my arm. It clattered to the floor, its contents spilling across the tile.

"You'd better calm your ass down or you'll end up in the psych unit if you're not careful."

"Get out," I said.

"You need to listen to what we're telling you—"

Caitlin chose that moment to walk in. She glanced at the tray, then at Randy, and finally at me. "What's wrong?"

"They're leaving," I said to her, and added, "Don't let the door hit you on the ass on the way out," to Randy.

"He needs to come home with us," Randy said. "We're his legal guardians, and we feel that you've put him in danger with those articles you're writing."

Caitlin appeared thunderstruck.

"Randy, I swear to God." I got out of the bed holding my side. "Get out!"

"I would never knowingly endanger him," Caitlin said.

"Knowingly—unknowingly—you have."

I could tell she was about to cry. "Can we please take this conversation out in hall?" she asked Randy.

"There's nothing to discuss. We don't have to have your consent."

"*NO!*" It hurt to stand up straight, but he was going to listen to me. "No," I said again. "She's my wife. She does have a say."

Now it was Randy's turn to look gobsmacked. And then he laughed—not a sound of amusement, but one of derision. "You are *not* serious!" He turned to Laurie. "Do you see what he's been up to? And you still doubt what we need to do?" Then he was back to me. "All right, John, here are your choices. You either get your ass to our house or we're filing a petition to have you involuntarily committed again, and I think all the crazy shit you've been up to since you left is enough to put you back in Broughton."

"Don't hold your breath."

"I can get an order to have you picked up."

"Get your god damned order then and *try* to have me picked up. And if you manage, you'd better hope they kill me, because if they don't, I *will* kill *you*. Now get out, get out, *GET OUT!*" I picked up the Gideon Bible from the little bedside table and hurled it at him. It bounced off the hand he threw out to deflect it, struck him in the center of the face, and fell to the floor. Never had a Bible been put to better use.

A trickle of blood snaked across his upper lip, but he still couldn't keep his big mouth shut. He pointed to Caitlin and said, "And you can be charged with taking advantage of a disabled person."

"*Shut up! Get out!*" I was panting, sweating, in a full-on rage, and I could hear voices outside the door and security being paged over the intercom in the hallway.

Caitlin's face colored. "I haven't taken advantage of anyone. Why are you doing this to him? Hasn't he been through enough crap?"

"Apparently not," Randy sneered, "because ever since he hooked up with you, he keeps getting in more. And I could ask you the same questions."

I shoved the rolling table in his direction, but it caught against the chair leg and crashed over. I really wanted to get my hands around his throat and tried moving toward him, but my progress was halted by the IV line and by Caitlin stepping between us.

He motioned Laurie out of the room. "Let's go. John, we'll be seeing you real soon."

When the door opened again a few moments later, I thought he'd come back to taunt us some more, and I yelled, "I told you to *get out!*" But it was a startled nurse followed by a security guard.

"Is everything okay in here?" the guard asked, looking around at the mess.

"We're fine," Caitlin said.

Breathing hard, each breath like a stab from the point of a knife, I sat on the edge of the bed. "Can I get some more pain medicine?"

"You're not due any just yet," the nurse said. "You've got another couple of hours before I can give you the next dose." So not what I wanted to hear.

I held a hand against my chest, trying to subdue the throbbing, and felt dampness. My fingers came away bloody.

"Why don't you let me check that?" She lifted my hospital gown. "Let me get some supplies and I'll take care of that for you."

Caitlin squeezed my hand. "While she does that, I'm going to make some phone calls. Will you be okay while I'm gone?"

I waved her on, too preoccupied with the pain to answer. The nurse changed the bandages and came back with my pain medication long before Caitlin returned. I didn't realize I'd dozed off until she shook my arm. "John, wake up."

With her help, I sat up in bed. The razor's edge of pain was gone, replaced by a chemical warmth and sense of well-being. "What took you so long?" I yawned.

"I had some people I needed to talk to. Listen, what would you think about leaving?"

"Leaving where?" I knew I sounded stupid, drugged.

"Leaving the hospital—now. AMA. Against medical advice. John, if Randy manages to get that order and you're still here, they can take you into custody."

"But he knows where we live now. What's to stop him from showing up there?"

She flashed me her sly grin. "The fact that you won't be there?"

"I like the way you think. And where will I be?"

"I could tell you, my love, but then I'd have to kill you."

"Help me get dressed, then."

"Just so you understand, if we leave now, we won't have access to any pain medication or antibiotics."

That gave me pause for thought, but I had no intention of returning to Broughton Hospital—voluntarily or involuntarily. The psychic pain would far outweigh any physical pain or risk of infection. "I'll take that chance then. Can you remove this IV?"

"I think so, but we need to be ready to hit the door once it's out. Lucky for you, I brought more clothes so you'd have some when they released you. Otherwise, you'd have to wear that thing out of here," she indicated the hospital gown and grinned, "and I don't want other women ogling my man's booty."

She helped me dress. When she had my few other belongings gathered and stowed in her purse, she said, "All right. Here we go." She worked the tape loose from the back of my hand and gripped the top of the IV. "Sorry in advance if it hurts."

"Go for it."

She pulled it free and an alarm immediately began sounding. She grabbed her purse with one hand and my arm with the other. "Let's get your shirt on quick before they come to check the machine." She helped work my arms into the sleeves. It hurt like hell to raise my left arm. Then we were out in the hallway, moving toward the elevator. When we passed the nurse's station, one of them looked up. Caitlin gave her a big grin and said, "He's starting to feel a little better, so we're going down to the cafeteria for a cup of coffee. See you in a minute." My nurse was not in sight, thank God.

The woman smiled and gave a little wave. "Enjoy."

"You're such a good actress," I said once we were in the elevator.

"One of the many things you love about me."

"I love *all* things about you, but especially your deviousness."

"I'll remember you said that."

We walked past the cafeteria and out the front door, to where I knew not. If leaving the hospital was against medical advice, it was also against common sense—just one more thing Randy could show the court to have me locked up again.

#

"We've got some hard decisions to make, babe," Caitlin said once we were in the car heading west on Highway 74. "I know you're not up to it yet, but we'll have to make them soon. Right now I've just got to get you where we're going."

"Where *are* we going?"

"You'll see. All in due time, my dear."

Still drowsy from the pain meds, I settled back in my seat, closed my eyes, and fell asleep. When I opened them again, Caitlin was parking the car. The area looked familiar but slightly off, as if I was seeing it from the wrong angle. Then I spied the log cabin below the ridge to the right of where we sat.

"Rev. Jack's?" I asked.

"Yes—surprise." She grinned at me.

I grinned back. "So we're staying here?"

"For the time being you are."

I felt my smile fading. "But—what about you?"

Her eyes left my face. "I'll see you on the weekends, but I have things to do in Kingsville."

"Caitlin, no. Not by yourself. Not with everything that's happened."

She took my hand in hers. "There is no safety in numbers. That should be fairly obvious."

"There's no safety anywhere, but I'd feel better if we're together."

"I don't know of any other options we have."

I heard Winnie's bark then and saw her chugging up the path to where we were parked. I looked toward the cabin and saw Rev. Jack standing on the porch. He waved his hand in greeting. I waved back and got out of the car. Winnie wriggled her body and gave an excited yap. Feeling angry about the situation, but powerless to ameliorate it, I reached to pet her, but lost my balance, and fell to the ground beside the right passenger wheel well. Caitlin hoisted me into an upright position.

"Are you okay?" she asked.

Shrugging my arm out of her grasp, I muttered, "Yeah" and headed for the house, Winnie snuffling along behind me. I shook hands with Rev. Jack and he said, "Have a seat. Have a seat. John, I heard about what happened, and I've got to say I'm glad to see you and glad you're okay now."

I flopped down on the porch swing, happy to see the old man despite what my being here meant. Winnie whined and scratched at my ankles until Caitlin picked her up and put her beside me.

"Looks like Winnie's glad to see you, too," he said, as she slurped my face, then settled in my lap with a contented sigh. The little dog made me feel ridiculously loved.

"I'm jealous," Caitlin said pinching my arm.

"Then don't go off and leave me," I muttered, "or you might find yourself replaced."

She pinched my arm again, a little harder this time. "That little bitch isn't getting my man without a fight." She put her arm through mine and thumped the dog lightly on the rump. Winnie growled.

Rev. Jack stood and said, "If you all will excuse me a minute, I'm going to check on dinner. Miss Cait, are you going to be eating with us? I fixed my world-famous lasagna."

"I guess I need to get on the road. I've got to be at work at 7:30 in the morning for a staff meeting."

"You have a safe trip back then, you hear?" Rev. Jack went into the house, leaving us on the porch.

I squeezed her hand. "Please don't go yet," I begged. I couldn't stand the thought of being without her.

"I've got to, sexy." She leaned over and kissed me, her mouth lingering on mine until Winnie growled again, and Caitlin pulled away. "I'd say someone is smitten."

"Besides me?" I reached for Caitlin's chin, pulling her gently back to me, and returned her kiss in kind. Winnie jumped down from my lap and looked at me in an accusatory manner.

Caitlin patted my face. "Besides me."

Winnie and I followed her to the car, and I stood next to her door as she cranked the engine.

"Oh, I almost forgot," she said, digging in her purse. "Here's the debit card in case you need anything, and here's your cell phone and charger. Will you please keep it on and keep it charged so that I can reach you?"

If she only knew how much I hated telephones and how much she was asking of me to tie myself to one; but I promised her I would anyway, and with another kiss for me and blowing a razzberry to Winnie, she drove off. Winnie chased her to the end of the drive, barking ferociously.

"Come here, girl." I snapped my fingers. The little dog came flying back to me, her long ears flapping, and we returned to the house.

Rev. Jack was standing at the screen door looking out at us. "Supper's ready."

I had gotten out of the habit of eating at 5:00 PM when I'd left Broughton Hospital. Caitlin and I didn't usually eat until after 7:00 PM, so I wasn't particularly hungry, but the lasagna was good and there was a salad of fresh lettuce and vegetables with a homemade red wine vinaigrette dressing. Winnie curled up under the table by my feet while we ate, and when I got up to clear the dishes, she followed me from the table to the sink.

Rev. Jack looked amused. "I've never seen her take to anyone else the way she's taken to you."

"It's my magnetic personality," I said. "I attract women, children, small dogs. Killers."

"Speaking of killers, I guess that was pretty scary. Do the police have any idea who might have shot you?"

"I haven't talked to the police since it happened. Don't particularly care to talk to them—" I stopped mid-sentence, not sure how much he knew about me or my situation.

He nodded his head and sucked his teeth thoughtfully. "No, I don't suppose I would either, under the circumstances. No sir, and I don't know that there would be anything more upsetting than being falsely accused of something and knowing that some people believed it of you for no other reason than the fact that you were accused."

"Thanks for not judging me." I allowed my eyes to meet his.

"Not my place. No one's place but God's."

"Rev. Jack, I've got to tell you, I don't know if I believe in God."

He smiled at me. "Well now, that's okay, because He believes in you, and it appears He's not finished with you yet."

CHAPTER FIFTEEN

BY WEDNESDAY NIGHT my reprieve from the Voices was over and they were back in all their hateful glory. The vitriol they spewed, together with the unrelieved pain, made for a bad couple of days. In addition, I had an out-of-control beard, no schizo meds, and no other clothing. When I commented on the ripeness of my shorts and shirt, Rev. Jack found me an old t-shirt and a pair of boxers still in their packaging.

"They're a size 38-40 waist, so they'll swallow you whole, but I'll find you a safety pin. Just hang your clothes on the doorknob to your room and I'll get a load going in the washer before I go to bed."

"No, sir," I said. "Show me how to work the machines and I'll do it." So he showed me which buttons to push and where to find the laundry detergent and bid me good night. I started the washer then got my cell phone and went onto the front porch to call Caitlin.

She answered just before I thought the call would go to voice mail and I heard a bunch of noise in the background—laughter, music, people talking. "Hello?" She sounded distracted and distant.

The mental image I had of her at home getting ready for bed did an abrupt fade to black.

"*Hello*?" she said again.

"Hey," I managed to say, then, before I could stop myself, "Where the hell are you?"

"Hi, babe. I had to work over, but I'm glad you called."

"I've really missed you." At the same moment someone in the background on her end said her name. A male someone. I felt heat rush to my face.

I heard her laugh and then she said to me, "I'm sorry, John—what?"

"Caitlin, who is that and where are you?"

She said something else to the person on her end and then to me, "John, can I call you back in a little bit? I'm having trouble hearing right now."

I ended the call without replying and sat in the dark, my face burning and the Voices raging. An hour passed, then two. I checked the signal. Three bars, and the battery—fully charged. I continued to check until I fell asleep on the porch.

Winnie woke me the next morning licking my ankles. Rev. Jack was in the kitchen rattling around and the smell of coffee wafted through the screen door. I stretched my legs and stood. The pain in my side gave me a sharp reminder that it was still very much in residence and not amused about having slept in a chair. Winnie yapped at me as if saying, "Come on." She bounded down the steps, spinning around to look at me.

"Okay, I'm coming," I grumbled. It was very early morning, and I figured there would be no one else out and about to be offended by the sight of me in boxer shorts, so I followed her into the yard. She wasted no time in shooting off through the brush, chasing a squirrel down the path which led to Caitlin's cottage. My conversation with Caitlin of the previous evening began replaying itself in my head, tormenting me with thoughts of what she was doing and who she was doing it with. I allowed myself to become angry once more.

We came out on the trail near the dock in approximately the same place I had seen the figure the night of the party. Had the assailant shot me then, I knew the medics would never have reached me in time. If he'd been intent on killing me, why hadn't he done so when he stood a better chance?

At the cottage, an unfamiliar car was parked in the drive and some inflatable beach toys and floats leaned against the screen porch. An unreasonable jealousy seized me, and I longed to bang on the door and order the interlopers to leave. I could imagine another couple making love in the bed Caitlin and I shared, could see them sitting on the dock in the evening drinking wine together, swimming in my cove, enjoying my Utopia. I hated feeling displaced—in essence, a man without a country.

I took a step toward the cottage door, my fist raised to pound on it, but Winnie chose that moment to come zooming back like a torpedo, barking as if possessed, saving me from an embarrassing faux pas. I laughed at her until I had to rest against a tree to get my breath. She sat at my feet until I was able to continue, then pricking her ears and wagging her tail, she zipped down the trail to Rev. Jack's. I followed her, my chest on fire, and slowly climbed the steps to the porch. In addition to coffee, I now smelled bacon, and Rev. Jack called out, "It's breakfast if you're hungry."

"No, thanks. I'd like some coffee, though."

He handed me a mug and waited until I had taken a seat at the table before saying, "I put the clothes in the dryer when I got up, so they should be about dry. I'm going into Sylva this morning. You ought to consider coming with me. Get out and about a little while."

I was preparing to decline the offer, then thought better of it. "If you'll give me half an hour, I think I will come with you."

"No hurry."

I took my coffee into the bathroom, sipping it as I started the shower. The hot water helped ease some of the pain and I stood under it until I felt more human. Stepping out, I glimpsed my hair in the mirror and a plan came to me.

In my bedroom, I saw that Rev. Jack had placed my now clean clothes on the bed. They smelled and looked measurably better. I dressed and made sure I had the debit card in my pocket, and went to wait on the porch, Winnie taking her place next to me in the swing. When Rev. Jack came to the door with his keys in hand, Winnie jumped down and began an excited dance around his feet. "Sorry, little girl. You can't go on this trip." He bent to scoop her up. She tucked her tail between her legs, her brow furrowed.

I patted her on the head. "Sorry about that, girlfriend."

He popped her back in the house and locked the door, and we climbed into his old Buick station wagon, headed for Sylva.

"Do you know a place where I can get my hair cut?" I asked.

He laughed and rubbed his bald head. "Been a while since I needed a barber, but we'll find you some place. Need to make a stop at Walmart, too. I dislike that store, but I figure I can get most of what I need there, if that's all right with you."

"Yeah, that's fine. I can get what I need there, too."

When we stopped at his bank, I noticed a hair salon across the street, so I got out of the car and said, "While you do your business, I'll go over here and see if someone can help me." In the shop, there was a waiting area in an alcove to my right, which intersected one side of a long narrow room with booths running along the left wall, and a row of hair dryers facing the work stations. There were two women in different stages of having their hair colored or cut, a couple of female stylists, and one other woman under a hair dryer.

I figured the salon catered only to women and was turning to leave when I heard a door open and a voice saying, "Well, hello, sugar. How can I help you?"

I turned and saw a man slightly older than me, dressed in a tight t-shirt tucked into tight jeans, wearing loafers with no socks. He smiled happily.

"I need a haircut, but I don't have an appointment."

He walked closer and looked me up and down. "I can do you."

I heard snickering from the other side of the room and one of the stylists said, "Marco, behave yourself before you scare off the clientele."

Marco stuck out his tongue in her direction, then turned his attention back to me. "I *mean* I have an opening," he said and there was more tittering from the stylists' booths and a voice said, "Yeah, and he never gets it filled."

"Don't pay them any attention," Marco said. "Bunch of menopausal bitches."

I was ready to leave and stepped toward the door, but Marco grabbed my arm and steered me to his booth. He pointed to the chair and I sat while he took out a cape and fastened it around me. I was trapped.

"Now, then, sugar," he said, running his hands through my hair, "what are you wanting done? A trim? Something new? Although you have some *gorgeous* hair."

He continued playing, pulling a section here, pushing a section there until I gave a shudder and said, "I want something new—I'm just not sure what. And can you shape up the beard and mustache?"

He studied me a few more moments then clapped his hands, making me jump, and said, "Sugar, have I got the perfect look for you!"

Out came his scissors. I watched my hair falling to the floor, and was beginning to have regrets about the whole business when he put the scissors down and picked up a tube of gel. He squeezed some of the product into his hands and rubbed them together. "Now this is the key to the whole look," he said, and wiped the goo in what was left of my hair. He worked furiously, pulling segments in different directions until I was sure I resembled a frightened hedgehog. He had me turned away from the mirror, though, so I was unable to survey the damage.

"Okay," he said after he finished, "now let's work on that beard." He grabbed a set of clippers off the charging base and went at my face with entirely too much enthusiasm. Finally satisfied with his work, he took a step back and said, "Oh, sugar, that is the look for you."

He yanked off the cape and spun the chair around to the mirror. I did not recognize the person looking back at me.

"Damn," I said, and he laughed.

The stylist in the next booth said, "Marco, you've outdone yourself this time."

"Haven't I just." He gave her a high five before leading me up front to the register. "Don't suppose a good-looking thing like you is available for a date," he asked as I handed him my debit card.

"I hate to disappoint you, Marco, but I'm not bent that way at all." I thought about Caitlin and how funny she would find this whole episode, and then remembered my attempted conversation with her the night before and the male voice in the background, and wondered what she would think if she knew I had offers, too.

I reached to shake Marco's hand before leaving, but he came around the counter and put an arm on my shoulder. "Sugar, if you ever decide to bat for the home team, you be sure and let me know."

"You'll be the first person I call," I assured him.

"Oh, wait," he called as I opened the door. He picked up a tube of hair gel from the counter and placed it in my hands. "A little gift from me to you."

#

Rev. Jack was waiting on a bench outside the salon and looked me over before saying, "Well, now, I was about not to recognize you."

"I was about not to recognize me either." I sat down beside him and shook my head.

"You don't like it?" he asked.

"No, it's not that. But in addition to attracting women, children, small dogs, and killers, I also attract gay guys."

He laughed and slapped his leg. "Out of the five, I'd think the latter would be the least of your worries," and he laughed some more.

I watched him a moment and said, "You're not like any preacher I've ever met before."

"Maybe that's because I represent a God you've never met before."

"You're not going to preach at me are you, Rev. Jack?"

"No, sir. I've always believed in teaching by example, not telling people how they ought to act. If you want someone to exhibit love, mercy, and forgiveness, they have to experience it first." He got to his feet and fished his car keys out of his pocket.

I followed him across the street to the parking lot, and girded myself for our foray into Walmart. I have been known to hyperventilate when forced to enter that unholy domain, known more affectionately to Walmartians the planet over as Wallyworld, and I usually made Caitlin go without me. Of course that was in her best interests, since she enjoyed shopping and I couldn't abide more than thirty minutes in the place before I was ready to commit homicide and/or suicide. But there was no Caitlin to go in my stead today, and if I wanted clothes to wear or any other necessities, I was going to have to brave the front line.

"Thirty minutes," I told Rev. Jack, "that's all I can take of this place."

"That's about fifteen minutes more than I can stand it," he replied.

I grabbed a buggy and went in one direction, while he did likewise.

Unfortunately, I was unable to move through the store as quickly as I normally did. In the men's clothing department, I grabbed a couple pairs of cargo shorts, a pair of jeans, two t-shirts, a short-sleeve button up shirt, a pack of boxer shorts, and socks before heading to cosmetics, excusing my way through a couple of family reunions in the middle of the aisles, and picking up a beard trimmer, some shampoo, body wash, deodorant, toothpaste, and toothbrush.

You would think that even a twenty-eight-year-old man recovering from a gunshot wound would still be able to move faster than a seventy-something-year-old man, but when I reached the front register, Rev. Jack was sitting on a bench at the exit, his bagged purchases in his cart. He smiled at me and tapped his watch.

"That's not humanly possible," I told him as we loaded our stuff in the back of his station wagon. "Twenty-four minutes is my personal best on a good day. You must have super powers."

"The prospect of having to spend time in Walmart is a pretty powerful motivator."

"I like that," I said. "Maybe instead of sending people to prison, they should be forced to spend time in Walmart."

"I'm sure there would be a lower rate of recidivism in that case. You want to go get some lunch? Jimmy Mac's back in Bryson City makes a good country-style steak."

"I'll pass on the country-style steak, but I could freaking kill a BLT."

We ate lunch and headed to the lake. As we were carrying things in from the car, I heard "One Step Closer" by Linkin Park playing from somewhere in the vicinity of the porch and it took me several moments to realize it was the ringtone for my cell phone that I'd left behind. Of course it stopped ringing by the time I located it between the cushions of the chair where I'd fallen asleep the night before.

I unlocked it and saw a message informing me that I had fourteen missed calls. All from Caitlin. As I was looking at the screen, it rang again. Startled, I dropped it on the floor. The battery popped out and skittered off the end of the porch. By the time I found and reinstalled it and tried to call Caitlin back, her phone was going to voice mail. I seriously considered taking the damned thing and slinging it far out into the lake. I tried calling her for an hour with the same result, and when my phone finally rang again and it was her, I wasn't very nice.

"Why the hell didn't you call me back last night like you said you would? Where the hell were you and who were you with?"

There was a silence during which I thought the call had dropped, and I really was going to launch the thing into the woods, but then she said, "Is that why you didn't answer? Because you were mad about last night?"

I stalked off the porch and away from the cabin so Rev. Jack wouldn't hear me yelling and cursing. "You told me you'd call me back. You didn't. Who the fuck were you with, Caitlin?"

"John, I told you I had to work over."

"That's bullshit! What I heard wasn't working—"

"John, will you shut up for a minute?"

"Don't tell me to—"

"John! Are you listening to me? There's been another murder."

I shut up.

"Are you there?"

"Yeah." Now it was hard to speak above a whisper. Then a thought occurred to me. "But I have an alibi. Right? I've been here with Rev. Jack."

"I wish it were that simple, John, but the murder took place before you were shot." She sounded close to hysteria. "Jesus Christ, could this get any worse? Randy knows you're gone from the hospital. He's been blowing up my phone. The Sheriff's Department is blowing up my phone. Kingsville Public Safety is blowing up my phone. I'm coming up tomorrow night and there are some things we've got to talk about. Will you please, *please* keep your cell phone on in case I need you?"

"Sure," I said. "Sure." She hung up before I could tell her that I loved her, nor had she said that she loved me.

#

Even though I knew Caitlin wouldn't arrive before 8:30 PM at the earliest, I nevertheless began watching for her at 8:45. When I wasn't staring down the driveway, I was checking my cell phone signal and charge. At 9:30, I moved from the living room to the front porch. I tried calling her, but of course the call went straight to voice mail. If I had *ever* been able to reach her on the damned thing when I needed her, I didn't remember it.

Shortly after 10:00, I heard the rumble of thunder and a breeze blowing through the trees. At 10:30 it began sprinkling and lightning flashed behind the ridge above the cabin. I pulled my phone out of my pocket to call her again, but was afraid she would be driving through a downpour when it rang and wreck trying to answer it, so I didn't.

Rev. Jack came to the door and said, "No disrespect to Miss Cait, but Winnie and I are going to turn in for the night. I'll leave the lamps on here in the living room for you."

"She'll be sorry she didn't get to speak to you, but she'll understand. Good night." I was secretly glad he would probably be asleep when she got there, because I had some very specific plans for her that involved the removal of all her clothing.

Listening to the rain and wind, I inadvertently dozed off sometime after 11:00, and woke to her hand on my arm. I struggled to sit up, trying to pretend I hadn't been asleep. "What took you so long?" I asked, and yawned despite my effort.

She was staring at me and several moments passed before she was apparently able to speak. "Are you growing a *beard,* and—oh my God—what happened to your hair?"

"You don't like it?"

"No—it's not that I don't like it, but it's just such a transformation. If I'd passed you on the street, I wouldn't have known you." She bit her bottom lip. "I really liked your hair long."

"It'll grow back," I said, "but I thought it would be better if I was less recognizable as John Colucci."

She sat in my lap and leaned her head on my shoulder. "You may have a point."

We kissed and I ran my hands under her shirt, cupping her breasts. We remained that way a few minutes until she yawned and said, "I'm so tired. This has been the day from hell. I really need to go to bed."

So much for my plans. We went into the bedroom, where I watched as she undressed and slid under the covers. Climbing in beside her, I held her against me, aroused from the heat of her naked body. "You know how difficult it is to go to bed without you every night?"

"As difficult as it is for me?" she murmured, pressing her face against my chest. She was asleep in seconds, and I lay beside her, listening to her breathe, touching her hair, not sleeping myself. Toward dawn, as the sun was beginning to brighten the room, she stirred and reached for me, and I made love to her, our bodies and spirits reconnecting.

"You know," she said when we had finished and she was cradled in my arms, "that beard and mustache are beginning to grow on me."

I laughed. "I hope not. That would be kind of freaky—a wife with a beard."

She slapped my arm. "You know what I mean. And the more I think about it, the more I realize that your new look is perfect for what I wanted to talk to you about."

"Which is?"

"We need to petition to have your competency restored."

"Didn't Webster advise us against that?"

"Yes, but that was before Randy's threats to have you committed again. I talked to Webster this week. He prepared the paperwork, and I brought it with me. You'll have to sign it in front of a notary, then I'll take it back to him to file. There has to be a hearing on it within thirty days."

"And Randy and Laurie will be served with a copy?"

She smiled. "Oh yeah."

I smiled, too. "Maybe I can come home then. Let's go find a notary." I got out of bed and reached for my shorts.

"John, there's more."

I tilted my head back and closed my eyes. "Isn't there always?"

"Detectives Whisnant and Samuels came by the office yesterday afternoon right at five o'clock. That's why I was so late getting here. They wouldn't leave. They kept asking about you, wanting to know where you were. They're convinced you're the murderer."

"Of course they are." She didn't have to explain what this meant—they would be looking for anything to tie me to the crimes. Okay, so be it. "Let's do this thing."

She shot me a pensive look as she got up and began gathering her clothing and toiletries. "Are you okay with this? After—well, after what Webster said about making the state's job easier?"

"Yes, this is something I need to do. But just so you know, there won't ever be a second trial."

She stopped sifting through her overnight bag and peered at me. "What do you mean?"

I looked at my hands. "Just what I said. If it gets that far, there won't ever be a second trial. I finally have something good in my life, a reason for living. If there's a possibility that will be taken away from me, well, that's where it will end."

She dropped what she was holding and came over to me. "You'd better not be talking about suicide."

This time I met her gaze and watched her eyes widen and her lips form a tight line.

Her arms went around me, and she held me crushed against her. "We can never allow it to get that far." She put her palm against my cheek. "Which means we're going to have to find out for ourselves who's doing this, and brings me to the next thing I wanted to discuss with you. How well do you know Peter Barrington?"

"Oh, no, Cait. This is dangerous."

"How could it possibly be any more dangerous than it already has been? How well do you know Peter?"

"I get the feeling I don't know him as well as I'm going to."

She gave me one of her impish little grins. "Ding, ding ding—we have a winner, folks. Very soon he's going to become your new best bud." She grabbed my hand and pulled me toward the shower. "But first we're going to have your competency restored."

We showered together, ate breakfast with Rev. Jack, then Caitlin and I headed into Sylva in search of a notary public, not an easy person to find on a Saturday. After searching close to four hours, we did finally locate one at a used car lot and she agreed to notarize the documents for me. If she paid any attention to the nature of the document, she didn't let on. I showed her my ID and she made a photocopy of it, then had me sign, affixed her notary seal, and we were done in fifteen minutes.

"That was rather anti-climactic," I said as we got back in the car.

"Just look at it as climbing the first rung of the ladder," she replied.

"May I live to reach the top."

"Amen, brother."

When we returned to the cabin, Rev. Jack's station wagon was gone and Caitlin and I took full advantage of his absence to participate in some vigorous bedroom activity, after which we walked down to the water frontage of his property. His place did not boast much of a beach, nor a dock or boathouse, and I couldn't help but compare it, unfavorably, to what I now thought of as "our" cottage. She went for a dip while I sat on a large rock that jutted into the water. I missed my swims but my breath was still too hard to come by and the pain too easy.

Caitlin made her garlic chicken for supper that night and we all ate on Rev. Jack's back deck, Winnie's pointy nose resting on my foot. I wished the weekend could go on forever, but it was over too soon and Caitlin returned to Kingsville.

CHAPTER SIXTEEN

SHE CALLED TUESDAY NIGHT while I was sitting on the porch with Rev. Jack listening to the crickets, whippoorwills, and screech owls before turning in for bed. I actually had my phone in my pocket for a change.

"Hey, sexy," she said. "We filed your petition today and it was delivered to the Sheriff's Department for service on Laurie and Randy. Second rung on the ladder."

"I'd love to be a fly on the wall when they get it," I said.

"Wouldn't you just? The hearing date is set for two weeks from Friday. I'll come down that Thursday to get you. You know the Clerk will probably order a multi-disciplinary evaluation and then there'll have to be another hearing after that."

"What's a multi-disciplinary evaluation? That sounds a little scary."

"It's not. It just means that you'll just be examined by a physician, a psychologist, and a social worker."

"You know how much I hate doctors."

"I know, but it's the third rung of the ladder. Keep your eyes focused on the top."

"Okay, I'm trying."

I was so eager for something positive to happen and so ecstatic about the prospect of being reunited with Caitlin, I thought the Friday of the hearing would never arrive, but when it did, I was inexplicably terrified. What if they denied my petition? Where would that leave us?

That morning I trimmed my beard and even remembered to use Marco's hair goo. Dressed in my suit, I made sure my tie was straight and there were no scuffs on my shoes, and went into the living room in search of Caitlin. "I'm as ready as I'll ever be," I said.

"I'll say you are," she grinned. "My God, you look handsome."

"I am so nervous," I held out my hands to show her how badly they were shaking.

She took them in hers and squeezed. "Don't be. Remember, this is the third step. You'll do just fine."

When we arrived at the courthouse, there were no parking places close by, so she dropped me off at the entrance and then went to park the car. I immediately noticed Randy slouching on a bench outside the Clerk's office. He glanced in my direction, his eyes sliding over me briefly before focusing on something else. His head then snapped back around and he sat up on the bench.

"I'll be damned," he said to me. "You clean up pretty good."

"Thanks." I was wary, it being my experience that he never gave anything to me with one hand that he didn't take away with the other. He didn't disappoint.

"Too bad it won't do you any good."

I was about to tell him to fuck himself but decided now was as good a time as any to stop rising to his taunts. I was relieved to see my attorney coming down the hall toward us. Webster nodded to Randy. "Officer Kimbell."

Randy tipped his head at Webster but said nothing. Neither offered to shake the other's hand.

Webster smiled at me and said, "John, you're looking great. Married life's apparently agreeing with you." I could see Randy chafing at this comment, but for once he kept his big mouth closed.

Caitlin entered the courthouse followed a few minutes later by Laurie, and Webster said, "If you all will come with me, we'll go ahead into the Clerk's hearing room."

I wasn't sure what I was expecting, but the room contained only two small tables and eight chairs. Caitlin, Webster and I sat on one side of the room, leaving Randy and Laurie to sit on the other. The Clerk of Court entered, introducing herself as Anne Jenkins. She sat behind one of the tables and opened the file she'd brought with her, flipping through the papers. "So, Mr. Colucci, you've filed a motion for the restoration of your competency?"

She looked up at me and I said, "Yes, ma'am."

"And as you've obviously retained Mr. Webster as your attorney, we can proceed with this hearing. Mr. Colucci, you allege in your motion that you now possess the capacity to conduct your own affairs, and to make important decisions regarding your person, your family, and property. Please explain to me what has changed since you were declared incompetent in December, 2004."

Where to start? I told her of my release from Broughton Hospital in January with Dr. Fremont's blessing, that I had been taking my medication on a regular basis (which wasn't technically a lie, since I took it when I had access to it), that I was able to manage money (again technically not a lie, although it was Caitlin's money), that I shopped, cooked, that I managed my own personal needs, that I saw to my own health care (okay, this was bordering on an outright lie), and that I had been married.

Here Randy couldn't keep his mouth shut anymore. He snorted and said, "It's a voidable marriage, and she's leading him around by his cock."

Webster shot forward in his chair. "Officer Kimbell, that is uncalled for!"

At the same time the Clerk said, "Officer Kimbell, you'll have your chance to speak in a minute."

Always one to have the last word, Randy sneered, "Just saying," which prompted Webster to say, "*Kimbell*," in a warning tone.

My face was on fire and I clenched my fists. Caitlin rubbed my knuckles, and whispered, "Third rung."

The Clerk returned her attention to me and said, "Is that all Mr. Colucci?"

"Yes, ma'am."

To Randy, she said, "Now, Officer Kimbell. I take it you have objections to the motion, but please keep your comments civil."

With relish, he listed all my faults and problems, throwing in the legal trouble I had encountered for good measure. He also added, "My wife and I feel that he is being taken advantage of by Caitlin Murphy and that he's incapable of protecting himself from exploitation. Furthermore, Ms. Murphy's been writing a series of articles for *The Kingsville Herald* that have endangered him. He was shot and very nearly killed just three weeks ago. He left the hospital against medical advice and nobody's known where he was until today."

Ms. Jenkins said, "Is this true, Mr. Colucci?"

If looks could have killed, I would have murdered Randy right then and there. I could feel my heart sinking, dragging my hopes with it. "Ma'am, it's true that I was shot and that I left the hospital against medical advice, and the reason I did so is because Randy—*Officer Kimbell*—threatened to have me involuntarily committed again. Caitlin is not exploiting me. Officer Kimbell has harassed us both and has quite simply made my life a living hell."

At this point, Laurie left the room, a tissue pressed against her face. Randy's face was a thundercloud ready to unleash a storm.

"And what about the pending charges you have against you?" the Clerk asked.

"One charge is assault on a government official—Officer Kimbell—which came about after he threatened me. He's bullied me ever since I was released from the hospital, and I snapped. I admit that I hit him and he hit me in return. The other charges are traffic related—"

"DWI and assault on a female," Randy interjected.

"Both of which are a huge misunderstanding," I continued. "I wasn't impaired and I didn't assault Caitlin."

Randy was cranking up again. "What he's *not* telling you is that the Sheriff's Department is looking at him for—"

Webster stood up. "Kimbell, you'd better be damned careful what comes out of your mouth next, or you'll be looking at some legal trouble of your own."

I would never have believed it possible, but Randy was completely and utterly silent.

The Clerk looked at each of us, waiting, then said, "Gentlemen, if that's all, here's what we're going to do. I will order that Mr. Colucci participate in a multi-disciplinary evaluation, with a report submitted to me within two weeks from today, at which time we will conclude our hearing."

Webster stood to address her, saying, "Madame Clerk, if it pleases you, we would also ask that Mr. and Mrs. Kimbell provide an accounting of Mr. Colucci's estate on that date."

"So ordered. Officer Kimbell, you'll have that accounting to us then, please."

Randy slammed out of the room and was nowhere in sight when we stepped into the hallway.

Webster shook my hand. "You did fine, John. You'll need to go ahead and schedule that evaluation at Kings County Behavioral Health Care and be here Friday after next at 10:00 AM."

Once in the car, I closed my eyes, leaned back against the headrest, and said, "Well, that was quite humiliating."

Caitlin cranked the car engine. "Randy is, without question, the biggest asshole I have ever had the misfortune of meeting." She leaned over to kiss my cheek, "But guess what?"

I opened an eye. "What?"

"We're on the third rung of the ladder, and we're getting ready to climb to the fourth."

The following Wednesday morning, I presented myself at Kings County Behavioral Health Center for my appointment; however, the evaluation was more excruciating than I had imagined it would be. A nurse took my vital signs and weighed me, recorded my height. The doctor then had me strip down to my undershorts to examine me, commenting on the bullet wound. He put the stethoscope against my chest and listened to my heart and lungs, saying, "I take it you're still having some shortness of breath." When I replied in the affirmative, he said, "What kind of follow up care are you receiving? Any type of respiratory therapy?"

Damn. "Uh, no."

"Hmm." He made a note on the laptop computer he'd brought into the examination room. "What medications are you taking?"

That, at least, I could answer confidently. "Thorazine. Twenty-five milligrams, three times a day." Usually.

He interrogated me for another twenty minutes before telling me I could get dressed and passing me off for the psychological evaluation, which took forever. The psychologist asked a million questions, then pulled out a bunch of test forms until I told her there was no way I could read the instructions, at which point she had to scratch around for alternative tests for morons like myself. When we finished, I was hungry and cranky and felt as if my brain were bleeding.

Then the social worker got her claws in me. She inquired about my past, my childhood, employment (or lack thereof), education, finances, legal issues, and my psychiatric history. The more information she demanded, the more dispirited I felt. It was after 5:00 PM by the time Caitlin picked me up, and I had a headache from hell.

"Bless your heart," she said when I got in the car. "Was it that bad?"

"There is *nothing,* absolutely *nothing* those people don't know about me now. I feel like I've been gang raped."

"I'd say you need a drink."

"I need more than one."

#

I couldn't sleep the night before the second hearing. I lay down in bed with Caitlin, but once she was out, I went back in the living room and switched on the TV, hoping to obliterate my fears. It didn't work. I rolled around on the couch thinking of all the worst case scenarios and driving myself crazier. I hadn't discussed any of my concerns with Caitlin, but I was afraid that she would see me as less of a man if my competency wasn't restored, and that Randy would then make good on his threat to have the marriage annulled.

I was already showered and dressed, sitting at the kitchen table, when she came in yawning. "Why are you up so early?"

"I couldn't sleep."

"Do you want me to fix something for breakfast?"

My stomach roiled at the thought of food. "No. No, thanks. Do you want me to make something for you?"

She came over to stand behind me and kneaded my shoulder muscles. "No, I don't want you to get anything on that suit. Babe, you need to relax. Everything's going to be okay."

"How can you possibly know that?"

"Because whatever happens, it's not going to change us. We'll just regroup and go at it a different way. Now let me get ready." She kissed the top of my head and headed for the bathroom.

By the time we got to the courthouse, I was close to being a basket case, and when Caitlin offered to drop me at the entrance, I told her that we would walk in together. I wasn't in the frame of mind to deal with Randy on my own. Of course, his hateful ass was the first person I saw when we came through the door. He and Laurie were accompanied by a man in a suit, who was obviously an attorney. I felt sick.

Randy gave me his customary nod and sneer. "John. Caitlin."

I looked around for Webster but didn't see him, so I pulled Caitlin down the hall toward the hearing room. There was a group of people standing around the doorway and it took me a moment to recognize them all—Rev. Jack, Dr. Fremont, Edie and Pat from the diner, Sandy, Jennifer and Mackenzie from the party, and Caitlin's editor, Will Lackey. Caitlin gave my arm a squeeze and said, "I told you—everything's going to be okay."

I couldn't believe that they had shown up to support me and for a moment I was touched. Then, when I thought of all the nasty things Randy and his attorney would be saying about me, I was equally horrified. I felt my hands trembling and I stuck them in my trouser pockets so that no one would notice.

Ms. Jenkins, the Clerk of Court, opened the door to the hearing room and, seeing all the people, said, "We may have to move this to the magistrate's courtroom. Let me make sure it's not in use. I'll be right back, folks." She then returned and told us all to follow her to a small-scale courtroom. I could feel myself starting to hyperventilate and my chest began throbbing. While everyone else filed into the room, Caitlin motioned me to one side of the door.

"Get a grip on it, babe," she whispered. "Fourth rung on the ladder."

"I missed a rung. I thought this was the third."

"No, the third was the evaluation. This is the fourth. We're getting closer to the top."

Webster came trotting up behind us. "There you are." He glanced in the room. "Who are all these people?"

"Witnesses for John," Caitlin said.

Webster looked in the room again and his mouth twisted. "I see Kimbell's got Harry Jablonski involved.

My stomach clenched and I broke out in a sweat. "I take it that's a bad thing?"

"I'll put it this way—it's not a *good* thing."

The Clerk beckoned us into the room and shut the door. "Ladies and Gentlemen, I take it you're all here for Mr. Colucci's hearing?" There were murmurs of assent, and she opened her file and began shuffling the papers inside. "Before we get started, I want to make it clear that this proceeding will be conducted in a civil manner." She looked pointedly at Randy. He gave her a smarmy smile in return.

"I have here the report from the multi-disciplinary evaluation, which I will share with the parties in just a moment. Mr. Kimbell, do you have the accounting for Mr. Colucci's estate?"

Jablonski stood up and said, "Madame Clerk, it may take a few more weeks for Mr. Kimbell's accountant to have that ready. We would therefore request a continuance of this hearing until such time that we can have that available for the court."

Webster stood also. "We would object to a continuance and ask that the Respondents produce what they have at this time."

"I'm not going to continue the hearing, Mr. Jablonski. Please produce what you have."

Jablonski handed up a sheaf of papers, which the Clerk glanced over. She placed one copy in the file and handed a copy to Webster. Webster reviewed the document and I saw his eyebrows raise a fraction.

Jablonski said, "You understand that is preliminary, and the actual amount is subject to change."

Webster replied, "We'll expect the final accounting within thirty days."

"Thirty days, Mr. Jablonski," the Clerk said. "Now, we will proceed with the hearing. Mr. Colucci, Mr. Webster, I understand you have some witnesses to call?"

"We call Rev. Jack Woodrow," Webster replied.

Rev. Jack came forward and took a seat across from the Clerk. In response to the questions from the two attorneys and the Clerk, he stated the length of time he'd known me, the length of time he'd known Caitlin, described his observations on my ability to care for myself, his opinion on my ability to manage money, and whether or not I appeared to be exploited. He didn't falter, nor did he become flustered, even under Jablonski's thinly-veiled badgering. They went through each of the other witnesses in pretty much the same manner.

Webster then asked the Clerk to excuse all of the witnesses except for Dr. Fremont. "Since we may be covering information protected by HIPPA, I think it would be best to have everyone else step out of the room."

The Clerk thanked those witnesses and dismissed them, and Dr. Fremont came forward. Webster and Jablonski started with the same questions they'd asked the other witnesses, but once those were out of the way, Jablonski jumped on him with both feet.

"Why was Mr. Colucci in Broughton Hospital, Dr. Fremont?"

"He had been diagnosed with undifferentiated-type schizophrenia, manifesting both positive and negative aspects of the disorder, and had a history of non-compliance with regard to his treatment and medication. At the time he came to the hospital, he was in the throes of an acute psychotic episode."

"But was there a precipitating event, something specific that brought him there?" Jablonski asked, knowing damned well there was.

"Again, sir, he was diagnosed with schizophrenia and was suffering an acute psychotic episode."

Jablonski tried for at least fifteen minutes to get Dr. Fremont to say that I had been committed to Broughton Hospital because I had murdered and molested children. Fremont would only say, "He was there because he was extremely ill. That's why we were treating him."

I remembered how frustrated I had been with him when he'd responded in kind to a similar question I had asked, and realized I was developing a new-found respect for him. He'd treated me for an illness; he would not brand me a murderer or child molester. He left that job to the courts, the press, and the public, all of whom were quite eager to do so. In his refusal to label me, he'd shown compassion.

Jablonski eventually gave up on that tack and Dr. Fremont continued his testimony under Webster's questioning. "I'm sorry to learn that John's relationship with his brother-in-law has been so acrimonious. Continued exposure to that type of environment would have a very negative impact on his mental health. In fact, he expressed a good deal of apprehension about living with his sister and brother-in-law when we discussed his release. At the time, there were no other options available to him. Now, apparently, there are." Here he smiled at Caitlin. "So, I would posit that, even were Madame Clerk inclined to deny the request for his competency to be restored, perhaps Mr. and Mrs. Kimbell are not the appropriate persons to act as his guardians."

When Dr. Fremont finished, Jablonski waved his hand in a dismissive gesture and said, "I have nothing further."

After he left the room, the Clerk opened her folder and handed out copies of the report. I didn't bother opening mine, but Caitlin grabbed hers and began scanning it. I watched her, trying to gauge whether it contained good news or bad. After several agonizing moments, she turned to the last page and her hand came up to cover her mouth. A tear slid down her cheek, and I closed my eyes, feeling the white-hot burn of shame. Sweat coursed down my back.

The Clerk cleared her throat and said, "As you can see, the multi-disciplinary team has examined Mr. Colucci and assessed his ability to manage his own affairs in the areas of residential needs, health care, financial matters, legal matters, and general community living." She flipped through each page as she spoke. "After reviewing the evaluation, it is my opinion that Mr. Colucci has demonstrated satisfactory ability in these areas. Furthermore, I've heard nothing here today that contradicts those findings. Therefore, I will order Mr. Colucci's competency restored."

I heard Randy snarl, "What a load of horseshit," as he stormed from the room, but Caitlin's arms were around me, and I could feel her tears on my neck.

Webster leaned over to shake my hand. "Congratulations, John." He handed me another paper. "Look this over when you get home. Don't forget, you've got court on that assault on government official charge next Monday, and we'll need to talk soon about your other cases, so give my office a call to set up an appointment."

I folded the paper and put it in my suit coat pocket. I shook his hand, while Caitlin hugged him, and then we went to Caitlin's favorite bar, where I drank an entire bottle of muscadine wine on my own.

#

The next hurdle—or to use Caitlin's analogy, the next rung on the ladder—was to face up to the charge for assaulting Randy.

Caitlin dropped me off in front of the courthouse that Monday morning. I felt like the place was becoming my new home.

"I'm sorry I can't stay with you," she said, "but I can't take off work today. Walk over to the office when you're finished to let me know what happens."

I think every other citizen of Kings County must have had court that morning, too, and the place was like Broughton Hospital during a full moon, only without the padded rooms and medication. I stood in line for twenty minutes for my turn to walk through the metal detector. The courtroom was jam packed, people crowded onto the benches and standing two or three deep all around the perimeter. I was one of the lucky ones who had to stand.

The air conditioning in the place was faulty at best. It had to be eighty-five degrees—and me wearing a freaking suit and tie. I tried to remember if I'd used any deodorant that morning and then decided it wouldn't matter if I had, since several people around me hadn't bathed in a while. Two more smelly armpits weren't going to matter a whole lot. I hadn't seen so many wretched people gathered in one place since leaving Broughton. Fortunately for me, the docket was called in alphabetical order, so I didn't have as long to wait.

The Assistant District Attorney called my name, and Webster stood and beckoned me forward. Randy and a group of other officers were already sitting on the bench behind the ADA. All of them stared at me as I took a seat beside Webster.

The ADA put Randy on the stand and asked him to describe the assault, the extent of his injuries, and the cost of his medical treatment. Then Webster got a turn at him.

"Officer Kimbell, what took place immediately prior to this alleged assault?"

"John and I were talking."

"Talking? Not yelling? You weren't deliberately provoking him? You didn't threaten to give him—" Webster consulted his legal pad, "—a 'major ass whipping'?"

"I remember John yelling, but then he tends to do a lot of that." There was snickering around the courtroom, most notably from Randy's pals on the bench behind the ADA. "And no, I don't remember threatening to whip his ass or provoking him."

"Yet you remember that he was yelling."

"Well, like I said—"

"Yeah, we get it," Webster said, "he tends to yell a lot. Tell me, did you hit him?"

"After he punched me in the face and broke my nose, yeah, I hit him."

"Have you ever hit him before? Ever given him a reason to think you might hit him?"

Randy squirmed a little. "I don't remember."

"And you say that this alleged assault took place in your home. Were you on duty, Officer Kimbell?"

Randy got quiet and still in his chair. "I had just gotten home."

"Well, now that doesn't really answer the question, does it? Were you on duty, Officer Kimbell?"

"No, sir, I had just gotten home at the end of my shift. I was off duty."

Webster put down his pen. "I don't have any more questions for Officer Kimbell."

Randy stepped down and the ADA called me to the stand.

"You've had some significant mental health issues, haven't you, Mr. Colucci? Spent eight years in Broughton Hospital?" Nothing like having your deepest, darkest secrets made known to half the general population.

"Objection," said Webster. "We're not getting into HIPPA protected information here without clearing the courtroom."

The judge said, "Sustained. We're not getting into that Mr. Dalton."

"Mr. Colucci, did you strike Officer Kimbell in the face, breaking his nose?"

"I hit him in the face, yes," I said. "I was provoked—he's hit me before—and I hit him first this time. I thought I broke his nose, but I don't know for a fact that I did." I was so hot and so nervous that my shirt was stuck to my body and it was for damned sure that my suit would have to be dry-cleaned before I could wear it again.

ADA Dalton looked satisfied with himself. "I don't have any further questions."

Webster shifted in his seat and said, "Nor do I."

I was excused from the stand and Dalton gave his closing statement, asking the judge to find me guilty of assault on a government official. Webster then said, "I would ask Your Honor to dismiss this charge against Mr. Colucci. My client admits that he did strike Officer Kimbell after being provoked and intimidated; however, Kimbell was not acting in his capacity as a public safety officer, nor was he even on duty at the time of the assault."

The judge was fanning his face with a handful of papers, and said, "We're going to take a thirty minute break, while I try to find someone to look at the air conditioner before we all melt."

I walked outside with the rest of the losers and bummed a cigarette. I'd hoped a smoke would have a calming effect, but it only made it harder for me to breathe, which made me that much more anxious. I crushed it out after a few drags. It was ninety-five degrees even standing in the shade, and we were all nice and ripe by the time the break was up and we trooped in once more. I knew I would reek of smoke and sweat by the time I made it back to Caitlin's office, provided I didn't go to jail.

Once everybody was situated in the courtroom, the judge addressed me. "Mr. Colucci, I don't want what I'm about to say to give you the idea that you've gotten away with something, or that it is ever acceptable to strike anyone, but as the state has charged you with assault on a government official who wasn't on duty or acting in his capacity as a public safety officer, then I'm going to dismiss these charges. However, I think you and your attorney will agree that it wouldn't be in your best interests to show up in my courtroom again on a similar charge.

I was so relieved that it didn't occur to me until I walked out of the courthouse, that I still had one assault charge to go. I prayed it would be in front of a different judge.

Pushing through the front door and onto the sidewalk, I removed my jacket and pulled off my tie. I was rolling up my shirtsleeves, when who should I see standing next to the building, but Randy?

He sidled up to me and said in a low voice, "I ought to take you behind the courthouse and beat your ass."

"Let's go," I said, gesturing to the steps leading to the rear parking lot.

He waved a hand at me. "Don't even think I'm going to give you another reason to run tell your attorney how abusive I've been to you." And he did what a lot of bullies do when someone stands up to them. He walked away.

I thought for a second about going after him, but he had the home advantage. I wouldn't put it past him and the Sheriff's Department to have concocted a scheme to provoke me into another assault so they would have an additional reason to hold and question me. When I saw Detectives Whisnant and Samuels walk out of the courthouse and start in my direction, I was convinced of this theory.

Whisnant held out his hand and said, "John, how're you doing?"

I didn't offer him mine. "What do you want?"

"Still just need to talk to you, find out what you might know about those murders."

"Leave me alone. I don't know anything." I tried to walk away but Samuels stepped into my path.

"We're close to being able to make an arrest. Talk now while you can still make a difference for yourself. Once we arrest you, we're done listening and we're done dealing."

I held out my wrists to him. "Arrest me, then. I don't have anything to say to you."

I became aware of a third man in a suit walking toward us, and I knew from the look of him that he was also a cop. It was going to be another gang bang with me as the honoree.

As he came abreast of us, he nodded to Whisnant and Samuels. "John Colucci?" he asked me.

"What do *you* want?" I was tired of all of them.

"Sir, I'm Detective Pendergrass with Kingsville Public Safety. We're investigating the shooting where you were injured, and I just needed to ask you some questions about that. I've been trying to reach you for a couple of weeks now and saw on the docket that you had court today, so I thought I'd take a chance on finding you here."

"Lucky me." I looked at Whisnant and Samuels, hoping they would get the message and leave. No such luck—they both looked very interested and they were sticking around for the show.

"You were shot?" Whisnant asked.

I snorted. "How can that have escaped your notice, with the two of you up my ass all the time? You call yourselves detectives?"

Samuels crossed his arms and leaned against the building. "Well, now, tell us about this."

I was determined to say nothing, but Pendergrass was more than happy to share all the gory details with them.

"Sounds like someone's pretty pissed off with you," Whisnant commented.

"Ya think?"

"You might want to reconsider your refusal to talk to us. If someone is after you, we might be able to help. The next bullet might catch you in the head."

"At which point, you won't know any more than you do now, and I'd be a whole lot better off," I said to Whisnant. And to Pendergrass, "If you want to talk, call my wife and give her a date and a time. Now, if you all will excuse me, I am about to burn the freak up." I walked away from them and managed the six blocks to Caitlin's office without being accosted by any more cops.

When I stepped into the bullpen at the newspaper, Caitlin got up from her desk and came over to hug me, then pulled away, frowning at my damp shirt. "You're sweaty."

"It's ninety-five degrees out there. Eighty-five in the courtroom. This suit is toast."

She pinched her nose closed. "I'll say. So tell me, how did it go?"

I couldn't help but grin. "The judge dismissed the charge."

She squealed and then yelled across the room, "Hey guys, the judge dismissed the charge!"

Clapping, shouts, and whistles went up all around, and Will Lackey came to the door of his office and looked out. "Who authorized you slackers to stop working?"

"The judge dismissed John's charges," Caitlin yelled to him and pumped her fist in the air.

"Great!" He waved me over and said, "That's good news, John. How've you been?"

"Good, although if I never see another courtroom again, it'll be too soon."

"I didn't get a chance to tell you congratulations the other day after your competency hearing. I'm pleased that went well for you. I told you, Caitlin's like a pit bull when she gets her teeth into a story. You've know, you've been really good for her."

I couldn't imagine any scenario in which I would have been good for Caitlin, but nodded and said, "She's been really good for me, too. I couldn't have done any of this without her. I don't even know where I would be if it weren't for her—probably back in Broughton."

Caitlin came up to us, her purse tucked under her arm. "If it's all right, Will, I'm going to take an early lunch."

"Sure, sure. Go celebrate." He patted my shoulder. "Take care, John."

Caitlin slid her arm through mine. "Do you want to go home to eat or go out somewhere?"

I looked down at my still damp shirt, "Are you brave enough to take me to a restaurant smelling the way I do?"

"Maybe we'd better eat at home."

"Yeah, that's what I thought."

At the apartment, she fixed lunch while I went to shower. We ate sitting next to each other on the couch while we listened to *The Heroin Diaries Soundtrack*. When she was getting ready to go back to work, I said, "By the way, can you take my suit by the dry cleaners? If it doesn't go today, we might as well burn it."

"As much as that suit cost? I don't think so. Grab it for me and I'll drop it off."

I brought it to her and she went through the pockets to make sure I hadn't left anything in them. She pulled a folded paper out of the inside coat pocket and opened it. "John, what is this?"

"It's something Webster handed me at the competency hearing the other day."

"You haven't looked at it?"

"I forgot about it until just now. What is it?"

"It's your estate accounting from Randy."

"And? What does it say?"

"It says you are the proud owner of $250,000 and a house located at 2526 Windflower Lane. No wonder Randy had such a hard-on for you to come back to them. They're living in your house."

CHAPTER SEVENTEEN

LATER THAT EVENING, I went into the spare bedroom where Caitlin had her home office set up. As usual, she was on the computer, with my discovery files open. I went over to kiss the top of her head and saw that she was playing the video of my initial arrest. It was like trying to look away from a really horrific car crash—I knew it wouldn't be pretty, but I stared anyway.

The camera was placed slightly above my head, pointed down. I saw my nineteen-year-old self on the screen and felt my gut tighten at the expression of terror on my face. A terror I now remembered well.

I'm alone again. They all file out of the room together, leaving me sitting here at the table to contemplate just how much shit I'm in. I think about my mother. She has no idea where I am—not that she ever does lately. I can't stand to be at home by myself, so I walk the streets. She tells me frequently, "If you keep refusing to take your medication and keep hanging around that part of town, something bad will happen. You're going to end up in trouble." And she's right.

Oh my God—oh my God. They think I killed a child. I found the doll; I rocked the doll; I wept over the doll. But I didn't kill a child. Did I? No, no, no. I didn't. I didn't. Jesus Christ, I can't think with all the Voices rioting. Time slips away from me. I start out each day with twenty-four hours, and then something happens to them. They disappear without warning, and I disappear with them. My thoughts jump from one subject to the next, often without my finishing the first one. I laugh when everyone else cries and cry when everyone else laughs. I become enraged over things that shouldn't matter. I withdraw into myself more and more. And now I've committed a murder. Or have I? How can I know for sure when the organ I use to determine reality from fiction is diseased?

I put my head in my hands and rock. Scared, scared, scared. This is a nightmare. Any minute I'll wake up, look around my bedroom in relief, roll over and go back to sleep to have a different nightmare. I close my eyes and open them again. Still the same room.

Murder, murder, murder. I'm a murderer. Oh my God. If only I'd listened to my mother, to Laurie. If only I hadn't been born. If only my father hadn't been born. If only my parents hadn't met. If only that one sperm hadn't met up with that one egg, then I never would have been. The state murders murderers, don't they? I'm a murderer. Therefore, the state will murder me.

The cops will be back any minute now to yell at me some more. Tell me what a piece of shit I am, how much trouble I'm in. They'll put me in jail; I'll never see my home, my mother, my sister again. I rock back and forth, back and forth, back and forth. If I can rock fast enough or long enough, it'll all go away and I'll be back home in my bedroom, listening to my music, my mother in the kitchen making supper. But no, she's usually at work in the evenings now. She has to work two jobs—ever since my fucking father committed fucking suicide. Bastard left us all behind. I'll be by myself. Always by myself. Always. I've scared away all the people who've been my friends. There's no one left to care. The rages, talking out loud to the Voices, repeating words and phrases over and over, over and over, over and over. Or talking about one thing and suddenly switching topics in mid-stream. I can follow the thread—why can't they?

And the medication. If I don't take it, the Voices shriek and bellow, rant and rave, until I'm doing the same. If I do take it, the side effects make me just as crazy.

"What is wrong with you, John?" The girl I was dating doesn't return my phone calls any more. What is wrong with me? What is wrong with me? What is wrong with me? I'm batshit crazy. Going off the deep end. Losing touch. Freaking out. AWOL. Fucking nuts.

Child murderer. Child molester. Child murderers, child molesters don't fare too well in prison. They're the most despicable of the despised. Despised. Despicable. Desperate. Desperately despicable murderer. Child-molesting, child murderer. Laughing now. Know I shouldn't be. Oh my God, how could anything, anything, ANYTHING about this be funny? Laughing harder, then, just as inexplicably, crying once more. Adding insult to injury and humiliation to shame, I feel a warm wetness at my crotch. I begin banging the table with my head.

I am so fucked. Bang. Bang. Bang. I am so fucked. Bang. Bang. Bang.

The door opens and Peter comes into the room. He avoids the puddle of urine and squats down beside the chair on which I'm sitting, puts his hand on my back. "Dude, get a grip."

I stop banging my head and look at him. "What's gonna happen to me? What are they gonna do to me?"

"Right now we're gonna get you to the restroom, get you cleaned up. Come on." He grips my arm, pulls me to my feet, walks me to the men's room. Another officer hands me an orange jumpsuit.

They bring me back into the interview room. The rest of them are there. The urine has been mopped up and the room smells strongly of disinfectant cleaner. Randy is watching me with more than his usual expression of disgust. I put my head in my hands. I can't look at him, at them. I can't.

"Why don't you tell us what happened?" one of the detectives asks.

Eyes closed, I have to try a couple of times before I can make my throat work. "The doll was broken when I found it."

"So, we're back to the damned doll again. If you're trying to set yourself up for an insanity defense, you're going to have to do a lot better than that. You just need to admit that you murdered that boy and this will all be over. Tell us what we need to know and you can go home."

I'm drowning in a sea of terror and I hang onto those words like a lifeline. Tell them what they need to know and I can go home. It will all be over. I'm crying again. "I killed him," I whisper. "I choked him until he stopped breathing."

"Did you have sex with him?"

I open my eyes. They are all staring at me. There is complete silence in the room. Disgust, hatred, loathing—I feel them like knife blades against my skin, preparing to slice me apart. The thought of sex with any child is repulsive to me, but the promise of home is strong. What am I supposed to tell them? What is the answer that will allow me to go home?

"Yes."

Randy rushes at me again, but Peter and the detective stop him before he can reach me. They're pushing him out of the room, telling him to go home. I've told them what they want to know; I want to go home, too.

"Can I leave now?"

"You need to write out a statement. Explain what happened on paper and sign it for us."

He slides a notepad and pen across the table. I pick up the pen and put it to the paper. I make a mark, then stop. What do I write? How do I form the words? The panic is about to drown me, and I realize that I can't remember the alphabet. I can't put together a word, let alone a sentence. I struggle, making random marks on the paper, but I am incapable of writing. My hands tremble as I push the pen and paper back to him. Will the degradation never end?

"I can't."

"You can't or you won't?"

"I can't. I lost the alphabet."

The detective rolls his eyes and sits down at the table, picking up the pen. He tells me to start at the beginning, but I don't remember what I told him earlier, so I have to make it up all over again. I remember nothing. Nothing. NOTHING. Except finding the broken doll. Holding it. Rocking. Rocking. ROCKING. The skin so cold. Lips blue. Bruises on the throat. Eyes open. Bloodshot. Staring. Staring. STARING. But not seeing. Anything. Ever again.

The detective says, "Describe the sexual assault."

I shudder convulsively, but I'm desperate to go home, and I make that up, too. Is what I'm telling them the truth or am I remembering a TV show? I don't fucking know. There are tears running down my face. There aren't any tissues. I wipe my nose with my hand, wipe my hand on my leg. There aren't enough tissues in the world for all my tears.

The detective reads the statement back to me. All lies. All of it made up, but I want to go home. "Is this accurate?"

God forgive me. "Yes." He hands me the pen and I sign the paper. "Can I go home now?"

He doesn't answer. Gets up, goes to the door and beckons to someone. A uniformed officer comes into the room.

"Can I go home now?" I ask again. "Please, I just want to go home."

"Take him down to booking. They may need to segregate him."

My blood runs cold and the sense of betrayal is mushrooming in my brain. "Wait a minute. You said I could go home if I told you what you needed to know. I want to go home."

"John, you're being charged with murder and aggravated sexual assault. You're not going anywhere for a long time."

"But—but you promised me!" The uniformed officer tries to force me from the room, but I'm pulling away from him, fighting him, screaming at them both.

"You fucking promised me!" After that, I'm just making sounds, not words—sounds of outrage. Fighting. More cops enter the room. I fight them, too. The bodies are moving around me, then I'm being lifted—or am I flying—and we're hurtling down the hall to the jail. They all but throw me into the cell and the door slams shut on my pathetic excuse for a life.

"John? Babe, you're hurting me."

Startled, I released my hold on Caitlin's shoulder. My palms were wet, hands shaking. "I've got to go out for a while." I had to get those images out of my head—shed the memories and emotions the video engendered. If I didn't, I might hurt myself.

She grabbed for my hand. "Please don't go by yourself. Wait a minute, and I'll come with you."

"No!" My voice was louder and harsher than I intended. "I'm going for a walk. I'll be okay." I didn't much care if the Mad Mauler had his laser sight trained on me. Kill me tonight, but catch me first.

I left the apartment walking fast; faster. Running. Running as if all the demons in hell were after me. But I'd never get away from them because they were all inside me. Seething, clawing, grasping, chewing. Sucking up the little bit of sanity I had managed to hold onto.

Block after block I ran, until my chest burned and my left lung was in flames. I stumbled, almost fell, and dropped to the curb, gasping for air. Rocking, crying. Dr. Fremont's prediction that I would remember more as time went on was proving to be correct, but I was beginning to wish he'd been wrong.

It was one thing to be debased and degraded. Humiliated. It was quite another to have your wife watch it all unfold in excruciating Technicolor detail. I wondered what she was thinking. She was probably packing all my stuff and changing the locks on the doors while I sat feeling sorry for myself. I couldn't imagine what it would be like to hear someone you loved describe committing such a monstrous act. The fact that I'd made it all up served to make the whole episode that much more repugnant. How could she stand to look at me?

A guy walked past and asked, "You okay, dude?"

I waved him on with a shaking hand, and he continued down the sidewalk. When he was out of sight, I lurched to my feet and crept back home. I was relieved not to find my stuff tossed out into the yard.

Caitlin was waiting for me in the living room, concern in her eyes. "You look like hell," she said as I fell onto the couch.

"Didn't you know? I *am* hell."

She sat beside me, her leg touching mine, and reached for my hand. "I'm sorry."

I shook my head. "No, I'm sorry. I'm sorry you ever had to see that. Sorry I ever had to see it, to be honest. How can you stand me—hearing that, seeing that. Doesn't it repulse you?"

She squeezed my hand. "What I saw is evidence of someone who was very sick and very scared. You made it all up, didn't you?"

"I was so desperate to go home, I would have told them I was the Queen of England if I thought that was what they wanted to hear. I honestly thought they would let me leave."

"Did you notice how Peter was hovering around you the entire time? Almost like he was trying to monitor what you were saying. He was acting awfully solicitous compared to the way all the rest of them were acting toward you."

I had never given any thought to this before, but now that she had voiced this observation, I had to agree. "He once told me that he felt sorry for me because of the way Randy treated me."

Caitlin put her arm through mine. "I think there's more to it than that. Did you notice the Band-Aids across the knuckles on his right hand? Watch it again, and I'll show you. I don't trust him. Something's not right there, John."

"No!" My pulse quickened at the thought of having to view the video again. "You said that before, and I'll take your word for it. I don't like him, but he's never been anything but nice to me."

"You're his scapegoat."

"I just don't see it. How could he get away with something like that for so long?"

"Because he's a cop."

The thought of a person in such a position of trust using that trust to molest and murder children was disgusting. "I'm not thinking about this anymore tonight," I said, though I knew I was lying, and it would be churning through my brain all night long.

She stood and yawned. "Well, here's a change of subject—Laurie called while you were out. She wants you to call her back. I'm going to soak in the tub for a while." She pulled me to her and kissed me. "Come join me when you're off the phone?"

I spent the next few minutes working up my nerve to call Laurie, hoping she wouldn't answer the phone because I didn't really want to talk to her. No such luck.

"What do you want?" I asked when she picked up. I wasn't in the mood for pleasantries.

"I'm sorry to bother you," she said. "I know you're not happy with us right now, but I need to know what you want to do about the house."

"I don't want to do anything about it."

"Well, we're going to be moving out by the end of the month."

"You don't have to do that, Laurie."

"Randy isn't going to be beholden to you."

I laughed. Rudely. "I'll bet that just chapped his ass, but if I wanted to be a dick about it, I would have told you to get out the minute I realized it was mine. I don't want it and I don't need the hassle of trying to sell it right now. So stay. Please. Seriously."

"We've already found another house, just the same."

"Fine," I said. "Let me know when you're out." I hung up on her and went to join Caitlin in the bathroom.

She was in bubbles up to her chin, eyes closed. I sat on the floor beside the tub and she opened one eye and said, "Well?"

"She wanted to tell me that she and Randy are moving out of the house. She said Randy wasn't going to be 'beholden' to me."

"I should say not, the way he's acted. Probably afraid you'd kick him out on his ass."

"They can have the damned house for all I care, but they've already bought another one. What am I going to do with it?"

She looked thoughtful. "Trying to sell anything in this economy is impossible. Speaking of economy, you know, even breaking the lease on the apartment, we could save money by moving there."

I shuddered. I didn't want to move into the house where Randy had lived and breathed his evil. "I don't want to move," I said, but resistance was futile when Caitlin stepped out of the tub, naked and inviting. Despite the day I'd had, I found myself aroused.

"Let's talk about it some more." She reached for my t-shirt and pulled it over my head. "The house is already paid for. It'll give us money to do something about the cottage."

She knew she had my attention then, but I felt obliged to offer one more protest. "I don't want to live in the same house where Randy lived—there are too many bad memories."

She reached for the button on my shorts. Slid the zipper down. "We'll make our own."

And that's how I found myself agreeing to a fourth move in less than a year.

CHAPTER EIGHTEEN

THE FRIDAY WE MOVED into the House from Hell was hot and humid. My shirt and shorts were plastered to my body after just the second trip from the moving van into the house. I was ill and out of sorts because I really hated the freaking house and the longer I was in it, the more upset I became.

"John, why don't you relax and let the guys I hired do their jobs and unload?" Caitlin asked, handing me a handful of paper towels to wipe my face.

"Because at the rate they're 'moving', they'll still be at it come midnight." I snapped, watching as two of the movers started into the master bedroom with our bed frame. "Hey, where are you guys going with that bed?"

"They're taking it where it belongs."

"It is *not* going in there."

She put her hands on her hips and stared at me. "Where else would it go?"

"It can go in one of the other bedrooms, but it's *not* going in there."

"Why in the world not?"

"Because that's where *he* slept."

"You're being ridiculous," she said, sounding dangerously condescending. "It's got an *en suite* bathroom, and it's as large as the other two bedrooms combined."

"I don't care, Caitlin. I'm not sleeping in the same bedroom that Randy slept in. It would be like sleeping with *him*. This house is swimming in negative energy anyway. It's creeping me out."

"John—"

"If you put the bed in there, you can sleep in it by yourself."

She sighed and instructed the movers to put it in the larger of the other two bedrooms. When they'd gone back out for another load, she said, "Are you okay? You're acting really strange."

"Stranger than usual, you mean?"

"Stop it. What is wrong?"

My anxiety got the better of me. "To put it bluntly, I hate this house! I hate, hate, *hate* this house. Okay?"

She looked totally bewildered. "If you hate it so much, why did you agree to move here?"

"Because apparently I'm really good at agreeing to things I have no business agreeing to."

"What do you mean by *that*?"

"Just what I said. I confessed to a murder I didn't commit because I thought that's what the cops wanted to hear. I agreed to move here because that's what you wanted to hear, but I hate this damned house."

Now she was looking pissed off. "If you didn't want to live here, all you had to do was say so!"

I was on a roll, though. "I did. I did say that, and as usual, you didn't pay any attention to me. I say no to something and you push me that much harder."

She gave me a frosty smile. "If I didn't push you, you would never move outside your comfort zone. You'd do *nothing*. You certainly wouldn't have had your competency restored."

I wanted to hit her, and that scared me. The fact that she was right didn't mean I had to like it or be gracious about it. I slammed out the kitchen door and onto the deck. I hadn't even been in this house two hours and I was already channeling Randy. I stood looking across the lawn and willed myself to calm down.

Adam Wade and his little brother were playing with super soaker-type squirt guns in their own backyard and presently he looked up, saw me. I waved to him, and he ran over, leaving his brother standing by himself. He stopped short of the steps and peered at me closely, saying, "John? I wasn't sure if it was you. I didn't think I'd get to see you again. I thought Mr. and Mrs. Kimbell moved out." He was talking in his usual breathless, run-on manner.

"They did," I told him. "Caitlin and I are moving in, though."

"Oh, cool." He beamed up at me. "Can you play with us? We're playing World War II."

"If you've got an extra squirt gun, we'll play as soon as I help get this moving van unloaded."

"Awesome!" He waved to his little brother. The smaller boy came running. When he reached the deck, I could tell that although he had the same blonde hair and fair skin as his brother, he had the round, flat face, almond-shaped eyes, and protruding tongue common to many people with Down syndrome. "This is my little brother, Gabriel. We call him Gabey. Gabey, can you say hi to John?"

Gabey smiled at me. "Hi, John."

My anger dissolved and I felt a twinge of compassion for the small boy, knowing myself what it was like to be considered different. I went down the steps to him and held out my hand, which dwarfed his palm as we shook. Squatting next to him, I realized how diminutive he was. "Hi, Gabey. Can I play with you and Adam?"

He nodded and licked his lips.

"Okay, if you guys can give me a couple of hours and find me a gun, we'll have one heck of a war." I figured a squirt gun battle would cool me off literally and figuratively.

"We'll be back later," Adam said to me. Then, his arm around Gabey's shoulder, "Come on, let's go find him a squirt gun. You'll like John. He's cool. He can do acrobatics and he's got some neat tattoos. Wait'll you see them up close."

A little over two hours later, with me rushing the process along, the van was unloaded and Caitlin was busy unpacking boxes. "I'll be outside for a bit," I told her and slipped out the back door before she could question me or protest.

Adam and Gabey were watching for me in their yard and came tearing over. "Are you ready to play, John?"

"I sure am. Do I get a gun?"

Gabey held out a squirt gun to me. "Here, John. It already gots water in it."

Adam said, "It leaks a little, but I let Gabey use the best one to make up for the fact he's so little."

"Fair enough." I tested the trigger and squirted Adam in the chest.

"Hey!" he laughed and pointed his gun at me. The fight was on. The battle took us all over the block and into the woods at the end of the *cul-de-sac* on the next street over. I had to surrender when I ran out of ammo first (due to my leaky weapon) and was marched back to enemy camp at gun point, a prisoner of war, where I was subsequently tortured (squirted) unmercifully to give up my secrets. I did not succumb to the torture, although I was liberated from the POW camp when the boys' mother called them in for supper.

Caitlin was not amused when I came back in the house soaking wet. "What the hell?" she asked as I squished across the kitchen in my wet shoes.

"Have you unpacked the towels yet?" I was dripping on the floor.

"No. Let me find them. Do not move off that tile."

In my wet clothing, with the air conditioner on, I started shivering before she could return. My teeth were chattering when she finally reappeared with a bath towel. "Take your clothes off right there." She unfastened my shorts while I pulled my t-shirt over my head. "May I ask how you got so wet?"

I hugged her to me. "I could tell you, but then I'd have to kill you."

She squirmed and pulled away. "You're freezing. What were you doing? Did you go swimming somewhere? In your *clothes*?"

"No. I was a German POW in World War II. I was captured by the Americans."

A funny expression flitted across her face and she looked a little scared. "John, have you been taking your medication?"

My restored good mood vanished instantly. I swear a negative entity possessed me. "I was playing with Adam and Gabey. Adam and Gabey Wade—the little kids who live behind us? You met Adam on our ski trip. I was having a water gun fight with them."

She crossed her arms. "Seriously? While I'm in here unpacking, you're out *playing*?"

I know when to shut up, admit defeat, and take it like a man. I headed for the shower. I had an idea she wasn't through with me, and when I came back out of the bathroom, dry and dressed, she pointed to a stack of boxes. I quickly got busy.

Time did not improve my feelings about the house however. I couldn't stand to be in it by myself and therefore played outside with Adam and Gabey a lot. I didn't know what I would do with my time when school was back in session. When I wasn't playing, I walked the neighborhood incessantly. Since it consisted mostly of young working couples, and I was at home during the day,

I seldom encountered anyone else. The rest of the time I spent sitting on the back deck going quietly insane.

It may have been coincidence, but the minute I walked back into the confines of the house, I felt my personality changing, and I snarled at Caitlin often. The Voices were more active, and I talked to them when I was alone or if I thought she wouldn't hear me. I never slept well to begin with, but I slept even less, except to doze while sitting on the deck. I went to bed with her, but when she fell asleep, I was up again, prowling the house or back outside with the summer night draped softly around me, miserable as hell.

I knew I was acting like the crazy person I was, but didn't realize the full extent of it until I walked into the kitchen one morning to find Caitlin counting my Thorazine tablets.

"What the hell are you doing?" I was supremely pissed off and more than a little ashamed.

She dropped the bottle on the counter and faced me, her cheeks coloring. "I was afraid you weren't taking your medication, so I was trying to see how many pills you had left. John, you *haven't* been taking it like you're supposed to."

"I keep forgetting." I hated having to explain myself like a child caught doing something wrong and I hated for someone to be checking up on me.

I could tell she was weighing her words carefully, probably afraid of setting me off. "Please take your medicine. I need you here. With me. Not at Broughton. Not with the Voices. I'm so worried about you. I think you need to make an appointment with your doctor." She appeared ready to cry, and I didn't know if I could deal with her tears, her distress. I could barely deal with my own. I felt my life going to hell, but wasn't sure I knew how to stop it.

"I'm sorry," was all I could manage. "I'll try to do better."

"I know you don't like the house," she continued. "If you're that unhappy, let's just list it for sale. It's not worth your mental health or our happiness to hold on to it. In retrospect, it was a bad idea."

"Are you sure?" I knew I sounded too eager, but it was the first good news I'd had since we'd moved in.

"Yes, I'm sure. It's probably not the best time to list, at the end of summer with kids getting ready to go back to school. It may take a while to sell, but we'll deal with it. I would at least like to throw a Labor Day cook out, though."

"A cook out is fine." I took her hands in mine. "Thank you. Nothing would make me happier than to get rid of this place."

"I just want you back." She leaned her head against my chest. "I really need you. Especially now."

#

For Caitlin's sake, I vowed I would try harder to remember to take my medication and not act so demented. I also promised myself that I would clean the house and have a meal ready when she got home from work each day, but despite my good intentions, by mid-morning most mornings the house was usually freaking me out, and I was walking the neighborhood until Adam and Gabey came outside, and we were playing war again.

On that particular day, we were still playing hard when their mother called them in, and I realized it was time for Caitlin to be home from work. I ran back to the house, knowing my ass was grass if she was already home, but for once luck was with me. I headed straight for the kitchen, figuring I probably had just enough time to poach a couple of chicken breasts and throw a salad together. I had everything ready to eat and my mess in the kitchen cleaned up before I heard her pull into the driveway an hour late.

I hugged her as she came through the door, and asked, "Where've you been?"

She gave me her mischievous smile, which I realized with a jolt I hadn't seen in a while. "I stopped to pick up something for you."

I was intrigued. "Like what?"

"Come on in the den, and I'll show you."

She gestured for me to sit on the sofa, kicked off her shoes, and set her purse down. Taking her tote bag from her shoulder, she set it on the coffee table. I saw the sides of it moving and said, "What the hell?"

"Wait 'til you see this." She opened the tote, reached in, and withdrew a small, wriggling body, which she placed in my lap.

A miniature dachshund puppy blinked up at me, yawned, and wagged its tiny tail.

Caitlin sat beside me and stroked the puppy's head. "Wilhelm, meet John. John this is Wilhelm. Willie for short."

Willie nuzzled my hand and licked at my fingers. "He's freaking cute. You got him for *me*?" I picked him up and held him against my chest. We watched as he sniffed at my shirt, and gave another yawn, which ended in a little squeak, causing us to laugh. He settled himself in the crook of my arm and closed his eyes.

"He is cute," Caitlin said, leaning her head on my shoulder. "I know how much you like Rev. Jack's little dog. I got him from Mackenzie. Her dachshund had puppies. Wilhelm was the last one of that litter. You remember Mackenzie from our party at the lake, don't you? I was worried about you being here by yourself while I'm at work. I wanted you to have a companion, a reason to get up and get moving every day. I thought a dog would be perfect."

I felt his little heart beating and his warm puppy breath against my arm. "I think you're right." I wanted to put my arms around her and hold her tightly, but couldn't bring myself to disturb Willie. The old feelings of inadequacy bubbled to the surface. "You're a lot better to me than I deserve."

She snuggled closer to me. "You're a decent man, John. You deserve good things. Please stop thinking that you don't." She yawned, too. "I'm so tired. I'm just going to sit here a minute and then we'll eat." Soon she was snoring softly in my ear, while Willie slept in my arm. Neither stirred for the next hour and although my arm was asleep, I didn't move for fear of waking them.

Caitlin finally sat up and looked around. "Good Lord, I didn't mean to nod off. I don't know why I'm so tired. Will dinner keep a little longer while I shower?"

"Sure. I'll take Willie out while you're doing that."

She handed me her car keys. "Can you bring in the stuff from the trunk? I bought a few things for him."

Willie explored the yard and did his puppy business, then pranced around sniffing bushes and rolling in the grass. He yapped at a couple of birds and dashed back to me, where he grabbed my shoestring, growling and playing tug-of-war with it.

"Silly dog." I scooped him up and went to get his stuff out of the trunk. I swear you'd have thought Caitlin was buying provisions for a baby. Not only was there a bag of food twenty times the size of the dog it would be feeding, there were also two other bags crammed full of stuff, an enormous box of dog treats, a dog bed, and a package of pee pads. "She's lost her mind," I muttered, trying to gather everything so I only had to make one trip.

In the house, I set all the doggie accoutrements on the coffee table to be sorted out after dinner, and Willie and I went in search of our mistress, who was curled up in bed, asleep once more. Now I was worried. I shook her gently.

"Did I fall asleep again?" She looked confused and sounded dopey.

"Babe, are you okay?" I sat on the bed beside her and put my hand on her forehead. She didn't feel hot or look feverish.

"Yeah." She gave a huge yawn. "I'm just so freaking tired. And starving. Can we eat?"

Once seated at the kitchen table, she held Willie in her lap while I plated everything and brought it to her. She ate so much and so fast that I stopped eating just to watch her. Only when I'd refilled her plate for the third time did she slow down and look at me.

"I don't know what's wrong with me tonight," she said, finally pushing her plate away. "What kind of salad dressing was that? It was delicious."

"Rev. Jack's red wine vinaigrette. He showed me how to make it when I was there in July."

She patted her belly and said, "I need to get back to working out—which reminds me. I signed us up at Body Tech Fitness."

"Wait a minute," I laughed. "How does *your* needing to work out translate into signing *me* up?"

"Well, you want to get your six-pack back, don't you?"

"I beg your pardon, but my six-pack has never *gone* anywhere."

She smacked my arm. "I know, and that's why I hate you! Now what's for dessert?"

"I don't think fat girls need to be eating dessert."

She squealed. "You are *so* going to pay for that remark!" She made sure I paid for it several times over that night.

#

We went back to our routine of working out in the evenings after Caitlin got off work. The first two nights I didn't think she would make it to the end of the workout, and when we got home, although it was only 7:30 PM, she lay down in bed and didn't move again until the next morning.

"I really think you ought to go to a doctor," I told her. "You're starting to worry me. It's not like you to sleep all the time."

"I'm fine." She stuffed a huge bite of bagel mounded with cream cheese into her mouth. "I've gotten out of the habit of working out, and it's kicking my butt. I'll be okay."

I didn't point out to her that the exhaustion started before the exercise had resumed.

She polished off one half of the bagel and began slathering cream cheese on the other half.

"Um—" I began, but when she narrowed her eyes at me, I didn't have the nerve to finish what I was going to say about the wisdom of eating the whole bagel, which was just as well, as I would have paid for that remark for a week.

"I'll pick you up after work this evening." She wiped her mouth on a napkin and stood on her tiptoes to kiss me.

"Don't you want to take a night off?" I asked.

"After the way I've been eating the past few days? I can't. See you this evening, babe." And she was off to work and I was stuck at the House from Hell.

After she left, I cleaned the bathrooms and vacuumed the floors and then the house was creeping me out, so I took Willie for a long walk around the neighborhood. Or I should say I took me for a long walk; I ended up carrying him most of the way since his little legs couldn't keep up. Adam and Gabey were waiting when I got back and were excited to see Willie. They tumbled around in the grass together, the boys laughing and squealing, and the puppy barking, until they were all worn out and the boys went home for lunch. I napped in the lounge chair on the deck, Willie curled up beside me, and woke with a start to find a man standing over me.

I scrambled out of the chair, tipping it over, and accidentally dumped Willie off, causing him to yip. Leaping to my feet, my heart hammering, I faced the man.

"Sorry, didn't mean to scare you," he said, extending a hand. "Detective Pendergrass, Kingsville Public Safety? We met before."

I shook his hand, although I was angry at having been startled out of a dead sleep. "Yeah, I thought you were going to call and let me know a time to come talk to you."

"Well, sir, I did leave a message, but didn't hear back from you, so I decided to take a chance and see if you were home. Your brother-in-law mentioned that you were living here now."

I made a mental note to thank Randy for revealing my whereabouts, although I would have expected nothing less from him. "Do you want to go in the house to talk or is out here okay?" I was really hoping he was okay outside.

"If we could step inside, that would probably be better," he replied, fanning his face.

Of course. I led the way into the kitchen. We took a seat at the table and he pulled a small notebook from his jacket pocket and flipped it open. "What can you tell me about the night of the shooting?"

Rubbing the sleep out of my eyes, I recited what had taken place. "We were later than usual working out that night. We came outside, and Caitlin and another couple were talking. I saw a red flash at the edge of the parking lot and turned to say something about it. Then I heard the crack of the rifle shot and felt as if I had been punched in the chest. The window shattered behind me, and I went down."

"You didn't see anyone? A car?"

"We were in the parking lot of a large apartment complex, there were cars everywhere. All I saw was the red flash."

"Red flash?"

"From a laser scope. Just like the night at the lake."

He looked up from his notes. "Wait a minute. What are you talking about?"

I told him about the night of the party, the shadowy figure standing on the shore, the laser beam pointed directly over my heart. I told him about the break-ins, both at the apartment and the cottage. About the notes and the sign. About the dead coyote.

"Why haven't you reported any of this before now?"

"Because I accepted a long time ago that nobody gives a shit what happens to me. You guys are so busy busting your humps to send me off for another murder, if someone were to take me out of the picture, you'd give them a medal."

"Mr. Colucci, I'm not looking to put you away for a murder. My job is to find out who shot you, but I need your cooperation. Anything you can remember would be a tremendous help, because, quite frankly, we're working at a big disadvantage here. So much time has passed since the incident. I interviewed the couple you were with, but they claim they didn't notice anything, and I haven't been able to get up with you or your wife. Do you have any idea who may have done this? I'm beginning to think maybe you're trying to hide something."

I could feel the anger blooming in my brain like a toxic flower. "I've been harassed by cops for *months* now. First my brother-in-law, then Kings County, and now you. You'll forgive me if I have a less than favorable impression of law enforcement and your ability to help me. As for who may have done this, take your pick from any of several thousand people—the family and friends of the first victim. Family and friends of the most recent victims. Everyone with a screw loose and a blood lust for ridding the world of child molesters, which I'm not, by the way...." I stopped as I recalled an image of Daniel's face, hovering over me, knife in hand.

Swallowing hard, I told him about Daniel's attack on me, his pantomime of firing a gun at me, and his words to me the day I left Broughton. *"Good luck, you pedophile. You know I won't be in here forever either. Be seeing you around."*

"What's Daniel's last name? Do you know where he lives?"

"I never knew his last name. I would assume he lives somewhere in North Carolina, but that's as much about him as I know. We weren't exactly best friends."

He pulled out a business card and slid it across the table, then closed his notebook. "Please let me know if you remember anything else. I probably shouldn't mention this, but the bullet we recovered from the scene has disappeared. There was no shell casing found. We're working with a whole lot of nothing here."

I was spooked for a number of different reasons after his departure—the fact that he was able to sneak up on me so easily, first of all, the idea that Daniel may be gunning for me, second of all, and then the disappearance of the bullet. But more importantly, I was bothered by the implications behind the disappearance. If Caitlin was correct, Peter would have been in a perfect position to dispose of it. Randy, too, for that matter.

Peter was an unknown factor, and although he'd never given me a reason not to like him, there was something about him I didn't trust. His appearance on the scene so quickly after I'd discovered the child's body was troublesome, almost as if he'd been waiting to snare me in a trap. And I'd walked into it so willingly. It was frustrating that I was unable to recall any more of that night.

Then there was the fact that although I hadn't previously thought Randy was responsible, I had royally pissed him off, and he would delight in fucking me over. And what better way to increase the chance that my would-be assailant was never caught and would remain free to make another attempt on my life than to cause the evidence to disappear?

I tried to force myself to stay in the house long enough to do a couple of loads of laundry, but I kept imagining that I could hear Randy breathing behind me or that I heard him stomping down the hall. Finally, I gave it up, and, scooping Willie from his bed, I headed out the door, going back in only long enough to change into my work-out clothes in time for Caitlin to be home.

I was sitting on the front stoop waiting for her when she drove up. She could apparently tell from the look on my face what kind of day I'd been having because she said, "You are going to have to get over your obsession about this house, John."

"It's not an obsession. There's an evil entity here," I retorted.

"You really need to see your doctor." She touched my shoulder as she moved past me into the house, but I pulled away angrily.

"For him to tell me what? That what I'm feeling isn't real? Because I assure you that it is. Just because *you* can't hear it or sense it doesn't make it any less real to *me*. You want to discount it because I'm schizophrenic, but that doesn't stop me from *feeling* it."

Her eyes widened and she blinked at me before saying, "Calm down. I'm sorry, but you really need to see your doctor. You have a right to your feelings, but you don't have the right to act like a dick."

That shut my mouth. "I'm sorry," I said when we were in the car heading for the gym.

"Apology accepted, but I want you to make an appointment with Dr. Steele. You never sleep anymore. I can't count how many times I've gotten up to go to the bathroom in the middle of the night and saw you sitting out on the deck. That's not normal."

I was trying really hard not to become angry again. "All right. I'll make an appointment tomorrow, but I want you to make one, too, to find out why you're sleeping all the time."

"There's nothing wrong with me," she began, then cut her eyes to me and started laughing. "Okay, deal. We make a fine pair, don't we? You can't go to sleep, and I can't wake up."

In the gym, she hit the elliptical trainer, while I headed for the fixed weight machines. I did my warm up exercises and then moved into my routine, working through the different muscle groups. I was in the zone, eyes closed and concentrating on proper breathing techniques as I worked on the reps for my abs, when I sensed someone standing next to me. Assuming it was Caitlin, I said, "See? My six-pack hasn't gone anywhere."

A male voice replied, "No, you're looking pretty good, John."

I opened my eyes and sat up abruptly to find Peter Barrington watching me. *Shit*! Where had he come from?

"Sorry," I stammered, feeling uneasy. "I thought you were Caitlin." I looked around but didn't see her.

"I think she's over on one of the treadmills. I didn't know you two worked out here." He was wearing only basketball shorts and cross-trainers and had a towel slung over his shoulder. I had never noticed before, but his trapezius muscles nearly touched his earlobes, and his biceps were almost the circumference of my thigh. He was a monster. I wondered if he used steroids and the term "roid rage" came to mind.

"Yeah, we just started a couple of nights ago." I'd discarded my t-shirt on the floor during my routine, but I reached for it now and slipped it back on. I felt like the proverbial ninety-pound weakling next to him.

"But you've been working out somewhere else, right? I mean you don't get that kind of definition sitting around watching TV."

Again I glanced around for Caitlin and finally saw her across the room watching us. To Peter, I said, "I swam a lot this summer and we worked out in the fitness room at the apartment complex where we used to live before—well, before I was shot."

"Oh, hey, I heard about that. Randy said you coded on them at Mission. Pretty scary stuff. Glad you're doing okay now."

"Thanks."

I was trying to think of a way I could politely sidle off, when he said, "Let me show you a good exercise for your quads." He laid his towel across a machine next to us while he set up my machine. Before I could make an excuse, he was demonstrating the exercise and soon had me doing the reps.

My thigh muscles burned and my legs felt wobbly after I finished. By that point Caitlin had done her time on the treadmill and came over to watch, striking up a conversation with Peter. They were soon joking and cutting up like old friends and I was feeling like a third wheel, but when he bent down to tie his shoelace, I saw her slide his towel off the machine and try to cram it down into the top of her tote bag.

I frowned at her, trying to figure out what she was doing, relieved when Peter looked up at the wall clock and said, "Got to get going, guys; got some errands to run before my shift starts. John, Caitlin, good to see you." He started to walk away, but then halted and looked around. Looking for the damned towel.

"What did I do with—" He spied it sticking out of Caitlin's bag. "I think you got my towel by mistake. Trust me, you don't want that stinky thing."

Caitlin laughed and returned it to him. "Sorry, I thought it was John's. Looks just like the one he had. John, what did you do with your towel?"

I played along. "I probably left it in the locker room."

Peter gave a wave and sauntered off.

"What the hell was that about?" I asked as we walked out to the car.

She didn't answer until we were actually pulling out of the parking lot onto the highway. "I'm going to get a sample of his DNA one way or the other."

"*What?*" I couldn't believe what I was hearing. "Have you lost your mind? And people call *me* crazy."

"He made a mistake and left some biological evidence behind at the scene of the murder you were accused of. This is the only way we're going to be able to prove it was him, and I'm going to get his DNA one way or another."

I hit the dashboard with my fist. "Oh, no, you are *not.*"

Her eyes flashed and I knew my manhood was in danger. She yanked the steering wheel to the right and pulled onto the shoulder of the road. "Let's get something clear right now. Don't ever tell me what I'm going to do and what I'm not."

I put my head in my hands and rocked for a minute to keep from saying something I knew would escalate the situation. When I thought I had a handle on my temper, I said, "Can you please try to understand how scared I am for you? I don't care anymore what happens to me, but if you get hurt because of this mess, I'm not going to be able to live with that. Besides, I think that if Peter is really the killer, it's going to take more than you to bring him down."

"I may not be able to bring him down on my own, but I can be the catalyst. And—news flash!—no one else is interested in clearing your name and finding the real killer. They're convinced it's you. The only way we can ever hope to prove that it's not is by getting Peter's DNA. And how are we going to get it since he's not going to volunteer it? We're going to *steal* it."

"And do what with it? Take it to the Sheriff's Department and say, 'Here you go guys. Have this tested.' And they're going to say, 'Oh, okay, yes we'll get right on that.'"

"You forget I have a friend at the state medical examiner's office."

"Caitlin, this is craziness. What if Peter figures out what you're trying to do?"

"We can't let him. He needs to become your new best friend. That will give us the access we need."

It was then that I remembered her making a similar remark previously. "Wait a minute. You've been planning this, haven't you?" She didn't answer and that infuriated me. "Seems to me you were doing a pretty good job of making him *your* best friend."

She glared at me. "I'm doing this for you. You need to calm down." She put the car in gear and stomped the accelerator.

When we got home, instead of following her into the house, I took off down the street. She and Willie were asleep in their respective beds when I returned. Neither stirred.

I didn't sleep again that night and called Dr. Steele's office the next morning to schedule an appointment. If I'd been having an emergency, they wouldn't have had an opening for weeks. Since I wasn't that thrilled about going, of course they had a cancellation for the next afternoon. I called Caitlin to tell her so she could make plans to be off work.

"We might as well make a day of it," she said. "I'll call Century 21 and see if we can meet with a realtor after your appointment to talk about listing the house for sale."

"Good idea." This excited me more than I let on. I was so ready to be rid of that albatross. I wanted to be at the lake full time. I could already imagine Willie and Winnie romping through the woods together, with me and Rev. Jack not far behind. Kingsville would be just a bad, distant memory.

At Dr. Steele's office, Caitlin came back with me to talk to him and detail all the problems I'd experienced: the sleeplessness, lack of appetite, anxiety, the belief that there was an evil entity in the house, the irritability and anger. I found myself wanting to rebut each symptom she listed, but instead I just sat there with my mouth shut except to tersely answer a few questions by Dr. Steele.

At the end of the session, he took out a prescription pad and scribbled out three scripts. Handing them to me, he said, "I want you to try these."

I couldn't make out what he'd written. "What is it?"

"I'm upping your dosage of Thorazine, and the other two are for Ativan and Ambien. The Ativan is for anxiety and the Ambien is to help you sleep."

I started to protest, but Caitlin cut me off at the pass. "You really need this, John. The least you can do is try the new prescriptions. You've got to calm down and get some sleep."

I was angry as we left his office, but it seemed that I stayed that way. "I don't want to take any more meds," I grumbled.

"Suck it up and at least try it," she said unkindly.

We stopped for lunch at the diner where Edie worked, and I sulked while Caitlin and Edie chatted and laughed.

"Who licked the red off your candy?" Edie asked me after a few unsuccessful tries to draw me into the conversation.

"His doctor and I did," Caitlin answered. "Stop acting like a prick, John."

I gave her a warning look, which she ignored. Wisely, Edie did not delve into it further and walked away to take another customer's order.

After lunch, we got my prescriptions filled and Caitlin insisted that I take the Ativan right then. Tired of the tension between us, I complied without argument. Whether it was the placebo effect or I was really experiencing an improvement, I did begin to feel calmer and less annoyed with the world. Or maybe it was just that I was away from the House from Hell.

We met with the realtor, discussed prices, and made arrangements for her to see the house. I was feeling ecstatic by then.

It was nearly five o'clock, the time when Caitlin would be getting off work anyway, so I said, "Let's go celebrate and get some wine." At the bar, however, she surprised me by ordering not muscadine, but a glass of orange juice.

When I remarked on this, she just shrugged, gave me an enigmatic smile, and said, "We'll be working out in a little while and wine makes me sleepy, so I'm going to pass. You might want to take it easy, too, especially since you're taking new medication."

I limited myself to just one, albeit rather large, glass of wine, wondering at her new resolve. Then I started feeling extremely sleepy and wished I'd followed her example. My butt was dragging in the dirt by the time we got to the gym.

Peter was there doing reps on the fixed weights. Caitlin steered me over to him and began chatting. I noticed, half amused, that he had with him a bright red towel with white embroidery in what I assumed was his monogram, "PBA". There would be no way Caitlin could pretend to mistake his towel for mine. There was a plastic water bottle next to the towel. Caitlin nudged me and pointed to it surreptitiously. I shook my head at her but she gave me "the look" and followed me over to the machine I had chosen.

"Try to get that water bottle," she whispered, leaning closer.

I turned to tell her that I wasn't going to participate in her crazy scheme, but she'd already headed for the treadmills. Damn it. I knew if I didn't agree, then she would be found doing it herself. So I set up my machine, keeping watch on Peter.

He finished his routine, gathered up his towel and bottle and came over to me. Waiting for me to finish my reps, he chugged down the contents of the bottle and once again showed me new exercises—this time for pecs and biceps—and coached me through them. While I went through the paces, he talked about competitive bodybuilding and the titles he'd won. He was seriously into it.

"I've entered the Hard Bodies contest in Asheville in November," he said, "and I think I stand a really good chance of coming in first place." I didn't see how he couldn't win. If there were guys more developed than him, I wasn't sure I wanted to see them. "Have you ever thought about competitive bodybuilding?"

I was about to laugh and tell him no way when I remembered that I was supposed to make him my new best bud. "I'd like to learn more about it," I said. "I don't think I could do it, but I enjoy watching the Mr. Universe and Mr. Olympia competitions on TV. And, of course, I've watched *Pumping Iron*." Honest to God, I don't know where that came from. I had never in my life been interested in bodybuilding and any competitions or movies I might have seen would have been because someone else was watching them when I happened to be in the same room. I was amazed that (a) my defective brain had stored that information, and (b) that I was able to recall it. Truth be told, I thought bodybuilders were narcissistic and more than a little creepy, and Peter fit right in with that perception. That was all the encouragement he needed, though.

He talked non-stop for the next forty-five minutes while I finished my workout, and I learned more about bodybuilding than I ever had a desire to know.

"You really ought to consider competing," he said. "You'd do well in the middleweight class. You don't have the bulk yet, but you've got a good start on getting ripped. If you want to give it a go, I'll be glad to coach you."

"I don't know how I'd feel about showing off my body in a room full of people," I said, although I *did* know how I'd feel about it, and I would *not* like it.

"Man, you should be proud." He looked me up and down.

Okay, I was getting *majorly* creeped out. "Let me think about it," I said, but what I was thinking was "No fucking way."

"Yeah, let me know." He put a hand on my shoulder, leaving it there just a beat too long. My skin was all but crawling, and I glanced around for Caitlin, relieved to see her headed toward us. Then I glanced around for the water bottle, but it was already clutched in his other hand—almost as if he knew what we had in mind.

"I'm glad you're still here," Caitlin said to him as she came up to us, and I saw her eyes cut to the water bottle. "John and I are having a Labor Day cookout and we wanted to invite you. I guess Randy told you we're living in the house where he and Laurie used to live?"

"Yeah, he mentioned that. A cookout sounds great. What time?"

"Come around 4:00 PM and stay until whenever. Bring a date if you want."

Please God, bring a date, I added silently.

He looked pleased to be invited. "Thanks, I'll be there. Talk to you soon." He headed for the locker room.

I'd been entertaining the idea of a shower myself, especially after being touched by him, but there was no way I was going in there now. I grabbed Caitlin's elbow. "Let's get the hell out of here," I said, pulling her to the door.

"Something wrong?" she asked as we got in the car.

"It's nothing." I was feeling distinctly dirty, but I wasn't going to talk about it with her. "I just want to get home and get a shower."

"You could have showered here. I would have been glad to wait."

"I don't know if I'll ever be able to shower there again." I shuddered at the memory of his hand on my shoulder and then another memory tried to push its way to the surface—

"Don't tell me you think it's haunted, too," Caitlin spoke, sending the memory skittering back into the shadows.

Frustrated because I had the feeling that the memory held an answer, and angry that it was once again out of reach and that she was making fun of me, I spoke without thinking. "Would you, for once in your life, *shut up*!" It was a chilly ride home, and I don't mean the temperature in the car.

CHAPTER NINETEEN

CAITLIN WAS ON THE COMPUTER looking at my discovery when I walked into the spare bedroom. I stopped just inside the doorway and said, "Can you turn that off?" and waited for her to do so before venturing further into the room. I'd made the mistake of watching the video of my arrest and had seen photos of the child's dead body and had no wish to see any more.

Her attitude toward me was still rather frosty. "I'm sorry," I said again. If I'd said it once since the previous evening, I'd said it a hundred times. I massaged her shoulders and felt her relax. The freeze out was, hopefully, over. I bent to kiss her cheek and she turned her mouth to mine. Progress. She stood and allowed me to sit, then perched on my lap. I was home free. I held her and we snuggled for a few minutes.

"I'm sorry, too," she said. "I shouldn't have made fun. I just wish you wouldn't talk to me that way."

"God, I'm sorry. It's my mouth that says these things, not my brain. They sometimes work at cross purposes. Don't make me feel like any more of a shit than I already do."

She smiled and put a finger on my lips. "Your mouth is going to get the rest of you in a whole lot of trouble. Sometimes it's good to feel that way. It keeps you humble."

"I'm the most humble guy on earth."

"You are actually."

"And since I'm so humble and I know I can't do this by myself, I'm going to ask for your help."

"You know I'll help you."

I took a deep breath. "I want to get my driver's license back, but I'll need your help to study for it. The lady at the driver's license office said they can give me an oral test, but that I'll have to be able to identify the road signs and, of course, I'll have to take the driving test."

"Not to rain on your parade, but won't you just get revoked when you go to court on your tickets?"

I nodded. "Yeah, but Webster thinks I may be eligible to have my license reinstated, and then he can at least get the charge for driving while license revoked dismissed. Too, I might be eligible for a limited driving privilege. It'll make me feel better about myself to be able to drive and not have to depend on someone else for transportation."

She put her head on my shoulder. "You know, I never stopped to think how it might feel if I couldn't drive myself where I needed to go. That would make me feel very dependent. I think it's a great idea to get your license reinstated."

She logged on to the computer and brought up the Department of Transportation website. "Let me find a copy of the driver's license handbook and we'll start now."

"And I want to get my own vehicle," I added.

She glanced up at me. "Okay. What kind?"

"I'd really like a Chevy Avalanche. Black or dark blue."

She grinned. "That vehicle is you. Okay, we'll shop for a truck, too."

We studied for the test the next several evenings after returning from the gym, where Peter was, thankfully, absent. We also found what looked to be a good deal on an Avalanche at a dealership in Hickory and made plans to drive there on Saturday.

Caitlin took off work another afternoon to accompany me to the DMV, but when we got there, they demanded to see proof of insurance and a clearance letter from my doctor stating it was safe for me to drive. We then had to contact Dr. Steele's office and wait two days for the letter. In the meantime, Caitlin added me to her insurance policy so we could obtain a DL-123 form from the agent.

Finally, clearance letter and insurance form in hand, I was ready to take the test. Initially, I missed a couple of the signs but the examiner just yawned and said, "Look at it again," and I got it right the second time. I nearly botched the driving test by not using my turn signal when beginning the three-point turn, but remembered to use it when pulling away from the curb. I was extremely happy and a little surprised when they told me I'd passed and to step in front of the camera to have my photo made. I was closer to becoming a normal human being, and I celebrated by driving home without getting arrested or ticketed.

#

As we drove to Hickory on Saturday, Caitlin was giving me details of the Labor Day cookout plans. "I've invited everyone from the paper and the diner. Oh, and some of the neighbors, including Adam and Gabey's parents."

I snorted. "I don't know why you bothered inviting the neighbors. It's not like any of them have ever gone out of their way to talk to us."

"John, you can't expect other people to do something you're not willing to do yourself."

"I think you're making a mistake to invite them. We're not going to be living there long enough for it to matter anyway."

"You don't know that. You heard the realtor. It could take a year to sell the house."

But I didn't want to think about that. "Let me put it this way. *I* won't be here long enough for it to matter." As soon as I had my vehicle, I was gone to the lake.

She looked wounded. "You would leave without me?"

"I don't *want* to," I explained. "But I just can't stay around here much longer, and I know you have to work. We could be together on the weekends for the time being." I cut my eyes toward her briefly. I definitely saw tears.

"That's not a marriage, John. That's not even much of a relationship, and you certainly didn't like us being separated after you were shot."

"And I don't want to be now. Let's just move to the lake and be done with it. Can't you work from home? They let you do that before."

"But what I write about is mainly in Kingsville, not Fontana Lake, not Bryson City. And I love Kingsville."

"I don't know what the answer is, Caitlin, except that I can't stay around here much longer. I just can't."

She wept silently, her face turned to the window. I put my hand on her thigh, but she didn't respond.

"I'm sorry." I seemed to be saying that all the time where she was concerned. I was an A-1 jerk and knew I didn't deserve her, didn't see how I could ever make her happy. She was destined to be unhappy from the moment she first spoke to me in the diner. She seemed to be sad so frequently now, or she went from happy to homicide in 0.6 seconds. I was sure her continued exposure to my mental illness was bringing her down, too, changing her from the upbeat, positive person she was into, well, a bitch.

At the car dealership, she was subdued, quiet. She offered no opinions, asked no questions, wordlessly proving to me how much I needed and depended on her, and I was left to negotiate the process on my own. Damn me and my big mouth. She did relent when it came to the paperwork, glancing over the documents and giving me the gist of the contents, but when the salesman handed me the keys, she walked out of the building, got in her car, and left without a word. I was going to have to do a whole lot of kissing her pretty ass when I got home. I gave some serious thought to driving straight to Fontana Lake, but knew I'd never get out of the dog house if I did, so after the salesman showed me some of the truck's features, and I familiarized myself with the controls, I pointed it toward Kingsville.

The drive home was therapeutic. I'd brought Caitlin's entire KoЯn CD collection and cranked the sound system up to 12, until the truck was vibrating from the bass and I probably wouldn't be able to hear for a week. I did a good job of singing along, although Jonathan Davis doesn't have anything to worry about. I enjoyed the feeling of freedom that being able to drive and having my own vehicle afforded.

When I got to the house, Caitlin's car was not in the driveway, so I drove back into town. I'm not sure why, but I decided to go past the gym and saw her car in the parking lot. She hadn't mentioned working out, so I pulled into the parking place next to hers and went inside. I didn't see her on any of the elliptical trainers or treadmills, and wandered through the building looking for her. I had almost decided she must be in the women's locker room and was heading back up front to wait for her, when I thought to stick my head in the juice bar.

She was sitting at one of the small café tables talking to Peter, her hand resting on his arm, their backs to me. The flood of emotions coursing through me at that moment threatened to propel me into the room, and it was only a phenomenal effort on my part that prevented me from storming in, grabbing her, and dragging her out to the car. Instead I stood there watching, trying to get a feel for what was going on, but knowing I wouldn't like it, whatever it was.

She leaned her head closer to his, murmuring something to him. They both laughed and he scooted forward, his knee touching hers. She didn't move away. They continued on in this vein for several more minutes until I could stand it no longer and I strode up to their table. Peter at least had the good grace to look guilty, and he slid back in his seat so that he was no longer touching her.

"You didn't tell me you were coming to the gym," I said, my voice betraying my anger.

She gave me a brittle smile. "You didn't ask, did you?"

I put my hand around her arm, forcing myself not to squeeze hard, and urged her to her feet. "Let's go," I said.

Pulling away from me, she said, "I haven't worked out yet. I'll be home when I finish."

I really wanted to slap her, but I'm not a complete idiot, so I choked down the impulse and gritted my teeth. "Fine. I'll wait for you."

Peter stood up and said, "I'd better be running. I'll see you at the cookout Monday." He snatched his cup off the table where he'd been sitting and beat a hasty retreat.

She scowled at me. "Thanks for screwing that up!" she snapped. "I could have had that cup for testing."

"You need to back off on that," I shot back at her. "You let me worry about getting it. I don't want him to have any reason to come after you. He could break you in half with one hand." I took her by the arm again and pulled her along to the door with me. This time she came somewhat willingly.

"We're going to have to get his DNA at the party somehow," she muttered as we walked to her car. "We're running out of time. The Sheriff's Department is saying that they're close to having what they need to arrest you. We've got to give them a reason to look at him." And she surprised me by bursting into sobs.

I wrapped my arms around her, pulling her tight, feeling her chest heaving against me. "We'll get it," I told her. "Somehow, someway, we'll get it, okay? Come on, I'll drive you home. We'll come back later for your car." I helped her into the passenger seat of the truck. She continued to cry during the drive home, and I was starting to worry about her mental health, which then turned into anger at myself, as it always seemed to do.

Once at the house, she went straight to the bedroom where she lay down and continued to cry. I tried to hold her but she shrugged out of my embrace and sobbed that much harder. Willie was whining to go out, and feeling helpless and hopeless, I reluctantly got up to take him. When he finally finished his business and we returned to the house, Caitlin was asleep, clutching my pillow against her. She didn't even wake up when I came to bed much later.

Early the next morning I thought I heard her in the hall bathroom throwing up but I fell asleep again and when I woke for the second time, I couldn't decide if I'd dreamed it or not. When I went into the kitchen, she was sitting at the table with a glass of orange juice. She didn't appear sick, so I figured it was my imagination.

"Hey." I kissed the top of her head and sat down beside her.

"Hey, yourself," she said back. "Do you want me to fix you something to eat?"

I yawned and reached over to hoist Willie onto my lap so he would stop scratching at my ankles. "No, I think I'll just make some coffee. Are you going to drink any?"

She gave a little shudder, which I couldn't interpret, and said, "No, I'm good."

I touched my fingers to her forehead. "Caitlin, are you okay? You are really worrying me. Did you ever make a doctor's appointment?"

"I've got an appointment for the week after next," she said, "but I'm fine."

I didn't see how she could think she was fine when she wanted to sleep all the time and she was so moody, but I knew better than to say anything more, so I got up to start the coffee. Once I had it brewing and got out my favorite mug, I turned around to speak just in time to see her jump up from her chair and race down the hall. The bathroom door slammed and I definitely heard her retching.

I went down the hall after her and knocked on the door when she stopped gagging. "Babe, are you all right?"

She opened the door, looking pale and shaky. "I'll be okay in about eight more months," she said and started bawling again.

I'm not a complete idiot, as I may have mentioned before, but I'm close. "What's going to happen in eight months?" I asked and then my defective brain, always slow on the uptake, put all the pieces together and I felt my guts turn to ice.

"You're pregnant," I said at the same moment she sobbed, "I'm pregnant."

"Oh fuck," I said as she fell against me weeping.

She made a sound that was a cross between a laugh and a sob and said, "Yeah, that's generally what causes it." And then she was throwing up in the hall, which caused her to cry that much harder. "Oh, my God, I've ruined the carpet!"

"Don't worry about it." I propelled her toward the bedroom. "Why don't you go back to bed? I'll clean up."

She climbed under the covers and said, "Will you come talk to me when you're finished? I want to know what you're thinking."

"Yeah, sure," I told her. "I'll be there in a few minutes." I went to get some old towels to blot up the worst of the mess and then located the foam carpet cleaner and the mop. I took my time because I wasn't sure what I would say to her that wouldn't cause her to cry more. I felt numb inside and a little sick myself, and I found myself wondering if this was the way my father had felt when my mother told him she was pregnant with Laurie, with me. Did it scare the piss out of him to think about fathering a child, knowing he was schizophrenic and knowing that he could pass that on to his son or daughter? Because it sure scared the piss out of me. How could I be a decent father when I couldn't even be a decent husband or human being? And what if I was arrested? How was Caitlin going to manage then? How would the child manage, growing up as the offspring of a suspected murderer and child molester? Would that make it the target of more than its fair share of bullying? It was my worst nightmare ever, multiplied by one hundred. One thousand.

I expected Caitlin to be asleep when I re-entered the bedroom, but she lay there looking sad and a little frightened, the comforter pulled up to her chin.

"I'm sorry," she whispered as I sat down beside her. "I know it's not what you wanted. I didn't do it deliberately. I just forgot to take the Pill a couple of days. I guess I don't have any business fussing at you about not taking your medication." Tears slid out of the corners of her eyes and into her hair.

I reached over and touched her face. "I guess that's a pretty good example for why it's important to take medication as prescribed."

She clutched my hand as if she were drowning and I was the only thing keeping her head above water. "What are we going to do?" she asked. "Do you want me to get an—" but she couldn't get the word out for sobbing.

"Shhh. No, I don't want you to get an abortion. Not if there's a chance we'll have a little girl who looks like you."

"Or a little boy who looks like you." She smiled at me through her tears.

"I'm just so scared." I nudged her to move over and slid under the covers next to her. "What if this mess with these murders isn't resolved and I'm arrested again? I can't stand the thought of you having to deal with this on your own."

She put an arm across my chest and her head on my shoulder. "I can't stand the thought of it either. That's why we've got to get something from Peter."

"And what if we do and it's not him?" I asked, and she got quiet and still.

"Then I don't know what we'll do, John. I just don't know."

"You know what keeps running through my mind? What could have been so bad in my father's life that he would rather eat a bullet than watch his son grow up? And how can I know I won't make the same decision?"

She twisted her head to look at me. "You make me so mad when you talk that way. Didn't you once tell me that your father was non-compliant with his medication, too? That's one way you can keep from ending up like him. Take your meds. Please. For me. For the baby."

I made a pact with her that I would faithfully take my meds as directed and that I wouldn't get angry about her checking up on me.

"So, are we going to tell everyone at the cook out tomorrow?" I asked.

"No, it's bad luck to tell before the end of the first trimester."

I kissed her. "You're a nut."

"It takes one to know one."

CHAPTER TWENTY

THAT NIGHT I DREAMED about my father.

I searched through my childhood home for him to tell him that he was going to be a grandfather. I went from room to room, but I was always behind him. I could smell his aftershave, his cigarette smoke in each successive room. The original house was only a thousand square feet, but the house in my dreams was never ending, or so it seemed as I followed my father's ghost.

Why was he avoiding me? I hadn't seen him in thirteen years. There was so much to tell him, best of all the news about the baby. I kept calling out, "Dad! It's me, John. Dad, wait up. I need to talk to you!" I was furious. Why couldn't he stop for just a minute? Didn't he miss me? Surely he wanted to see me, talk to me.

Then the atmosphere changed, and instead of being angry, I was scared. I had to find my dad before—before it was too late. I knew what he intended to do, and had to find him and tell him the news, for I was sure this would give him a reason to live, a reason that his own son couldn't provide.

I stumbled through the dream house. "Dad! Dad, wait—listen to what I have to tell you. Dad, don't. Please. I love you. You're going to be a grandfather. Whatever pain you're in can be fixed. I know I disappointed you, but don't you want to see your grandchild? Dad!"

Then I heard the shot, the shot that had blown my father's head into several pieces and my fifteen-year-old life to shreds. I ran into the next dream room and there he was, exactly as I had found him in our garage thirteen years ago, half his face gone. Brain matter and blood covered part of the wall and ceiling where he'd been standing.

I sat up in bed screaming, sweating, shaking. I looked around wildly. Caitlin was not there. I heard the bathroom door open and her footsteps pounding down the hall toward the bedroom.

She stopped in the doorway. "What's wrong? Are you okay?"

I was crying now. "I had a dream about my dad. I found him dead, just like that day he…." But I couldn't finish because the mental images were still too fresh, too bloody. God, I could even remember the smell—the brains, blood, excrement, urine—and I gagged, which in turn caused Caitlin to gag and sent her racing back to the bathroom where I heard her retching once more.

I wiped my sweaty face on the hem of my t-shirt, staring at the clock. 6:47 AM. There would be no going back to sleep now, Ambien or no. I pulled on my jeans and stumbled to the kitchen to start the coffeemaker. Willie roused from his dog bed in the laundry room and came over to me, blinking sleepily as if wondering what was going on. Caitlin came in a second later, got a whiff of the coffee, and immediately returned to the bathroom. When she reappeared, looking a little green around the gills, the coffee had finished brewing.

"Sorry. I didn't even think. Guess I'm going to have to give up coffee for a while," I said as she sat down.

"You might have to, at least until I get past the morning sickness."

Willie snuffled at her ankles and she picked him up and placed him in her lap. "Hey, little guy." She stroked his head and he curled up and went back to sleep. "I never knew you were the one who found your dad. I can't imagine how horrible that must have been," she said after a moment.

"It was like something out of the goriest horror movie you've ever seen. I couldn't believe it was even real at first." I stopped myself, remembering her delicate stomach.

"It wasn't your fault, you know. I can sense that you blame yourself, but you shouldn't."

I felt the tears rising unbidden. "You want to know the last thing I said to him? I called him a crazy motherfucker and told him I hated him and wished he was dead." My voice broke on the word 'dead', and I was crying again, the dream and reality both still fresh in my mind.

She grabbed my hand, kissed my fingers. "He was sick, John. You were sick, and you were a teen-ager. I bet there's not a person alive today who didn't say that to their parents at one time, or at least thought it."

"One day our child will say all of that to me."

"And he'll get his mouth washed out with soap!" Caitlin squeezed my hand and smiled.

"Or she."

She shook her head. "No, it's a he. I've just got this feeling." She kissed my hand again. "I'm going to get a shower before the equipment rental people get here to set up for the party."

She handed Willie to me and I got him settled in my lap. I finished my coffee and sat there imagining the life growing inside her and wondering how a father could care so little about his child that he would kill himself. My child wasn't even born yet and already I knew I would do anything to protect its life, keep it from harm, from angst. It wouldn't be fair to consider suicide as a solution to the many problems which were plaguing me, but how unlovable had I been that my father hadn't felt the same way? It was a question that had begged an answer for thirteen years.

Returning Willie to his bed, I went in search of Caitlin and found her still in the shower. Yanking off my clothes, I stepped in and pulled her to me, holding her tight. I wanted to assure myself of her love and assure her of mine. She raised her face and I could tell that she had been crying.

"What's wrong now?" I asked.

She put her arms around me. "Hearing about your father makes me sad. Knowing that you found him like that—I can't stop thinking about how you must have felt; how your mother and Laurie must have felt."

"I'm telling you, my life is a train wreck and unfortunately for you, you're on board now."

"Well then," she said, "I'm going to do everything in my power to keep it from being derailed." Her mouth met mine and the shower devolved into my favorite activity. Minutes later, however, the equipment rental truck pulled into the driveway and we scrambled to dry off and get dressed.

Things got crazy after that. When the chairs, tables, and canopies were set up to Caitlin's exacting standards, she had me running last minute errands prior to the arrival of the caterers. By the time I finished, it was 3:45 PM and guests were starting to arrive. Unloading bags from the truck, I looked up to see Caitlin's editor, Will Lackey, getting out of his car. I raised a hand in greeting and he beckoned me over. He had a grim look on his usually jovial countenance.

"Something wrong?" I asked.

"Yeah." He sighed. "I'm assuming you haven't seen a copy of *The Asheville Journal* today?"

I knew what was coming. "No, we've both been so busy getting ready for the party…"

"I'm sorry to have to bring up this ugliness, but I thought you and Caitlin needed to know."

He reached into his car and pulled out a folded newspaper. He opened it up and showed me the front page. The headline screamed, "Sheriff's Department Close to Making Arrest" and there was a photo of me, a recent photo—shorter hair, beard, mustache—not one of the ones they'd previously used. I felt the bottom of my stomach drop. I had no idea where they'd gotten it and it gave me a creepy feeling to know someone was photographing me without my knowledge.

"Oh, hell," I said.

"Yeah." Will looked miserable. "The article mentions your street address."

"I appreciate you telling me," I murmured. My brain was reeling with all the implications. "Caitlin is going to be devastated. Will, please don't mention this to her right now. I'm just not sure how well she'd take it since—" I stopped, remembering that she hadn't wanted to tell anyone our news yet.

"She's pregnant, isn't she?"

Damn, he was good. "How did you know?"

"I remember how my ex-wife got when she was pregnant with our two kids. Moody, tired all the time. When she wasn't throwing up, she ate like a horse. Bitch from hell doesn't begin to describe her disposition. Of course, the bitchiness during pregnancy was just a taste of the bitchiness to follow, which is why she's now my ex-wife. Emphasis on the *ex*. I lost the office bet, though."

"Bet?"

"Office pool. No offense. Whenever anyone gets married, we start a pool to see how long before they turn up pregnant. I figured Caitlin was good for a couple of years. I lost."

"It wasn't planned. She forgot to take the pill a couple of nights and the rest is history." I didn't know why I was sharing this information with Will except that I now considered him my friend. "Please don't tell Caitlin you know. She'll think I told you and my life won't be worth living. Not that it is anyway."

"You didn't tell me. I guessed. But okay, I'll keep it to myself."

Several more cars parked along the street, the occupants making their way to our house. "I guess it's too late to call off the party."

Will took one of the bags from me, stuffing the newspaper down inside it, and steered me toward the house. "Look at it this way—anyone who saw the article and was bothered by it isn't going to show up for the party. So try to enjoy yourself."

Caitlin was in the kitchen when Will and I walked in. She gave him a hug and a kiss on the cheek, then looked from him to me and said, "Okay, what's up?"

I tried to downplay it. "Nothing to worry about right now." I handed her the bag I was holding.

She turned to Will. "What isn't he telling me?"

"Enjoy your party, Cait. We can discuss it later."

She crossed her arms and tapped her foot. "I'm not going to enjoy anything until you two tell me what's going on."

"You may as well show her," I said to Will. I should have had better sense than to think I could hide anything from her eagle eyes.

Will pulled the newspaper out of the bag and flipped it open. I watched her face blanch and her lips set in a hard line. Tears formed in the corners of her eyes.

"Where did they get this photo?" Her voice quavered. "Have they been *spying* on us?" She snatched the paper from Will, marched over to the trash can, and crammed it in. "Damn them."

"Will's right," I said. "Let's just enjoy the party." I knew it was useless to try and that neither one of us could enjoy it now, but I was desperate for her to stop being so sad, and I was desperate to stop feeling so guilty for dragging her down in the cesspool with me. I viewed everything that had happened since I'd confessed to that murder almost a decade ago as the beginning of an avalanche that was now racing down the mountainside to obliterate my life and Caitlin's.

How could I have been so stupid as to say I'd murdered and molested a child and expect there to be no permanent and dire repercussions? But I remembered that all-consuming panic, the dread, the terror, how frantic I had been to go home. They'd used my illness against me, knowing if they pushed the right buttons, I'd say what they wanted to hear. And, if Caitlin was correct, as she usually was, Peter had set me up. He was not only responsible for the murders, he was responsible for the hell my life and Caitlin's had become. He was responsible for the tears on Caitlin's face right now and I was suddenly possessed of a burning desire to bring him down. To see him screaming, broken and bloody on his knees in front of me while I pounded him into the ground.

"I will get his DNA tonight," I whispered in her ear, "or I'll die trying."

"Don't talk of dying." She put her palm against my cheek. "Just please get a sample from him."

I ran into the bedroom and changed clothes, took my Ativan tablet, then I was back outside greeting guests and watching anxiously for Peter to make his appearance. When, at last, I saw him heading toward me, I couldn't help but smile inwardly. *You're mine, asshole*, I thought.

He clasped my hand. "John, how are you?"

"Fine." The touch of his flesh against mine made me want to squirm. I forced myself not to jerk my hand out of his. "Come on and I'll introduce you to everyone. You want something to drink?"

"A beer would be good," he said.

I grabbed a bottle of beer from a huge tub of ice and my own obligatory glass of muscadine wine and then took him around to make introductions to the people whose names I could remember. Fortunately, the ones I couldn't remember were more socially adept than I and introduced themselves, saving me from embarrassment.

Before I realized what I was doing, I'd chugged down the wine and found myself working on a refill while Peter merely sipped on his beer. Almost immediately, I felt the effects of combining the Ativan with the alcohol. I put down the glass but I was already dizzy and my tongue felt too thick for my mouth.

"Have you thought any more about competitive bodybuilding?" he asked.

"I'd like to try it, if you're willing to coach me," I lied.

"You've got a good start." He gave me a look that sickened me and I fought to keep my face from showing the revulsion I felt. I had never claimed to be an actor and had my doubts that I could get through the night without puking or punching his lights out, but knew I had to try. I was sticking to him like a tick and it was going to take an industrial-sized pair of tweezers to remove me. The minute he put down the beer bottle, I would grab it and put it in a safe place until Caitlin could get it to her friend at the medical examiner's office. Except that the son of a bitch wouldn't turn loose of the bottle.

I followed him all over the yard as he spoke to different people. Finally, in desperation, I reached for the bottle and said, "Let me get you another beer. That one's got to be hot by now." How long did it take to drink one beer anyway?

He smiled and moved his hand out of my reach. "No, thanks, John. I'm good. I have to limit myself since I'm competing, and I have to work third shift tonight, too."

I gritted my teeth and continued to follow him around like a puppy dog, but other people kept stopping me, talking to me, and he managed to get away. When I spotted him again, the beer bottle was gone and he was helping himself to a plate of food at the buffet. I wasn't sure what kind of DNA a lab could get off of a plastic fork, provided I could even get my hands on it. I strode toward him nevertheless, determined to attempt it.

"John!" Mackenzie and Edie stepped into my path, laughing, both carrying glasses of wine.

Edie put an arm around me and hugged me. "You're going to be a daddy, aren't you?" Oh God, if Edie knew, then everyone at the party would eventually know.

"Will told you, didn't he?" I was aggravated to think that he had broken his promise not to say anything.

Mackenzie squealed. "Told us? Then it's true?!"

Edie looked smug. "So I was right! I knew it."

Throwing her arms around me and spilling some of her wine on my shoulder, Mackenzie said, "Congratulations." She and Edie ran off to blab the news to everyone else, while I hit myself in the head with my fist, realizing I had been duped into confirming their suspicions.

By this time, Peter was gone again, so I made my way through the multitude of people, looking for him. Edie and Mackenzie had been at work, however, and the word was spreading like wildfire, so everyone was stopping me to offer congratulations, hugs, kisses, and handshakes. Then Caitlin caught up to me.

"I thought we agreed we weren't going to tell anyone yet," she growled into my ear as she pinched the tender flesh on the back of my arm.

"I didn't do it intentionally," I said, grabbing both her hands in mine to prevent any more pinches, and explaining to her what had transpired.

She began laughing. "I don't suppose Will would be in charge of a newspaper if he didn't have some clue what was going on around him, and I should have warned you about Edie. She could have been CEO of the Spanish Inquisition. I guess we might as well make the announcement, then, hadn't we? We won't let her steal all our thunder."

She pulled me over to the buffet table and once she had everyone's attention, she said, "John and I want to share our news with everyone, although Edie and Will have already sussed it out. We're pregnant!"

There were shouts and applause and Will made a toast, then the people who hadn't already offered personal congratulations were pressing toward us and it was another thirty minutes before I thought to look for Peter again. As it was, he found me.

I felt his hand on my shoulder. "Congratulations," he said as I turned around. "You and Caitlin have been busy, haven't you? Married in April and already expecting in September."

"Well, I've never been one to waste time when I see something I want," I replied and gave him a look I hoped he found meaningful. Unfortunately, I was successful.

He jerked his head for me to follow him and we walked around to the front of the house where it was quieter. "Listen, are you and Caitlin interested in a three-way with me because I'm getting these vibes from both of you. I swing both ways, you know, but I'm really more—well, more into you."

I vomited a little in my mouth and swallowed reflexively. I could only stare at him for a few minutes. I hated him, but I couldn't refuse the opportunity in case my efforts of tonight weren't successful. "Yes." I managed to force the word out of my mouth, and I hated myself even more. If I wasn't already in hell or going to hell for confessing to a murder I didn't commit, then I would surely go to hell for the lies I was telling now. I really wanted to punch him in the face and keep punching until there was nothing left. He moved closer to me and ran his hand down the length of my arm. I felt myself tensing. Any minute now I was going to explode like an atomic bomb. I pulled away from him. "Not here," I said, looking around and praying no one else had seen.

"That's fine," he murmured. "I understand."

No, you don't, I thought, *but you are damned well going to*. Out loud I said, "Caitlin may take a little more convincing, so I wouldn't say anything to her just yet."

"No problem; no pressure. I'm looking forward to it."

"Me, too," I said, but we were *not* talking about the same thing. "Let me get you another beer." I led the way around to the backyard again, grabbed another beer out of the tub, uncapped it, and handed it to him. Put your mouth on it, I silently urged him and was rewarded when he complied. God willing, I *would* get this bottle.

But God did not will, for I was once again distracted, this time by a small pair of arms encircling my right leg and a hand tugging at my left arm. I looked down to find a blonde head on either side of me and Adam and Gabey smiling up at me. They were a welcome distraction from the nastiness of Peter and I found myself grinning, happy to see them. "Hey, where did you guys come from? I wondered where you were."

"We just got back from the beach," Adam beamed, "and Daddy said we could come to the party for a while."

Gabey patted my leg and said, "I gots sunburned, John."

I picked him up and looked at his red little face. "You sure did. I missed you guys. I'm glad you're back."

"We missed you, too," Adam said. "You ought to see the seashells we got and we found a piece of driftwood shaped like a dinosaur and we got you a surprise, too. Gabey got knocked down by the waves and it scared him and I had to help him. We saw jellyfish and a dead shark but it wasn't as big as the one in *Jaws*! Guess what? I'm gonna play Mitey Mite football! Our team has the same colors as the Green Bay Packers." The child amazed me the way he could talk without drawing a breath.

"Sounds like you had a good time." I rubbed Adam's head. "I'll have to come watch some of your games." To Gabey I said, "I'm sorry you got knocked down by the waves. I guess that was pretty scary for you."

Gabey nodded his head solemnly. "They tumbled me 'round and 'round. I cried. Can you play with us?"

I gave him a little hug. "Sorry, buddy, I can't right now, but we'll play tomorrow, okay? Can you wait for me until then?"

Gabey nodded again and I stooped over to set him down next to his brother. When I straightened up, I saw the boys' mother and the man I took to be their father headed toward me. I had seen their mother a handful of times but had never talked to her, and I had never laid eyes on their father before.

I held out my hand. "Hi, Mr. and Mrs. Wade. Glad to meet you finally. I'm John Colucci."

The mother nodded at me. "I'm Pamela and this is Kevin." She indicated her husband.

He stuck out his hand and we shook. I saw an expression flit across his face as I introduced them to some of the other guests and to Caitlin, and noticed that he was staring at me openly. I was getting a really bad feeling.

Caitlin was saying to them, "I'm sure you knew John's sister and brother-in-law, Laurie and Randy Kimbell, who used to live here," and that's when everything blew sky high.

"Wait a minute," Kevin said, his voice rising. He pointed at me. "*You're* Laurie's brother? The one who molested and murdered that child?" He was shouting now and everyone in the vicinity stopped talking. Heads swiveled to look at us. He turned to his wife. "*This* is the John you've been letting our boys play with? You've been letting them play with a *child molester*? A *murderer*?"

"I didn't know. Kevin, I swear I didn't know." Her eyes were wide and she acted stunned.

The boys looked from their father to their mother to me. Gabey screwed up his face and began crying.

Adam pulled at his father's hand. "Daddy! Daddy, don't be mad at John. He's our friend."

"This man is *not* your friend, Adam!" Kevin shouted at him and the little boy flinched. "This man is a murderer. He does bad things to little boys."

Caitlin had heard enough. Her eyes flashed, but Kevin didn't recognize danger when it was staring him in the face. "My husband is not a murderer, nor has he ever molested a child. He was never convicted of *anything*. His only crime is having a mental illness and confessing to something he never did." Her voice was low and steady, but only someone who knew her would recognize the peril they were in.

"Well, excuse me," Kevin continued to shout. "My apologies. He's a *crazy* child-molesting, murdering monster. That certainly changes things!"

I was starting to seethe. "I'm not a monster and I'm not a child molester or a murderer! All I ever did to your children was be a friend to them, play with them. Maybe you should try doing a little of that yourself. They're obviously starved for attention."

"Don't you dare tell me how to parent my kids, and don't you *ever* come around them again." He stopped only long enough to draw a breath. "Maybe you think everyone's forgotten by now, but I remember what you did. If you aren't a child molester or murderer why did you confess to it? What kind of idiot would confess to something they didn't do?"

I couldn't respond because there wasn't anything to say that wouldn't take hours to explain. And even then it would make no sense. I looked down at the ground.

"Yes, that's what I thought. What have you done to my kids?" He stepped into my personal space, crowding me. Trying to provoke me. I took a step backward. I really didn't want to get into a physical altercation with him, which appeared to be what he was seeking now. He raised a fist. "You'd better tell me what you did to my kids! For God's sake, Gabey's handicapped. What kind of freak are you?"

"I've never done anything but be their friend and play with them." Adam and Gabey were both squalling at the tops of their lungs by this point.

"'Play', that's what your kind always calls it. Then you pull them into your sickness and destroy their innocence. Kevin turned to Pamela. "Take them home. *Now!*"

She grabbed each child by the hand and raced across the yard to their house. I could only imagine what the poor little guys were thinking and I ached for them.

"I haven't done anything to Adam or Gabey," I began again, but he put his hands on my chest and shoved me. I staggered but didn't fall and then Peter was standing beside us.

"Back off, Kevin," he said. I'd forgotten until that moment that he knew Adam and therefore must know his family as well. I also remembered that Peter had worked with the Police Athletic League at Adam's school and there was a very real possibility that he had already tried something with Adam or would do so eventually if he wasn't stopped. I could not stand the thought of that. I wanted to tell Kevin all of this, but who would believe me—a self-professed crazy child-molesting, murdering monster? We had to get DNA from Peter and we had to stop him without alerting him as to what we were doing. Anything less and he would be lost to us and remain in a position where he could prey on other kids. And I would be in a position of being blamed for it. Neither position was tenable.

"Peter." Kevin dialed his machismo back a couple of notches. "Don't tell me you're at this freak's party."

"Calm down. These are friends of mine."

"Don't tell me to calm down. You don't know what he might have done to Adam. To Gabey."

"You don't either," Peter replied. "Get out of his face."

The irony of the situation was almost more than I could bear. Kevin was indeed in the presence of a monster, but it wasn't me. Instead of calming down, he seemed to grow angrier.

"I want to know what you did to my kids!" He launched himself past Peter and grabbed me in a headlock. We were down on the ground rolling around, punches flying. He got in a few licks, popping me once in the mouth and once above my left ear, making my head ring. I got a foot in his nuts, which slowed him down long enough for Peter to yank him off of me.

Standing the man upright, Peter panted, "Kevin, if you make another move toward him, I will take you in on assault charges."

Kevin was breathing hard, too, and I'd never seen such loathing on a person's face.

I stood up, brushing off my clothes. I was feeling a lot of anger and hatred myself, and when Kevin spit on me, I fell on top of him swinging, fully intending to beat the shit out of him, except that now Peter was grabbing me and Will suddenly appeared and grabbed Kevin.

Peter pinned my arms behind me and muttered in my ear, "John, I'll haul your ass in, too, if I have to. Are you going to chill or do I need to handcuff you?"

I wrenched out of his grasp as Will frog marched Kevin through the yard and back to his house, Kevin shouting, "Leave this neighborhood, you perv, or, by God, you'll wish you had! Get your ass out of here or you might find your house burned to the ground!"

There was dead silence among the crowd, and I noticed some of the guests heading for their cars.

"Do we know how to throw a party, or what?" I said and there was laughter and gradually some of the noise resumed. Caitlin's friends made a valiant effort to keep the festivities going, pretending that nothing extremely mortifying had just taken place, and I came to the realization that they were now my friends, too. I was done just the same and wished everyone would go the hell home.

I got another glass of wine and went to sit at one of the tables. I hadn't yet eaten, but had no appetite. Peter sat down across from me, his knee touching mine. I didn't bother pulling away. The sooner this was over with, the better.

"I'm sorry about that mess," he said in a low voice.

I looked him in the eye. "I'm getting used to it."

The bastard couldn't meet my gaze, and he glanced away as he said, "Do you want to take out criminal charges against him for assault? Communicating threats?"

"And have to go to court?" I asked. "Or risk him taking out cross warrants against me so your buddies or the Sheriff's Department can have another go at me? Fuck that shit."

"Right, I wasn't thinking." It could have been my imagination, but he was looking distinctly uncomfortable, and I found that I was enjoying this.

"You don't know what hell I've been through," I said. "Being arrested for murder. Spending eight years in a mental institution. Knowing people hate me and want to see me dead. And now the articles in the paper." I wasn't lying, of course, but I admit I was reciting my litany for his benefit.

"What can I do?" he asked, finally meeting my eyes.

"I think you know," I replied and this time he didn't look away.

CHAPTER TWENTY-ONE

THE PARTY FROM HELL on the day from hell at the House from Hell ended with me being unable to find my cell phone. We turned the house and both vehicles upside-down looking for the damned thing but were unable to locate it. We tried calling it from Caitlin's cell phone, also with no result.

"Where did you last have it?" she asked, sounding annoyed.

"It was on my nightstand. I swear I left it on the charger."

"Well, obviously you didn't."

"I *did*. It was—"

Caitlin yawned and flapped her hand at me. "Never mind. It's not worth arguing about. Let's just go to bed. If you don't find it tomorrow, I'll buy you a new one—and I'll be sure to buy insurance on it, too."

It was after 2:00 AM before we finally got to bed, much too late for me to take an Ambien, and I knew I wouldn't be sleeping. I was so unsettled anyway after the fiasco of a party, that I doubted the Ambien would have had much effect. Lying together, Caitlin snuggled tight against me, I said, "Can you understand now why I can't stay around here?"

"You're not going to talk about leaving me again, are you?" she asked, her breath warm against my chest.

"I'm talking about *us* leaving. I'll crack somebody's skull before I put up with any more crap, but I'm not going to leave you to deal with the crazies on your own."

"Promise?"

"Promise."

"I guess it's pointless to ask if you were able to get anything with Peter's DNA or lack thereof?" She placed her palm on my face and I placed my hand over hers.

"No. I swear he must know what we're trying to do. I tried to get the bottle away from him, but it was like he was guarding it with his life, and then I kept getting distracted or interrupted. It was a comedy of errors. But get this—he asked if we were interested in a three-way with him."

Instead of shuddering against me, as I thought she might, she grew still, and I figured she had dropped off to sleep. "What did you tell him?" she asked after a few moments, making me wonder if she was seriously considering his proposition.

In the dark, I couldn't see the look on her face. "I told him we were interested, but that you weren't one hundred percent committed and to give you time."

"Did you, now?" She got quiet again and this time she had fallen asleep.

I dozed off briefly right before dawn and woke to the now familiar sound of retching. I got out of bed, only to discover—with my foot—that Caitlin had thrown up before reaching the bathroom.

"Watch where you step," she said as she met me in the hall.

"Now you tell me," I muttered. "You know this carpet is history, right?"

"Well, if we were in the *master* bedroom, we'd have an *en suite* bathroom and I wouldn't have as far to go." Just like that she was crying.

"Hey, I'm sorry." I pulled her to me, smoothing her hair. "Listen, stop crying. I'll move our bedroom furniture into the master bedroom today, all right?"

She smiled at me tearfully. "You'd do that for me?"

"Babe, I'd do *anything* for you. I'm sorry I was such an ass about the bedroom. Just please stop crying."

I got her calmed down and she went to shower and get ready for work. I clipped Willie's leash to his collar and we went out the front door for his morning walk. Almost immediately he stuck his nose to the ground and began sniffing, straining toward Caitlin's car. I allowed him to lead me in that direction, not realizing until we were standing next to it that the tires on this side were flat.

I walked around my truck. All the tires were flat. On my hands and knees, I could see a gash on the sidewall of the right rear tire, and immediately thought of Kevin Wade. My first impulse was to march over there and drag him outside for a fist fight. But the neighbor's cat chose that moment to saunter by and Willie lunged, yanking his lead from my hand as he zipped across the yard in hot pursuit.

Fifteen minutes and eight of the cat's nine lives later, I returned Willie to the house. "Bad dog." I scooped some kibble into his food bowl and refilled his water dish and went to tell Caitlin about the latest disaster.

She switched off the blow-dryer as I walked into the bathroom. "What's wrong now?"

"You must have ESP. You always know when something's up."

She gave a little laugh. "No, I don't have ESP, but you probably shouldn't ever take up poker playing. What's wrong?"

"Can one of your co-workers pick you up this morning?"

"Why would they need to?"

"We've got eight flat tires."

Her eyes flashed. "Flat tires? Mine are almost new and yours *are* new. Can you tell if they were cut or did someone just let the air out?"

"At least one of them has been slashed, but I don't know for sure. The valve stem caps are still on."

"I'm not going to work until I've called the cops and we've made a report."

"What's the point? We both know it was Kevin, but they're probably never going to prove it."

"That may be, but I'm tired of this. We're going to fight back, and if there's a chance they might find out who it was, it'll send a message to the rest of these redneck assholes."

She called her office to say she would be late and then dialed Kingsville Public Safety. I prayed Peter would already be off duty and the report wouldn't be assigned to him, but my prayers mainly fall on deaf ears, and of course he was the one who pulled up in a patrol car forty-five minutes later. Reluctantly, I followed Caitlin out of the house to talk to him.

"Good morning," he said. "Didn't think I'd be seeing you two again quite so soon. So what's the problem?"

I gestured to the vehicles. He walked slowly around both and knelt down to examine each of the tires. He stopped his inspection at the back of my truck. "Did you notice this, John?"

We joined him. Scratched into the paint on the tailgate of my brand new truck was the word "Murderer".

"I'm going to be a murderer before this is all over with," I muttered, and to Peter, I said, "You know Kevin Wade did this."

"Don't worry. I'm going to be having a talk with him. Let me get my report forms and camera out of the car and I'll be right back."

He made copious notes and took more photos than the situation probably warranted and finally had Caitlin sign some of the forms as registered owner of her vehicle. She handed them to Peter. "Well, if that's all you need, I've got to get to work." To me she said, "I'm going to call Mackenzie. She promised to come get me when I was ready," and went inside, leaving me alone with him.

He continued writing for a few moments, then held his clipboard out and indicated where I should sign. "I work a twelve-hour shift today," he said, "so I get off at 11:00. If you want, I'll come back then and help you take the rims off so you can get them to a tire store."

My first inclination was, of course, to refuse his help, but I knew if I did, it would be one more lost opportunity to hijack his DNA. "Thanks. I'd appreciate that." I gave him what I hoped passed for a grateful smile, trying my damnedest to hide what I was really feeling.

"Good. See you shortly after 11:00. Let's grab some lunch afterward."

Great. My lunch date with a killer. The title of a cheesy novel.

I found Caitlin at the bathroom vanity, swiping a mascara wand over her eyelashes. "Everything settled?"

"He's coming back after 11:00 to help me take the wheels off so we can get new tires. He asked me to lunch. I don't think I'll be able to eat anything."

"Please be careful."

"Don't worry," I assured her. "I don't want to end up as another one of his victims. But if this charade goes on too much longer, I *will* become a murderer. I want to take him down—make him suffer the way I have."

"Thank God you're not a little boy. You'd be totally at his mercy."

"Damned straight." Something tickled my memory. As soon as my mind tried to seize on it, though, it crawled back into its hole and try as I might to coax it out again, it would not come to me.

Caitlin raised her eyebrows. I could only shrug in response. She rearranged a tendril of hair. "I wish you had your phone. I'm going to be worried about you. For God's sake, please be careful."

"I will," I promised.

Her own cell phone chirped to indicate a new text message. She glanced at the screen and said, "Mackenzie just pulled up." She gathered her purse and tote bag from the console table in the foyer, and I trailed her out to the driveway.

"Please be careful," she said again, "and call me if you find your phone."

"Absolutely." I kissed her. She squeezed my ass. "Hey," I grinned, "you keep that up and I might just have to keep you home today."

Mackenzie beeped the horn and rolled down the passenger window. "You two might want to get a motel room."

"Hush," Caitlin said. "You're just jealous."

"I am, actually," Mackenzie admitted as Caitlin slid into the seat.

I waved as they pulled away and drove off down the street. Returning to the house, I spent another hour looking for the phone. It was just nowhere to be found. Giving it up for a lost cause, I busied myself with removing the drawers from the dresser and chest preparatory to moving them into the master bedroom. With the help of a couple of furniture gliders, I was able to transfer them from one room to the other, then worked on dismantling the bed.

Willie watched from the hallway, occasionally dashing into the room to bark at me or worry my shoelaces. I nearly tripped over him twice and finally decided I'd better walk him before Peter returned. When we got back, Peter's pick-up was already parked in the driveway and he was busy jacking up one side of the Avalanche.

Willie went apeshit. He strained at his leash, barking and snapping as if suddenly possessed, and lunged for Peter's heel. I managed to snatch him up just before he opened his tiny mouth to attack. I had never seen him act that way toward any other living thing, even the neighbor's cat, which he hated with a passion.

"Whoa, killer," Peter laughed, and I bustled Willie into the house.

The puppy continued to snarl until the door closed between us and Peter. I shut him in the laundry room and forced myself to return, dread slowing my footsteps. I was creeped out and on edge.

Peter already had one side of the Avalanche up on a jack stand, wheel off, and was working on the other side. "Grab the lug wrench there," he said, "and go ahead and loosen the lug nuts, then I'll finish jacking it up."

I did as he directed, wishing I could take the lug wrench to his skull instead. He slid the jack stand in place, then removed the wheel and rolled it around to the back of his big black sport pick-up truck.

"If you're cool with it, we'll drop these off and get some lunch while they're putting on the tires, then we'll do the other two. Once we get the truck taken care of, we'll work on Caitlin's car."

"Sounds like a plan." I ran into the house to grab my wallet and lock up.

He filled the travel time with talk of bodybuilding competitions he'd competed in, laughing about the attempts of the participants to psych each other out. He was slightly obsessed.

We dropped off the rims, and he asked, "King's Tavern?"

"That's fine." It was Caitlin's favorite pub and I knew the food was good, although I had my doubts about being able to eat anything.

"What'll you have to drink," he asked as we got settled in a booth. The lunch crowd was packed into the place and the noise level was rising.

"I'm going to stick with iced tea." I didn't need wine slowing me down—I had to be at one hundred percent, or as near as somebody like me was ever likely to get.

He shrugged. "Suit yourself. I think I'll have a beer, though."

"Go for it." I hoped it would make him less vigilant so I could be done with this once and for all.

The waiter brought the drinks and took our lunch order. Peter chose a huge-ass sandwich that would have made two meals for me and Caitlin—at least two pre-pregnancy meals. She could probably eat it by herself in one sitting now. I ordered my old stand-by—a BLT—since I knew it wouldn't sit too heavily on my stomach in case I felt the overwhelming urge to puke before the day was out.

I watched as he downed the beer, but as I was wondering how I could manage to get the bottle away from him, the waiter popped up, asked, "Another, sir?" and, when Peter declined, whisked it away. Any other time we could have sat there all day without being offered refills, but today I was fortunate enough to have the most efficient waiter in history. Now what? Paper napkin? Would that possibly work? He hadn't used any silverware, so that was a no-go. He hadn't touched his water glass either. Ok, paper napkin it was. Now if I could just filch it without him noticing—but I'll be damned if he didn't stuff the thing in his pocket as we were standing to leave.

I had never in my life been around someone who was so meticulous and so obviously paranoid. Even my fellow schizophrenics at Broughton Hospital weren't as paranoid. It defied belief, and I despaired of ever getting a sample from him.

After lunch, we picked up the new tires and installed them on the front of Avalanche. We were loading the rear wheels into Peter's truck when I heard him say, "Ow! *Damn it*!"

I looked up to see him grasping his left forefinger tightly in his right hand. "What's the matter?"

"The rim slipped." He opened his hand and I saw blood.

"Is it bad?" I had a hard time keeping the eagerness out of my voice.

"I sliced it pretty good."

"Come on and we'll get it cleaned up." Seizing his arm, I pulled him into the house and down the hall to the bathroom where I grabbed a wad of tissues from a box on the counter and pressed them into his hand. He wrapped them around his finger, blotting up the blood, while I switched on the faucet and adjusted the water.

"Here, let me see." I took his hand and peeled back the tissues, casually dropping them into the wastebasket next to the counter and shoving it with my foot behind the toilet. There was a good-sized gash on the thumb side of his index finger.

"You may have to get some stitches to close that up." I pushed his hand under the running water.

"Nah, I've had worse. Got any butterfly strips? That and a couple of Band-Aids ought to do."

I rooted through the drawer and found a tube of antibiotic ointment, bandages, and a box of butterfly strips. He finished cleaning off his finger and held it out to me. As I opened the drawer to replace the box, he reached for my hand and held it in his.

For one dreadful moment, I thought he would try to kiss me, and I knew if he did, the jig would be up. There was no way I could pretend to abide that. But he just gazed at me and said, "I'm ready when you are."

There were several different ways I could interpret this—most of them didn't bear contemplation. I applied some of the ointment to the wound, then placed three of the little closures up and down the cut, followed by two Band-Aids.

We finally finished and got the last two tires to the store before it closed. I was relieved to find Caitlin at home when Peter dropped me off, nearly $1,500 poorer. I thanked him for helping, assured him I could manage the last two tires by myself, and watched impatiently as he drove off before running into the house to greet Caitlin and let her know we finally had a sample.

I raced into the bathroom to snatch up the trashcan. The *empty* trashcan. I looked in the floor. In the corners. Behind the toilet. Nothing. "*Fuck*! Fuck, fuck *fuck*!"

She came to the doorway and stood peering in at me. "John, what are you yelling about?"

I held the empty trashcan out to her. "Where are the tissues that were in this trash can?"

"I flushed them. I didn't want to have to look at your bloody tissues every time I came in here until you emptied the trash. Why didn't you flush them to start with?"

"Because they weren't *mine*, goddamn it! They were *Peter's*!"

"Oh, my God. I didn't know. I'm sorry—I'm so sorry."

I wanted to cry. Instead I pounded my fist against my forehead until Caitlin grabbed my hand and forced it down by my side. "Do you understand how hard it was to get that? Do you have any concept what I went through—" but I stopped the tirade because, of course, she did, and because she was tearing up on me. And if there was one thing I could not stand, it was to see her weeping.

"I didn't know." She looked bereft.

"Of course not." I put a hand on her shoulder. "You couldn't have. It's just— I don't know when we'll get another opportunity. I can't pretend much longer. He's really freaking me out. We're messing with a killer here, for God's sake." I couldn't tell her about his attraction to me and how revolting I found it.

A tear coursed down her cheek and she brushed it away, but another quickly followed.

"Please don't cry," I begged her. "I'm not blaming you. I'm just at my wit's end, and I'm scared that any day Whisnant and Samuels are going to show up on our doorstep with a pair of handcuffs and an arrest warrant."

"We'll get the sample, John. I promise."

"I don't want you trying to get it on your own," I told her. "Especially now that you're pregnant."

Unshed tears were still brimming in her eyes, but she gave me her sweet little smile. "Being pregnant doesn't automatically make me helpless, you know."

I pulled her to me, enveloping her in my arms. "No, but it makes you doubly precious to me."

CHAPTER TWENTY-TWO

I WAS ACTUALLY in a good mood the next morning despite the fiasco of the previous two days, mostly owing to Caitlin's early morning booty call. For a change, she wasn't puking her guts out first thing.

"Thank you for moving us into the master bedroom," she whispered as we lay together afterward.

"You're welcome." I loved early mornings like this—her soft, smooth body pressed against mine, the sight, smell and taste of her filling my senses. "Can you go in late one more morning?" I was getting my second wind, ready to go once more.

"Well, maybe just a few minutes late." She reached for me and made me happy all over again.

I was still smiling, humming to myself, as Caitlin headed for the shower. I dressed and went to the kitchen to set out some breakfast stuff for her and get Willie for his morning walk. He danced around my feet, yapping and eager to go. He wriggled impatiently until I clipped his leash to his collar, then turned a summersault down the steps in his excitement to get outside.

"You want to go running this morning?" I asked as we trotted toward the street. He managed to keep up the first fifteen minutes or so and when he started lagging and his little tongue started lolling, I slowed it down to a fast walk, then dialed it back to a leisurely stroll.

I saw the first sign posted near the subdivision entrance and, although aware that subdivision by-laws prohibited such, I assumed it was for a yard sale. I was almost past it when I glanced over and stopped dead in my tracks. Willie bumped into my heel and plopped down on his haunches. The size of a realtor's sign, it was printed on neon orange poster board with black magic marker and consisted of five words. "Child molester/murderer this way" with an arrow pointing in the direction of the House from Hell.

I stared at it for several long minutes, feeling dread and shame flooding my body, then found myself looking around for the culprit, though it was hardly likely the person responsible for erecting the sign would still be present. I yanked it out of the ground and tossed it behind some shrubs, tucked Willie into the crook of my arm, and set off at a run.

The second sign was posted further down the next block, and contained the same message with the added words, "Getting closer". There were six more scattered along our return route, not including the one taped over the "For Sale" sign in our own yard, which read "The murdering bastard lives here." I set Willie down in the yard and numbly ripped at the poster board. By this time I was shaking with fury. I knew that the minute I set foot in the house, Caitlin would know something was wrong and badger me until I told her. I did *not* want to tell her and watch her cry. I wanted this shit to be over. One way or the other, it had to end, and I was really beginning to doubt that it would be in my favor.

I took the remnants of the posters around to the garbage bin and tossed them in, covering them with a bag of trash so that Caitlin wouldn't accidentally see, and spent a few minutes working on my poker face. When I thought I had managed to mask my feelings sufficiently, I whistled to Willie.

Caitlin's reprieve from morning sickness had not lasted very long. I heard her retching the moment I walked into the house. I stayed in the kitchen to give myself additional time to practice pretending nothing was wrong. Knowing she wouldn't be eating anything now, I packed a cup of yogurt and a container of strawberries and blueberries in a bag for her to take to work—if her stomach settled down.

Thankfully, she was too preoccupied to pay much attention to me. She took the bag, gave me a kiss, patted Willie on the head, got her stuff and left.

As soon as she was out the door, I got the keys to my truck and drove around the neighborhood, where I located eight more signs. My anger increased exponentially with each one I confiscated. I checked the rear entrance to the subdivision—yet another. I drove out onto Sheridan Boulevard. There was a much larger sign posted before the turnoff to the main entrance. How Caitlin had managed not to see them, I didn't know, but for once I was grateful for the distraction of morning sickness. I pulled the truck onto the shoulder of the highway and jumped out to grab the last sign when I noticed a man standing across the highway next to his parked car, pointing a camera in my direction, following my moves.

I yanked the sign out of the ground, slung it into the truck bed, checked for traffic, and started across the five-lane highway toward him. Before I could reach the center turn lane, he'd gotten in his car and started it. By the time I'd reached the driver's door, he had it in gear and was pulling away, squalling his tires.

"Yeah, run away, you bastard!" I yelled after him.

I drove to the house, ran into the kitchen, grabbed a roll of tape and a black Sharpie marker from the junk drawer, and went out to the truck. Taking one of the signs from the truck bed, I pulled the poster board from the metal frame, flipped it over and began writing a message of my own. I taped it to the frame and drove around to Kevin Wade's house.

There were no cars in their driveway and no sign of life inside the house—it was past time for 9 to 5 people to be at work—but it wouldn't have mattered if there had been. I put the truck in park, got out, reached for my revised sign, and pushed the metal pronged feet into the lawn. Once I had it positioned for maximum effect, I grabbed the other signs, piling them all into the middle of Wade's yard. When I was finished, I stood back and surveyed my handiwork, smiling to myself as I re-read my sign. "The asshole lives here."

#

I obsessed about the signs the rest of the day and Willie got more exercise than he bargained for. As of 5:00 PM, no other signs had been posted and I took Willie back to the house so I could begin preparing supper. He immediately went to his dog bed in the laundry room and flopped down, not moving even when Caitlin came home.

She and I went to work out at the gym and returned around 7:00 PM. While she showered, I cooked off the pasta to go with the sauce I'd made earlier, toasted the garlic bread, and dressed the salad. We had just finished eating and Caitlin had gone into the den to watch television, leaving me to clean up, when I heard the doorbell ring.

"I'll get it," she called.

"Thanks," I yelled, rooting through the cabinets for containers in which to put the leftovers, eager to get everything cleared away and the dishwasher loaded so I could watch TV with her.

I heard some murmuring and a couple of male voices, and several minutes later, Caitlin was saying loudly, "Sir, I think you need to leave. Now."

I dropped what I was holding and ran to the foyer. "What the hell is going on?"

There were two men poised just inside the front door. One was balding, with a fringe of gray hair encircling his head, the other was red-haired with freckles. Both wore Dockers and polo shirts, which just proved that bad fashion never goes out of style. The balding guy's face was red and his companion shifted his feet uncomfortably. I had never seen either of them before. Caitlin looked ready to eat them both alive.

"Who are you?" I walked up to the men, getting up in the bald guy's face, forcing him to look up at me. I stood about a head taller than him and he looked soft and pudgy, like a marshmallow. He took a step backward but found the wall preventing his retreat.

"Bob P-Patterson," he stammered. "I'm president of the neighborhood homeowner's association."

"What do you want?" I asked, not moving from in front of him. "What did you say to my wife?"

He swallowed and cut his eyes to his companion. The other man did nothing to help him out; he just stood there mute, his eyes wide.

"I'm waiting," I said. My heart was beating fast. "If you don't start talking, I'm going to start busting some heads." He didn't know how unlikely that was and this was the only situation I could think of where my ill repute could be used to my advantage. It was apparent from his reaction that he believed me capable of it.

"We—we came to ask you to move," he blurted out. "N-no one wants you here. No one wants you around their children."

"We're working on that," I said. "Or didn't you see the 'For Sale' sign in the yard?"

"Yes, sir, we saw it. But the other homeowners want you gone immediately."

"We'll leave when the house is sold." I would have liked nothing better than to walk out of the House from Hell at that precise second and never look back, but now it was a matter of perverse principle.

"Sir, you need to just—" Bob began.

"Don't tell me what I need to do," I shouted in his face, taking pleasure in seeing him flinch. I reached for the handle on the front door and flung it open. I pointed and said, "I think you'd better heed my wife's advice and *leave*."

Bob and his companion didn't wait for me to tell them again. They left. Quickly. I slammed the door behind them.

Caitlin watched me with a funny expression on her face before finally saying, "Who are you and what did you do with John?"

"It's the new and improved John," I said. "You like?"

She laughed. "I like. I like a *lot*, but I don't think Bob liked."

"There's goes my upstanding reputation in the neighborhood."

#

If my reputation in the neighborhood or the county or, indeed, Western North Carolina wasn't tarnished enough, there was a smarmy article in *The Asheville Journal* the next day about the signs posted in the subdivision, accompanied by the title "Neighborhood Fights Back Against Suspected Sexual Predator". Of course there were photos of the signs posted around the development, obviously taken before I found them, and one of me yanking the sign off the side of the highway. For the one or two people who didn't yet know all the dirt on me, there was a rehash of the murder I had confessed to and been tried for. For those same one or two people who didn't yet know where I lived, the paper helpfully provided my address. The reporter also did an excellent job of pointing a finger at me for the most recent murders.

"Why didn't you tell me about the signs?" Caitlin asked after reading the article to me. She shook the paper in my face. "Didn't you think I should know? John, you wanted to leave, and I think now is the time we should do that. You were right. Let's just go."

It was going to be a bad day. First the Voices had started in on me, now her. I'd taken my meds, but I may as well not have bothered for all the good they were doing. As calmly as I was able, I replied, "We are not going anywhere until this house is sold. You're the one who said we should fight back. Well, I'm ready to fight now and God help the first person who gets in my way."

"You don't leave me any choice then." She handed me a folded document on vellum-type paper. "I was going to wait and give this to you for our six-month anniversary, but in light of our situation, I decided now was as good a time as any."

"Divorce papers?" I was only half joking.

"You wish. You aren't that lucky."

I unfolded the paper and tried to decipher what I was holding. The word "deed" leaped out and then the word "grantee" followed by my name and Caitlin's— Caitlin Murphy Colucci. It was the first time I had seen her name printed that way, and it gave me a weird tingly feeling. Further down the page was a long paragraph containing numbers and symbols such as "75° 25' 15" East 455 feet…" None of it made any sense to me. "What is it?" I asked.

"It's the deed to the lake cottage. I bought out my cousins' interest. It now belongs to you and me."

"You're kidding." I turned away from her so she wouldn't see how choked up I was. She reached for my hand and placed it on her abdomen and that choked me up even more.

"You're fighting dirty. I've given you nothing but headache and heartache," I said when I was able to speak without my voice breaking.

"That's just not true. You've given me you. You've given me our baby. Nothing can compare with those gifts. Certainly not a cottage that's close to seventy-five years old. But let's just go there and leave this all behind."

I was so tempted. It was all I had ever wanted since first laying eyes on the place, and yet here I was refusing. What the hell was wrong with me? "I want to enjoy my life. I want to enjoy us—our baby, but I don't want to spend the rest of my life paying for something I didn't do. Being ostracized and vilified, knowing people hate me. I can't live that way, and I'm not going to take this ass-fucking anymore. If I'm going down, I'm taking someone with me. I want you to go to the cottage. I want you out of here, 'cause this shit's going to get ugly."

She was shaking her head before I even finished speaking. "I'm not leaving without you. No way."

I took a deep breath and attempted to get a handle on my frustration. "Did I ever tell you how crazy you make me?"

"It can't be any crazier than you make me."

#

We were in bed, lights out, and I had almost dropped off to sleep when Caitlin said, "I'm going to have a girl's night out tomorrow night, so I'll be late getting home, okay?"

I was sleepy for a change, so I just grunted in consent, turned over and drifted off, not thinking to ask where she was going and who she would be with. Whenever I took Ambien, I always had trouble remembering anything that happened between the time I took it and waking up the next morning. I hated having to take it, but I hated not sleeping even worse. It wasn't until the next evening when it was time for her to be home from work and I had supper ready and was wondering where she was at, that I had a vague, dreamlike recollection of her telling me she was going out. I pulled out the new cell phone she'd purchased for me to replace the one I'd lost and tried calling her to confirm, but her phone went straight to voice mail. Of course.

So I went ahead and ate, fed Willie, and took him out, discovering that someone had put up more friendly neighborhood child molester signs since we'd walked earlier in the afternoon. I went back to the house for the truck and spent a while removing them. A couple of the neighbors were watching me, but when I shouted, "What are *you* looking at?" they went back in their houses. I wasn't even pretending to be nice or sane anymore.

After disposing of the newest signs, Willie and I settled down on the sofa in the den to watch TV. There wasn't much worth watching—not that there ever is—and I found myself dozing off and on until around 11:00 PM, when I gave it up and went to take my Ambien. I was in bed and asleep by 11:30.

I'm not sure how many times my cell phone rang—the new ringtone incorporated itself into my dreams flawlessly—before it filtered through my sleep-fogged brain and I woke up. It stopped ringing before I could coordinate my thoughts with my limbs. I reached for it belatedly, my heart beating a fast tempo. The time was 3:17 AM, and I didn't recognize the number of the missed call. I looked around. Caitlin wasn't in bed. My heart beat faster.

I hastily pulled on my clothes and walked through the house, phone in hand, stopping to look out the living room window. Caitlin's car was not in her parking spot. My heart ceased beating. Where the hell *was* she?

As I stood there in an Ambien stupor, trying to decide what to do, two things happened simultaneously. My cell phone rang again, and I saw a car turning into the driveway. I pressed the talk button and put the phone to my ear, at the same time pulling back the sheers to get a better view. I could already tell it was not Caitlin's car.

"Hello?" I said, feeling my heart at the back of my throat.

"Mr. Colucci?" a crisp, professional female voice asked.

"Yes, this is John Colucci. Who is this?"

"Sir, I'm calling from Kingsville Memorial Hospital."

"My God, something's happened to Caitlin."

The bell rang and I went to it, flipping on the porch light and throwing open the door. It was Will Lackey.

The voice on the phone was speaking again. "You wife is being treated in the emergency room and she needs for you to come down."

"What's happened to Caitlin?" I addressed the question to both her and Will. I was going to be very, very sick. "What's happened to her?!"

"Sir, do you have someone who can bring you to the hospital right away? Your wife's being treated—"

"Oh my God." My first thought was that the Mad Mauler had gotten to her. My blood was freezing in my veins.

"—she's not critically injured, but we need for you to come immediately. Do you have someone who can bring you, Mr. Colucci? You probably shouldn't try to drive yourself."

"Yes, there's someone here now. I'll have him bring me. I'll be right there." I hit the end button and looked at Will. "That was Kingsville Memorial. Caitlin's in the emergency room. What's going on? What are you doing here?"

"Come on, John, and I'll drive you. Caitlin had them call me when they couldn't get you to answer the phone. All I know is that she was assaulted."

"No, no, please God, no." I put my head in hands and felt a cold rage building, but Will was pulling me to the door, pushing me down the steps and into his car.

I remembered nothing of the drive to the hospital, but as soon as he pulled up to the emergency room entrance, I was out and running toward the door and the reception desk, demanding to know where Caitlin was.

I waited an agonizing fifteen minutes for them to locate her and send someone to take us to her. It seemed like several lifetimes. Will stood silently by my side, while I tried unsuccessfully to fight back tears. People in the waiting room were watching me with interest, obviously intrigued by the drama playing out before them. I wanted to scream at them to mind their own business.

A nurse finally came to get us and led us back to one of the treatment rooms, pulling aside the privacy curtain as we entered. Caitlin lay there on the gurney, her eyes closed. I had imagined all kinds of horrible scenarios—bruises, lacerations, disfigurement, broken bones—but I could see nothing visibly wrong with her. She opened her eyes as we came into the room, tears welling on her lower lids.

I knelt beside her, taking her hand and kissing it. I pushed her hair behind her ear. "What happened? Are you okay?"

Before she could even answer, a female deputy stepped into the room with a nurse behind her. I stood warily. The nurse came over to Caitlin and introduced the officer as Lila French of Kings County Sheriff's Department. She patted Caitlin's shoulder and said, "We've got to do a rape kit now, honey, and Officer French is here to take custody of the evidence."

My brain locked on the word. "*Rape*?" A tremor shot through me. "You were *raped*?"

Will moved beside me and placed a hand on my arm. "John, let's walk outside while they finish. Okay?"

I shook his hand off, but he gripped my arm again, tighter, and tried to push me toward the door. "No! I want to know what happened."

"John, *now*. Let them treat her. We'll get the details when they're done."

I looked at the nurse. "My wife is pregnant. Please tell me that she's going to be okay—that the baby's okay."

"They're getting ready to examine her, sir. Someone will speak with you when they're done. Your wife is not in any medical danger." The nurse beckoned to me and Will to follow her into the hallway and pulled the door shut behind her. "When you talk to her, you need to try and remain calm. She's going to need your support, and getting upset isn't going to help her right now."

"What happened?" I asked again. "What the hell happened? How could she have been raped? She was just going out with a couple of girlfriends." But I realized as the words left my mouth that I didn't know *who* she had gone out with or where she had gone.

Will and I were led back out to the waiting room and left with assurances that someone would return for us as soon as the examination was finished. More than two hours later we were still waiting, and I was pacing a hole in the linoleum, ready to grab the first person in scrubs and demand a report.

"How could my life get any worse?" I muttered.

Will shook his head. "I'll be the first to admit that you've had more than your fair share of trouble. You've had a hard life."

"I've had a *fucked* life, Will! There's a monumental difference. And the fucking continues every single day, except that now it's branched out to

Caitlin." I was breathing hard. Any second the rage would burst forth and annihilate everything in its path.

"I don't know what to say, John, except the nurse was right. It's not going to help Caitlin for you to have a meltdown. I know you're upset and angry, but you're going to have to help her get through this and you can't do it if you're losing your mind. Come on, take a big breath."

I remembered Caitlin telling me many times to breathe deeply when I was stressed out. Breathe deep, hold it, breathe out. So I concentrated on breathing. The exercise didn't eliminate the rage, but it kept me from acting on it. At least for the time being. Breathe deep, hold it, breathe out. Breathe, damn it, breathe. I noticed people watching me again, and went over to a corner of the room, where I sat, eyes closed, so I wouldn't have to see their staring faces.

At long last, a voice at my elbow said, "Mr. Colucci? Mr. Lackey?" and I looked up to find another woman clad in scrubs. "Would you come with me, please?"

She led us to an empty examination room and introduced herself as Dana Barnes, a sexual assault nurse examiner. "You're Caitlin Murphy's husband and father?" she asked us. I didn't bother to correct her about Will's relationship. Close enough.

I nodded, impatient. "Is she okay? Is the baby okay?"

She smiled at me reassuringly. "She's fine. The baby is fine. In some cases of rape, there's very little physical trauma and that appears to be the situation here. The majority of the trauma is psychological, and often the victims blame themselves. We've done the rape kit and she's been interviewed by law enforcement." She continued, but I couldn't pay attention. I wanted to see Caitlin and hold her. Ask her who had done this unspeakable thing to her. Find that person and punish him in ways that would have him screaming for mercy, which would not be forthcoming.

Ms. Barnes pressed some pamphlets into my hands and encouraged me to make sure Caitlin saw her obstetrician immediately and followed up with a rape crisis center for counseling.

"Yes, okay," I said, interrupting her, "but can I see her now? Please?"

"Of course." Down the hallway we went and into the room where Caitlin was being treated. She was sitting up on the edge of the exam table, wearing a hospital gown.

She held a wad of tissues in her hand and pressed them to her face as we came in. Her hair was now wet and her skin looked red, as if she had been scrubbing at it. "They let me take a shower, but I still feel dirty." She plucked at the hospital gown. "They took my clothes for evidence, so I'll have to wear this home. Can I please go home now?"

Ms. Barnes said, "Absolutely, sweetie. Let me get your discharge summary and you'll be all set."

I put my arms around Caitlin, pressing her face against my chest, holding her while we waited. And waited. Finally, Ms. Barnes came back carrying another handful of papers, which she handed to me, for all the good they would have done me.

After wrapping Caitlin in another hospital gown, worn like a robe to keep her backside from being exposed, we were ready to leave. She refused the offer of a ride in a wheelchair. "I'm not waiting another half hour while they find one," she muttered to me under her breath. "I want to go home *now*. Take me home." So we took her home.

Will came in the house with us long enough to help get her settled, then left after promising to check in with us later on. I tried to get her to go to bed but she insisted she wanted to take another shower, so I followed her into the bathroom, feeling useless.

She pulled off the hospital gowns and dropped them in the floor beside the shower stall while she adjusted the water temperature, and I saw what looked like a bite mark on her right breast and bruises on her thighs. I felt my heart seize and I went over to her, caressing her shoulder.

She pulled away and turned her back to me. "Not now, John. Please. Can I be alone for a while?"

"Sure." I managed to reply in a calm manner, but anger at her assailant coursed through me until I thought it would burn my flesh from the inside out. Reluctantly, I left her in the bathroom alone and went to take Willie for a late walk.

When we returned, I went to check on Caitlin. She was still in the shower and as I stood at the bathroom door, I could hear her sobbing, "God, please forgive me."

I knocked on the door and went in without waiting for her to reply. I got the largest, fluffiest bath towel I could find from the linen closet, and turned off the water. I wrapped the towel around her and had her step out onto the bathmat while I dried her off oh-so-gently. I took her favorite nightgown from the hook on the back of the door, slipped it over her head, and directed her to the bed. I covered her up and knelt down in the floor next to her.

"Are you able to tell me what happened?" I smoothed her hair back from her forehead.

She stared at me for several long moments and I couldn't read the expression on her face. Fear? Dread? Shame? There were tears in her eyes when she replied. "We finally got a biological sample from Peter."

CHAPTER TWENTY-THREE

WILL CAME BY the next morning bearing a bag of doughnuts, coffee, and the day's edition of *The Asheville Journal.* For a pleasant change of pace, instead of articles and photographs in which I figured prominently, *The Journal* sported the front page headline "Kingsville Public Safety Officer Accused of Rape," and there was a photograph of Peter.

Caitlin came into the kitchen as Will finished reading the article to me. She was dressed for work.

"You are *not* going to the office today." I was rewarded with her go-to-hell expression. Time for some backpedaling. "I mean, I don't think you should go in today." I turned to Will for support.

"No, ma'am. You're not working today. In fact you're taking the rest of the week off." He was either immune to "the look" or he just didn't care. Then again, he didn't have to live with her.

I tried one more time. "Why don't you stay here and rest? Or we could go to the lake for a couple of days and just hang out."

"Listen to him, Caitlin. Take the rest of the week off."

There was a stubborn set to her jaw. "I'm going to work and that's the end of it." She glimpsed the headline on the newspaper and held out her hand. "May I?" She scanned it and returned it to Will. "As usual they got some of their facts wrong." But rather than elucidate, she gathered her purse and keys and said, "I'll see you shortly, Will." She kissed me but still wouldn't meet my eyes, and again I got the feeling that there was something she wasn't telling me.

She paused at the door. "Oh, John I need for you to start putting some of the stuff we don't use every day in storage. That way there's no clutter when the realtor is showing the house, and we can leave it until we decide where we're going to live." She gave me directions to the unit and dug the key from her purse. By the time she left, she almost had me believing it was just a normal day and nothing horrific had happened a little over twenty-four hours earlier.

Will folded the paper. "I'd better get to the office as well. It probably goes without saying, but you and Caitlin need to be careful. Kingsville Public Safety isn't going to appreciate this."

"I'll be as careful as I can. I guess I need to get busy, too. I'm already up shit creek without a paddle. It won't do if I'm nct finished by the time she gets home."

After Will left, I went out to the garage where we'd stowed all the empty boxes after moving in a few short weeks earlier. Originally planning to take them to the recycling center, I was glad now that I hadn't. In the living room, I started packing books, CDs and DVDs. Then worked on kitchen stuff—God what a bunch of crap we had. We might have used only ten percent of it on a regular basis. If we were going to live at the cottage, we'd have to jettison most of this junk; there was simply no room for it.

I hauled the first load to the storage unit, then came back for another. This time I worked on seasonal clothing, packing most of our summer stuff away since the days and nights were beginning to cool off. The majority of the clothes were Caitlin's. Despite having to replace her entire wardrobe earlier in the year after the break-in while we were in Vegas, she could have single-handedly stocked a clothing boutique on her own. The closet in the master bedroom was a generous 8 X 8 with a custom organizing system. Out of sixty-four square feet of space, I was allotted maybe four.

Just for fun, I counted my wearing apparel. Not including t-shirts and shorts and other items in my dresser, I owned one suit, two dress shirts, five pairs of jeans, five long-sleeved and five short-sleeved button-up shirts, a winter coat, a jacket, and a zippered, hooded sweatshirt. One pair of boots, a pair of dress shoes, a pair of Topsiders, and a pair of cross-trainers. I was seriously lacking in the wardrobe department by Caitlin's standards.

I packed several boxes of clothing, then turned to Caitlin's shoes. No kidding, fifty-two pairs. Sandals constituted about half of the inventory. On to the purses. Seriously, why does any woman need twenty purses?

I thought I had most of the shoes packed when I noticed two larger boxes shoved to the back of the top shelf. I almost decided to leave them where they were and say the hell with it, but knew when it came time to move again, I'd be glad I'd packed up as much junk as possible.

As I reached for the boxes, one slipped from my hand and fell to the closet floor. The lid popped off and photographs and newspaper articles spilled out. I squatted down, sifting through the mess. My own face stared back at me. There were dozens of photographs, all from my trial—me entering or leaving the courtroom clad in an orange jumpsuit and a bulletproof vest, surrounded by deputies, shackles on my wrists and ankles, a chain around my waist connecting the two. Photos of me sitting in the courtroom, head in my hands in some, staring into space looking drugged in others, my face wet with tears in yet others, my hair wild, my eyes wilder. Why did Caitlin have them?

I tried to read some of the articles but that, of course, was beyond my ability. There were numerous small notepads, the pages full of Caitlin's handwriting, some with dates nine years earlier. I slowly gathered everything, trying to make sense of it, trying to understand why she had saved these articles. Yeah, sure, she was a reporter, but she wasn't a reporter *then*. She was only a few months older than me. She would have been twenty years old at the time of my trial—still in college.

I took the box into the kitchen, set it on the table, and stared at it for a while, trying and failing to come up with a reason for Caitlin to have this stuff. I arranged the contents on the surface of the table, so that every square inch was covered by an article or photograph, then went back to packing.

I was ruthless. If we hadn't used an item since moving into the House from Hell, then in a box it went. I was sure to get bitched out over a few things, but so be it. I loaded the truck and whistled for Willie. He came running and nearly lost his little doggie mind when he realized he was going for a ride. He climbed up on the passenger seat and sat at attention while we drove to the storage facility. Once the boxes were unloaded, I took him to the dog park near the house and let him run, watching as he raced around the enclosure and played with a Shih Tzu and a Border Collie. But I still had work to do, so after thirty minutes I chased him down, stuck him in the truck, and headed to the house.

The siren call of the shoebox proved irresistible, however, and I sat down at the table, scrutinizing the photos and articles yet again. When the doorbell rang, I went to answer it without thinking twice. I no sooner flipped the latch on the deadbolt and turned the knob, when the door crashed inward and a large uniformed figure pushed his way in. A pair of hands grabbed the front of my shirt. Randy.

I broke free and lurched toward the kitchen, thinking to escape out the back, but I was met by two other police officers entering through the French doors. They half-dragged, half-pushed me to the living room sofa, where they turned me loose so quickly that I fell. Before I could right myself, Randy yanked me around to face him. From the window I caught a glimpse of three police cruisers parked in front of the house, lights flashing. Randomly, I wondered how long it would take for word of this to get back to the homeowner's association and Bob to come knocking on my door, demanding that I vacate the premises. Soon, I hoped.

"I don't know how you did it," Randy snarled, "but you managed to hook up with someone who is crazier than you are."

It didn't matter whether or not I responded. He was going to beat my ass regardless. My choices were between having it beaten now or getting it beaten later, so I sat on the sofa, hands clasped between my knees where Randy couldn't see them shaking.

"What does your crazy whore of a wife think she's doing?"

Okay, I couldn't let that slide. "She's *not* a whore."

"Yeah, John, she is. She screwed Peter behind your back. That qualifies as a whore in my book."

"Peter *raped* her. That doesn't make her a whore." I attempted to stand but he shoved me back down.

"Rape? You've got a lot to learn about that little wife of yours. She's *claiming* Peter raped her. What she didn't tell you is that she went out on a date with him. I don't know what kind of sick game she thinks she's playing, but she has fucked up big time now."

"She didn't go on a date with him."

"She did, and that's exactly what she told the detective. It's in the report. Ask the slut and see what she tells you."

Had I not previously gotten the impression that she was holding something back, I would have defended her with my dying breath. The black seed of doubt was planted now—already thoughts of Caitlin in bed with Peter were eating at my brain, but I couldn't let Randy know. I didn't want to believe what he was telling me; however, that feeling in my gut told me I was hearing the truth. My gut was also telling me that Caitlin and I were heading for a major confrontation, but first I had to survive this showdown. He hadn't come to gloat over the fact that my wife was unfaithful to me with a murderer. He never did anything unless he could intimidate, terrorize, and humiliate in the bargain, and he had only just arrived.

"What do you want, Randy?" If I hoped to come out of the ordeal with all my teeth intact and no broken bones, maybe it was best to get right to the point.

"I want to know what kind of sick game that bitch is playing. Peter's been on the police force for fifteen years. His record has been exemplary.

Unblemished. Now he's been suspended until this shit has been resolved—arrested on nothing more than the word of that whore you're married to!"

"Don't call her a whore!" Never mind I was thinking the word to myself, I couldn't stand to hear him say it. I attempted to rise. Again he shoved me backward.

"Caitlin picked the wrong person to fuck with. If you think your life was bad before, just wait. It's about to get one hundred times worse than you ever imagined. Every cop in Kingsville is gunning for the two of you. Get her to recant that accusation. Get her under control, John."

"I don't control her. Not like you try to control Laurie."

The expression on his face was particularly nasty. "If *you* don't get her under control, then I will, and I will enjoy every second of it."

As angry as I was with her and as much as I wanted to punish her myself, my blood ran cold at the thought of what he or the others would do to her. "Randy, no. Don't hurt her, please. She's pregnant."

He graced me with his customary sneer. "So I heard. And that's great. Just what the world needs. A triple dose of crazy. Neither one of you is fit to raise a child, and I think a judge would take one look at your record and agree. I'll see to it that you never get the chance. Laurie and I would love a baby."

"You won't raise *my* baby. I'll see you dead first. I'll see us all dead!"

Randy addressed the other officers. "You guys heard him. He threatened to kill me, kill himself."

The two officers voiced agreement.

When would I ever learn to keep my mouth shut around him?

"Sounds to me like he's getting out of control. Maybe he needs to be tased."

Time to talk fast. "Listen to me, Randy. Peter is the one who committed the murder I was arrested for. He's also the one behind the recent murders, and the biological evidence is going to prove that."

"What the hell are you talking about? The biological evidence has already proven that you did it, genius."

"It only proved that I was at the scene, not that I committed the crime. The other evidence points to Peter and the evidence from the rape will confirm that."

His face turned an angry crimson. "You are not going to lay this at Peter's feet. You are *not!* Caitlin put you up to this, didn't she? She has filled your head with such bullshit. Get her to recant, John, or by God, you will wish you were back in Broughton. She's using you, but I'll be damned if I can figure out why she felt it necessary to marry you, unless maybe she was afraid you'd run off before she could finish her story. Let me ask you this, Mr. Genius. How do you even know that baby is yours? You'd better ask for a paternity test when it's born."

With crystal clarity, I remembered my telephone conversation with Caitlin in July when I was at the lake and she was in Kingsville, the man's voice in the background calling her name. She could have gone out for a drink with some of her co-workers, or she could have been on a date with another man. With Peter. I didn't want to doubt her about the baby. I didn't. So why did this make me so angry?

"Shut up!" I screamed at Randy. "Shut up! Why do you hate me? What have I ever done to you?"

The other officers moved in closer. Close enough for me to read their name tags. M. Levitt and D. Hopkins. Levitt took a contraption from his utility belt. It looked like a plastic toy gun.

"Drive stun?" Levitt asked Randy.

"Yeah. We'll start with that and move on to the barbs if that doesn't produce the desired results."

Beads of sweat gathered across my forehead and my armpits were suddenly damp. "There are rules against stuff like this," I said like a moron.

Randy grinned at me. "Rules against what? We're just having a little chat. Don't think that's against any rules." He looked to Levitt and Hopkins. "You guys know of any rules against that?"

Levitt shook his head and held the taser toward me. "Nothing wrong with chatting."

I tried moving out of his reach, but in a practiced move, Randy grabbed me in a headlock, and Levitt touched the taser to my shoulder. The sensation that followed was akin to what one might feel after slamming into a brick wall at a hundred miles an hour. I uttered an involuntary howl of pain and went down in a heap. Willie began barking frantically in the laundry room.

Before my scrambled brain cells could transmit a message to my legs to stand, Randy was on top of me, pinning me down. "I don't think you and Caitlin comprehend what you're dealing with here, John."

It was difficult to answer with Randy's knee at the back of my head, mashing my face to the floor. "I do, I do," I attempted to say, but I sounded drunk. They all laughed at me.

"Let's make sure he gets the message." Levitt touched the taser to my back once again and held it there until I thought I would pass out. It took a moment for me to recognize the strange keening filling the room as my own voice. Willie yelped in response and scratched at the baby gate which kept him confined to the laundry room.

"Get her to recant," Randy said again, his mouth close to my ear, "or *we* will get her to recant. Your choice." He stood, relieving the pressure on my chest, but then turned and kicked me savagely in the side, and I was unable to breathe for several agonizing moments. The door slammed shut behind them.

I didn't move, waiting to make sure they didn't return. Finally satisfied that they were gone, I picked myself up from the floor. The pain in my side was excruciating and the mere act of drawing a breath was an ordeal. No doubt I had a broken rib or two. The words to КоЯn's "Coming Undone" ran through my head, and I was, indeed, coming undone, my brain ticking like a bomb, set to detonate. The first casualty would be my lovely wife.

Perching gingerly on one of the kitchen chairs, I waited for her return from work. Randy had timed his departure well, for it was only a matter of fifteen minutes or so before I heard her car pull into the driveway.

"Hi, babe." She dropped her keys and purse on the console table in the foyer and came into the kitchen. "John?" She hesitated in the doorway when I didn't respond, then came into the room. "Are you okay?" She laid an arm across my shoulder, leaning over to kiss me.

I recoiled from her touch.

"What's wrong? What is all this?" She picked up one of the photos and I saw her face tighten and color. She glanced across the tabletop, taking it all in. Her eyes met mine briefly before shifting away. "I guess I owe you an explanation."

"I guess you owe me more than one." My tone was not kind, and I stood, with difficulty, and went to stare out the French doors.

She apparently noticed the way I was moving. "Are you hurt? What happened?"

"I had a visit from Randy and two of his buddies today."

She pulled my hand away from my side—I hadn't even realized I was holding my ribcage—and lifted my shirt. "Jesus, John. Randy did this?" She still couldn't look me in the eye.

"Yes, he did. And before kicking the shit out of me, he told me something, Caitlin."

She covered her face with both hands, her shoulders shaking.

"I think you know what that something was."

"Oh my God. I'm so sorry. I was going to tell you—I just hadn't worked up my nerve. It was the only way I could think of to get his DNA and get it quickly."

My skin was on fire, but my inner core was ice. "So it's true, what Randy said. You went on a date with that son of a bitch. You fucked a *murderer*. You weren't raped at all."

"John, please. I did it for you, for us. So we could get his DNA."

"*No!* I told you not to do anything on your own and you defied me. You've always got to do things your way!" I grabbed her by the shoulders, wanting nothing more than to choke her within an inch of her life. Her eyes widened and I saw true fear there for a split second before I pushed her away from me. Ignoring the stabbing in my side, I hobbled to the bedroom closet and grabbed a suitcase. My meager wardrobe would fit into it quite nicely.

Caitlin followed me into the room. "John, please let me explain. It's not what you think. Please stop and talk to me for a moment." She snatched the clothing from me and before I could think better of it, I popped her in the mouth with the back of my hand.

"I'm tired of talking to you," I spat. "I talk and talk and you do whatever the hell you want without consulting me, without caring. I've talked all I'm going to talk. Now get out of my way."

Stiffly, I retrieved the clothing from the floor and went to the dresser for the rest. When I turned around, she'd upended the suitcase and was sitting on it. I attempted to pull it out from under her.

"Get off." I tried pushing her, but my ribs were having none of it. "I said move." I tried one more time to dislodge her, but she wouldn't budge.

"Please listen to me," she begged.

Physically and emotionally exhausted, I sat on the bed. "Talk. Then I'm gone, and you'd better not get in my way, Caitlin, or I won't be responsible for what I do to you."

"I'm not proud of what I've done, but the only sure, quick way to get his DNA was to have sex with him. Then the only way to get anyone to do anything with it was to claim he'd raped me. And the only way to get to that point was to go out on a date with him. The evidence is being sent to my friend at the state medical examiner's office. She's going to put a rush on it and they should have the results back within two weeks. We're two weeks away from nailing his ass to the wall, John."

All I could envision was her in bed with that pervert. My wife. In bed with another man. And not just another man, but a murderer—the man who was responsible for my having spent eight years in a mental institution. I wasn't thinking about the procurement of his DNA. "Did you enjoy it? Was he good? Was it a thrill fucking a murderer?" Wounding her didn't assuage my pain.

She whipped her head from side to side . "No, John, no. I didn't enjoy it. Please believe me—I did it for you."

"You'll understand if I don't thank you. And you still haven't explained all those photos and newspaper articles. What the hell is that about? Was that for me, too?"

"You know I went to UNC School of Journalism and Mass Communication?"

"Yes. So?" I had seen her diploma and awards.

"During my sophomore year one of our projects was to cover a murder trial. We were supposed to report on the trial, which I did, but I saw a collateral story in your case—mental illness. You were so breathtaking, so heartbreaking, so tragic, and I was going to write about your plight and set the world on fire. I was going to make people aware of the misconceptions about the mentally ill, the lack of funding for treating and housing the mentally ill, for aftercare when patients were released from hospitals, the stigma of mental illness and having committed a serious crime. I was going to win the Pulitzer. I followed your trial, found out what I could about your background. I was in the courtroom the day they found you not guilty. I watched that man jump over the partition after you, and I saw the look on your face as they were dragging you out. That haunted me for months, John. And then…then I got bogged down with other assignments, and I met someone and started dating him. Thought maybe I'd marry him. Thank God I didn't. I think he and Randy must have been twins separated at birth.

"I kept all my notes, my photographs, because I still intended to write those articles, but I graduated and started working and forgot about it. Until one day I looked up and saw you sitting there in the diner, looking even more breathtaking and tragic, and I knew I had to write about that. It was like God saying, 'This is your assignment.' And John, Will says I may be nominated for several awards. Not local or even regional, but national."

My day just kept getting better and better. Perhaps she deserved congratulations, but the sense of betrayal was so strong, that what came out of my mouth was, "So let me get this straight. My trial was a *field trip*? My mental illness was a way for you to get recognition for your writing?" The Voices were back with a sudden, malignant vengeance.

Well, well, well, John. What did we tell you? She was after an award. Not woman of the year, but ace reporter of the year.

That's what she saw in you. She saw that plaque hanging on the wall, and you, my boy, were the means to an end.

You loser.

She didn't want you. She just wanted your story, and you handed it to her on a silver platter tied up with a pretty bow.

She married you so Randy couldn't snatch you away before she was finished with her project.

Now she's got a whole new story to pursue. She's fucking murderers and telling you she did it for you.

And you're so stupid, you'll believe it.

Wonder what kind of story she'll write about that?

I stood up. "You wanted the discovery from my criminal case for your articles, didn't you? It had nothing at all to do with helping me and everything to do with helping you. You *were* exploiting me. Worse than that, you let that creep put his—put his sickness inside you."

"John, please." She began crying. For once I was unmoved.

I ran my hands through my hair, my mind racing and the Voices yammering. "Shut up. I don't want to hear anything else out of your mouth. Just shut up."

She ran from the room. I finished packing my stuff, gathered some things for Willie, loaded him and the suitcase into the truck, and headed for Fontana Lake.

CHAPTER TWENTY-FOUR

GOING ON DAY THREE at the cottage, I confess I was not doing too well. I hadn't bathed or changed clothes in that time, and although I remembered to feed Willie, I had eaten very little myself. My cell phone rang at intervals or chirped to indicate a new text message. Caitlin. I didn't bother to answer or respond, nor did I bother to take my medicine. I was back to not sleeping and the Voices were regaining control of my thoughts. The water was still warm enough for swimming during the day, but the rib injury made that difficult, so I mostly just sat on the boat dock, wandered through the woods like a zombie, listening to the conversations raging in my head, or rocked on the screened porch.

I pondered where I would go and what I would do next. I knew I would sign the cottage back over to Caitlin. It had been in her family for years and I had no claim to it, but it would pain me if I could never return here, where I had been so happy, so alive, even if only for a brief period. It scared me to be without any support, but if the choices were between that or being Caitlin's project, then I supposed that was how it would have to be. As far as the baby, I wasn't stupid enough to think that a judge would ever give me joint custody or unsupervised visitation, even if this mess with the murders was cleared up. I would be stuck with whatever Caitlin allowed—a two-hour a week dad. If that. My train wreck of a life had finally derailed.

With this happy thought, I heard rustling in the brush at the edge of the yard. Willie barked at the intruder, and I thought perhaps a raccoon or possum had come to forage, but presently Rev. Jack's little dachshund snuffled into the clearing. She was followed a few moments later by Rev. Jack himself.

"Well, now, there you are, John. You've got Miss Caitlin real worried about you." Spying Willie, he added, "Who might this be?" He came up onto the porch without waiting for my invitation. Anyone else I would have told to fuck off. I was glad to see him even if I didn't want to talk to him. He held the screen door open for Winnie, laughing as she and Willie nosed and patted paws at each other excitedly, and said, "Aren't you a cute little fella?" When Winnie had finished greeting the puppy, she stopped next to me and yapped once, but I couldn't stir myself enough to pet her.

"You didn't have to come all the way over here just to check on me." I sounded as morose as I felt.

"Yes, sir, I did. Miss Cait said she's been trying to call you but didn't get an answer. She's mighty worried about you, especially given the circumstances under which you left. That girl loves you, you know." He scooted the other rocking chair closer to me and sat down.

"That girl is afraid her chance at glory grew a pair of balls and ran away," I snapped.

Winnie settled by my feet and Willie plopped down beside her, as Rev. Jack got himself comfortable and studied me. I could only imagine how I looked to him. Rumpled clothing, wild, dirty hair, dark circles under my eyes. The epitome of crazy.

"Don't sit downwind of me." I was trying to be funny, but there was no humor in my voice. No humor in my entire body.

He sucked on his teeth and nodded his head. "You're hurting."

Boom. I was sobbing, head in my hands, taking him and myself completely by surprise. I couldn't seem to stop. I felt Winnie and Willie licking my ankles, commiserating. I had spent the past three days being angry, but now as I finished watching my life fall apart, I was overcome with grief.

Rocking, Rev. Jack waited until the worst of it had passed, his hands resting on his stomach. "I need you to do something for me," he said when I was calmer.

I wiped my face on my shirtsleeve. "What?"

"Go get yourself a shower and get some clean clothes on. Then we're going up to my cabin to get some supper. I've got a pot roast in the crockpot, and it should be about ready."

"Thanks, but—"

"No, sir. I'm not asking. I'm telling." He stood and put his hand around my arm, urging me to my feet. "Come on." He steered me into the cottage, into the bathroom, where he pulled back the shower curtain and turned on the water. He adjusted the temperature, and said, "You get on in there, now, and I'll fetch you some clean clothes."

He was sitting in the living room waiting on me when I'd finished. "Where do you keep your prescription bottles?" he asked. I gestured at the kitchen counter and he walked over, picked them up, and placed them in his pocket. He glanced at his watch and added, "About time to dish up the roast."

Not possessing the energy to argue, I trudged through the woods behind him to his cabin, Winnie and Willie bringing up the rear as if they didn't quite trust me to go last.

"Why don't you find us some music to listen to while I bake up some yeast rolls?" He pointed to a shelf full of vinyl record albums and a stereo. I sifted through the stack half-heartedly, finally choosing an album entitled "Westward Ho", which professed to be "an American adventure recording" published by the National Geographic Society. It was a collection of melancholy Western folk songs which suited my mood perfectly.

"That's one of my favorites; one of my granddaughter's favorites, too," he said, taking the rolls from the oven.

When we sat down to eat, I noticed that he'd put a huge slab of meat on my plate, along with a mound of potatoes and carrots and two rolls. He'd also placed my Ativan and Thorazine tablets on the mat next to a glass of tea. I picked up the pills and swallowed them. The tea was cold and sweet and I drained every drop, then cut a small piece of roast and put it in my mouth. It was so tender I didn't even need a knife. I couldn't eat all of the food he'd piled on my plate, but I managed to put a dent in it just the same.

"There's apple cobbler and ice cream for dessert," he said, clearing away the dishes.

"Maybe later. I don't think I could handle it right now."

He finished putting away the leftover food. "Let's go sit on the front porch for a bit."

The late afternoon sun filtered through the leaves, giving the woods a golden glow, reinforcing what a beautiful part of the state this was, and I felt crappy all over again, knowing this was my last time here. Rev. Jack settled in an Adirondack chair, and I lifted first Winnie and then Willie onto the porch swing next to me.

We sat quietly for a little while, then Rev. Jack said, "I've talked to Caitlin on the phone a couple of times and she's filled me in on what's been going on since you were here in July. John, I have to believe that things happen for a reason, and that reason is God's plan. I know you say you don't believe in God, but He has a hand in your life nevertheless. You and Caitlin connecting wasn't coincidence. It was meant to be, and it had the added bonus of you falling in love, marrying, and now starting a family of your own. Congratulations on that, by the way."

I wanted to cry again. My family was over before it began.

He shifted in his seat and continued, "I've preached funerals for young men and women who were estranged from their families at the time of their deaths. I've provided grief counseling for those families when they couldn't turn loose of the regret and the guilt. You don't want to have to live with regret like that. Neither does Caitlin. You need to go to your wife and embrace her. Cherish her. Those Christian vows you told me you recited at your wedding? Repeat them to each other every day.

"I can understand that you feel she's been unfaithful to you and how you could think she's used you or that's she been dishonest with you, but I think her motives are pure. She loves you. She wanted to help you, and she wanted to make a difference by writing about your plight. She can't change what happened in your past, John, but she might be able to change the lives of other people by bringing attention to the way you were treated.

"There's been a lot of talk going on. Those articles have stirred people into action. I've read of at least two churches in Kingsville and the surrounding area that are looking into sponsoring halfway houses for mental patients, and two more that are holding fundraisers to help provide medication and treatment. Your wife is making a difference for people, and that's just on the local level. Her articles have also been picked up by major papers."

I walked to the edge of the porch, looking down toward the lake. I was nowhere close to letting her off the hook. I just couldn't rid myself of the feeling that she had used me in a big way. Neither could I turn loose of the anger and the hurt. And there was the matter of Peter. Would I ever be able to make love to her again without thinking about that? I wasn't sure that I could. Intellectually, I almost believed she had done it for me, to help me. Emotionally, I didn't care. She had gone too far. I had no doubt that she would do so again if the spirit moved her, and I didn't know if I could live with that. I loved her; I depended on her, but my trust in her was destroyed.

Feeling the flood coming again, I left the porch and walked down to the shore, the dogs following me. Randy was right about one thing—I wished I had never left Broughton Hospital. The old adage: "It's better to have loved and lost than never to have loved at all" simply wasn't true. If I had never loved, I wouldn't be feeling this agony right now. If I had never left Broughton, I wouldn't have known happiness, but I wouldn't have known this misery either.

Refusing Rev. Jack's second offer of dessert and his exhortations to spend the night in his guest room, I said good-bye. "I'll be checking on you tomorrow," he called as Willie and I started down the path.

"You really don't have to do that. I'm fine." I wondered if there was a special kind of penalty in the afterlife for lying to a preacher.

"I'll be by just the same." He lifted his hand in a wave and went back into the cabin. I knew he was as good as his word.

Back at the cottage, nothing on TV held my interest, so I switched it off and wandered out onto the screened porch, where I leaned against the railing and listened to the night insects drone. I thought about the baby and Caitlin and suicide, in that order. After Caitlin told me she was pregnant, I promised myself that suicide would never again be an option for me. Now I wasn't sure I could abide by that promise. Besides, if the child never knew me, then he—or she—would never miss me. And there was a distinct possibility that it wasn't even mine. With me out of the picture, Caitlin was free to hook up with the real father, and the child could have a normal life. Whatever that was. It was something a child would never have with me.

Taking a flashlight, I walked up to the woodshed, searched until I found the whetstone located there, and carried it back to the screened porch. I set it on an old kitchen towel, got the bottle of mineral oil from the bathroom, and coated the top of the stone with the oil.

My dad had shown me how to sharpen a knife when I was just a little older than Adam, when we still did things together besides yelling at each other…before everything went bad. My mother was angry when she discovered that he had allowed me to handle knives, and she forbade me to do it again, but my dad whispered, "Good job," and I was secretly proud of myself.

From my pocket, I pulled the folding hunting knife I'd found shoved in the back of a kitchen drawer two days earlier. I flipped it open, enjoying the heft of it in my hand. Would I still remember how to do this? I placed the blade flat against the stone, tilted it to what I thought was the correct angle, and drew it across.

"Listen for the sound. You'll know if it sounds right." He pulls the blade across the stone. It makes a perfect 'swoosh'. He demonstrates the way not to do it. It sets my teeth on edge, and I shudder. He laughs. "Remember, John. Whatever you do to one side of the blade, you have to do to the other. Watch." He makes a few more passes. "Six strokes on one side, pushing away from your body in a curving motion, so that you're drawing the tip of the knife across the edge of the stone. Now, six strokes on the other side, pulling toward you. Here, you try it. Careful." He hands the knife to me.

It takes me several minutes before I get the hang of it, then I, too, am making the blade swoosh across the stone effortlessly. When I finish, Dad holds up a piece of newspaper and runs the knife across it. The wicked sharp blade slices the paper in two and one piece flutters to the floor.

My eyes teared as I drew the blade back and forth and heard the swoosh that told me I did, indeed, remember how to do this correctly. Six strokes in one direction, six strokes in the other. Flip the stone over. Oil it. Repeat the actions. When I was done, I held up a paper towel and swiped at it with the knife. The severed piece drifted downward.

I cleaned the oil from the blade, then moved closer to the living room window, so that the lamp light shone on the steel. I ran it lightly along my skin, tracing the outline of a vein in my forearm. If I slit my wrists, would it take a long time to bleed to death? I thought it might. Too much of a chance someone would find me in time. Maybe an overdose of meds. Then I realized Rev. Jack had kept them. Too bad I didn't own a gun. There would be no screwing up a gunshot through the roof of my mouth. Bam. Done. Over.

Holding the knife to my left wrist, I pressed down. Watched blood well around the blade. Pressed a little harder. Repeated the procedure with the opposite wrist. Blood oozed from the cuts and dripped onto the porch floor, but I couldn't force myself to make the cuts any deeper. I wiped the blade on my shorts, folded it shut, and returned the knife to my pocket. Tomorrow was as good a day to die as any.

I stretched out on the swinging bed and pulled Willie up beside me. He snuggled against my hip and sighed happily. All was right in his little doggie world. I wished it were in mine. I stroked his silky head. His soft snuffling calmed me and I fell asleep.

#

I slept like the dead, rehearsing for the real thing. I probably would have slept a lot longer except Willie began barking. It took me a couple of beats to get my head together and realize where I was. Swinging bed. Screened porch. Cottage. Lake. Morning. I sat up, startled to find Rev. Jack sitting in a rocking chair, Winnie lolling on the floor by the door.

"Some watchdog you've got there. Been here ten minutes and he just now barked."

"He's still in training."

Rev. Jack studied me as I stretched. Belatedly, I realized that he was taking in the cuts on my wrists, the twin lines of dried blood, and I lowered my arms.

He didn't comment on the marks, instead gesturing to some covered dishes and a thermos sitting on the picnic table. "I brought breakfast. Appreciate it if you'd eat with me. Mostly I like being up here by myself, but I take spells where I like company."

"I'm afraid I'm not much better than no company," I mumbled.

"Well, now, I wouldn't say that at all. I enjoy your company, John. You talk when you have something to say and keep your mouth shut when you don't. My wife and I were married fifty-two years, and I loved that woman dearly, but she could talk the ears off a concrete elephant. The older she got, the more she talked. I could leave the house with her talking, go to the store, come back half an hour later, and she'd still be going. Didn't matter if anyone was there to hear her or not."

Married fifty-two years. I hadn't even been married six months and my marriage was over. What was the secret? I guess it helped if you weren't crazy.

"What was your wife's name?" I was curious about this woman he'd loved so much for so long.

"Elizabeth. Lib for short."

My heart squeezed. "Elizabeth. That's Caitlin's middle name."

He grinned. "One more thing we have in common. I go by Jack, but my first name is John. John David."

"John Edward."

"I knew you were good people the first time I met you."

"Same here."

He uncovered the dishes. "Come on and eat before it gets any colder." He unscrewed the top from the thermos, and I could smell rich, fragrant coffee. Willie had remained on the bed next to me, but now jumped down, stretched, and greeted Winnie with a nuzzle, then trotted over to the table. Rev. Jack chuckled and patted him on the head. "Don't you worry, little fella. You'll get a bite."

The plates were heaped with eggs, scrambled with cheddar cheese and mushrooms, sausage patties, and hash browns with onions and peppers. He'd even made biscuits. Breakfast at the hospital had always turned me off and therefore I seldom ate, but I was hungrier than I wanted to admit, and I dug into the food. Finally I pushed the plate away and treated Willie and Winnie to half a sausage patty that I couldn't finish.

"That was really good," I said, as Rev. Jack poured more coffee into my cup.

"Thank you. I don't cook like that often. I enjoy having someone besides myself to cook for. Oh, here—before I forget." From his pocket, he pulled a plastic zip top bag containing the day's dosage of medication.

I reached for the bag, and noticed that he was looking at the inside of my wrist again. Feeling foolish, I turned my hand palm-down on the table. "I appreciate you doing this. You didn't have to. I don't want to be a bother to you."

"Glad for your company. No bother to me at all, although I'd like to ask a favor if I could."

"Sure."

"I need to go to Walmart for some dog food and birdseed. I usually get the forty pound bags when I can, so I don't have to go as often. Only trouble is I have trouble lifting them. Would you consider going along to schlep them for me?"

I wasn't really in the mood to go to Walmart and suspected this was a ploy by him to keep an eye on me, but I couldn't refuse to help him.

"Of course. When did you want to leave?"

"Is eleven okay with you? I'll treat you to lunch at Jimmy Mac's in Bryson City afterward."

"Eleven is fine, but no, you won't treat me. I'll treat you."

"Well, I appreciate that very much. I'll drive down to get you then."

He began to gather the dirty dishes but I told him to leave them. "I'll wash them and have them ready for you when you come back."

He smiled and I felt my mouth trying to smile in response. It occurred to me that I loved this old man.

"See you in a while." He snapped his fingers for Winnie and headed home.

I took the dishes into the kitchen, ran the sink full of hot soapy water and put them in to soak while I took Willie for a quick run through the woods. When we returned, I washed everything, wincing at the sting of soapy water in the cuts on my wrists, and then went to take a shower.

Waiting for Rev. Jack, I pulled out my cell phone and checked the voice mail. "You have 27 new messages," the robot lady told me. Okay, screw that. I *really* wasn't in the mood to listen to 27 voice mail messages from Caitlin, so I scrolled through the text messages, starting with the day I'd left. Luckily they were abbreviated, since she knew I had trouble reading anything more than a sentence or two.

9/16/2013	5:47 PM	J, I'm sorry. I love u. C
9/16/2013	6:28 PM	J, plz answer. Love u. C
9/16/2013	8:15 PM	Plz let me nc ur ok. C
9/16/2013	9:46 PM	Txt me 2 let me no ur ok.

There were more messages of a similar nature, then:

9/16/2013	11:56 PM	Good nite, slave. Sweet dreams. Love u. C

That one made me cry and I had to turn off the phone. Damn her.

#

On the way to Sylva, I studied the scenery. If I didn't decide to end it all in the next few days, I was going to need somewhere to live. Even after the sale of the house, I knew I wouldn't have enough money to buy a place on the lake, so that was out. Bryson City might be my next best option. I'd be close to the lake and I could visit Rev. Jack, and perhaps the price wouldn't be as steep. Hopefully Caitlin would agree to rent the cottage to me until I could decide what to do.

Our first stop was Walmart. I'd have thought business in the store would be fairly slow late on a week-day morning, but no, there were the usual crowded aisles and family reunions throughout the store. It took us considerably longer than our last shopping trip together, but we got the dog food, bird seed and a few other items, and checked out.

Back in Bryson City, he said, "I need to run to the bank and pay a few bills. Do you want to tag along or just meet me at Jimmy Mac's in about half an hour?"

"I'll meet you at the restaurant. I think I'll wander around a bit." There was a realty company two doors down from where we'd parked, and I took a real estate brochure from the little kiosk on the sidewalk and sat down on a bench to peruse it. Not much I could afford. I might have to think about renting.

Someone plopped down on the bench next to me and said, "Well, bless my buttons! Sugar, where have you been keeping yourself?" Startled, I glanced up to find Marco grinning at me.

"Marco, how are you?"

"I'm doing great, sugar. Headed to the salon. I have a one o'clock appointment coming in. Look at you, letting that beautiful hair grow back out. I think I like it better long."

"Yeah, my wife wasn't happy when I had it cut."

"Where is the lucky little lady?" He glanced up and down the street expectantly.

I hesitated, feeling depressed all over again. "We're—we're separated."

"Oh, sugar, *no!*" He gripped my forearm in one hand and patted it with the other.

Had any other man touched me that way, I would have been pissed off, but with Marco, it was strangely comforting.

Do not cry, do not cry, I said to myself, but that didn't stop my eyes from tearing.

He wrapped his arm around me and pulled me to him, patting me on the back. Releasing me, he said, "I'm in the same boat. My partner of ten years up and walked out on me a couple of weeks ago. I was *devastated*. He found a younger, prettier man and he just came in one night and said, 'I'm outta here, bitch,' and that was that. I couldn't stop crying for two days! What happened with you? Did she find another man, too?"

"It's a long, sad, complicated story, but suffice it to say she screwed another guy." I felt guilty somehow for not telling him why she claimed to have done it.

Marco stroked my arm. "Sugar, if I had you in my bed, everyone else could cease to exist. I could have made you a happy man. I could *still* make you a happy man."

He raised his eyebrows hopefully, but I shook my head. "Sorry—"

"I know, I know," he pouted. "You're not bent that way. Well, it's an open invitation if you change your mind. So what brings you into beautiful downtown Bryson City?"

"Just tagging along with my neighbor. He had to run some errands, then we're going to have lunch at Jimmy Mac's. Would you like to join us?"

"Ooohh! A lunch date," he squealed, but quickly shifted to his pouty face. "I'd love to, but I've got a perm coming in fifteen minutes. One of my regular little old ladies. She'll get her granny panties in a wad if I'm a minute late. Tell you what, though, let me get your phone number and we can get together for dinner tonight."

"I don't even know my own freaking number," I admitted. "I just got a new one and the only person who ever calls me on it is Caitlin."

Marco rolled his eyes. "Here, let me see your phone." He messed with it a minute and said, "Here it is." He showed me how to look up the number, programmed his into my phone, then pulled out his own phone and entered mine into his contact list.

"I've got you saved under 'Cutie'. What is your name, by the way?"

"John Colucci."

"An Italian-American stud. Well, sugar, I *will* be calling you about dinner."

He continued on up the sidewalk to the salon, but paused before entering and waved to me. I waved back.

#

Marco called at 5:30 and said, "Can you be at my place around 7:30? I'll fix a London broil. What kind of wine do you like?

"Moscato, muscadine, scuppernong. The sweeter, the better."

"I know an excellent scuppernong." He gave me directions to his house. "I'll see you at 7:30."

I fed Willie around 6:15 and took him for his evening walk. At 7:00, I went out to the Avalanche, programmed Marco's address into the GPS system, and hit the highway to Bryson City. After stopping to get gas, I pulled up in front of a pretty little bungalow around 7:25. The front yard was immaculate and well-landscaped. Marco sat on the front porch in a white wicker chair.

As I came up the steps, he stood and hugged me. "Have a seat, sugar. I don't know about you, but I'm ready for a glass of wine." He uncorked the bottle resting in a silver caddy on a side table and poured a glass for each of us. "To new friends."

"Amen." Friends were exactly what I lacked in my life and what I sorely needed. I sipped the wine, which was sweet and crisp. I drained my glass, and he refilled it. "This is great. What brand is it?" I would definitely purchase some for myself.

"Duplin." He held up the bottle. "Made in the eastern part of the state. So tell me about yourself. Where do you live? What sort of work do you do? You're a model or an actor, right?"

I laughed. "No, I'm not, but my sister is. She did some of the Mom's Homemade Soup commercials."

"That's your sister? Okay, okay, I see it. You two look a lot alike. Why in the world aren't you modelling, too? I'd buy anything you advertised!"

It always came down to questions that weren't easy to answer. Things about me that other people didn't necessarily need to know; things they probably wouldn't want to know. I hated to lie, but I hated to tell the truth. I didn't know Marco well enough yet to judge whether or not my truth would scare him off, so I gave my pat answer, "I'm disabled, so I don't work. I was living in Kingsville until—well, until the separation. I don't know where I'll be living now."

"Bless your heart. I hate that for you. Does that mean you'll be moving to Bryson City?" He looked hopeful.

"Maybe. I haven't decided yet. But I'm considering it."

He grinned. "What can I do to help you decide 'yes'?"

"Well, I'd have to find a place I can afford. Right now I'm staying at the lake, but that's not a long-term option, unfortunately. I really love it out there."

Marco considered this, sipping his wine. "Would you be open to a place that needs some work?"

"Yes, but nothing extensive. I don't have the funds for a major renovation."

"I might know of a place. Let me check with the owner, and I'll let you know. Right now, though, I'm going to check on the food. Come on in and make yourself at home."

The inside of the bungalow looked professionally decorated in what I'd seen referred to as shabby chic or cottage-style. A lot of soft, comfortable upholstered pieces, painted wood, and pastel colors.

Marco opened the oven door and peeked in. A delicious aroma wafted out.

"Perfect." He removed the dish and set it on the stovetop. "It needs to rest a few minutes and then we'll be good to go."

He poured us another glass of wine, plated the food, and we sat down to eat. I'd just put a bite of London broil in my mouth, savoring the flavor, when my cell phone rang. "Sorry," I said and hit the ignore button. It rang again a minute later. I glanced at the screen and switched it off.

"The wife?" Marco asked.

"Yes. She averages about ten calls a day and about twenty texts."

"She wants you back and she's sorry."

"That's about the gist of it."

"Maybe you should give her another chance."

"Maybe. And maybe she should have thought about the consequences before she—" I stopped and unclenched my fists, realizing how angry I sounded.

"You love her a lot," Marco observed.

"I do," I admitted. "And she's pregnant, which makes everything that much more complicated."

Marco put down his knife and fork. "Sugar, if she's pregnant, you've got to work things out. You can't just walk off and leave that baby."

"I don't even know if the baby is mine, and I don't know if I can ever make love to her again without thinking about what's she's done. But there's more to it than that."

He cut his eyes at me. "We all screw up, and where would any of us be if the other people in our lives weren't willing to forgive?"

"Right now I can't."

He patted my arm. "Right now you're hurting."

"Be careful—the last person who said that had to listen to me crying for half an hour."

"Sugar, if you need to cry, here's my shoulder."

We talked for a long time after supper, moving to the living room, where Marco pointed me to a recliner. We finished off one bottle of wine and started on another. At some point he got up to go to the bathroom. I was feeling drowsy and knew I needed to get home, but thought, *I'm just going to close my eyes for a minute.*

When I opened them again, the sun was shining in the windows and I sat up like a shot. "Shit!" I threw off the blanket that Marco had apparently placed over me sometime during the night and fumbled in my pocket for my phone to check the time. I vaguely remembered switching it off while we ate and turned it back on now, waiting impatiently for it to power up. 8:48 AM.

Almost immediately it began ringing. I pushed the talk button. "What is it, Caitlin?"

"Hello, to you, too. Please tell me you're in Kingsville."

"No, I'm at the lake. What do you need? I just woke up."

"You didn't get my messages? My texts? I called Rev. Jack around 7:00 last night and he was going to remind you, too. Please, God, don't tell me you forgot."

"Forgot what?"

"Are you kidding me? Oh, crap."

Marco walked into the living room, yawning. "Wife?" he mouthed.

I nodded, and he gave me the thumbs up sign and moseyed into the kitchen. "Forgot *what*, Caitlin?" I asked once more.

"That you have court today on that second assault charge? Oh my God. Webster was sure they would dismiss it. I planned to testify on your behalf."

I leaned back in the recliner, feeling defeated. "What do I do now? There's no way I can get there before noon."

"I don't know. God, let me call Webster and see what he suggests. Keep your damned phone on and *answer* it when I call you."

"Okay, okay." I returned it to my pocket.

Marco came back in the room and asked, "Something wrong?"

"Just a typical day in my life." I rubbed the sleep from my eyes. "I'm sorry to cut and run, but I've got to head back to Kingsville. I've missed an important appointment."

"That's what they all say, sugar." He pretended to pout, then laughed at the look on my face. "Don't worry about it. You want me to make some breakfast? You can shower in the guest bathroom if you want."

"Thanks, but I don't have time to eat or shower." I was glad I'd worn jeans and a long-sleeved button-up shirt instead of my usual cargo shorts and t-shirt, and equally glad I hadn't done anything to get sweaty and stinky in the interim, even if I had slept in them.

I hit Highway 74, merged onto Interstate 40 and kept the speed at 72 miles per hour, except for the construction zone through Morganton near Exit 105, stopping only once to use the restroom and buy some coffee in Hickory, where I left 40 and headed north on 321. I turned into the courthouse parking lot at 12:20 and realized, as I parked, that Caitlin hadn't called me back. I yanked the phone out of my pocket. *Fuck.* The battery was dead. I plugged it into the car charger and scrolled through the text messages.

11:13 AM	R u on ur way?
11:26 AM	J, answer ur gd phone 4 Christ's sake.
11:44 AM	I NO ur not ignoring me when I'm trying 2 help u!
12:02 PM	Ur on ur own, u dick.

I tried to call her. Yep. Straight to voice mail. I left the phone charging and walked into the courthouse. All four courtrooms on the criminal court level were empty. To the Clerk's office. "Court has recessed for lunch, sir." Back in the truck. Check the phone. No new missed calls. No new text messages. I called her again. Voice mail. I drove to the newspaper office and met Will as he was coming out the door.

"Caitlin's not here. She was supposed to be in court with you," he said in answer to my query, and it could have been my imagination, but he seemed a little cool toward me. Caitlin had, undoubtedly, shared our trials and tribulations with her co-workers.

"I was late getting to court and I can't find her. Do you know where she might have gone?"

"Sorry, no. If the court recessed for lunch, then I'm guessing she went to eat."

I thanked him and walked up the street to her favorite pub. It was full but Caitlin wasn't among the patrons. I walked on to Webster's office, but his paralegal said he was gone to lunch. He hadn't told her anything about my case, but he had to be in court again at 2:00 for other cases and I could try talking to him then.

Truck. Phone. No calls; no texts. I headed for the house. Her car was not in the driveway. I didn't know what else to do, so I drove back to town and parked across from the newspaper building to see if she reappeared. When she hadn't done so by 1:45, I returned to the courthouse and got in line for the metal detector.

Webster eventually entered the courtroom, and I managed to get his attention. The bailiff convened court and the DA called the next Defendant. Several cases were disposed of and then Webster addressed the judge about my case.

"Your Honor," he said, "my client, John Colucci, is now here and ready to proceed with his case if it would please the court to strike the failure to appear and order for arrest issued this morning."

"Mr. Colucci," the judge said, "come forward."

I went to stand by Webster.

"Why weren't you in court this morning, Mr. Colucci?"

"I'm sorry, Your Honor. I forgot—"

"I'm not striking the order for arrest. Bailiff, take Mr. Colucci into custody."

"I'm sorry, John," Webster said.

"Not your fault," I muttered as the bailiff handcuffed me and led me out of the courtroom.

While the deputy and I waited for the elevator, I saw Caitlin at the other end of the hallway. She looked at me, frowning, and I held my arms out so she could see the handcuffs. She shook her head, then turned and left. I hoped she was planning to bond me out, but once at the jail, no one was in a big hurry to process me. They left me shackled to a bench in booking, and I realized why when my good pals, Whisnant and Samuels, entered grinning like Cheshire cats.

"What brings you around, John?" Whisnant unfastened me from the bench and propelled me down the hall to my home away from home—the interview room.

Just another fucked day of a fucked life.

CHAPTER TWENTY-FIVE

"AM I MICRO-CHIPPED OR SOMETHING? When I walk through the door, does it activate an app on your cell phone to let you know I'm in the building?" I asked Whisnant as he shoved me into a chair.

"Something like that." He grinned and perched on the edge of the table. "Been a while since we talked, hasn't it? You been missing us?"

"No…no offense."

"That hurts, John. I thought we meant more to you than that. Why haven't you been in to talk to us?"

"Nothing to say."

"A little birdie told us that you're claiming Public Safety Officer Peter Barrington is responsible for the murders."

"Shutting up now."

"We've found an interesting piece of evidence at one of the murder scenes recently."

Silence.

"Something that we can tie to you."

More silence.

"Don't you want to know what it is?"

Still more silence.

"Are you missing something that belongs to you? You fucked up big time, John."

He wasn't expecting me to laugh. I wasn't expecting to laugh either, to tell you the truth.

"You think this is funny?"

"There's not much about my life I find funny, Detective."

"It's about to get more unfunny for you."

"If you're so sure it's me, why haven't you arrested me? All you ever do is talk. It's a waste of my time and yours. Because—and get this through your heads—I haven't done anything. I never did anything. I confessed to a crime I never committed because I was young and scared and sick. I won't do that again. Peter Barrington set me up. You'll find out when the evidence from the rape comes back. That's all I'm saying. Let me call my lawyer. I want a lawyer. I didn't know to say that when I was nineteen, but I'm saying it now. Lawyer."

"Why do you want to call a lawyer if you haven't done anything wrong?" Samuels interjected.

"Lawyer," I repeated, and then again in case there was any misunderstanding. "*Lawyer.*"

"Go ahead and take him back to booking," Whisnant said to Samuels. "We'll be seeing him again soon enough and he'll talk then if he knows what's good for him."

Caitlin had me bonded out by 7:00 PM, at which point I was in a very crabby mood.

"I should have let your ass sit there a few days," she said as we walked out of the jail.

"Then why the hell didn't you?" I snapped.

She stopped in her tracks. "I'm only trying to help. I just had to put up a $2,000 secured bond for you. Please stop acting this way."

I took a deep breath and tried to turn the volume down on my annoyance. "I'm headed to the lake. I'll talk to you later." I started to walk away but she grabbed my arm.

"Do you have to go tonight? Come back to the house and get something to eat, get some sleep. You can go tomorrow morning."

"Willie's been by himself all day. I've got to tend to him."

"Rev. Jack's got him. I called him earlier. He's got a key to the cottage. If I know you, you haven't eaten anything. I'll fix us something. I can sleep in the spare bedroom if you want me to. Please, John."

I was exhausted and hungry, but if I spent the night, she might misconstrue my reason. "I'd better not."

"Please. I'm begging you. I won't ask more of you than that." The expression in her eyes pulled at my heart.

I hesitated. What the hell. "All right. Just for tonight. And I'll sleep in the spare bedroom."

At the house, I showered while she started supper. For a while I could pretend that nothing had changed, and decided I would just go with it. Tomorrow I'd be back at the lake and I could worry then about what my future held. Or didn't hold.

Having washed off the jail stench, I sat at the kitchen counter and watched her cook. Her movements were fluid, purposeful. Sexy. Her breasts strained the tight t-shirt she wore, and I found my gaze focused on her butt as she bent over for this thing or reached for that thing. In spite of my anger and disappointment, I was aroused, and I was thinking maybe I wouldn't sleep in the spare bedroom after all.

She chattered all through dinner, but I attempted—unsuccessfully—to tune her out. When we'd finished, I helped clean up the kitchen and load the dishwasher, and then she took my hand and said, "Come on in the den." She sank down on the couch next to me and I caught a whiff of her perfume—my favorite.

"I want you to know how sorry I am," she whispered.

"I don't want to talk about that right now."

"We've got to talk about it. It can't just hang out there forever, and the longer we *don't* talk about it, the harder it will be *to* talk about it. If I could take it all back, I would. I was so focused on getting that DNA, I didn't consider how you might feel. My whole life I've always just taken the bull by the horns to get what I need, personally and professionally. I'm sorry. I can't tell you that enough."

"I don't know what to say."

She squeezed my arm. "You don't have to say anything. Just come home. I know I've damaged your trust in me, but please give me the opportunity to repair it." She leaned over, covering my mouth with hers, and placed her hand between my legs.

I crushed her against me, our lips grinding.

"You've missed me," she laughed, pulling away long enough to slip off her t-shirt and unfasten her bra.

"Oh my God how I've missed you," I breathed, pulling first at her jeans and then my own. After that we were down on the floor and I was inside her and we were riding our way toward forgiveness. At that moment I didn't care what she'd done with Peter. She was mine. *Mine, goddamn it.* Neither of us slept in the guest room that night. In fact, neither of us did much sleeping, period.

#

While we were certainly on the road to forgiveness, we hadn't yet reached our destination.

"Where were you the night before last?" Caitlin asked me at breakfast.

"Why do you want to know?"

"Rev. Jack said you never came home that night. I was just curious."

"Are you afraid I was out screwing around, too?" I just couldn't help myself sometimes.

"All right. I deserved that, but can you try not to be quite so nasty about it? How long do you intend to punish me?"

"It's too early to answer that question."

"John, stop. I get that you're hurt."

My anger returned, swift as a bolt of lightning and just as destructive. "No, you don't get it! I've spent the last five days thinking that our marriage was over and contemplating suicide." I held my wrists out for her inspection. "This isn't going to go away overnight and I can't just let it go overnight. I'm still pissed as *hell* about it!" I stopped and swallowed. "But I love you," I continued in a quieter tone. "That's why it hurts so damned bad."

"I'm sorry. It's not easy living with someone who has a mental illness. I forget that you don't always process things the way other people do."

"You knew all about that when you got involved with me. In fact, you knew far more about me than I've *ever* known about you. And it sounds like you're saying that if I wasn't mentally ill then it wouldn't bother me that my wife slept with another man, and that's just not accurate."

She touched a finger against my lips. "Shh. I'm not complaining and that's not what I'm saying. I'm just saying that I have to stop and really give some thought to how something might affect you. I'm afraid I haven't been very diligent in that regard."

"Yeah, well, whatever. I'm going to get a shower, then I need to get back to the cottage."

"I'm coming with you."

"To shower or to the lake?"

"Both."

Though my brain may not process things the way other men's do, I'm pretty sure my body does, and like most men, I've found that it's hard (pun intended) to stay mad at a woman when she's rubbing her wet, naked body against mine. Harder still when she's on her knees with her mouth wrapped around me. But I digress.

After we finished in the shower, she packed some things in a carry-on bag. We locked up the house and set out for the lake, stopping for lunch at the Jarrett House in Dillsboro at Caitlin's request. After eating all that carb-heavy country cooking, I was wiped out, and she drove the rest of the way to the cottage while I dozed in the passenger seat.

The afternoon had turned off hot, so I retrieved Willie from Rev. Jack and took him for a walk, then went down to the boat dock for a swim. Willie jumped in after me, and I laughed as he dog-paddled along behind me, although he tired long before I did. He swam to the shore, curled up in the sunshine, and slept, and Caitlin came to join me, wearing a super sexy bikini.

"Are you trying to kill me?" I asked when she swam out to where I was.

She laughed. "Death by sex. What better way to go?"

"I can't think of one, but I don't believe I can oblige you right now. I'm empty."

"I've never known you not to rise to the occasion." She pretended to sulk. "But I'll give you a break," she added when I opened my mouth to protest. "Although, just so you know, this will probably be my last chance to wear a bikini for a while. The weather and John, Jr. will soon put an end to my bikini wearing days."

"No juniors. You're not cursing the poor child by naming it after me."

"I love your name."

"No one else loves it. Besides, a little girl named John is going to have issues."

"I'm telling you it's a boy."

We discussed baby names without coming to a decision, then swam before joining Willie on the dock for a nap, and for just a little bit it was almost like my first time at the lake, that same tentative sense of peace, happiness. It occurred to me that short snatches of bliss may be all I could ever hope to experience in this life and I may have to be content with that. Would it be enough to sustain me?

Rev. Jack and Winnie came over for supper that night, and although it was too cool to eat on the dock, we were comfortable on the screen porch after the sun went down. Caitlin began yawning around 9:30 and finally apologized and excused herself to go to bed. Rev. Jack and I sat in the rocking chairs talking until 10:30.

After he left, I cleaned up the kitchen, washed all the dishes, and took Willie out one last time before bed. I was getting undressed when I heard Caitlin's cell phone buzzing from the charging station in the living room where we kept our phones. There was no way I was going to wake her up at this point, but unable to contain my curiosity, I went to check it anyway.

I picked up her phone. No new texts; no new voice mail messages. I frowned and picked up mine. One new text message from a number I didn't recognize. Okay, must be Marco. I clicked to open the message.

11:58 PM   Recant or coming after her 1st. Adam Wade = insurance.

I stared at the screen stupidly while my brain computed the message, my hands shaking. No. No, no, no, *no*. I put the phone down. Started toward the bedroom. Stopped. Went back and picked the phone up again. Stood there trying to decide just what the hell to do. Caitlin was safe. For now. But Adam. I needed to call Adam's parents. How? I didn't have their phone number. I stepped out onto the porch to keep from disturbing Caitlin and dialed 411. Asked for a number for Kevin Wade, Kingsville, NC. No listing. *Damn!* I couldn't think of the wife's name. It just wouldn't come to me.

I scrolled through the contact list Caitlin had programmed into my phone, looking for Laurie's number. Hit send. Laurie answered, and I blurted out, "Do you have Kevin Wade's phone number? I need his phone number."

Laurie yawned. "John? What? Kevin who? Oh. He lives right behind you—why do you need his number? It's too late to be calling him now."

"I know it's late, but I need their number. I think Adam may be in danger. I got this text message from Peter—I mean I didn't recognize the number, but I'm sure it's Peter. He said if Caitlin doesn't recant, he's coming after her, and Adam is his insurance. Do you have their number?" I knew how crazy I sounded, but I didn't have time to explain. There was silence and I said, "Hello?"

"Are you taking your medication, John? Is Caitlin there? Could I speak with her?"

"Laurie, listen to me. I need the Wade's number. I'm not home right now, or I'd just walk over to their house—"

"Given what happened between the two of you a couple of weeks ago, that would not be a good idea, John, and you know it. Why don't you try to get some rest tonight, and I can call him in the morning. See if he's willing to speak with you."

I wanted to yell at her, but I was trying to keep my voice low so I wouldn't wake Caitlin. "Adam's in danger. I need to speak to Kevin *now*."

"Go to bed, John. I'll call you in the morning." She disconnected the call.

Damn it! The only other plan of action I could come up with was to return to Kingsville to warn the Wades in person and take care of the Peter problem once and for all. If I left now, I could be there in plenty of time to talk to Kevin before 9:00 AM. But I couldn't leave Caitlin alone, so I hatched my next plan. I would have Rev. Jack stay with her, which meant I had to get him now. I looked at the clock. 12:08 AM. If he hadn't already suspected it, he would know without a doubt that I was insane when I showed up on his doorstep after midnight.

I tiptoed to the bedroom, dressed quietly, and carried my shoes to the living room before putting them on. In the kitchen, I took a flashlight from the drawer, tested it to make sure it worked, and stepped out onto the porch.

A ten-minute walk through the night woods later, I was standing at Rev. Jack's front door. I hated to disturb him at this late hour since he was probably already asleep, but I wasn't leaving Caitlin by herself, and I had to get back to Kingsville to warn the Wades. If I took her with me, she might try to prevent me from confronting Peter, and worse yet, she would be where he could get at her easily. So I knocked on the door, hearing Winnie's sharp, excited barking from within the house.

The porch light blinked on and Rev. Jack eased the door open. He answered much more swiftly than I would have thought, given the late hour and his advanced age. "Is everything okay?" He motioned me into the living room.

"I'm really, really sorry for bothering you, but I've got to head to Kingsville—something just came up and I have to go now—but I didn't want to leave Caitlin alone. She can't be alone right now." I prayed he wouldn't demand to know why.

He rubbed a hand over his bald head. "You need me to come back down to the cottage?"

"Would you mind? That way I don't have to wake her up, too. She'll just want to argue with me and I need to get on the road."

"All right. Let me get dressed. Give me just a few minutes."

"Thank you. You don't know how much I appreciate this."

Another ten minutes later we were on the path to the cottage, Winnie huffing along behind us, no doubt wondering what in the world we were doing. The night air was cool, and I hadn't put on a jacket, so I was shivering by the time we returned, but I wouldn't risk going into the bedroom for fear of waking Caitlin.

"I really appreciate this," I told Rev. Jack again, keeping my voice low. I retrieved the truck keys from the rack in the kitchen. "The bed in the guest room is made up. You're welcome to use it."

He sank down onto the sofa, kicking off his shoes. "Winnie and I will be good right here. You have a safe trip now. Don't be falling asleep at the wheel."

"I'll be careful," I assured him. There was no way I was falling asleep.

In the truck, I turned on the heat but couldn't stop shivering. Once I got to the highway, I put KoЯn's latest CD into the sound system and cranked the volume. I would get to Kingsville in the wee hours and watch the Wades' house until I saw signs of life, then I would go talk to them, warn them of the danger Adam and Gabey were in. At least that was the plan. As for Peter, well, one way or the other, it appeared I was destined to go down in history as a murderer, now as a cop killer, but I would not stand idly by and allow him to harm Caitlin or the boys. And it also appeared that, one way or the other, my baby was destined to grow up without a father.

I indulged in a little self-pity for several miles, but given the mess that was my life, I could hardly expect anything different. If I accepted that, the rest should be easy to swallow. But it wasn't. Not really. So then, I spent a few more miles railing about the injustice and unfairness of it, for all the good it did me.

I pulled into the driveway of the House from Hell at 4:00 AM. I walked around to the back and looked across the yard at the Wade residence. No lights. Obviously everyone was still in bed. It was much too early on a Sunday for anyone to be stirring.

I let myself into my own house, started the coffeemaker, and went to shower while it did its thing. Once I was clean and dressed again, I took a mug of coffee into the den and switched on the TV. *Whatever Happened to Baby Jane* was playing on TCM, but it was hard for me to concentrate on it. I kept getting up to check the Wade house for signs of life. Gradually, the sun rose and at last I saw movement through the kitchen window. Here went nothing.

The phone rang just as I put my hand on the doorknob, however. Caitlin. I answered and she started in on me.

"I can't *believe* you just left me with no transportation in the middle of nowhere. What is going on? What are you doing that you couldn't wait until morning—that you couldn't take me with you?"

I gritted my teeth. "Caitlin, I don't have time for this."

"Is she with you now?"

"What? Is *who* with me?"

"Whoever you were with the other night when you didn't go home."

She had apparently lost her mind, too. "What are you talking about? Oh...I was with Marco the other night."

"*Margo?*"

"*Marco!*"

"You cheated on me with a *guy*?"

"Oh my God. No. I don't have time for this. And might I add you're a fine one to be worried about me cheating. I'm trying to stop a freaking killer." I told her about the text message I'd received and heard her sharp intake of breath.

"John, no! Don't do anything yet. Please. Wait until I get there and we can talk about this. We'll go to law enforcement together. I called Mackenzie—she's on her way to get me. Please don't do anything yet."

"I'm not waiting three hours for you to get here, babe. Adam is in danger, and I've got to let the Wades know. Stay with Rev. Jack. You're safer there."

"No! Please don't do anything yet."

"I'm hanging up now. I love you."

"Don't you hang up on me!"

Feeling like a bastard, I pushed the end button. Almost immediately it began ringing again. I thumbed it off, crammed it into my pocket, and set off across the yard to the Wades' house. Once at the back door, I hesitated, dreading a face-to-face conversation with Kevin, but then I thought about Adam or Gabey dying at Peter's hands, and I knocked before I could chicken out.

I heard footsteps pounding toward the door and it swung inward to reveal Adam standing there in his pajamas. He grinned at me. "Hi, John!"

He pushed the screen door open and I stepped into the kitchen, which smelled of cinnamon rolls and bacon. "Hey, buddy. How's it going?"

He threw his arms around me at about the same time Gabey came clattering into the room. He, too, raced over to me and embraced my leg. I reached down to give him a quick hug. God, I had missed those little guys, and it was good to know they had missed me, too.

"Come play with us, John," Gabey said, pulling on my pants leg.

"I'd love to, guys, but I really need to talk to your mom and dad a few minutes. Can you let them know I'm here?"

"Mama just left a few minutes ago with Aunt Lee Lee," Adam said, "and Daddy's in the shower. Come play with us while you wait for him." They pulled me into the living room, where hundreds of Lego blocks were scattered across the floor.

"Help us build a pirate ship." Adam shoved a pile of blocks at me and I knelt down in the floor next to him, stacking the blocks into some semblance of a ship, listening for Kevin. Nervous.

When I heard a door opening elsewhere in the house and heavier footfalls in the hallway, I stood, my heart beating a little faster. The expression on his face when he stepped into the living room was pretty much as I had anticipated, and it was not welcoming.

"What the fu—what are *you* doing here?" His face flushed an angry red.

His little boys watched him, happiness and contentment replaced by anxiety, and when Kevin bellowed for them to go to their room, they didn't argue nor waste any time. The bedroom door shut behind them, and Kevin turned to me. "I'll ask you again before I call the cops. What are you doing here?" He reached for a cordless phone sitting on a shelf of the entertainment center inside the doorway.

"I think Adam may be in danger."

"You're damned straight he's in danger. From you. You need to leave."

"Not from me. From Peter Barrington."

Kevin snorted. "Bullshit. Your sister called to warn me about you."

"*Warn* you?"

"She said you were off your medication and that you may be trying to contact me. Your brother-in-law said if you came around then I should take out a no contact order. You need to leave. Now. I'm calling 911." He punched three numbers into the phone, his finger poised above the send key.

I tried to remain calm, to make him see reason. "Kevin, listen to me a minute. Please." I talked fast, explaining to him about Peter and the text message I'd received the night before, but I could hear for myself how crazy I sounded. I stopped, frustrated, and reached into my pocket for my cell phone, meaning to show him the text message.

"*No!*" He must have thought I was reaching for a weapon and his panic was obvious as he hit the send button on his phone, and gave his information to the 911 operator.

Damn it! I didn't even want to think what it would mean for Caitlin, for Adam, if I got locked up before I could stop this screaming disaster. Before I could put a stop to Peter.

I tried once more. "Kevin—"

"You need to send someone quick," he spoke into the phone. "This guy is a former mental patient, and the Sheriff's Department is looking at him for these latest child murders. He's broken into my house and he's after my son."

I wanted to pound him. "Kevin!" I shouted, my calm evaporating, "I'm not *after* Adam. I'm trying to *save* Adam!"

"He's out of control and he's in my house," Kevin said to the dispatcher.

Fuck it. I pushed past him, running for the door. Fine. I'd try to enlist the help of law enforcement, too, but instead of waiting for them to come to Kevin's house and lock me up, I would go to them and try to get them to listen to me, take me seriously. After that, I was out of ideas.

Back in my own driveway, I jumped in the Avalanche, took off with a squall of tires, and drove straight to the Sheriff's Department, where I gave the desk sergeant my name and asked to speak with Detectives Whisnant and Samuels.

"What do you need to see them about?" he asked from behind his bulletproof barricade.

"They'll know."

"Have a seat." He waved in the general direction of a sitting area in a corner of the lobby. I went over to slouch against the wall, nervously jingling my keys in my pocket.

Twenty or thirty minutes later, after I'd paced the length of the room many times over, Det. Whisnant sauntered into the lobby, raising his eyebrows at me. "Well, I didn't believe it, but he was right. So, you've come to your senses and you're ready to talk?"

"Yeah. Can we do this in private?"

He patted me down before motioning the sergeant to buzz us through the locked door and ushering me into the inner sanctum. He pulled me to a stop at the doorway to an office—Det. Samuels', according to the nameplate by the door—and pointed to me, saying, "Look who's come to tell us what he knows about the murders."

Samuels raised his eyebrows, too, and followed us down the corridor to the interview room. They were probably close to orgasm, thinking I was about to solve their murders with an admission of guilt, and I hated to be a cock tease, but I knew they wouldn't listen to me unless they thought a confession was forthcoming.

They each took a seat across from me and waited eagerly for me to get settled. Whisnant smiled at me. "So John, are you ready to admit responsibility for these murders and let us try to help you?"

"I want to help *you*. Peter Barrington committed the murders. Now he's threatening the life of another child, and I think I have the proof you need."

The happy expression on Samuels' face morphed into a scowl. "John, are you off your meds? This doesn't sound like an admission of responsibility to me. This sounds like you trying to shift suspicion onto someone else."

"Why the hell does everyone keep asking me if I'm off my meds? Why can't you just accept that what I'm telling you is the truth?"

"That might have something to do with your past and the fact that you confessed to a murder nine years ago, don't you think?"

"A murder I *told* you I didn't commit. I explained to you why I confessed."

"Yeah, you were young, scared, etc. Nice try, but you know the evidence tied you to the crime. Your attorney managed to make a jury believe that you were crazy. You got lucky. That won't happen again."

I gripped a fistful of my hair in each hand and closed my eyes. Took a deep breath. Opened them again. "Please, listen to me. Peter Barrington is who you want. Not me."

Whisnant slammed the tabletop with his fist. "Stop with the Barrington shit, John. No one is buying it. This is your very last chance to come clean. The grand jury is meeting this week. We're confident that they will indict you based on the new evidence we have, and we will enjoy putting your ass away very much."

This was *not* welcome news, and it distracted me from my real purpose. New evidence? A grand jury indictment? I felt my gut cramping in fear and I spent a few minutes fighting off a nearly overwhelming sense of panic.

Samuels gave me a smarmy grin, goading me. "Your days as a free man are almost at an end." He sat forward in his chair. "So—unburden yourself. When we come for you this week, no amount of talking in the world is going to help you then."

"I haven't done anything. I swear to you." I pulled my cell phone from my pocket and turned it on, scrolling through the messages until I found the one about Adam and shoved it at Whisnant. "Adam Wade is in danger, and if you don't do something about it, Peter Barrington will kill him, too."

Whisnant looked at the screen and passed the phone to Samuels. "What makes you think this is from Barrington? Is this his number?"

I attempted to explain Peter's connection with Adam, with myself. The evidence attributable to Peter found at the scene of the murder of which I had been accused. His being first on the scene of that murder. Caitlin's claim that he raped her and the biological evidence being processed as we spoke— evidence that would prove he was the murderer. "I don't know if it's his number or not," I concluded, "but do you think I sent the damned message to myself?"

Samuels looked up at me. "Quite frankly, yes, I do. You'd do anything to get the attention off you because you're getting ready to go down."

I was angry now. "Why don't you trace the number and find out where it came from? I was in Bryson City when I got the message. If it came from Kingsville, then there's no way I could have sent it to myself."

"You could have had someone send it for you."

"But I didn't! Listen to me for Adam's sake. At least get someone to watch him."

"I can understand why you don't want to admit it now. You've had your competency restored and you know you'll get the death penalty this time around, but this is your last chance to be a man and stop being a coward, John."

I leapt to my feet. "I'm done here."

Samuels and Whisnant stood, too, and Whisnant opened the door.

"We'll see you soon," Samuels sneered.

In the truck, I leaned my head against the steering wheel. No one was going to listen to me. All right, accepted. My only dilemma now was how to stop Peter. He was a pro at the killing game. And despite my claim to the contrary nine years earlier, I was not a killer. Peter had access to guns, tasers, pepper spray; he had police training on how to subdue and control people. All I had was the knife I'd found in the woodshed and my hands. He was stronger and bigger than me—his freaking muscles had muscles—but I had crazy on my side. Crazy would just have to be enough.

CHAPTER TWENTY-SIX

A KINGSVILLE PUBLIC SAFETY patrol car was waiting in the driveway when I returned, an officer standing next to it. He was not one I'd had the pleasure of meeting before. I took a deep breath, trying to quell the wild beating of my heart, and approached him warily.

"Mr. Colucci?" He kept his hand on the butt of his gun, as if he thought I might try to attack him, and I supposed, given what he'd probably been told about me, he fully expected me to.

I knew it would not be wise to make any sudden moves. "Yes, sir?"

"I understand you've been at Kevin Wade's house this morning?"

"Yes, sir."

"Mr. Wade said that he's instructed you not to come around his family. Do you remember that, Mr. Colucci?"

"Yes, sir, but—"

"Sir, if Mr. Wade told you not to come around his family, then by going to his home, you were essentially trespassing. Wouldn't you agree?"

"Yes, sir, but—"

"Do you want to be arrested for trespassing, Mr. Colucci?"

"No, sir, but—"

"This is your official warning. If you go back on his property, you will be arrested. Mr. Wade has been advised to take out a no-contact order against you, and he intends to follow through with that. Once the paperwork is served on you, you are to have no further contact whatsoever with him or any of his family. If you then violate that order, you will be arrested. Do you understand?"

"I just wanted to warn him—"

"Mr. Colucci, do you understand what I am saying to you? It's a yes or no question."

"Yes. I understand." My face felt hot, flushed with embarrassment. I said nothing further.

The officer inclined his head, got into his cruiser, and pulled out of the driveway. I glanced at the Wade's house and thought I saw Kevin watching me from his kitchen window. I gave him a one-finger salute.

Kevin proved to be a busy man that morning. Barely more than two hours later, a deputy from the Kings County Sheriff's Department came to the door and served me with the civil no contact order, making sure to point out the court date less than a week hence. Great, another court date. At least it wasn't another criminal charge. Yet.

I sat down on the sofa in the den. *Whatever Happened to Baby Jane* had gone off and *Psycho*—one of my favorite movies—was now being broadcast. Janet Leigh's character was eating a sandwich with Anthony Perkins' character in the back room of the motel office, so the infamous shower scene was not far off, but I was too exhausted, too discouraged to watch it. And I needed to find Peter. I wasn't sure where to even start, since I didn't know where he lived.

According to what Caitlin had told me, he had been suspended from the police department pending the outcome of the investigation into the rape claim, so it was useless to look for him there. Randy and Laurie knew where he lived, but I also knew they would refuse to tell me and would then warn him that I was on the hunt. Like they had "warned" Kevin. Caitlin had various methods of tracking people down, but I was loathe to ask her, because she would try to talk me out of it, and I could *not* be dissuaded. After racking my brain, however, I could come up with no other way to get the information I needed, so I sat back to wait for her.

Upon her return, she flew into the house with a frantic look on her face. Her relief was evident when she found me in the den, and for a moment, I thought she was going to cry.

"Thank God," she said. "I'm glad you waited so we can talk to the sheriff's department together."

"I didn't wait, Caitlin. I tried talking to Kevin Wade, but he called the cops on me. So I went and talked to Whisnant and Samuels. They told me to stop being a coward and confess. Then, when I got home, Wade had me served with a civil no contact order. No one is going to listen to me. No one is going to listen to you. I've got to find Peter before he does something to you or to Adam. I need you to help me find him. Now. We don't have the luxury of time."

"You can't go after him, John. He'll kill you. Let's go to the Sheriff's Department together—"

"Caitlin. Did you hear what I just said? Nobody believes us. Whisnant told me the grand jury will issue an indictment against me this week and they are going to arrest me. Time's up, babe."

She turned her face from me, and I knew she was indeed crying. I let her, not because I didn't care, but because I didn't know what else to do. When she finished, I put my arms around her. "Help me find him," I whispered into her ear, "or I'm afraid our baby will never be born."

My words had the desired effect. She pushed away from me, fierceness in her eyes, and wiped a sleeve across her face. "All right, damn it. Come on."

She pulled me down the hall to the spare bedroom/office, where she booted up the computer and got on the internet.

"Let's try this first." She typed Peter's name into the search engine. "Okay, that's no good. Over one million results." She scrolled through a couple of pages of text—page after page of information I couldn't read. "All right, let me narrow it down." She typed "Peter Barrington, Kingsville, NC." That produced over 435,000 results, none of them germane. "I'll try some online directories for Kingsville, encompassing a thirty mile radius. He couldn't live any farther away than that because he's required to live within the county."

No matches found.

"I'm going to check the public safety department website, not that I expect there to be any information, though."

There wasn't.

She checked a couple of other websites.

Nothing.

I was ready to admit defeat, when she said, "Let's try the county tax records. Peter owns a truck, if not a house."

She pulled up the website for the Kings County Tax Office and then a screen that invited her to "Tax Search View Pay." She ticked several boxes and typed in his name.

Success.

She clicked on the first record, then "view bill," and I leaned forward eagerly. He owned two vehicles—the 2011 black Honda Ridgeline I had seen him driving and a 2009 Jeep Grand Cherokee. The address on both bills was a post office box.

Next record.

He also owned a house. Billing address, same P. O. Box.

Failure. Damn, damn, damn.

"Hang on a second," Caitlin muttered, clicking on her favorites again to pull up another Kings County site called WebGIS. She clicked and typed and finally said, "Hell, yes!" She hit the print button, snatched the paper out of the machine almost before it finished, and handed it to me. Most of it made no sense; however, I had no trouble discerning the property address: 10105 Cedar Brook Lane, Kingsville, NC.

"What are you going to do now?" Her voice quavered.

"I'm going to find his house, then I'm going to put a stop to him."

"John, it's too dangerous. He'll kill you."

"I guess I'll just have to take that chance. Adam's in danger, but I'm the only one who seems to think so. Somebody's got to do something, and I guess that's going to be me."

She took my hands in hers. "Thanks to you, his daddy is going to be keeping a very close eye on him today and Kevin's probably asked for officers to drive through the neighborhood just to be on the safe side. It's public knowledge that Peter has been suspended, so he wouldn't dare show his face. Tomorrow Adam'll be in school until 3:00 o'clock. You don't have to do anything today. Besides, we have our first appointment with the obstetrician tomorrow morning. Promise me you'll wait until after the appointment."

Reluctantly, I promised Caitlin that I would accompany her to the doctor's appointment. I would get to listen to my child's heartbeat for the first and possibly only time. Then Peter or I one would die.

#

In bed later that night, our arms wrapped tightly around each other after an almost feral lovemaking session, Caitlin said, "I was thinking about what you said earlier. Do you think our baby won't get the chance to be born?"

I weighed my words carefully, but there was no kind way to say it. "I think there's a chance none of us will make it through this alive. And you know if I kill Peter then I'll spend the rest of my life in prison, so it doesn't much matter if I get out alive or not."

I felt her swift intake of breath. "Sometimes I wish I had never gotten pregnant. I hate the thought of bringing a child into a world where police officers rape and murder children and terrorize innocent people." She cried some more, but I could offer no comfort. I simply held her until she fell asleep, and when her arms relaxed, I slipped out of bed, pulled on my jeans and shirt, and went to the den where I checked my cell phone to make sure there were no more text messages.

Tucking the phone into my pocket, I went to the kitchen to take my Ambien. I was filled with apprehension about what tomorrow would bring and not the least bit sleepy, despite not having slept the previous night. I hesitated and shook another tablet out of the bottle, then one more. Three should guarantee some sleep, although eight hours was probably still too much to hope for.

I sat in the den to give the Ambien time to work its magic, ended up almost dozing off in the chair, and stumbled back to the bedroom, where I fell into bed, still clothed. Pulling Caitlin to me, I breathed the scent of her hair, her skin, and kissed her lightly on the forehead. She sighed in her sleep and snuggled closer to me. Too late I remembered I hadn't put up the baby gate at the laundry room door to contain Willie. He might wander around the house and end up piddling in the floor before the night was out, but I was too far gone to do anything about it now. Oh well, one night wouldn't kill any of us, and the carpet had to be replaced anyway.

I closed my eyes. It seemed that any thoughts of or discussions about the baby always brought memories of my own father to the surface of my brain. The dream started the way it always did....

I chased him from room to room, pleading with him to stop and talk to me. I followed along, always one room behind him. Except...the next room I entered, there he stood, his back to me.

"Dad?" I trembled from excitement, fear, joy.

He turned slowly and gazed at me, the love in his eyes unmistakable. "John. Son."

I was afraid to touch him. Afraid he would disappear. I was crying tears of joy. "Dad. My God, I've missed you."

"I've missed you, too."

I wanted to hug him and never turn him loose, but I was frozen, unable to move.

He was crying as well. "I'm so sorry for what I did. For leaving you behind. Can you ever forgive me?" He took a step closer to me.

"Yes, I forgive you. You didn't even have to ask."

He smiled at me through his tears. "Thank you. I don't deserve your forgiveness, but thank you."

"Of course you deserve it. You're my father. Hey, did you hear? I'm going to be a father, too."

"I'm so glad for you."

"But I'm scared, Dad. I don't know if I have what it takes to be a good father. How will I know if I'm doing it right?"

He put a hand on my shoulder. I could feel the heat of his palm through my shirt, growing hotter by the minute. "You won't know while you're busy doing it. You'll only know after your child is grown, and you can only work with what you have. I'm afraid I didn't give you much to go on."

"Don't say that! You were a great dad. I just wish you hadn't—" A loud, annoying buzz interrupted us. "What is that?"

The room in the house faded abruptly and became the garage. The garage where my father had ended his life. I knew what came next—I'd had the dream often enough. The gunshot, the blood and gore. But this time, instead of the smells of a ruined body, of death, I smelled gasoline. Not just the faint odor of gasoline you smell in any garage, but gallons of it.

My father lit a cigarette and took a pull on it.

"Dad, should you be smoking around so much gasoline? Besides, smoking will—"

He laughed. "Will kill me?"

The buzzing continued. "What the hell is that?" I asked.

"That's the wake-up call for the rest of your life. Heed it. Don't make the same stupid mistakes I did. Get out alive. Don't leave your son without a father." He turned to go and as he did, I heard Caitlin calling for me, her voice frantic.

Between her and the perpetual annoying buzz, I was getting very angry. I just wanted to talk with my father.

"Don't go yet, please. Why do you have to leave so soon? I've missed you so much." The sound continued. The cigarette smoke was so thick that I couldn't breathe. I coughed. "Please don't go," I said again and heard Caitlin screaming my name. What was wrong with her?

"I can't stay," he replied. "You can't either. You need to go. Take your wife and go."

That damned noise just wouldn't quit, and I was choking from the smoke and gasoline fumes. "I love you, Dad."

He reached out to touch my face and vanished into a column of smoke.

I awoke to a horror show. Alarms blared. Smoke filled the room. Struggling to understand what was happening, I sat up, looking around in confusion, and saw the reflection of flames on the wall outside our bedroom door.

"John! Get up!" Caitlin sobbed, pulling at my arm. "John! What is wrong with you? The house is on fire—get up!" She shook me again, her terror palpable. "Hurry!" She shrieked as something fell at the other end of the house with a horrific crash.

Lurching to my feet, I grabbed her arm and pulled her toward the door, but once at the threshold saw that the hallway between us and the safety of the living room was in flames. There was no way to get to either the front or rear doors. I pushed her back into the room and over to the closest window, where I ripped at the curtains, yanked the louvered blinds from their mounting, flipped the lock, and nearly tore the window from its sash. I lifted her, shoved her through the opening, and dove after her, jamming my shoulder when I hit the ground.

We both scrambled to our feet, Caitlin sobbing. "Willie! *Where's Willie?*"

Oh my God. Where was he? A sick feeling washed over me. "I'll get him," I said and dragged her around to the front of the house.

The next door neighbor was standing in his yard. "I've called the fire department. Are you okay?" he yelled.

"We're fine!" I shouted, and to Caitlin, I said, "Stand over there with him. I'm going in after Willie."

She didn't listen to me, though—big surprise—and clutched my arm as she followed me to the front of the house.

I tried forcing the steel security door open, but being the former residence of a police officer, it would naturally have nothing less than a top-of-the-line deadbolt lock. Next bright idea. I grabbed a good-sized rock from the flower bed bordering the foundation and lobbed it at the living room window. The glass broke but didn't give way completely and I wasted precious seconds bashing at it to make an opening large enough so that I could reach in and unlock it without cutting myself. Finally, I hoisted myself in and rushed to the front door to open it—which in retrospect was a very poor decision, because the moment I did, the fresh air fueled the flames and the fire blazed up around me.

Caitlin darted in behind me, pushing past to get to the kitchen. "Willie! Willie, where are you?" Sparks rained down around us, then a chunk of ceiling and smoldering insulation, just missing her head.

"Get the hell out of here NOW!" I grabbed her, and marched her to the front so fast, I don't think her feet had a chance to touch the floor. She managed to snag her purse and cell phone as I shoved her past the console table and onto the stoop, where someone pulled her away from the house. They shouted and gestured for me to come out, but once I was certain she was clear, I returned to the kitchen.

"Willie!" With the flames crackling and alarms shrilling, I couldn't have heard him if he was barking right in front of me and he probably couldn't hear me. The smoke was heavy and I could feel the heat on my skin as I moved further into the kitchen, glancing under the table—anywhere a little dog might hide. I only got as far as the island—the entire wall between the two rooms was on fire. If Willie was still in the laundry room, well, he wouldn't be alive, but I couldn't live with myself if I didn't at least try to get to him.

The smell of gasoline permeated my nostrils. I coughed some more and gagged. I tried to suck oxygen into my lungs and experienced a flashback to the time I was shot. It was that same feeling of breathlessness—needing air and unable to get it.

I turned back to the door just as another portion of the ceiling crashed down beside me, nearly knocking me off my feet, a blazing two by four falling against my forearm, setting my shirtsleeve on fire. Frantically, I slapped at the flame searing my flesh. Okay, I was starting to panic now. Time for retreat. But just as I was about to give the poor dog up for dead, I saw a small shadow dart under the sofa in the living room.

"Willie!" I ran to the sofa, dropped to my knees and shoved my arms underneath, feeling for him. Nothing. I moved farther down and at last felt his trembling body. I pulled him toward me as something else crashed in the kitchen. I felt his sharp little puppy teeth sink into my hand, but at that point I didn't care. I had him in my grasp, and I was on my feet running for the door.

Caitlin was standing in the middle of the front yard, and I shoved Willie into her outstretched arms and staggered into the driveway, needing to put some distance between myself and the smoke. My eyes watered so fiercely that I couldn't see well, and I coughed so hard I was afraid I might disgorge a lung. There were people and emergency response vehicles everywhere. All the flashing lights made my head swim. The effect was of a dream sequence from a movie—everything out of focus, blurry, indistinct. My arm was still on fire; the burning sensation intense. My mouth and throat felt coated in soot, bathed in smoke. I wanted nothing so badly as a big drink of water.

So many damned people, so much noise and confusion. All my "neighbors" were standing in their yards in their bathrobes, no doubt thrilled that, come daylight, the monster in their midst would be vanquished, banished to the netherworld forevermore. Reduced to ashes and rubble. I tripped on the curb and nearly fell. A hand gripped my left elbow and a voice spoke. "We need to get you checked out."

I faced a firefighter in full gear. He steadied me when I stumbled again. "Let's get you where you can sit down. Then we'll get a paramedic to look at you." He walked me away from the House from Hell—or what was left of it—to the back of a dark-colored sport pick-up truck parked farther down the street. He opened the tailgate, pointed and said, "Sit. What you need is something to drink. It'll help get that taste of smoke out of your mouth." He reached into the cab of the truck and came back with a bottle of water. He removed one of his gloves—a gesture that seemed vaguely familiar—twisted off the cap, and handed the bottle to me. I drank it in three gulps.

"More?"

I nodded, grateful, and he placed another in my hand. I took two swallows and felt suddenly and dreadfully ill. The bottle fell from my hand and I swayed on the tailgate, pitching forward.

He reached out to break my fall. "Whoa, there." He got a shoulder under my arm, hoisting me enough to walk me around to the cab. He reached with one hand to open the door, steadying me with the other, and eased me into the seat. For some reason, I seemed to have lost all muscle tone and slumped against the console while he swung my legs into the cab and reached across to fasten the seatbelt around me. He slid one hand under my head and the other under my shoulder, then repositioned the seat so that I was now recumbent. I attempted to sit up, but my brain and my muscles weren't communicating anymore, and I felt sick. So sick. I retched, but didn't vomit.

The passenger door shut and I was trying unsuccessfully to right myself when the driver's side opened, and I heard him fumbling with his gear. It took a phenomenal effort to lift my head even an inch off the headrest—I didn't possess the strength to sit up on my own. The smoke inhalation and oxygen deprivation had affected me more than I realized. He must be planning to drive me to the hospital.

He slid into the driver's seat and started the engine, then leaned over into my field of vision. My shitty luck had finally run out. I found myself staring into Peter Barrington's grinning face.

Chapter Twenty-Seven

I DIDN'T WAKE UP so much as gradually become aware of my surroundings once more, and my first thought was that I would never take more than the prescribed dose of Ambien in the future. I was uncomfortable in the extreme, but couldn't move. My limbs were numb, as heavy as if they were made of concrete, and the skin on my right forearm burned. My head throbbed with each beat of my heart and I was nauseated. I was also parched, my mouth so dry it felt as if it had been glued shut. And why the hell did I smell smoke? I wanted to open my eyes, but the mere effort of raising my eyelids was more than I could manage at that moment. I was cold, too, but then many mornings I woke to find Caitlin hogging the blankets, so that was nothing new.

This was ridiculous. I had to get up. I had to piss, I needed a drink of water, and I needed to stretch my arms and legs. Again I tried to shift position, except that my body still didn't obey the commands of my brain. I wasn't taking Ambien any more. Period. The amount of effort it took to force my eyes open was astonishing, but it was energy wasted, because once I had them open, I could see nothing. Complete and utter darkness.

I would have to rouse Caitlin, get her to help me. She would be cranky, but it was either that or wet the bed. I attempted to say her name, but the only thing that came out of my mouth was a cross between croak and groan. I tried again and managed to utter something that sounded vaguely like "Caitlin." No response. I couldn't hear her breathing, couldn't sense her beside me. I listened in case she had gotten up to go to the bathroom herself. No water running or toilet flushing. No hum of the refrigerator, no ticking of the grandfather clock in the living room. I could usually hear street noise from Sheridan Boulevard, even in the wee hours of the morning, but now, absolutely nothing. My ears were working no better than my eyes or my muscles.

I finally managed to roll over onto my back and with great difficulty stretched out my arm, feeling for Caitlin. Only a wall. Wait a minute. Neither side of our bed was against the wall, nor was the bed in our spare bedroom against a wall. The mattress was harder than any of ours—barely more than a little padding on what felt like a cement floor. Where the hell was I? I thought about the previous evening. Yes, I had been at home. I had gone to bed—my bed—with Caitlin.

I was able to shift my shoulders, and the faint scent of smoke wafted up. *Fire.* Images came back to me. *Smoke, heat, flames, trying to get my breath, choking, gasping, panic, searching for Willie.* None of it seemed real, but it must have been. Then—*then that meant the image of Peter was real, too.*

Oh, God. A surge of adrenaline shot through me, propelling me to a sitting position, which I immediately regretted. My stomach did a flip, and I gagged. Why did I feel like I had been run over by a truck?

And then I did hear a noise. A faint click and the scrape of metal on metal. A steel door opening. A slice of light moved across the floor and I saw a silhouette in the doorway. A fluorescent light burst on and I covered my eyes instinctively until they could adjust. When I was able to keep them open, it was to discover Peter squatting beside me, studying me. "I was worried about you," he said, his fingers brushing across my cheekbone as he pushed some hair behind my ear.

I jerked away from his touch, but my movements were slow and uncoordinated, and I ended up falling back on the mattress.

"It's about time you snapped out of it," he said. "I guess I shouldn't have given you that much." He yanked me upright again.

"Shouldn't have given me that much what?" Control of my vocal cords was no better than control of my muscles.

"Rohypnol. Ever hear of it?"

He waited while I processed that information.

"Isn't that the date rape drug?" Not all of the information processed quite so quickly. "Why would you give me—" I stopped as the implication became clear.

Peter smiled and made a "come on" gesture with his hand. "Finish the thought, John. Why would I give you a date rape drug? Why do *you* think? Tell me, do you feel violated?"

I shook my head, refusing to accept it. "No. No, you didn't."

He gave me that same sickening sly smile. "Do you know for sure? You were out of it. You've been out of it for hours." He watched my face for a few minutes, then laughed. "You're right. I didn't. Yet. But I will love doing to you what your wife claims I did to her, and I will then enjoy showing her the difference between consensual sex and rape. I'm an equal opportunity rapist. Most of all, I will enjoy killing you both. Of course the media will portray it as a murder-suicide."

In a mock TV announcer's voice he continued. "In other news, today a Kingsville man, previously accused of murdering a child in 2004, killed his pregnant wife before taking his own life." He shifted on his haunches. "This couldn't have worked out any better if I'd planned it. No one will have trouble believing it of you. You have charges against you for assaulting your brother-in-law and your wife. You have a no-contact order against you by the family of one child. And then, of course, you've already confessed to another murder. People will be talking about you for a long, long time."

He stood and moved to the door. "I'll be back after a while."

I heard the deadbolt turning in the lock. Only then did I take in my surroundings. The room was, of course, windowless, the floor, concrete. It was obviously soundproofed, as no noise filtered through. I had been lying on a thin, narrow mattress, covered with disgusting reddish-brown stains. It smelled rank.

There was nothing else in the room save a metal plate with an inverted u-shaped hook bolted to the floor and a chain fastened to the hook. The other end of the chain snaked toward me, ending at a metal cuff around my ankle. I stared, unable at first to comprehend the significance. Once it sank in, I spent several futile minutes pulling first at the cuff and then at the metal plate.

Because the concrete floor was so cold, I sat back down on the nasty mattress. I had no socks, no shoes, and part of my right shirtsleeve had a huge hole in it where it had burned, the skin beneath red and blistered. I had a memory of Caitlin standing in the middle of the front yard, Willie clutched in her arms. I wondered where she was now, what she was doing, if she had kept her doctor appointment, if she had gotten to hear the baby's heartbeat. She would be frantic, knowing I hadn't left on my own, but no one was going to listen to her when she tried to tell them about Peter. Whisnant and Samuels would be sure to claim that I'd left to avoid arrest. And now I was a prisoner anyway. I never thought the day would come when I would wish I was in the custody of the Sheriff's Department.

Without intending to, I fell asleep and woke to find him standing over me once more. I didn't know how long he'd been there and I hated the look on his face—a mixture of lust and sadistic pleasure. He crouched down next to me and put a hand on my cheek. I moved as far away from him as the chain would allow, but he merely waited until I'd reached the end of the slack and advanced once more, cupping my chin in his hand. He leaned forward and put his mouth on mine. I attempted to turn my head but he held my face in his grasp, squeezing my chin tighter, trying to force his tongue past my lips.

I flailed and kicked at him, but he pinned me beneath his bulk, his weight crushing me. "That's right, fight me," he said, grabbing a handful of my hair and yanking my head back. The tone of his voice chilled me. I forced myself to stop resisting and lie motionless when it occurred to me that the more I fought, the more aroused he became. I thought of the children he had subjugated. How terrified they must have been. I couldn't hold my own against him—the boys would have never stood a chance. They were completely at his mercy, and he had none.

"I've wanted you for a long time," he said into my ear. "You don't remember the first time we met, do you?"

The recollection came rushing into my head like a bullet train. The memory that had been trying to leap the synapses in my misfiring brain for months.

Thirteen years of age—I'm not terribly sophisticated, nor wise. I'm cognizant of the fact that there is something not quite right about me. I have very few friends, and those few aren't high caliber. Desperate to belong, to fit in somehow, that means hanging with lowlifes, which I guess makes me a lowlife by association. It also means experimenting with drugs and alcohol.

I need something to take my mind off the fact that my father is doing another stint on the psych ward at Kingsville Memorial Hospital. I'm ashamed of his behavior, ashamed of the fights he and my mother have, leading up to her having him involuntarily committed. I'm angry with her; angry with Dad for acting in such a way as to make his commitment necessary; angry with my sister for being in New York City on modelling jobs and auditions, thus removing herself from the drama that is our dysfunctional family. I hate the feeling of powerlessness and I'm angry about the situation over which none of us has any control. The anger takes on a life and personality of its own. I want to punch something, to hurt someone, and drugs and alcohol seem to be the only method by which I can deaden the emotions I'm experiencing.

Justin, one of my so-called "friends," tells me of a police officer who exchanges drugs for "favors". "Any kind of drug you want, man, he'll get it for you. You've just got to perform for him."

"Perform?" Performing, to my way of thinking, is singing or dancing, maybe magic tricks.

"You know," Justin says, giving me a significant look.

"I don't understand."

He rolls his eyes. "Sex, you moron. You give him a blow job or let him screw you and he'll pay you in drugs. The more you're willing to do, the more he'll give you."

"That's sick." I reply, but I'm desperate.

Justin shrugs, and I sense his disdain. He's only a year older chronologically, but decades older in experience. "Dude, it's just sex. Where else are you going to get OxyContin so easily? At least let me introduce you to him. You can take it from there. Or not."

I'm so anxious to prove myself worthy of his dubious friendship and not appear a total dweeb, that I go along with him. I agree to meet him in the alleyway behind an abandoned building at the edge of town. A lamb to the slaughter.

I expect the police officer to be an older man, creepy-looking and creepier acting, but he's young, attractive and personable. I'm tall for my age and on the skinny side, and the muscular young police officer makes me feel like an Auschwitz survivor. He separates me from the others, walks me over to a corner of the dark room, talking, laughing, joking, trying to put me at ease. He slips me a couple of pills, his hand lingering on mine for a moment. He motions for me to take them. "No strings," he murmurs. "No pressure, but you can't tell. If anyone finds out, you'll go to juvenile detention."

I swallow the pills with a huge swig from the bottle of Jack Daniels he offers, shuddering at the taste of the liquor. In short order, I begin feeling more relaxed. The officer sits beside me on an old wooden bench, his leg touching mine, but when he unzips my jeans, puts his hand on my junk, and begins fondling me, I squirm out from under him, stand up, and say, "I've got to take a leak." I walk out the door, zipping my pants as I go, and keep right on walking until I get home, where I go straight to my room. I don't dare tell anyone what's happened.

Another sharp tug at my hair brought me back to the present, and Peter growled into my ear, "You walked away from me then. You're not going to walk away from me again."

#

I came awake when I heard his key in the door and was on my feet by the time he got all the way into the room. He had that nasty grin plastered on his face.

"Morning, lover," he said and tried to kiss me on the cheek, laughing when I pushed him away. He held up his iPhone. "Most people only get fifteen minutes of fame. Looks like you're getting forty-five. I downloaded this for you. Watch."

He pressed the screen several times, scrolled with his finger, and then held it up to my face. It was a news broadcast from a Charlotte TV station, showing a male reporter standing in front of the smoldering remains of the House from Hell. The caption at the bottom of the screen read, "Vigilante Justice."

"I'm standing in front of what's left of the residence of John Edward Colucci, the man Kings County Sheriff's Department detectives believe is responsible for the murders of five boys ranging in age from seven to thirteen years old over the past nine months. Nine years ago, Colucci confessed to the murder of eight-year-old Hunter Jernigan. He was eventually found not guilty of that murder by reason of insanity or mental defect. Though never charged, he was also a suspect in the murder of nine-year-old Gavin Beasley, which occurred around the same time. He spent eight years at Broughton Hospital in Morganton and was released this past January. The Sheriff's Department has confirmed that arson is responsible for the fire which destroyed Colucci's home and believes it may be related to threats of vigilante justice against Colucci. According to Detective Michael Pendergrass with the Kingsville Department of Public Safety, Colucci was shot by an unknown assailant in July and suffered serious injury. The Sheriff's Department says Colucci disappeared from the scene of the fire and hasn't been seen since. It's feared that he may be the victim of foul play. They're asking anyone who may have information regarding his whereabouts to contact them at (828) 555-1212."

They showed a recent photo of me—the same one used in the last newspaper article. I somehow doubted that they would be inundated with phone calls from citizens concerned for my safety.

Peter said, "But, wait. It gets better." He tapped the screen a few more times and held it up to me again.

The same reporter was now standing in front of the Sheriff's Department and the caption read "Breaking News" in red letters on a white background in a running banner across the bottom of the screen. "Good evening everyone. This news just in—according to the Kings County Sheriff's Department there is now a manhunt underway for John Edward Colucci, 28, of Kingsville. It was at first believed that Colucci may have been the victim of vigilante justice after he vanished from the scene of the fire which destroyed his home last night; however, we've just learned that Colucci was indicted by a Kings County grand jury today for the murders of five boys within the last nine months, and it is now believed that he is attempting to avoid arrest. Colucci is also wanted in connection with the disappearance of eight-year-old Adam Wade, who vanished from a football game at his school this afternoon." The screen cut to a school photo of Adam. "Adam Wade's father recently took out a civil no-contact order against Colucci—a neighbor of the Wades—after Colucci forced his way into their home in what may have been an attempt to abduct the boy last Sunday."

I didn't wait to hear the rest. "What have you done to Adam?" I knocked the phone out of his hand, where it skittered across the concrete floor, and I lunged for him. He stepped back out of my reach, laughing when I jerked to a stop at the end of the chain.

"You'll see him soon enough," he sneered. "In fact we're going to have a family reunion of sorts."

"You'd better not hurt him."

"And what are you going to do about it?" Peter looked pointedly at the cuff encircling my ankle.

Even at the height of my conflict with Randy, I'd never before had such an urge to hurt someone. I swung at him, but he grabbed my arms, pinning me spread-eagled to the wall, his knee between my legs.

"You and I are going to have some fun right now," he breathed into my ear, "and then tomorrow we're going to invite Caitlin and Adam to join us."

He stepped back and I jerked away from him, but of course, there was only so far I could go. He caught me by the waistband of my jeans, yanking me off my feet, and spun me around.

"Take off your clothes," he said.

My heart seized. "What?"

"You heard me. Strip."

"No, please—"

"You or Adam. Your choice."

I knew there was no guarantee that he hadn't already raped Adam or that he wouldn't rape Adam anyway, but I had no other option if there was even the slightest chance of Peter sparing him. My hands trembling, I removed my shirt and undid my zipper, but I couldn't go beyond that.

He put his hands on my shoulders, moved them across my chest and down my stomach, stopping at the opening of my jeans. He pushed them down my hips, then put his hand between my legs.

"Peter, don't do this." I tried to move away from him, but he had me backed into the corner and there was nowhere to go.

He began to remove his own clothing. "Get on your knees."

"Oh my God—"

He grabbed my chin and squeezed. "Shut up and do it. You or Adam. I'm not telling you again."

I dropped to my knees. "Please, please, please…."

"Bend over." He moved around behind me and placed a hand on my right buttock. His body was hard and hot against mine.

There was nothing left to do but fight for my life and what little remained of my sanity. So I did. I twisted around and unleashed a volley of punches, getting in a few good blows to his head and a feeble kick to his crotch. He let me fight, let me wear myself out. Then, when he was sufficiently aroused by my struggle, he overpowered and handcuffed me.

As with his other victims, he showed no mercy. The only other time in my life I had ever been so completely and thoroughly humiliated was at the time of my arrest. The strip search had been unmerciful. In essence, Peter had raped me twice.

It was only after he'd turned off the light and left the room that I allowed myself to break down, the pain and the horror of the assault replaying in my mind like a particularly vivid nightmare. And it was only then that I understood why people hated me for what they thought I had done. It was the first time I had ever fully contemplated the extent of the crimes perpetrated against those children—things that made their murders seem like a mercy killing. What a mercy it would have been if I had died during the assault. I could imagine the white-hot rage of parents who learned that these atrocities had been committed against their child. How could a parent ever recover from such a thing? How could I ever recover from such a thing?

Even if Caitlin hadn't admitted to falsifying the rape claim against Peter, there could now be no question in my mind as to whether or not he had really assaulted her. If he had, she would not still be the same person. I would never be the same person. I hoped that his victims hadn't suffered for long, but having felt the brunt of his sadistic nature firsthand, I knew that hope was in vain. I feared for Adam and Caitlin. I knew I could not allow Peter to do those things to them.

Randy's words came back to me. "By God, you will wish you were back in Broughton." I wished fervently I had never left, because I feared I wouldn't be long in returning. I did the only thing I knew to do. I slipped into that place in my mind reserved for just such an emergency. The place with the titanium shell, where no one could follow. It was a place I had utilized many times in the past and, in all likelihood, would use in the future. To gain access, all I had to do was rock. Back and forth. Back and forth.

Rock. Pain. *Rock.* Hunger. *Rock.* Thirst. *Rock.* Cold. *Just rock.* Don't think. *Just rock.* Don't feel. *Just rock.* Don't cry. *Just rock.* Don't bleed. *Rock.* Hatred. *Rock.* Rage. *Rock.* Fury. *Rock.* Vengeance.

Vengeance is mine, sayeth the Lord. No, Lord. Vengeance is *mine*.

The Voices were back, and this time the vitriol was not for me, but for Peter. It was the first time I had felt them to be my allies. Normally, I did my best to ignore them; shut them out. Now, I was glad for their company and I listened intently to what they had to say.

You know the motherfucker has to die.

Sick shits like him don't deserve to live.

He's gotten away with this perversion for at least fifteen years and no one's stopped him yet.

Somebody's got to stop him—put an end to his reign of terror.

You know what he is. What he's done. What he's capable of.

But the bastard is going to fuck up, and when he does, you have to be ready to administer the coup de grace.

He cannot be allowed to defile another child.

You know he has Adam.

You know what he will do to Adam if he gets half the chance.

Pray to God he hasn't done anything to him yet.

See to it that he doesn't get the chance.

See that he never gets the chance to hurt another child.

Ever again.

You can do it.

You have to do it.

You must do it.

No one else has the balls to do it.

The motherfucker has to die.

Peter returned to the room much later. He spoke to me, but I didn't respond, which undoubtedly infuriated him. He jerked my head around to face him, but when I wouldn't meet his eyes, he slapped me. I continued to rock, while the Voices sang, "Die, motherfucker, die." I grinned to myself as he left the room.

The next time he appeared, he brought a bottle of water and a pack of peanut butter crackers, which he held out to me. I stared through him and continued to rock. My God, I wanted that water so desperately, but I would not give him the satisfaction of reaching for it. He remained in the room watching me for a long time. What he didn't understand was that I was an old pro at this. I had gone for weeks at a time without speaking a word or even acknowledging that there was a world beyond the confines of my own mind. I had the upper hand in this contest at least.

He nudged the bottle of water toward me with his toe and said, "Drink. I know you've got to be thirsty. I know you want it."

Rock. Rock. Rock.

"Did you hear me, John?"

Rock. Rock. Rock.

"Take it. Finish that and I'll bring you more."

Rock. Rock. Rock.

He left the room, and I continued to rock. And wait. When he didn't return, I grabbed the bottle and drained it. Honestly, you'd think I would learn, but no. The heaviness fell over me again.

#

The drug wore off much quicker this time, perhaps because I hadn't taken three times the prescribed dose of Ambien beforehand. I was no longer on the disgusting mattress in a small room with a chain around my ankle, but my situation hadn't improved. Not by a long shot. I was now in another basement, on an equally disgusting floor, my hands cuffed behind me.

After a short struggle, I was able to sit up so that I could survey the room in greater detail. The basement was immense, no doubt an abandoned warehouse or factory. A partial wall bisected its length, the far end shrouded in darkness. No natural light entered the space. The only illumination came from a few flickering fluorescent tubes, the wattage inadequate for the vast area. I became aware of a strange odor. I knew instinctively that it was the smell of death. The feeling of dread that overcame me was exacerbated by the discovery of what looked like a pile of clothing in the darkened corner to my left.

I could make out a small football cleat attached to a small leg encased in green and yellow sock and matching yellow football uniform pants. Oh Christ, it was Adam, and he wasn't moving. I could hear Peter grunting and dragging things around on the other side of the basement. I could not imagine what he was doing, but knew I had to find out if Adam was all right. Awkwardly, I managed to scoot across the concrete floor on my ass, trying to ignore the pain, grit biting into the palms of my hands as I propelled myself along. I reached him after halting every few minutes to make sure Peter hadn't heard or stopped what he was doing to check on me.

Adam was lying on his side, one arm outstretched and the other curled under him, one knee bent toward his chest. In this corner the light was even dimmer and I couldn't see his face clearly enough to tell whether he was injured or bleeding. He made a funny sound as he breathed. I put a foot on his thigh and jostled him gently, saying, "Adam!" as loud as I dared. He continued to snuffle, and I kept rocking him, repeating his name. After five or ten minutes I saw him twitch and then his leg straightened and I heard him whimper.

"Adam, shhh..." I whispered. "It's me, John. Are you okay?"

He began stirring and then sat up. As he moved into the light, I could see well enough to tell that his nose and upper lip were swollen and his glasses were sitting crookedly on his face. The sight of him made the ice in my gut turn to fire. He looked at me and whimpered again. "Peter hurt me, John."

"Shh." I scooted closer to him. "Come sit next to me."

"I'm scared." He trembled, tears running down his cheeks.

"I know," I told him. "He's got me in handcuffs, dude, or I'd give you a hug. Here, put your arms around me. You hold on to me."

He did just that. In fact, if he could have crawled inside me, I think he would have done it. There was a loud bang and a curse from the other side of the basement and Adam jumped, grabbed me tighter, and cried a little harder.

Peter appeared from behind the partition, saw us sitting together and came striding over.

"Stand behind me, Adam," I said.

Peter sneered. "He's not gonna save you, Adam, 'cause they're gonna find him with a bullet in his brain."

"No!" Adam screamed. "You leave him alone! You're a bad man!" His fingers dug into my shoulders as he clutched me.

Peter leaned toward him, and I took the opportunity to scramble to my feet, leveraging myself against Adam, catching Peter with a head-butt to the stomach. He hit the floor on his ass.

"Run, Adam!" I roared and we both took off for the door.

Peter got me in a flying tackle and down I went, my head slamming onto the concrete floor and the already dim lights in the basement went out.

CHAPTER TWENTY-EIGHT

MY HEAD WAS THROBBING when I came to. I tried to sit up, began feeling sick to my stomach, and decided to abandon that course of action. A small hand on my shoulder told me that Adam hadn't made it out either, and I wanted to give up.

"John, are you hurt?" he whispered.

"I'll be okay," I whispered back, but to be honest, it wasn't looking real good for either one of us at that point.

"Shut up, both of you!" Peter bellowed. "You—come here." He rolled me over and jerked me to my feet. I swayed dizzily, and he yanked me by the arm again to keep me from falling. He dragged me to the back of the basement where, in the farthest corner, exposed pipes ran from floor to ceiling. He removed the cuff from my wrist and fastened it around one of the pipes.

Grabbing Adam by the back of his football jersey, he lifted him bodily and brought him over to stand with me. "If you move," he said to Adam, "I will blow John's brains all over this basement with you watching, and then I'm going to blow yours out. You understand me?"

Tears ran down Adam's face, but he nodded.

Peter went back to what he had been doing, which I could now see was moving several wooden crates into a row. I had no idea what he planned to do with them, but was fairly certain it wasn't anything good. As I watched, I realized that I could see what looked like two small pairs of legs on the floor on the opposite side of the crates. These legs were not moving, and I got the creepy sensation that they would never move again. I prayed that Adam couldn't see them.

After a few more minutes of dragging and pushing, Peter stopped and pulled something from his pocket. Judging from the neon green cover, it was my cell phone. He stabbed the screen with his finger, looked at it and grinned.

"Caitlin just sent a text. Our guest of honor will be here any minute. The party is about to get underway."

"No, damn you!" I threw myself at him, though tethered to the pipe by the handcuff, I couldn't reach him. "Leave her out of this! This is me and you. *Me and you!* Not Caitlin, not Adam."

"Well, now, I've always said the more people at a party, the merrier. Let's see if we can't get us some female company down here." He raised his hand in front of my face, and I flinched, but he only patted my cheek and laughed. He went out the basement door, and I heard his footsteps in the stairwell, echoing on the metal treads.

I wiped my hand across my face, surprised to find it wet. "Adam," I said, "I need you to look around for another way out. See if you can find a door or a window."

"I don't want to leave you," he whimpered.

"Adam! Do what I'm telling you. Go! *Now!*"

He raced around the basement trying to find a way out. Too late I remembered to warn him away from the area where the two small bodies lay. He stopped short, staring at the floor. "John?" His voice was tremulous. "There are two little boys over here. They smell funny." He reached down to touch them. "They're cold. I—I think they're dead!"

"Adam, don't stop now! There's nothing you can do for them. Keep looking!"

Adam pulled himself away from them, and I saw him wiping his face with his sleeve. "I don't see any other doors," he sniffled, "and the windows are covered with boards."

I closed my eyes and took a deep breath, then opened them again. "Okay, Adam, listen to me. We're playing World War II, all right? You're the American soldier and Peter is the Nazi Stormtrooper. The only way to win is for you to get out of here. I want you to try that door he just went out. If it's open, then run like hell, but don't let him see you. Do it, now!" Even though he risked being caught by Peter, it was our only hope.

Adam sprinted for the door. I thought I would hyperventilate when it opened to his touch. "Hurry! And don't stop until you find help!"

He hesitated. "I don't want to leave you, John. He said he's gonna kill you."

"Adam, you've got to get out of here. I'll be okay." But I was lying and he knew I was lying. He'd seen the dead bodies.

"Okay." He gave me a teary smile. I could tell he was trying hard to be brave. As brave as an eight-year-old boy can be when faced with death. "Bye, John! I'm gonna get the soldiers!"

After he left, I wasted precious energy yanking on the pipe, but it wouldn't budge and the handcuff cut my wrist so that blood ran down my hand and dripped onto the floor.

Footsteps pounded back down the stairs, and the door slammed into the wall behind it with a bang. Peter. Looking panicked.

"Why did she bring Randy?" he muttered, and for a moment he acted as if he didn't know what to do.

I was suddenly, deliriously happy. If Caitlin had brought Randy with her, then all hope was not lost. It would be the only time in my life I would actually be glad to see him.

"Why would she bring him?" he asked again, staring at me. "It's not like he gives a shit about you." He looked around and it must have finally registered that Adam was gone and everything was falling apart in front of him. He strode over to me, wrapped his hands around my throat, and squeezed, lifting me so that my feet barely touched the floor.

I clawed at his fingers with my free hand, but couldn't dislodge them. Pinpoints of light danced in front of me. A few more seconds and I would pass out. I thought I heard sounds coming from the stairwell, but with the roaring in my ears, I couldn't be sure. Peter released me and moved behind the partial wall.

Caitlin and Randy entered, and my heart sank. Randy wasn't in uniform; no radio. He wasn't on duty, then. In the dim light, I couldn't tell if he was armed or not. We were all fucked. Caitlin looked around as if suspecting that someone was playing a practical joke on her. I could guarantee that this would be one she would never forget.

"All I know is that John sent me a text message to meet him here," she was saying as they moved further into the room.

"He's in some really deep shit. I don't think either one of you understands just how serious—" Randy began, then saw me in the corner and froze. "What the hell?"

Caitlin quickly turned and saw me. "John?" she asked, confusion in her voice. They both started toward me. "What the hell is going on?"

"Kind of what I asked myself when I caught him in the act again," Peter said, coming up behind them.

Caitlin jumped, terror on her face. Randy was clueless as usual, but how could she not have guessed what was happening?

Peter keyed the deadbolt lock on the door, trapping them in my Hell. "You haven't seen the worst of it yet. Have a look." He placed a hand on their shoulders, propelling them forward into the space where the little bodies lay.

First through the opening, Randy stopped in his tracks and tried to push Caitlin back out of the room. "No, you don't need to see this."

Caitlin pushed back. "What is going on? What are you talking about?" She shoved past him, looking behind the crates. She gasped and whirled to stare at me, and I don't know what she read in my expression, but she began crying.

"I'm sorry," I said. She paled, her head shaking frantically from side to side, and I could only guess that she took it the wrong way.

Randy's face was pinched. "Jesus Christ, this can't be happening again. Have you called it in?"

"Homicide's on their way," Peter said.

"Oh my God." Randy ran a hand over his face.

"I don't understand," Caitlin whispered. "What's going on?"

"Isn't it obvious?" Randy snapped. "Your dear husband has murdered two more kids!" Then he seemed to remember that he was a cop first and an asshole second and added, "We've got to get you out of here. You can't be around a crime scene." But he stopped and turned to Peter and there was a different tone to his voice. "Barrington, why the hell would you bring her in here?" He fumbled with his belt, then I heard the unmistakable sound of a gun being cocked.

That's when Peter's gun came up. The sound of the shot exploded in my ears, blasting my eardrums, and reverberated interminably throughout the vast basement.

"*No!*" I strained against the handcuffs, sobbing, my ears ringing, a frenzied animal caught in a trap.

Randy stopped and swayed unsteadily on his feet, then staggered toward me. I caught him with my free hand, using my body to break his fall, but I couldn't continue to hold him up, and we sank to the floor together. He babbled something and I heard an object hit the concrete, but was distracted by Caitlin as she stood in the middle of the room, trembling.

Peter came up behind her and put his hand on her shoulder, squeezing, pulling her to him. Leaning close, he licked the back of her neck and placed a hand over her breast. She shuddered.

"The party has officially started, and I must say, this one promises to be a blast." He brought the gun up and held it to her head, forcing her to face him. "Ready to have some fun?" he asked her. "We're going to play a game. You like games, don't you? You and John are real good at playing games."

Gun pressed against her temple, he pushed her to her knees and, with his free hand, unzipped his pants. "Open your mouth." *Jesus Christ, he was going to rape her right in front of me.*

Caitlin's eyes were locked on his. Slowly she shook her head. He grabbed her chin and jammed the handgun under her nose. "Open your damned mouth, bitch. You've been flapping your lips all over town. Don't stop now. You sure didn't mind sucking my cock that night you went out with me. Open your mouth, or I'll open it for you." He slapped her.

Randy squeezed my fingers and mumbled gibberish—something that sounded like, "Bygone. Bygone."

I looked down at him, wincing at all the blood. "I don't understand."

He spoke again, this time with great effort, and his words, although fainter, were clear. *"My gun."*

I could not be that lucky. Was he hallucinating as his brain and body shut down? "Gun? What gun? Where?"

"My foot."

I glanced toward his feet, seeing nothing at first but shadows. Then gradually I could discern a darker shadow in the shape of a gun. But the fucking thing might as well have been on the moon for all the good it did me, because there was no way I could reach it. "I can't get it!"

He squirmed around, trying to slide it closer to me. He attempted to straighten his leg, but missed entirely on his first pass, and I could tell any movement on his part was excruciating.

"Try again, Randy. Try to get it closer to me so I can grab it," I pleaded.

He groaned with the effort, but after a few tries, he was able to scoot it nearer.

"That's it. Keep trying."

He moved his leg once more and this time his effort put the gun just outside of my reach.

"That's great. If you can move it just a couple more inches, I've got it!" I leaned forward, ready to snag it, when Peter bellowed, "Don't even try!"

Randy kicked his leg a final time and the gun came skittering toward me. Peter and I both lunged for it.

He came up empty, sputtering, his own gun pointed at my face. "Give it to me."

"Here you go," I said, raising it level with his crotch. I pulled the trigger. He screamed—an ungodly screech that would be sure to haunt my sweat-soaked nightmares for years to come—and grabbed himself, but that shot didn't kill him. "That was for every kid you've ever raped. And this is for *me*." I shot him in the face. His head jerked backward and his cheekbone shattered, spraying me with blood and bone fragments. He went down hard, what was left of his head connecting with the cement floor in a sickening splat. I'm pretty sure that shot did kill him, but to be on the safe side, I pulled the trigger three more times.

The silence afterward was profound and painful. None of us moved for several minutes, and I felt blood and gore slowly oozing down my face. With the intensity of a seismic jolt, I realized that I had just become one of the very things I had fought so hard to prove I was not. My sorry excuse of a life had come full circle.

Here's your chance.

You've waited long enough for it.

Don't pass up this opportunity.

Do you think your life is ever going to be worth living?

Especially now that you're a cop killer.

Twenty-eight years of misery.

Isn't that enough?

Without thinking about it, I brought the gun up to my own head, pressing the barrel against my temple. I closed my eyes. I should have done this a long time ago.

Release yourself from this hell.

End this train wreck once and for all.

All aboard!

Have your tickets ready!

This is a one-way trip, folks!

My finger tightened on the trigger.

"*No!*" I felt Randy twist beside me, felt his hand on my arm, scrabbling for the gun. It fell from my hand, clattering to the floor.

Then Caitlin was there on her knees in front of me, sliding it out of my reach, hugging me. She kissed me, even though it meant that she had to have tasted Peter's poisonous blood and flesh on my lips. As she had no doubt tasted and enjoyed other parts of his anatomy. I shivered, unable to force myself to return her embrace.

Randy stirred beside me and moaned. We tried to help him sit up.

"Don't try to talk," I told him. "Adam's gone to get help. Just hang on."

"I've been so unfair to you." His voice was a hoarse sob and there was a peculiar rattle in his chest now. I knew that even though he was dying, this was as close as he could ever come to an apology.

"Yeah, well, life's a bitch," I murmured. I hunched closer, struggling to shift him into a more comfortable position, finally managing to maneuver his head, shoulders, and chest onto my lap. The hatred I'd always felt for him was inexplicably gone, replaced by a hollow dread.

"Yeah, I know—life's a bitch and then you die." He tried to laugh, but a groan was all that he could manage. Suddenly he looked up at me, tears sliding down his face, and said, "Oh God. I'm dying, aren't' I?" His hand tightened on my fingers.

There was banging at the door and a muffled, "Kings County Sheriff's Department. Open the door or we're breaking it down!"

"Open up now!" Bang. Bang. Thud.

"Break it down already," I pleaded.

Thud. The door vibrated in its frame, then crashed open. Cops spilled into the room, guns drawn.

"Hang on," I said to Randy, squeezing his hand. "Help is here. Just hang on a few more minutes."

There was a delay while they checked to make sure no one was waiting to blow them all away, and then they were rushing toward us.

"Jesus Christ," said the first cop to reach us.

I sat silently and made no attempt at explanations. One officer knelt down to examine Randy, speaking into his radio to request an ambulance, saying the words no cop ever wants to say or hear. "Officer down." He turned to Peter, grimacing. He felt for a pulse, then placed his jacket over Peter's ruined face.

"Are you hurt?" he asked me, his voice not betraying whatever emotion he might be feeling. I suppose it was hard for him to tell whose blood was whose. I wanted to ask him to define 'hurt', but I only shook my head. He helped me to my feet and unfastened the handcuffs which had secured me to the pipe. Like an automaton, I turned to face the wall and assumed the position.

"Turn around, son," the officer said. "You're not under arrest."

The ambulances arrived in short order and Randy reached for my hand as they were loading him onto a stretcher. "Good job," he wheezed. Words I never expected to hear from his mouth with regard to me. That made me cry, but it also made me angry because I'd been deprived of any kind of relationship with him. Now that he knew the truth, of course, it was too late. Much too late for either of us. I listened to him take a last few rattling breaths, his hand clutching mine, as if I could keep him tethered to this world. Briefly, I thought that it was too bad he was the one leaving it and not me.

Ironically, the same sexual assault nurse examiner who treated Caitlin was the one to examine me. She asked me to disrobe and explained that she needed to take swabs and gather evidence.

"I don't know why it matters now that he's dead, now that his head's decorating the basement of that abandoned building. It's not like *he's* going to spend eight years locked away from everyone he'd ever loved!" All the trauma caught up with me at that moment, and I was hysterical, on the verge of cracking. When the nurse put a hand on my arm in an attempt to calm me, I slapped it away. "Don't touch me. *Don't fucking touch me!*"

It took five hospital staff members to get a sedative in me (no doubt as much for their own protection as my distress), and, heavily medicated, I eventually allowed them to take their swabs, samples, fingernail clippings, and photographs. The nightmare would never end—Peter was raping me for a third time. No one seemed to know what to say to me, and I ventured a guess as to say that they had dealt with very few male victims.

They took my clothes, placing my shirt, underwear, and jeans into evidence bags, and allowed me to take a shower. I made the water as hot as I could and scrubbed frantically at my skin, sobbing the entire time, but I couldn't get clean. I stayed in so long that the nurse came in after me. After coaxing me out, she gave me a pair of baggy scrubs to wear. A police officer came into the exam room and thanked me for cooperating, explaining that they needed as much evidence as they could get, in case there was a way to tie Peter to other unsolved crimes.

Whisnant and Samuels showed up on the heels of that officer's departure and went at me as hard or harder than they ever had when I was their number one suspect. I understood the necessity of debriefing—they had to learn everything they could about Peter's crimes. I agreed because I wanted the families of the victims to have some closure and because I wanted the world to know that I wasn't the monster who'd murdered them.

Exhausted after an hour of intense interrogation, though, I begged to stop. When I stood to leave, Samuels opened his mouth to protest, but Whisnant put a hand on his arm and said, "Thank you, John. We appreciate it. We're glad you've helped us put an end to this. It was nothing personal, and I hope you understand why we suspected you for so long." Like Randy, I knew it was as close to an apology as I was ever likely to get from him.

I paused with my hand on the doorknob. "I understand that you don't know nearly as much as you think you do."

#

"Mackenzie says we can stay here with her as long as we need to." Caitlin sat on the couch next to me and leaned her head against my shoulder.

I tensed involuntarily. It took every ounce of effort I possessed to stop myself from pushing her away. I had struggled with the decision, wanting to make sure it wasn't just a kneejerk reaction to the trauma, and this seemed as good a time to tell her as any. "That's nice of her, but I'm not staying in Kingsville, Caitlin."

She peered up at me, annoyance flitting across her face for a brief instant. "I can't go to the lake right now. Not with this story breaking and this business with the house and—and everything else."

"I'm not talking about *you* going. I'm talking about *me* going. *By myself.* I'm not staying here. I told you months ago I didn't want to live here, and I'm not going to live here any longer. I don't know how to say this..."

She put a hand over her mouth and her eyes teared. "No, John, no."

I found the nerve to untangle my arm from hers and got up to stare out the window. I kept my back to her so that she wouldn't see how close I was to breaking down. "I think we're through." My voice quavered.

"No! Why are you doing this?" She came over to me and placed her palm against my chest, and I did pull away from her that time.

I couldn't stand for her to touch me—couldn't stand the thought of anyone touching me ever again—and in an instant, I was furious. In the week that had followed the kidnapping and rape, I could go from severe depression to uncontrollable rage in the space of five minutes. "Why am I doing this? Do you think it could have anything to do with the fact that we began our relationship on a lie? I was a school project for you—a story—an award—not a husband!"

"Stop," she whispered. "Stop. I do love you. Our relationship may have started out as my curiosity about your case, but I fell in love with *you*. I'm having your baby for God's sake!"

"You never listen to me, do you? Just more proof that nothing I say makes any difference! And here's another example! I told you to back off on Peter. I told you, but you pursued it anyway. And look what happened..." I stopped. I had no idea if anyone had told her he'd raped me. Both the cops and hospital personnel insisted I tell her and advised me to seek counseling immediately at a rape crisis center, but I hadn't. It was bad enough that I kept remembering that moment, the things he said to me as he did it, the sick feeling of his skin against mine. I no longer felt like a man, but a casualty of war, conquered, my dead body cast into a ditch. I would be damned if I gave her a reason to see me in that light, too.

"I'm sorry." Her face was a mask of misery. "You can't begin to know how sorry I am."

Not sorry enough, I thought. I drew a deep breath, trying to calm myself, and slid my hands into my pockets to keep her from seeing how they trembled. "I won't fight you over possession of the cottage. It belonged to your family and I won't make any claim to it. I'd just ask you to give me a little time to figure out what I'm going to do. And I'll split the proceeds with you if the insurance company ever settles on the House from Hell."

"I'm not worried about any of that, John, but I'm begging you not to go."

I glanced away, unable to tolerate her pained expression. I pulled the truck keys from my pocket. I had no luggage—there was nothing left to pack. Nothing left on so many levels. I whistled for Willie. He came scampering, eager for an adventure. It was just another day in his happy little doggy world.

"Please, don't go," Caitlin pleaded. "You really shouldn't be by yourself right now."

"I've always been by myself," I said, and Willie and I went out the front door.

Epilogue

I'D LIKE TO REPORT that we all lived happily ever after from that point forward, but no one is stupid enough to believe in fairy tales. Even me.

I'm coping the best I can, but the Voices make it hard. My nightmares are the waking kind. I'll be watching TV and suddenly I'm seeing Peter's face exploding on the screen or I see my clothes covered with his flesh and blood. Dr. Steele says that I should take it easy and in time the images will be less frequent. The new medication has helped a little.

Everyone assures me that I was justified in killing Peter. I haven't discussed it, but my only regret was that he didn't suffer enough. If there had been any way possible, I would have prolonged his agony indefinitely, but I couldn't take the chance that he would live to rape and murder again. At least that's how I rationalized it to myself. Mostly I just wanted to see him dead. I don't like to contemplate what that says about me, nor the fact that I enjoyed killing him immensely, and that I pulled the trigger even after I was certain he'd drawn his last breath because the adrenalin rush reminded me I was alive.

Adam doesn't seem to be too much worse for the wear, although at our visits he tells me he still has nightmares and his parents make him go to counseling even though he'd just as soon not. "I'm scared to say this to anybody else, John," he confessed to me, "but when they told me you'd shot Peter in the face, I was glad. My Grammie says I should never be happy when someone dies, even bad people, but I'm glad he died, and I wish I could have shot him." He and his family have appeared on several morning talk shows describing his ordeal, his narrow escape, and his heroism.

I haven't spoken with Laurie since the night before Randy's funeral. When I tried to console her at the receiving of friends, she pushed me away, saying, "Maybe one day I'll be able to look at you and not blame you for Randy's death." I didn't tell her that Randy and I had made our peace with each other, such as it was, and at her request I didn't attend the funeral.

Whisnant and Samuels said they figure Peter intended to use the wooden crates for makeshift coffins and that he planned to set the basement on fire with the oil-soaked rags and the gallons of gasoline he had in the back of his truck. Based on that, they've also attributed the arson of the House from Hell to him. They think they've tied him to the murders of twenty children going as far back as fifteen years, and they've exonerated me.

Caitlin cries each time I see her and begs me to come home. I feel it in my heart like a knife blade, but I can't do it. She's also being hailed as a hero in bringing about an end to Peter's criminal career. She's been making the rounds of morning talk shows, too, and she and Adam have even appeared on a couple together. I'm told that her paper will be doing a series of articles on the matter and that the public will be made aware that I've been cleared, but honestly, at this point it's a cold comfort.

The End

Additional Advance Praise for *Cold Comfort:*

In *Cold Comfort*, E. W. Abernathy takes readers into John Colucci's chaotic world. Through his eyes we experience emotional extremes from despair to hope, through love and danger, to a shocking climax. A well-paced thriller delivered in masterful prose and with believable characters, this novel is one to devour—and keep to read again. It's that satisfying.

—RLB Hartmann, author of the Cordero Saga, *Tierra del Oro*

www.ingramcontent.com/pod-product-compliance
Lightning Source LLC
Chambersburg PA
CBHW060155260626
47160CB00001B/284